# Escaping the pit

There was a soft hiss as the rope began to race down the well, slithering into the water around her. Then it stopped. She was knee-deep at the bottom of a well, and there was no one holding the other end of her rope.

Evie's heart began to pound. She dropped the torch, which hissed into the water, then began feeling along the walls. There were plenty of rough joints in the mortar between stones, but everything was coated with the slippery slime of decades of dripping water. She began to climb, carefully. She knew it was only a trick of the mind, but she couldn't stop picturing a furious dwarf looking up from the shadows beneath her. The face in her mind grew clearer and closer, though she knew it wasn't really there at all. Her foot slipped off a stone and she nearly plunged all the way back to the bottom, but her dragon childhood had strengthened her fingers and legs in ways other humans never knew.

## Other Books You May Enjoy

# THE WARRIOR PRINCESS OF PENNYROYAL ACADEMY

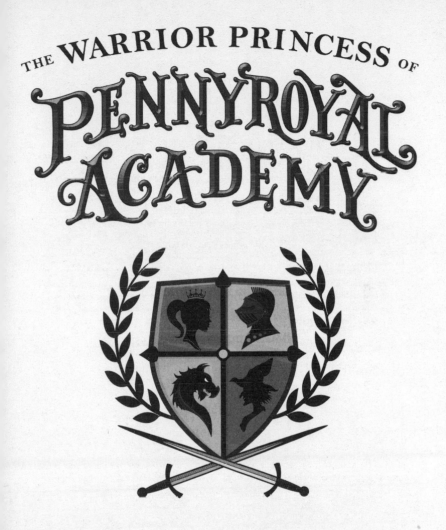

# M. A. LARSON

PUFFIN BOOKS

PUFFIN BOOKS
An imprint of Penguin Random House LLC
375 Hudson Street
New York, New York 10014

First published in the United States of America by G. P. Putnam's Sons,
an imprint of Penguin Random House LLC, 2017
Published by Puffin Books, an imprint of Penguin Random House LLC, 2018

LIBRARY OF CONGRESS CATALOGING-IN-PUBLICATION DATA IS AVAILABLE

Puffin Books ISBN 9780399545733

Printed in the United States of America

1 3 5 7 9 10 8 6 4 2

Design by Annie Ericsson

*For Scarlett*

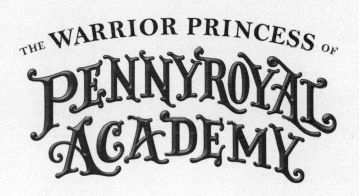

THE WARRIOR PRINCESS OF

PENNYROYAL ACADEMY

A CLEAR TRAIL of spittle ran from the corner of Basil's mouth. He snorted and stirred but didn't wake.

"Again! He didn't hear you!" whispered Demetra. She was on the verge of tears from holding back laughter.

The sun had just broken over the eastern forest, where birds sang by the hundreds. It was the dawn of what was certainly the most exciting day on the Pennyroyal Academy calendar. Yet in the early-morning hours, campus remained as still as it had been all night.

Except, of course, for three figures clad in gray huddled outside the storehouse behind the Leatherwolf Company barracks.

"Poor Bas," said Maggie, fighting off laughter of her own. "Do it again, Evie."

*It isn't as easy as it looks,* Evie thought. *I've no idea how loud I'm being.*

She peered through the window. The storehouse was scattered with axes and barrows and brooms and shovels. Across the room, Basil lay on a small straw pallet in the corner, his too-long hair feathered across his slender face. With each rising of his chest, there came a faint snore.

Evie opened her mouth to speak, and Demetra broke out in laughter. Evie smacked her on the arm, then looked back through the window to make sure Basil hadn't woken. When she finally did speak, her mouth moved, but no sound came out. In the storehouse, however, Basil shot up out of bed.

"Evie?" he said, his voice muffled through the window. "Evie, where are you? I can hear you laughing. Hang on, how can I hear you laughing? Have you got your voice back?"

"Again!" Demetra clutched her stomach, her voice a squeaking whimper.

Evie started speaking, but no sounds came from her mouth. There was a great crash inside. Demetra collapsed onto Maggie's lap, trying to hold in her laughter.

"A witch attack? Now?" said Basil. "Evie, where are you? What is going on? How are you talking?"

Evie suddenly began to shout. "Get out of there, Basil. Calivigne's coming!" Somehow, her voice had come from inside the storehouse.

There was a humongous clatter as garden implements went flying and Basil let out a shout. Now Maggie toppled to the ground, crying with laughter.

"Run!" shouted Basil. "Witch! Witch!" He burst out of the storehouse wearing only his breeches, panic on his face. "Calivigne is com—OOF!" He fell to the dirt as he struggled to pull on a boot.

"Cadet Basil!" came a furious squawk from the front of the Leatherwolf Company barracks. Evie's eyes shot open. It was Princess Copperpot, their House Princess, and she was spitting mad. She'd had a hard run of luck with witch curses over the years, giving her a wooden leg, two left arms, an eye patch with heavy scarring creeping out from underneath, and a nosy rooster named Lance, who followed her everywhere. "What is the meaning of this?"

Evie grabbed Demetra and Maggie. Their laughter was cut off as though hacked by a woodsman's blade, and they ducked against the wall of the storehouse. No one dared even to breathe.

*Go away, Lance,* thought Evie. *Back to bed with you.*

"I'm sorry, Princess, I . . . ." They heard Basil scramble to his feet. "I must have had a bad dream."

"Bad dream, is it?" said Copperpot. Her speech was punctuated with strange bursts of volume. "You're lucky this is the last day of the year or I'd give you some real nightmares!" From the front of the storehouse, Lance *buhgawk*-ed.

"Yes, Princess. I'm sorry, Princess."

"At least put some clothes on, will you?" said Copperpot.

Evie's hand vised down on Maggie's leg as Lance's bobbing red head appeared around the side of the storehouse. "Come, Lance!" shrieked Copperpot. "We've much to do before the ceremony!"

Thankfully, the rooster strutted away before he had a chance to notice the three girls huddled in the dirt.

"Sincere apologies, Princess," called Basil with a nervous chuckle. Then, after a moment, he hissed, "Evie! I know you're here! Show yourself!" The door to the storehouse opened, and he went back inside. "Evie!"

Demetra and Maggie resumed their battle against laughter. As Evie's lips moved, her ghostly voice came from inside: "Basil . . . this is the spirit of Evie . . . you must do as I command . . ."

"You're such a child, Evie. Come on, where are you?" Suddenly, his face appeared in the window. He pushed it open with a small metal rod. "Hilarious. I ought to march you right over there and turn you in—"

"Basil!" came Evie's voice from behind him.

He screamed and jumped, dropping the window closed. A moment later, he reappeared. "How in blazes are you doing that?"

Demetra could barely walk from laughing so hard. Maggie had to lead her inside and deposit her on a rain barrel so she could catch her breath. Evie stepped past the shovels and hoes that Basil had knocked over in his panic. She removed a delicate, beaded silk neckband from beside his pillow. She tossed it to him, and he studied it in confusion. The stones of the neckband were nicked and tarnished, badly in need of a polish, but it was otherwise unremarkable.

"That's my new voice—"

Basil threw the neckband like it was a talking snake.

4

Demetra began to cry with laughter until she fell off the barrel. Evie picked up the neckband and clasped it around her neck. The blackish-brown stones matched the dark waves of her hair, making her eyes gleam as green as a forest after the rain.

"See? I've got my voice back." Finally, it seemed to be coming from her own body again. "The nurses found this enchanted neckband for me in Cumberland Hall."

"Cumberland Hall?" said Basil. "You mean that's a . . ."

"Incredible, isn't it?" said Maggie, stepping over to admire the neckband. "Evie's got an honest-to-goodness fairy tale artifact there."

"Blimey!" he said, leaning in for a closer look. "How's it work?"

"They took a bit of my spit and a bit of my blood and mixed it in here." She tapped a tiny reservoir hidden amongst the polished stones on the front of the collar. "Princess Wertzheim wasn't sure if it would work, but . . ."

"I'd say it works brilliantly," said Basil. "Scared me half to death."

"Sorry about that. It was Demetra's idea."

Princess Wertzheim, the chief caregiver at Pennyroyal Academy, had nursed Evie to health after a particularly close call with the Vertreiben, a secret society bent on capturing Princess Cinderella. Evie had succeeded in helping the most famous princess in the land escape, but she had nearly lost her own life in the process. As a girl raised by dragons, she had learned enough from them to be able to start a small fire with her breath. Thanks to some enchanted trees, the fire she'd started had grown into a conflagration, scattering the Vertreiben into the forest and allowing Cinderella to flee. Unfortunately, Evie's human body wasn't yet equipped to handle the heat of dragon's breath. The act of breathing fire left her throat so severely burned that she couldn't eat or drink or speak. The medical staff had given her an array of poultices and potions, though none did much to ease the pain. Finally, after six days, the nurses managed to all but eliminate the agony of the burns. Evie had even successfully eaten some small bits of pear, a blessing to her empty stomach. Everything was starting to return to normal. Except, that is, for her voice, which was showing no signs of coming back. Princess Wertzheim had remembered the enchanted neckband from a visit she'd made years earlier to Cumberland Hall, the Academy's storehouse of magical and bewitched items. With a little bit of practice, Evie had finally managed to start speaking again.

"Princess Wertzheim says I'll probably be wearing this for the rest of my life, but at least we managed to get Cinderella out of here."

"What fantastic timing," said Basil. "With your voice back, you can go home for the summer after all, can't you?"

"Yes . . . but I'm thinking I might go to Sevigny with Maggie instead." She turned to her friend. "If that's all right."

"Are you mad? I've been asking you that for two years!"

"Uh, not to be the voice of reason," said Basil, adopting the earnest, scholarly tone that always made him seem older than his years. "But what about your family? Won't they worry? Especially after what happened at the Drudenhaus?"

"I haven't spoken to them in nearly a year," said Evie. "I doubt they'll notice."

Basil considered. "I wish I had that problem."

"Bas," said Demetra. "I'm sorry for teasing you with Evie's voice. I hope you understand that it had to be done."

"I consider it my punishment for being friends with you lot," he said with a laugh. Suddenly, his eyes popped open as he realized something. "Hang on, if you're out of the Infirmary, Evie, does that mean you can come to the ceremony?"

"It does indeed."

"Fantastic!" he said, looking from Maggie to Demetra. "Well then, shall we go have our final breakfast as second-class cadets?"

Demetra and Maggie, arm in arm, walked out into the morning sun. Basil reached up and touched the stones of Evie's silk neckband, his mind working. "You must let me borrow this someday. I could scare the pants off my brothers."


The Headmistress General's face looked like an unimpressed owl's: sunken eyes and humorless beak beneath a crown of choppy white hair. She was addressing the assembled second- and third-class cadets in the Queen's Tower, a translucent spear that rose high above the rest of campus. The walls were immense bricks of stone, yet somehow sunlight shone through, giving the hall a magical glow.

". . . and it has certainly not been an easy year, yet you have all persevered . . ."

The cadets were arranged by company, creating a colorful patchwork of girls and boys. Two tiers of balconies ringed the hall, filled with proud parents and siblings. And in front, atop a dais lined with ancient thrones, sat the Academy's staff, all dressed formally in matching cloaks.

During those long, boring nights in the Infirmary waiting for her body to heal, a thought had taken hold in Evie's mind. Maybe she wouldn't go home after all, even once the nurses declared her healthy. When she'd last seen her mother and sister, all they'd done was argue. Perhaps it would be better for them to have a bit more time away from her. Perhaps it would be better for her to be around other humans outside the Academy. Perhaps, though it hurt to think it, she simply didn't want to go home.

"Let me close by saying congratulations on an excellent year. You have worked hard, and now is the time for your reward. Third-class cadets, I hereby proclaim you second-class cadets."

The back half of the hall erupted in cheers. The balconies rippled with waving, clapping hands. Beatrice, without so much as a smile, raised her hands for quiet. Slowly, the new second class began to settle, though excitement still crackled through the hall.

"Cadets of the second class, I hereby proclaim you first-class cadets. Well done."

The wave of excitement now hit Evie's company, as well as the other princess company and the two knight companies who had just been advanced. Though they were equally as euphoric as the younger cadets, they managed to hold their composure a bit better, exchanging hugs and smiles instead of delirious screams. Evie felt a rush of pride as she embraced her company-mates. She had done it. Against all odds, she'd made it through her first two years of princess training. Only one more and she would be commissioned a Princess of the Shield, a sworn defender of the realm from all wicked witches. Shivers raced down her arms at the thought.

"When you return in the fall," intoned Beatrice, and the joyful buzz fizzled away, "you must endeavor to make it your best year yet. The road only grows more challenging. The witches only become more real. Take these months to reflect on your enemy. Remember those we lost to the Vertreiben. And then return to us refreshed, renewed, and ready for battle." She surveyed the hall with sharp eyes and pursed lips. "Now, there is one final thing I should like to leave you with. As you know, the first-class cadets will receive their commissions in a separate ceremony later today. Since they aren't here now, I don't feel too terribly guilty sharing this with you." Her face threatened a smile, but she managed to suppress it. "Cadets, you shall have a very important duty awaiting you in the fall.

For the first time in nearly twenty years, Pennyroyal Academy will play host to a royal wedding."

A flurry of voices rippled across the hall as the day's delight reached a fever pitch. Beatrice, meanwhile, did her best to speak above the noise. "Each of you will be heavily involved in the planning and execution. This is a rare opportunity for us all, and we must represent Pennyroyal Academy to the best of our abilities." The thrill could no longer be contained. Voices grew increasingly louder. "All this will be *in addition* to your regular training," she nearly shouted. "Lest you think a royal wedding is purely pleasure, let me assure you it is not. This will be hard work, ladies and gentlemen, but it will also be a remarkable opportunity to learn how an event of this magnitude comes together."

"Who is it?" shouted one of the younger girls, which prompted a host of other curious voices. "Who's getting married?"

Beatrice let her silence do the talking. She didn't speak again until the hall had gone completely quiet. "We will be hosting the wedding of King Nordstrand to one of the most celebrated graduates of recent years: Princess Middlemiss."

Chaos broke out. Evie, however, didn't move. Since she first arrived at Pennyroyal Academy as the child of dragons, Princess Middlemiss had served as her own personal touchstone of how to navigate through humanity. In Lieutenant Volf's histories, Middlemiss was a girl as riddled with doubt and as questionable a cadet as Evie imagined herself to be. Middlemiss lived somewhere along the One-Shore Sea, which wasn't terribly far from the Dragonlands. This made her feel something like Evie's local princess, since none existed beyond Griselda's Tears, where dragons roamed freely. During the long summer nights between her first and second years, when all she wanted was to come back to the Academy to see her friends, she used to disappear for hours at a time into Volf's tales of Middlemiss, of witches fought and treasures won. And now that same storybook princess would be having her royal wedding right here at the Academy. And Evie would get to help. It made the summer looming ahead seem as endless as the sea itself.

"Cadets, please!" shouted Beatrice, though now the excitement had reached something of a rolling boil. "Cadets!"

"Straighten those spines, you lumbering cows!" came an incongruously sweet voice that sent a dagger of fear straight into Evie's heart. It was Leatherwolf Company's fairy drillsergeant. She zipped amongst her cadets, shouting for order. Other fairies did the same. Trails of shimmering dust began to stripe the air. Within moments, the cadets were back at attention, and the fairies floated gently back to the sides of the hall, furious scowls on their tiny faces.

"Thank you. Now, if you'll excuse me, Commander Muldenhammer is here to tell you a bit about exit procedures." She nodded gracefully, then shuffled away from the lectern.

Her assistant, the lumpy, snarling Corporal Liverwort, met her, and they disappeared out the back.

Commander Muldenhammer, an immense man with long white hair, began to drone on about the importance of leaving the barracks in pristine condition for the summer. Evie's mind drifted to thoughts of what her final year at Pennyroyal Academy might be like. She had learned and experienced so much already during her first two years in human society. Next year was already promising to be the most exciting one yet, but it was still four months away.

Beneath an enormous statue of a princess and a knight atop the courtyard fountain, one coach after another full of cadets and staff circled through, then rumbled into the forest. Evie watched them go, but she resisted boarding one herself.

She, Maggie, Demetra, and Basil stood together, laughing and joking and speculating about their final year. There would be no mystery about which company they would join or who their House Princess might be. The first class had only one princess company—Crown Company—with elegant silver tunic dress uniforms. And the woman in charge was Princess Rampion, one of the most respected princesses on campus. Evie had seen her many times and had always found her warm, kind, and overwhelmingly intimidating. Rampion was as distinguished as a princess could be, a serious-minded warrior who thrived on creating Princesses of the Shield.

Finally, when the sun had begun its slow descent toward the horizon, casting a halo of light through Demetra's golden hair, she let out a sigh. "We can't stay any longer, I'm afraid. Camilla will leave without us if we're too late."

"Oh, Camilla's there?" said Maggie. Camilla was Demetra's older sister, a commissioned Princess of the Shield, and someone whom Maggie idolized. Unlike Demetra, who could be impulsive and flighty, Camilla had already established a reputation as a skilled, pragmatic Princess of the Shield. Both girls, however, shared a natural magnetism that made them quite popular with their peers.

"She's waiting for Basil and me in Waldeck so we can all ride back together. But patience is not her strong suit."

After saying their goodbyes, Evie and Maggie stood and watched their friends board the coach. Once it was full, two men in plated armor with giant swords hanging heavily around their waists climbed aboard. The sight of them gave the happiness of the day an unwelcome hint of unease. The Vertreiben had been scattered to the wind, and their leader, Princess Javotte, had been killed, but the staff was still concerned enough to provide armed guards for each coach's journey back to Waldeck.

After another hour of watching cadets and staff leave, a tiny voice sounded behind them. "How long are you two layabouts going to keep this up? Don't you have somewhere to be?"

Evie and Maggie turned to find the Fairy Drillsergeant floating behind them. In place of her usual scowl, they found a rare smile. "Nowhere better than this, Fairy Drillsergeant," said Maggie.

The fairy surveyed the winding streets of the Academy, the hulking stone buildings, and the soaring towers. "I do love it when it's empty. Such a peaceful place."

Despite the Academy's beauty, Evie found herself instead staring at the Fairy Drillsergeant. *She's happy. That's why she's acting so strangely.*

"Will you be here through the summer, Fairy Drillsergeant?" asked Maggie.

"Indeed I will. Busy summer, girls, very busy indeed. After that mass of new cadets we had this year, and then with the royal wedding next year, we're due for a restock like never before. That's why they've sent all the staff home early." She nodded to a group of princess and knight instructors boarding one of the coaches. "A quick pop home to visit family, then back again with coaches full of supplies."

The last knight instructor climbed on board, and the horses pulled the coach away.

"Right, off you go, girls. Last coach of the day."

"Yes, Fairy Drillsergeant," they both said.

The Fairy Drillsergeant turned and zipped away into the Academy, presumably to think up new ways to torture her cadets in the fall.

"Look," said Maggie. "It's only staff left, apart from us and her."

The courtyard was nearly empty, save for a small pocket of the younger princess and knight instructors. And there, sitting at the edge of the fountain, was Cadet Sage. Early in their first year, Sage had been one of a group of three who had tormented Evie and her friends. Another, Malora, had turned out to be Evie's stepsister, and also a witch. The third, Kelbra, had perished in the battle with the Vertreiben less than two weeks earlier. And now Sage sat alone, perhaps the only girl at the Academy immune to the excitement of joining Crown Company. "She looks so sad," said Evie.

"Well, she has had a horrible time of it, hasn't she? Maybe a harder couple of years than any of us." Maggie stepped forward and called out, "Sage! Over here!" Sage looked up. Her hair was a fountain of tightly packed curls above a blank face. Maggie gave her a wide smile and waved her over. Without changing her expression, Sage picked up her knapsack and walked across the cobblestone courtyard to join them.

"What." Like Evie, Sage had also been cursed by a witch, leaving her with no sense of humor. The medical staff was still trying to find a cure.

"Why don't you ride with us? We're all Crown Company girls now."

"All right."

"So," said Maggie, leading her to the open door of the coach, "excited for the royal wedding?"

"No."

And with that, they disappeared inside, followed by the rest of the staff members. Two heavily armed men waited for Evie to board, but she lingered there for another wistful moment. She wanted to let the image of the empty campus, washed orange with the sun, burn into her mind. The Fairy Drillsergeant was right. It was peaceful this way, without a soul there to see it aside from her. Birds sang from unseen trees in unseen baileys hidden behind castles and towers. The stone walls of the buildings seemed to settle with relief at another long year completed.

"Come now, lass!" called the coachman, waving to her from the coach stair. "She'll still be here when you get back!"

Evie took one last look, then boarded the coach. Only about a third of the benches were occupied. Still, she suddenly felt quite self-conscious to be one of only three cadets amongst so many staff, some of them her former instructors.

"Come on, lassies, step lively!" called Professor Adelbert, the rotund teacher of Applied Courage. Ordinarily, his sharp mustache and beard made him quite intimidating, but today he was in a brighter mood than the girls had seen him all year. "I've got two weeks at a cabin on the lake and I'd like to begin them forthwith!"

"The first round is on me when we reach Waldeck!" announced Princess Leonore. "In honor of Princess Beatrice and these delicious little days off she's given us!"

Evie and Maggie stifled laughter as they found benches in

the back, but the teachers' merriment still couldn't penetrate Sage's curse.

"Right, everyone, here we are, then," said the coachman, an angular man with bushy hair coming out of his cheeks. "Everyone's aboard . . ." He trailed off as the guardsmen pushed past him and sat in the first benches, two giant heaps of steel. "Right, *now* everyone's aboard. As the last coach to depart, we won't reach Waldeck until well past nightfall. But there'll be plenty of rooms at the Hoxford Arms, so don't fret about that, and they do a mutton so good a sheep would eat it."

"And the second, third, and fourth rounds are on me!" called Captain Ramsbottom, a knight company commander. The rest of the staff cheered. Even the coachman chuckled.

"Now," he continued, "there's only one rule on my coach: no singing 'Josephina with the Dark Blue Eyes.' It gets caught in my head and drives me absolutely bonkers."

"You've just put it in my head!" called Professor Adelbert with a wheezing laugh. "*Oh, Josephina, how long I've yearned to find you . . .*" he sang.

"No more, no more!" The coachman ducked outside and climbed into the driver's box, where he gathered his reins. As everyone settled in for a long, bumpy ride through the Dortchen Wild, the massive enchanted forest that surrounds the Academy, the coachman urged the horse team forward. They circled the fountain and eased into the dirt wheel ruts that headed down the hill. At the bottom, a low stone wall separated the campus from the enchanted forest, marking an invisible barrier of fairies' magic. Once they passed through, the only way back in was with a fairy's help. Luckily, Evie had no intention of returning, at least not until after several months of fun at Maggie's. Though leaving was always bittersweet, and she still felt the slightest bit guilty about not going home, there was no doubt that she was excited to visit Sevigny. It was a snowy, frozen climate, farther south than the Dragonlands were north, a place unlike any Evie had seen. She also knew that Maggie, despite her sunny disposition and extra-wide smile, was desperate to have a friend in her homeland, where no one much cared about princesses. Well, this summer, there would be one person who did.

As the team pulled to the right and followed the road that ran along the outside of the wall, the teachers began to sing "Josephina with the Dark Blue Eyes" at the tops of their lungs. Evie laughed, staring out her window at the Academy sitting atop the hill. The Queen's Tower glimmered in the late-afternoon sun, the tallest and most iconic structure of them all. It rose high above the jagged walls of the keeps and the sprouting towers of the castles like a mother bird in her nest. Soon, before Evie was quite ready for it, the coach veered to the left and disappeared into the enchanted forest.

"It's a bit sad what the Fairy Drillsergeant said, isn't it?" said Maggie.

"How do you mean?"

"About all the staff going to visit their families. I reckon Cinderella was her only family. Now she's got no one to visit."

Evie furrowed her brow. She'd never considered feeling sorry for the Fairy Drillsergeant before, but Maggie was almost certainly right. While the rest of the faculty sang their way home, the Fairy Drillsergeant was one of a skeleton crew left knocking about in an empty, silent kingdom.

Maggie cupped her hands and blew into them. "I can't believe I'm saying this, but I wish I still had that riding hood my grandmother gave me. It's cold out here."

"Oh no, have you left it?" asked Evie.

"It's at home, actually. I can't stand the bloody thing. Grandmother always thinks that because I've got red hair, everything I own should be red as well. Wait until you see my bedroom."

Evie smiled and turned back to her window. The air had gotten significantly darker beneath the canopy of the Dortchen Wild. As they bounced along through the undergrowth, the trees became a hypnotizing blur of green and gray and black. Evie rested her head on the cool glass. She could see the faint reflection of her own face and, beyond that, the dramatic swoops of the hills and valleys of the forest. Slowly, her eyes began to fall closed. Maggie said something else, something about seeing her father again, but Evie was too tired to hear it. Her second year of training had finally caught up with her. She fell asleep.

Her mind began to pull images and feelings together into the soupy beginnings of a dream. There was a royal wedding.

A castle hall festooned with flowers. And there was, of course, Remington.

Remington, tall and confident, with a charming half smile and a quick wit, was the first human Evie had met since the dragons had taken her in and raised her as one of their own. She had rescued him from a wicked witch on their way to enlistment that first year. There was some disagreement on that score, however, as he claimed it was he who rescued her. Whatever the case, he had been there with her throughout most of the first two years, never judging her peculiarities as she tried to integrate into human life. In fact, he even had a few peculiarities of his own. Remington was the great-grandson of the famous Frog King, and he was able to transform himself into a hopping amphibian whenever he liked.

For nearly two years, every time she thought of him, her stomach did flips. Until, that is, he had been discharged from Pennyroyal Academy. Remington had easily been the most famous cadet in Evie's class, heir to one of the most influential and wealthy kingdoms in all the land. When they'd arrived together to enlist, everyone had recognized him. And then, near the end of their second year, he had been sent away for trying to protect her.

*I wonder what his parents said when he came home early.* Based on what he'd told her about the royal family, his discharge was bound to be a massive disappointment, a significant black stain on his character. He could still be king, of course, but his rule wouldn't be quite as lustrous as they'd hoped. Perhaps they'd even do something rash and pass him over for his younger brother.

As her dreams fluctuated from royal weddings to royal disagreements, she found herself being lulled from her waking sleep back into the real world. Her eyes opened and she sat up straight. She hadn't even been aware she was asleep until she wasn't anymore. The singing had stopped, replaced by the murmur of quiet conversations.

Out the window, darkness was gathering and fog floated between the trees like ghosts. Maggie and Sage were engaged in a discussion with a third-class instructor who had just finished her first year on staff, so Evie settled back in her bench and watched the passing forest. For a moment, the sun fought through the clouds and the forest glowed yellow-green. Beams of magical light diffused through the thick fog. Then they were gone, and the forest went dark again.

She sighed and reached down for her knapsack. Inside, she found the dragon scale necklace she'd been wearing since she first left home for Pennyroyal Academy. The scale had belonged to her dragon father, who had gone missing that same day. When she'd first found it, it had been broken off in a wall of stone, streaked with his blood from a horrible crash. Dragon's blood was infused with the magical ability to show visions of the possible. Anything seen in a dragon's blood vision could come true, if all the right conditions were met. Some of the visions Evie had seen had been borne out, like Remington's near-fatal encounter with Countess Hardcastle, one of the most powerful of the wicked witches, at the end of their first year of training. Others, such as the suggestion that Evie was the Princess of Saudade, seemed to be possibilities that would never come to pass. But now the bloodstain had faded away. As she turned the scale between her fingers, a small piece of it crumbled off.

"Oh no!" In a panic, she tried to fit it back together, but it was no use. She carefully removed a small piece of canvas that was tucked inside the back and a bit more crumbled away. The canvas was a picture of her human father, King Callahan. She put that into her knapsack, then examined the scale. There was dust all over the palms of her hands. It was falling apart before her eyes. With a helpless sigh, she gently placed it inside her knapsack—

*WRAAAACK!*

In an instant, Evie felt herself go weightless. The coach twirled through the air, rocked by a deafening explosion.

Screams rang out. The horses whinnied outside. Evie's body slammed off the wall, then fell to the roof, which had now become the floor.

The coach rolled one last time and skidded to a stop, finally settling on its side right at the drop into a great valley. Evie lay motionless. Hooves thundered as the horses scattered into the forest.

"Is everyone all right?" shouted one of the knight instructors.

"What's happening?" yelled a princess.

Outside, there came a sound like metal shredding, followed by another explosion.

"*Ambush!*" someone screamed. "It's the witches!"

As Evie stood, her foot shattered the window beneath her. The coach was dark, with only a flickering orange light to help her see. It took a moment to realize that it was fire. Outside, the trees were ablaze.

She could make out the silhouettes of people near the front of the coach. They were piling onto one another's shoulders and climbing out through the roof. *It isn't the roof,* she thought, *it's the door. We've landed on our side.*

There was a sinister, dry-throated laugh from outside the coach. Then another. Then a whole chorus of them, like a howling pack of wolves. The horrible cackling scared Evie so badly, it forced her out of her groggy confusion.

"Maggie!" she yelled, her head throbbing from the crash. "Maggie!"

But there was no answer. There were screams all around the coach, people shouting to hurry and climb, and more bone-chilling cackling. Cackling that never seemed to end.

Evie grabbed her knapsack and staggered to the front of the coach. Every bench was empty. There was broken glass everywhere, scattered with people's belongings.

"To the trees! Hurry, everyone!"

She reached the front of the coach and found two princess instructors lifting people up through the door.

"Come on, love, up you go," one of them said. Evie stepped onto their intertwined hands. They lifted her through the opening, where she was met with the smell of pine and smoke. The sounds were sharper outside, more immediate. People shouting and witches cackling. And there, above it all, she heard her own name in the distance.

"Evie!" It was Maggie. Her voice was coming from the fog-draped trees.

"Maggie! I'm over here!" She reached back down into the coach and grabbed one of the instructors' hands. The princess emerged and clambered aside. Together, they pulled the final princess free.

Ten feet from the coach, sword raised and feet at a run, was the stone statue of one of the guardsmen. Beyond him, flames crawled up the pines. Just as they had with the fire at the Drudenhaus, the enchanted trees whipped and twisted to try to escape the flames, spreading a relatively small fire all around the woods. A horse ran past, tack dangling from its neck.

"Come on!" shouted one of the princesses. The three of them scrambled to the edge of the coach and dropped to the dirt.

"Look!" said Evie, pointing back down the road. In the glow of the burning trees, black forms began to float down from the treetops. Each of them was cackling.

"This way," said the second princess. She and her friend raced to the edge of the road and vaulted over the side, disappearing down the sharp drop into the valley. Evie was about to follow when she heard a soft voice.

"Help . . . help me . . ."

It was the coachman. His leg was trapped beneath the mounting step. He was sprawled in the dirt, agony written across his face. She glanced at the witches staggering up the road, then back to the coachman. She ran to him, heaving the mounting step with every ounce of her strength.

The first of the witches had arrived, slinking around the back of the coach. Her eyes were wide, locked directly on Evie. The loose, gray flesh of her face stretched into a broad grin. Evie pulled harder than she ever thought possible. The coachman screamed as finally his leg slid free.

Two more witches had joined the other, slim and frail figures covered in tattered cloaks. Their dim yellow eyes scared Evie to the bone.

She hooked her arms around the coachman's chest and dragged him to the road's edge. The witches lurched toward them, grinning. One reached out with long, skeletal fingers. Evie threw herself backward over the small lip of grass, dragging the coachman with her. They careened down the side.

She lost her grip on him almost instantly as she tumbled through the ferns and saplings and vines that clung to the steep stone walls of the valley. Finally, she bounced to a stop at the bottom of the hill.

She was sprawled out on her back. Her eyes fluttered open. There, at the road's edge, several dark figures peered down into the valley, looking for her. She scrambled farther into the basin, running for the dense fog that rested there like smoke in a cauldron. She scanned the darkened valley for somewhere to go, some sign of one of her traveling companions, but all she found were more shadows, more trees, and more fog.

*The coachman.* When she turned back for him, she realized she had already become hopelessly lost. The forest looked virtually identical in every direction. Except for one.

She bounded across a patch of moss-covered fieldstones and ended up at the base of an imposing bluff. Vines and roots protruded from the black wall of soil beneath a stony outcropping forty feet above. A gust of wind sent a spray of leaves fluttering down. There were shouts in the distance. She had no idea from which direction they might be coming. She wheeled, searching the fog and shadows for her coachmates. And for witches.

Up ahead, an ancient oak tree sprawled into the late-evening sky like a giant's rib cage. Evie's breathing was as quick and shallow as a fox in a hunt, but she couldn't do anything to slow it. Fear had taken hold.

Occasional flashes of white flared in the darkness.

Somewhere out there, the princesses were fighting back. But for every flash of white, she also heard the telltale crackle of a witch's spell.

*All right, Evie, think. Which way is the Academy?* She scanned the trees, but twilight had arrived. Her eyes fixed on a patch of sky visible through the canopy. It was still more blue than black. *So I'm facing west.* That meant she'd have to go over the bluff to get back to the Academy.

"Eh-heh-heh-heh-heh-heh . . ."

The laughter was chillingly close. Evie's breath caught, her heart thundering in her chest. Her eyes dissected the forest, looking for the witch. There, in the trees on the hill from which she'd just come, two dim golden eyes stared back at her.

"Eh-heh-heh-heh-heh-heh . . ."

More flashes of magic lit up the fog-draped forest. "Go!" came a distant shout. "Hurry, Carmelita, run!" A moment later, the earsplitting sound of a witch's spell rippled across the valley.

In the shadows, those malevolent yellow eyes never left Evie.

Just as she made up her mind to flee, something caught her attention. There, on the ground, only a few feet in front of the witch, sat a glinting piece of jewelry. Evie's hands shot to her throat and found it bare. She had lost her enchanted neckband. And that meant she had lost her voice.

The witch stepped forward from the shadows. She was hunched and formless, with two thick, hairy arms clutching the neck of her cloak. Her voice slithered out from a sharp grin of cracked teeth. "*Eh-heh-heh-heh-heh-heh . . .*"

Evie cast about in her mind for an idea. The one that came to her was a bit mad, but she didn't have time to think of another. *If this doesn't work, I'm blaming Demetra.*

"Hey! Witch!" she screamed as loudly as she could. Her own voice echoed back to her from the neckband. The witch reeled in surprise. She tumbled over, falling heavily on one of the fieldstones with a shout. Evie sprinted toward her.

"You'll pay for that, you wretch!" screeched the witch, who was struggling to right herself.

Evie grabbed the neckband on the run and bounded into the trees. Up she ran, her feet plowing through the soft, damp earth as she struggled to circle back to the top of the bluff. Behind her, the witch was growling with rage as she floundered on the jagged stones.

Finally, Evie reached the top. She peered over the stony out-cropping and saw the black form of the witch down below. With an immense feeling of relief, she stepped to the ledge that faced south. She found herself above the canopy, the valley dropping away in front of her. Even more enchanted forest stretched into the distance beyond that. Above the fog, the sky was awash with silver stars.

"*Eh-heh-heh-heh-heh-heh . . .*"

Evie wheeled so quickly that she nearly fell over the edge. Another witch stood behind her, not fifteen feet away. Her eyes emanated a dark yellow glow from the hollows of her skull. Pale, mottled skin hung from her cheekbones like seaweed on a mooring. A gurgling sound came from her chest with each breath she took.

A wisp of black smoke appeared in front of her. More tendrils came, like snakes emerging from their eggs. Evie was paralyzed with fear, even though she knew what she needed to do. She'd been training for this. But without a moment to catch her breath, to organize her thoughts and gather her courage, she was just stumbling from one horror to the next. The witch must have sensed it, because her grin stretched even wider, revealing small points of teeth and black gums.

The neckband fell from Evie's hand.

The witch's grin disappeared behind a plume of black smoke. *Run!* Evie screamed at herself. But before she had a chance, there was a primal shriek as loud as clashing steel. A large bird soared down from the sky and slammed into the witch's head with both talons opened wide.

Evie couldn't believe what she was seeing.

The witch collapsed as the bird—some sort of hawk, with piercing yellow eyes and a razor beak—beat its wings about her head.

"Have you considered running?" shouted someone in the forest to Evie's right. There was a girl standing there. She was dressed in the silver uniform of Crown Company. It was a new graduate, one Evie hadn't seen before. She was beautiful, with soft brown curls flowing down her back beneath a jewel-encrusted tiara. In this moment of terror, Evie couldn't imagine any sight would ever be so welcome. But despite the joy in the princess's smile and the twinkle in her eyes, something about her struck Evie as somewhat deranged. "Seriously," she said. "You need to run."

Evie grabbed her neckband and glanced at the witch, who swatted desperately at the hawk. "Get away, you fiend! I'll bite your head off!" Then Evie bounded toward the forest to join the princess.

"The name's Marline. *Princess* Marline. Of the Shield, of course." She gave a proud nod. "Let's be off, shall we?"

The hawk's wings fluttered as it abandoned the witch and lifted into the air. Marline turned and dashed into the fog. Without a glance at the witch, Evie sprinted after. As they tore through the trees, the hawk swooped down from above and landed on Marline's shoulder in stride, as gently as a feather on a stream.

"Wait!" came a panicked voice from the darkness. "Wait! Take me with you!" Another cadet came barreling out of the fog. She was wearing a Leatherwolf uniform.

"Sage?"

Sage raced toward them, her eyes wide with fear. "Evie! Evie, it's—"

Suddenly, there was a horrific rending of the air. A stream of black magic rippled through the forest and struck Sage.

"No!" screamed Evie, but it was too late. She could already hear Sage's horrified cries fading to echoes as her skin became cold gray stone.

Marline clicked her tongue, and the hawk lifted away into the night. Moments later, it dove with a screech and began clawing the witch's eyes with its talons.

"Hurry," said Marline, who seemed to be enjoying the thrill of it all. "Before she really does get a bite of my bird."

"But . . ." Evie stared at the statue sitting only ten feet away. "My friend . . ."

"That's not your friend. That is a four-hundred-pound hunk of stone." She pointed at the scrum happening next to Sage's statue. "And that is a witch who'd like to make the same of us." She grabbed Evie's arm so hard, it caused a jolt of pain. "Now let's go."

Evie took one last look at Sage, her company-mate, the fear of her last moments rendered forever in stone. Then she turned and followed.

The journey back to campus was a blur. Evie's mind was a jumbled mess. Everything had been so joyful, and then . . .

*Thank the Fates for Marline,* she thought, following tightly behind the Princess of the Shield. Marline was as decisive as she was fearless. There were several times when a battle broke out nearby and she instantly ran off toward the flashes to help her fellow princesses, leaving Evie to wait and hope she would return. Each time, she did.

Finally, the Queen's Tower appeared in the distance. It was aglow with a strange blue shimmer that reminded Evie of the ghostly lights she often saw dancing across the winter sky in the Dragonlands. She had never seen it lit up that way before. *It's a beacon,* she thought. *They know what's happened out here, and they're trying to call us back.*

By the time they reached the wall, Evie's entire body felt as numb as if it had been frozen in ice. A small contingent of Pennyroyal staff waited there. Princess Rampion, Princess Copperpot, and several shield-bearing knight instructors called them to hurry, scanning the trees for any witch attackers. Evie nearly fell when the hawk came screaming out of the sky. It landed on Marline's shoulder just as she ducked beneath the magical barrier a fairy was lifting with her wand.

"Come on, lass!" shouted Princess Copperpot. Evie sprinted the rest of the way, then collapsed to the dewy grass, her muscles spent.

"Hoo!" called Marline, doubled over to catch her breath. "Now, that was fun!"

Evie glanced over at her. She looked down with a wild smile, her hawk staring with yellow eyes.

"She's here!" barked Copperpot. "We've got her!"

"Thank the Fates," said Princess Rampion, kneeling next to Evie to inspect her for damage. "So they've failed at their mission."

"Get out of here, girls. Keep this hillside clear!" shouted

Copperpot. Lance strutted toward where Evie lay, clucking softly. With Rampion's help, she scrambled to her feet.

"*Buhgawk!*"

"Come on, then," said Marline. She twisted her hips, sending a crackle down her spine, then started up the road to campus.

Evie staggered after, though she kept her eyes on the wall. Three of the younger princess instructors, not far removed from receiving their own commissions, raced down the hill and blew past her, each outfitted for battle in dresses and tiaras.

"All right, ladies?" shouted Copperpot. "Most have been coming in from the northwest, so that's where our teams have gone. Warrior Princess is back, so now it's strictly rescue and recovery, yes? Headmistress says three coaches, with up to twenty unaccounted for."

"Yes, Princess," they replied in unison. Copperpot gave them a nod, and they raced through the gap in the wall, then disappeared into the forest.

"Move, Cadet!" barked Copperpot when she caught Evie staring.

Evie turned and hurried up the road toward campus. She joined Marline at the top of the hill, just as they split from the main road and veered to the right. The Dining Hall's arched roof was fringed in silver moonlight, with two bursts of flame flanking the doors.

"Thank you," said Evie. Her voice was thin and wobbly. "I'd still be out there if not for you."

"Rescue the Warrior Princess not a half day after I'm commissioned," said Marline, her own voice as carefree as a sailor arriving at port. "Proper good start to my career."

As they neared the Dining Hall, Evie heard something that seemed totally out of place amidst the harrowing night.

"Is that . . . music?"

"Oh good, you hear it, too," said Marline. "I thought I was losing my mind."

They reached the door. Marline pulled it open, and the music poured out. So, too, did the warmth of the roaring fires and the aromas of a hot supper. They gave each other a puzzled look, then stepped inside. Evie was completely unprepared for what she found.

The hearths and braziers were aglow with fire. Candles covered every table. Two young knight instructors played a stringed instrument and a pipe of some kind. Though very few of the benches were occupied, those who were there were enjoying a cozy, festive Pennyroyal Academy meal service.

"Well, it appears the whole world's lost its mind!" said Marline with a hearty laugh. Her hawk flew off and landed at an empty table, where it began picking apart a steaming golden turkey. "If it means supper, I say we join the madness. Come on."

She nodded hello to some of the people at a nearby table. They were as filthy and battered as Evie and Marline were, though they all had smiles on their faces. Evie recognized many of them: princess and knight cadets, mothers and fathers who had come for the ceremony earlier that day, Pennyroyal staff.

"Evie!" came a scream from the center of the hall. She looked up to find Maggie bounding toward her. She was smiling ear to ear, a dark bruise coloring the left side of her face. There was a significant scratch through the middle of it.

"Maggie!" She ran between the tables and hugged her friend as tightly as she'd ever hugged anyone. "I thought I'd lost you! What's happened to your face?"

Maggie gently touched her bruise. "It's a miracle this is all I've got. What about you? How did you make it out?"

Marline strode up, gnawing on a massive turkey leg. "Hiya."

"She's how I made it out," said Evie. "Maggie, this is Marline. *Princess* Marline."

"Been a Princess of the Shield for nearly twelve hours," said Marline. "Already saved the ol' W.P."

Maggie looked confused. "Warrior Princess," said Evie self-consciously.

"Ah," said Maggie. "Well, I'm very pleased to meet you. Thank you for looking after my friend. Come, they've just brought fresh stew." She led Evie and Marline to one of the tables. Though Maggie was the only one there, it had been set for a feast. Marline sat backward, leaning against the table and chewing on her turkey leg.

"What's going on here?" said Evie. She took a place across from Maggie and began dishing food onto her plate. "It's like some sort of celebration."

"I dunno. I've only just got back myself."

"Ah, there you are!" said Princess Moonshadow, skittering over to their table. She was a second-class instructor with dark features and a slightly spooky air. She always smelled of rain. "Cadets Magdalena and Eleven, if I'm not mistaken?"

"That's right," said Maggie. "And Princess Marline."

"Looking well, Moonshadow," said Marline with a casual salute.

"Thank you." The princess began scrawling their names on a parchment. When she finished, she looked over her list. "Excellent! Nearly everyone's made it back."

"Not everyone," said Evie. "Cadet Sage of Leatherwolf Company was turned to stone."

"What?" said Maggie, her hands shooting to her mouth.

"Oh," said Moonshadow. "I'm terribly sorry to hear that." She shook her head sadly as she noted it on her chart. "We'll find her just the same and get her into the Infirmary. Still, with you three back, that's only"—she looked over her list, then flipped to the next parchment—"nine left unaccounted for." Her face fell. "Eight, with Cadet Sage."

"How do you know how many are missing?" said Maggie.

"We've confirmed that only the last three coaches to depart were attacked. And nearly everyone on board those three has made it back. But don't worry, girls. We've got teams out there now finding the rest." She tried to give them a reassuring smile, but it came across as creepy. Then she wandered away.

"Only three coaches," said Evie. "That's not so bad. It felt like the whole forest was filled with witches."

"Demetra and Basil will have made it through. They probably don't even know what happened."

Near the Dining Hall doors, there was a flurry of activity. Five new survivors entered and were greeted with hugs and smiles.

"Now it's only three," said Maggie.

Evie turned to scan the faces but didn't recognize them. They were family members who had come to cheer on their cadets at the ceremony. One of the princess instructors ushered them to a table. The musicians began a new song. Evie smiled ruefully when she recognized it as "Josephina with the Dark Blue Eyes."

Marline gave a sharp whistle, and her hawk flew over, landing heavily next to a bowl of potatoes. "Leave some for the others, you old buzzard," she said. The hawk turned its back to the food and sat at the edge of the table. Maggie's eyes shifted to Evie in amazement.

Just then, Princess Beatrice burst out from the kitchens pushing a cart with a steaming roast on top of it. Her assistant, the lumpy, snarling Corporal Liverwort, followed with another cart. Watching Beatrice smile as she surveyed the Dining Hall only added to the surreal atmosphere. "Take over for me, will you, Princess Moonshadow?"

Leaving her cart to Moonshadow, the Headmistress swept toward the front of the hall, arms held wide. "I'm told we have new arrivals! Welcome, everyone! Fill your plates and cups. There's plenty for all!"

A group of parents that had been huddled near one of the fires closed in on her, all speaking at once.

"Please, please, ladies and gentlemen, do try to remain calm." Evie studied the Headmistress. She was surprised to find herself feeling somewhat angry. Beatrice spoke to the parents in an entirely different tone than she used with the cadets— with them she was warm, even *friendly*. "It's been a trying night, but I've just been told that nearly everyone has been found. Of the three who remain missing, two are Princesses of the Shield. I have no doubt that we shall recover them quickly."

*Tell that to Sage,* thought Evie ruefully.

"I know you were expecting to be home in your own beds by now, but it seems the Fates had other plans."

"The witches had other plans!" yelled the father of a third-class cadet.

"Indeed, but you must rest assured that we here at Pennyroyal Academy have things well in hand. Hug your families tightly and enjoy a warm meal. You are safe now. With respect to the witches, we have seen it all before. Birds have been dispatched to our surrounding kingdoms. Before long, help will arrive to assist in clearing and holding the roads to get you back to your homes. Until then, take comfort in the fact that you are almost certainly safer here behind our wall than anywhere else. Now, please, enjoy our hospitality and leave the rest to us."

The buzz of voices started up, punctuated by bouts of laughter. Beatrice's speech had worked. Families hugged and shared stories about the frightening experience, their fears put to rest by the steadying hand of the Headmistress General.

"Seems to me they should have been ready for this," said Marline, taking another bite of meat.

"How could anyone have predicted it?" said Maggie. "It was a sneak attack!"

"They put the bloody Warrior Princess on an ordinary coach only one year removed from graduation with guards to protect from the Vertreiben but not from witches. That's tossing meat in a bear's den." A huge chunk of turkey came off in her teeth and flopped against her chin.

Evie's stomach began to sink. "Are you saying this happened because of me—er, I mean, the Warrior Princess?"

Marline shrugged, sifting through some peas with her fingers and pulling out the carrots. She popped a few in her mouth, then tossed a few over to her hawk. "What, you think it was some random attack like Beatrice over there? All I know is I've just spent three years being told how cunning the witches are and how they can't stand working together. But that looked awfully coordinated to me."

Evie crinkled her forehead, trying to make sense of everything that had just happened. It was terribly difficult to do with such happy music playing.

Suddenly, the doors burst open. Another group entered, though this was altogether different from the last. Three heavily armored guards came through first, followed by a man in black armor and furs. Behind the man was a first-class knight cadet with dark, longish hair and a doublet embroidered in the scarlet and black of Huntsman Company.

"Look!" said Maggie. "It's Forbes!"

"Beatrice!" called the man in the furs. He was cut from granite, with a silver beard and a sour, sneering face. Evic recognized him from the end of her first year of training. His name was King Hossenbuhr, Forbes's father, and if the stories were to be believed, he was a rotting lemon of a man. "What is the meaning of this? Why have I found my boy in the woods, cowering from witches?"

Forbes's face dropped in embarrassment.

"King Hossenbuhr!" said Beatrice. She left the group of parents she was with and went over to him. "You weren't listed on our coaches. What are you doing here?"

"I've only just arrived. I had the novel idea of seeing my son advance with his class. I never expected witches to be my welcoming party."

"Yes, well, you're safe here now behind our wall. Come, please, have some supper. One of our knight cadets will clear space for you in the barracks."

"Barracks?" He glanced back at his guardsmen with a face like a dried-out sponge. "I'd prefer something a bit more . . . defensible, if it's all the same."

"We are behind an impenetrable field of magic, Your Majesty," said Beatrice. "You are safer here than in your own kingdom."

"Yes, well, I'd have to be, wouldn't I? Diebkunst has fallen."

"Oh . . ." said Beatrice, flustered. "Oh, I'm so terribly sorry."

Evie glanced at Forbes, who was staring at the floor. Her heart went out to him.

"If you'd like something with more traditional defenses," said Beatrice, "you are more than welcome to stay in Copperhagen Keep."

"Fine. And I'll take my supper there as well, if you please."

"O-of course," stammered Beatrice. "Corporal Liverwort, show the King and his men to Copperhagen Keep, please. Send some food round as well."

"Aye, Mum."

The King and his retinue turned to go. Forbes's eyes met Evie's, then quickly looked away as he ducked out into the night.

"For a man whose son used to be a pig," said Maggie, "the King seems to have awfully little faith in magic."

"I don't know," said Evie. "You can't really blame him for wanting thicker walls if his kingdom's just fallen." She swirled her fork through her potatoes without eating any. A moment later, Beatrice strode up to the end of their table, a prim smile on her face.

"Well, then, ladies, how are we getting on? Have you been to see Princess Wertzheim in the Infirmary?"

"Not yet," said Evie.

"After supper, then." She tapped her fingers lightly on the table. "Listen, girls, I'd like to ask a favor of you."

Evie glanced up at Beatrice, utterly flummoxed. "A favor? From us?"

"Of course, Headmistress," said Maggie. "Anything we can do to help."

"I'm afraid our nerves are all a bit frayed. We could really use your help making everyone feel welcome here at our home. I've been asking cadets, knights, and princesses if they wouldn't mind showing our guests around a bit tomorrow. Give them a feel for what we do here. Maybe lead them through a training exercise or two—"

Marline snorted out a laugh, then quickly recovered. "Sorry, Princess."

Beatrice scowled, but continued. "Many people spend their whole lives without encountering a witch. Though they are all fine now, this has to have been difficult for them. It will put quite a lot of hearts at ease if they can see how well prepared we are for such things. And I'm sure many of them have always wondered what our training regime looks like."

"Right, I'll just say it," said Marline, an incredulous smile on her face. "You want us to play at being princesses to entertain these people? Sorry, Mum, but that's madness."

"Cadet, that is—"

"I'm not a cadet. I'm a princess, same as you," said Marline, though she was only a year older than Evie and Maggie.

"Be that as it may, this is still my command," said Beatrice, her face suddenly clenched into its usual stony glare. "And get that bird off my table."

Marline stood. She gave the slightest nod, and the hawk bounded off the table and landed on her shoulder. "You lot can play princess if you like," she said, her eyes still fixed on Beatrice. "I'm going down to the wall to see if I can't help find those last three." She strode away, leaving Beatrice fuming.

"We'll help however we can," said Maggie.

Beatrice's cold stare followed Marline out of the Dining Hall. Only then did Maggie's words register. "Thank you. None of us would choose to be here under these circumstances, but the least we can do is make it bearable for our guests. Help them find a nice bunk, get them situated in the barracks, and do whatever you can to keep their spirits light, yes? Show them that not only do we prepare for our enemies here at the Academy, but we also enjoy a bit of fun."

"Of course, Headmistress," said Maggie.

"Excellent." She turned to go.

"Headmistress?" said Evie. "I know we're safe now, but it was pretty bad out there . . ." She didn't know how to finish the sentence. Thankfully, Beatrice seemed to understand her meaning anyway.

"Every single bird in the Mews has been sent, Cadet. I wouldn't be surprised if help arrives before dawn. But even if it does take a bit longer, the wall is here to protect us. As long as we're patient and keep our spirits up, we'll be absolutely fine." She gave them both a nod, then moved on to the next table. Evie looked over at Maggie and raised an eyebrow.

"What? You don't believe her?"

"If everything's going to be fine, why send every bird we've got?"

Maggie sighed and shook her head.

"What? It doesn't sound a bit desperate to you?"

"It was probably just a figure of speech. I'm sure she doesn't mean *every single bird*."

Evie's eyes fell to the table. Something was niggling at her, but she couldn't place what it was. "Sage was turned to stone right in front of my eyes. I do believe Beatrice, but . . ." She took a deep breath and shook her head. "It's still scary."

"Well, that is certainly true," said Maggie. "Scariest night of my life."

"Mine, too." A chill ran through Evie's body as a thought entered her mind. *Scariest night of my life until the next one.*

**3**

"THAT'S IT, MOTHER!" called Cadet Nadele, one of the girls who had been with Evie since her first day in Ironbone Company. "You look just like a real princess!"

They were gathered at the Marketplace, an open-air reproduction of a typical high street found in any of the major kingdoms. The packed dirt road was lined with replica stalls offering everything from fresh produce to carved walking sticks, all beneath a blanket of white clouds. This was where first-class cadets would hone their instincts, trying to detect which of the hand-painted "merchants" was a witch in disguise, thanks to an enchanted cloak that simulated the feel of a nearby witch. The cadets would practice using their courage as they walked the Marketplace, but the parents and siblings would have to make do with small rocks.

"It's quite creepy!" said the woman currently attempting the exercise. She had her stone at the ready and a smile on her face. "I think I might feel something rather dark up ahead."

"That's it!" called Nadele. "That's the witch! Remember, she'll look like anyone else, so you've got to trust your instincts."

The first spring-loaded merchant popped forward, causing the woman to scream and fall to the dirt. When she saw it was only a piece of wood painted to look like a flower seller, she laughed with embarrassment. The rest of the crowd was abuzz, eager for their turn at the princess training exercise. Evie and Maggie, however, stood far at the back, their arms crossed, their faces glum.

"It sounded like a fine idea last night," said Maggie, "but this is just silly."

On that, Evie could agree. Through a gap between a castle and a cathedral, she could see the whole of the Pennyroyal Castle courtyard. There, beneath the giant statues and the fountain, stood Princess Beatrice. She was addressing her staff. Evie could see the backs of some of those with higher rank: Princess Rampion, Princess Copperpot, Sir Schönbecker, and a handful of others. She knew what they were talking about, and yet she longed to hear about the attacks with her own ears.

Another merchant sprang out. Everyone screamed, and then everyone laughed. Evie kept her eyes on Beatrice and her team. She had done some figuring while her fellow cadets entertained their families. She estimated that there were roughly forty cadets on campus, almost evenly split between princesses and knights. That number included those who had graduated only yesterday and were not technically cadets any longer. In addition to that, there was a slightly larger number of parents, grandparents, and siblings of the cadets, perhaps fifty in total. But the staff . . . the staff she couldn't quite get a handle on.

"Maggie . . . where is everyone?"

"Huh? What do you mean?"

"Look over there." She flicked her chin toward Beatrice and her group. "I know there are more down by the wall, but is that the entire staff?"

Maggie looked at Beatrice and her group, disturbed. "Well, they did send loads of them home early, remember?"

The crowd cheered as the woman hit a wooden merchant with a stone, but neither Evie nor Maggie looked over.

"There are a few deadly ones, like Rampion and Copperpot, but look at the rest of them. They're all either fresh out of the Academy or have one foot in retirement." Most of those gathered were indeed very young or very old. These were the administrators apprenticing in the Crown Castle or broken-down knights many years removed from their last dragon battle. Young or old, these people were more familiar with quills and parchments than courage and compassion at this stage in their careers. Evie recognized a few of them—Sir Osdorf, the uptight knight who had taught the cadets how to dance for the Grand Ball; Princess de Boncouer, the quiet second-class instructor who was one year from retirement; Princess Rahden, an administrator only a few years older than Evie who was already deeply versed in the mountains of paperwork that made the

Academy go. The others she had only seen in passing. "Where are all the fairies? Where are the trolls?"

"Good question," said Maggie with a sigh. "Of all of them, I wish Princess Hazelbranch was still here."

"Me too. If she said everything was all right, I might actually believe it."

Through the voices of the crowd, they could hear distant shouting from somewhere deep in the forest. Beatrice and the others craned their necks toward the wall. There were more faint shouts. Several of the gathered staff began to run down the hill.

"What's going on?" said Maggie. The cathedral blocked their view of the road and the wall and whatever was down there causing the commotion.

"Help!" came a distant shout, this time as clearly as a raven's squawk.

Evie's eyes shot open. "That's Marline!"

"Come on!" said Maggie. They raced away from the Marketplace and blasted past Beatrice and the others. "Look! Evie, that's Demetra!"

Sure enough, down at the break in the wall where the coaches passed through stood two figures. One was Marline. The other, screaming and terrified, was Demetra. There were a handful of staff there as well, but they were inside the magical barrier.

Evie and Maggie sprinted down the rutted road. "Demetra!" shouted Evie.

"Hurry!" screamed Demetra, her eyes wide in horror. "Help us, please!"

As Evie and Maggie reached the bottom of the hill, where it evened out and sloped gently through the grass all the way to the wall, they could see the small contingent of knights and princesses fumbling helplessly to lift the magic. "We need a fairy!" bellowed one of the princesses. "Someone get us a fairy!"

Two more figures broke out of the forest and raced toward the wall. Then a handful more.

"Basil!" shouted Evie.

"Lift the wall!" he screamed. "Let us in!"

"Where are the bloody fairies?" bellowed Princess Copperpot. "We've got to get these people inside!"

"I didn't come out here to rescue these people only to die at the wall!" yelled Marline through a mad smile.

"The fairies are coming!" said Princess Rampion, racing down from campus. "Hang on, cadets!"

It was chaos. The group trapped beyond the wall pressed against the invisible curtain of magic designed to keep them out. Inside, no one could do a thing to help them. Then, deep in the forest, there came a violent rumble. Evie's breath caught in her throat. The ground vibrated again, followed by several immense *cracks* . . . ancient trees snapping at their trunks.

"They're right behind us!" screamed Demetra. "Please!"

"Who's right behind you?" Evie had never felt so helpless. Her friends were just there, nothing between them but an invisible magic barrier. Then she noticed a face amongst the group that she hadn't expected. "Remington!"

"Hello, Evie," he said with a smile, though it barely masked his panic. "Any progress on that fairy?"

"This is unacceptable!" shrieked Copperpot. "Never have I tasted such foulness!"

Another earth-shaking rumble sounded in the distance. Evie felt it more than heard it. "What is that?"

"There!" shouted Basil, pointing up the hill. "There she is!"

"Coming! Coming!" came a small, thin voice. It was the Fairy Drillsergeant. When she arrived, she looked a mess, as though she hadn't slept in days.

"And just where were you?" bellowed Copperpot.

"Sorry, Princess, our fairy on duty fell ill and she'd only just come to tell us. We hadn't had the chance to relieve her yet—"

Another deafening *snap* echoed through the forest, this one closer than the last.

"What is that?" said Evie in horror.

The Fairy Drillsergeant wielded her wand, and a faint shimmer rippled through the air. The survivors pounced through the opening in the stone wall, and the Fairy Drillsergeant lowered her wand, sealing them all inside.

Trees broke apart and thundered to the ground just inside the forest.

"Run!" screamed Demetra. All of them bolted up the hill. Evie, however, found her feet rooted to the spot. She stared with wide, horrified eyes at whatever was coming through the trees.

And then it emerged, knocking over pines like marsh reeds. It was a giant. He stood nearly as tall as the tallest trees and wider than most of them. His arms were enormous, bulging so thick that his shoulders nearly swallowed his head. Around his waist, he wore breeches comprising hundreds of furs and animal skins. He was shirtless and so utterly swollen with muscles that he didn't appear to have a neck. His entire body was slashed with scars. A matted red beard poured down over his chest beneath a slobbering mouth littered with black teeth. His head was a bald lump peeking out from between his shoulders with two bulging eyes staring straight across the forest to where the Academy stood.

He glanced down at Evie with delight. Then, in two strides, he was at the wall, nose pressed against it, his slobber dribbling down the invisible shield.

"Ah!" he bellowed happily. "There you are! A'right, mate?"

Evie stood stunned beneath the enormous beast. She felt a hand wrap tightly around her arm.

"Evie, step away from the wall." It was Remington, and his face was as serious as she had ever seen. She let him lead her up the hill, though she couldn't look away from the hideous giant leering in at her.

"Aw, come back, love!" he shouted.

They reached the top of the road, where a rather large crowd had formed. Princess Beatrice stood in front, her lips parted and her eyes wide as she stared at the giant. All of them, cadets, family members, and staff alike, had looks of abject horror on their faces.

Then, slightly to the east, the tops of the trees began to shudder as another enormous creature shouldered through the forest. Ancient pines, taller than most castle towers, fell like sticks.

"*Mith aigle dheo ár greadh . . .*" came an otherworldly voice, only this one was singing. "*Mith aigle ti sléibhe . . .*"

Then, just a bit farther to the west, yet another giant appeared. While the red-bearded monster paced at the wall, grinning with thick, broken teeth, the other two smashed down trees and sent resonant thuds echoing across the forest. Finally, all three of them were there, leering at the tiny crowd at the top of the road. Only a transparent layer of magic kept them out.

"Blimey, they're big," said Maggie in awe.

"Well, they are giants," said Basil, earning himself a dirty look.

"Which of you lot up there is in charge?" bellowed the giant with the red beard. The one to his left was just as big and just as ugly. One of his eyes was fused closed, and he had a burst of course black hair atop the nub of his head. The other one was covered in pink-and-white scabs, which he scratched compulsively.

"I'm in charge," called Princess Beatrice, stepping forward. The air of positivity she'd exhibited the night before was gone, and her icy hardness had returned.

"You?" The giant bellowed with laughter, his muscular arms

clutching his stomach. The other two grunted their amusement as well. "Listen here, you little ant, you're in charge? How 'bout this, how 'bout I bust down this wall and have you for morning tea with some cream and jam?"

"I want one!" yelled the black-haired giant.

"Me! Me!" bellowed the other, scratching his raw cheek.

"So here's your current situation, right?" said the red-bearded giant, pointing a finger as thick as an ox at the group. "My name's Galligantusohn. That there is Blunderbull," he said, pointing to the one-eyed giant. Then he aimed his finger at the scabby one. "I've absolutely no idea what his bloody name is. And the three of us is gonna wait out here and make sure none of you lot go nowhere without being eaten by us, yeah? So that's pretty much the tall and the short of it. What d'you think of that?"

The itchy giant let out an approving laugh.

"They've forgotten how to talk!" boomed the one-eyed creature, Blunderbull.

Evie glanced at Princess Beatrice, whose eyes were as thin and hard as the slits in a knight's jousting helmet. Her jaw worked back and forth in barely suppressed rage.

"Do not engage them," said King Hossenbuhr, standing at the back of the crowd with Forbes. "I've dealt with giants before. They're simple creatures, but they're quite skilled at needling people and forcing mistakes. Fatal mistakes. It's best to ignore them."

"Ha!" shouted Galligantusohn. "Look at this bloke! Thinks he knows all about us lads!" The other two joined in his laughter. Hossenbuhr's face tightened into a snarl.

"I agree with King Hossenbuhr," said Sir Schönbecker, one of the leaders of the knight brigade. "The fact that there are three of them indicates that they have been quite handsomely paid. Otherwise, they'd be tearing one another apart."

"Ah, let 'em play in their castles a bit," said Galligantusohn, waving a huge hand at them. "It'll build my appetite. I'm taking the north, and neither of you whumps better touch my food." After fixing the other two giants with a threatening glare, he stumbled back through the forest and found a piece of ground he liked. With deafening crashes, he began to clear away trees. The other giants did the same, one moving east, near the knights' barracks, and the other west, near the princesses' barracks. Like dogs scratching out patches of dirt, they prepared their areas and made themselves comfortable. Between the three of them, they had the entire northern end of campus under watch. Blunderbull continued to hum the song he'd been singing earlier.

Beatrice turned to face the crowd. "These giants will lose interest within the hour. They'll be off in search of food before the—"

*Crash!* There was a thunderous explosion in the sky overhead. A tree as big as a dragon smashed against the invisible wall, branches splintering off in every direction. Blunderbull bellowed with laughter. He reached down and began to work another tree free from the ground, then hurled that one at the wall, too. Several cadets screamed.

"I hate fairies!" the giant roared. The other two snorted with laughter.

Beatrice turned back to the crowd. She was trying to force a brave smile, but it was clear she'd been shaken. She looked around at the families huddled together, the cadets holding one another for comfort, the instructors paralyzed with fear.

"Headmistress," said Evie, "none of these people were on the last three coaches—"

"This changes nothing," said Beatrice, trying her best to sound resolute. "A whole host of our birds will have reached their destinations by now, and help is imminent. As you can see, the wall repels giants as well as witches. All we need to do is wait."

"But, Headmistress, if they weren't on the last coaches, then the witches' attack had to be bigger than—"

"That is all, Cadet."

There was silence in the courtyard. Blunderbull's heavy tones rumbled softly up from the forest: *"Bydd i lahg pøb ghlentÿn . . ."*

"What is that?" came a high-pitched shriek. One of the cadets' mothers pointed down the hill to the wall. Soon, everyone was gasping in horror. Even the giant stopped his song. Beatrice stepped toward the edge of the hill, her mouth hanging open in astonishment.

Like breath on iced glass, dozens of witches clad in black

robes began to appear in the trees. Each had a hideous grin on her gray-skinned face. They stepped to the wall and stood as unmoving as the stone before them.

"What's in their hands?" said Maggie.

Then, at the bottom of the road where the wall opened to allow carriages to pass, the witches stepped aside to let another come forward. This one towered above them all. Where the sinister grins of all the others could be seen, along with their yellow eyes and decaying skin, this one kept her face hidden beneath a heavy black cloak.

"Mercy . . ." said Beatrice softly.

"That isn't Calivigne, is it?" said Basil. "Blimey, is that really her?"

Then, one by one, the witches revealed what they were carrying. Each tossed a heavy stone object to the ground.

"What are those?" said Demetra.

"I suspect," said Princess Rampion with a gulp, "that those are our birds."

The line of witches stretched from one end of the horizon to the other, with Calivigne looming in the center. In front of them was a collection of lifeless stones that had been meant to carry pleas for help to the surrounding kingdoms. While everyone's eyes were fixed on them, Evie glanced at the Headmistress. She, too, looked horrified. But there was something else in her eyes. Something Evie couldn't quite place.

The witches, a wall of leering, evil grins, began to recede into the forest. No one moved.

"What's the matter, never seen a thousand dead birds before?" yelled Galligantusohn. Then he bellowed with laughter.

"Well," said Remington, "next I suppose the moon will fall from the sky and crush us all."

Evie kept her eyes fixed on the Headmistress. Beatrice was staring straight at Calivigne, who lingered after the other witches had gone. And still there was that strange, unplaceable . . . *something* in Beatrice's eyes.

"To the castle," she finally said, once Calivigne had faded into the forest with the rest of her witches. She cleared her throat and tried again. "To the castle."

She turned and trudged across the courtyard, leaving a field of stone birds just outside the wall.

"Right, er, everyone, why don't we head to the Dining Hall and see if we can't find some tea and cakes?" said Princess Rahden over the din of the increasingly frantic crowd.

"Tea and cakes?" shouted an old man. "I'd rather have some answers, thank you very much!"

Beatrice and the other top-ranking staff were halfway to the castle when Princess Wertzheim approached with several other nurses. "All of you who've just arrived, come with me to the Infirmary, please."

Remington locked eyes with Evie and tried to give her a reassuring smile. It didn't work. "I'll see you after, all right?"

She nodded, then he, Demetra, Basil, Marline, and the others trooped up the road to have the nurses look them over after their ordeal in the forest. The panicked crowd began to follow Beatrice across the courtyard with a frenzy of questions:

"What do we do now, Headmistress?"

"They've captured all the birds!"

"Where's the bloody Queen? Why hasn't she come down?"

Beatrice wheeled. Her face was granite, hard as stone and cracked by time. The anger in her eyes froze the crowd. "What we are going to do now is carry on," she said, her nostrils flaring. She ran her narrow eyes across the crowd and her demeanor slowly began to soften. When she spoke again, her voice had lightened. "You must all keep your heads, ladies and gentlemen. Even if they did intercept our birds, help will still be returning with our supply convoys. I know that the prospect of giants in our woods is somewhat frightening, but you must understand that we have extensive experience with all manner of beasts. All will be well if you'll—"

"That's what you said last night!"

Beatrice took a deep breath and closed her eyes. "All will be well if you'll trust in my staff as I do. We're here, all of us together, safe behind the wall. Our final three missing were recovered in the night, and we will get to the bottom of these new arrivals as soon as they've been cleared by the medical staff. Nothing has changed. In very short order, you'll be back in the safety of your own homes with quite a story to tell. Now, why don't you go with Princess Rahden and have a spot of tea?

Perhaps she can take you to see Swansdown Castle when you've finished." She nodded to Rahden, who nodded back. "It's a sort of museum to the great heroes who have passed through our halls. If anything can reassure you that we are well prepared for the monsters of this world, it will be a visit to Swansdown."

The hysteria seemed to have gone out of the crowd. Though there was still fear on every face, Beatrice's words clearly had a calming effect. "Tea might be nice," said the old man. "Warm the bones a bit."

"That's the spirit," said the Headmistress. "Allow me and my staff to assess this new information and make certain we've got every box ticked. In the meantime, enjoy what our Academy has to offer. Forget the giants. Think of them as nothing more than very large pests."

Several people chuckled nervously. Cadets began to lead their parents away to the Dining Hall. Beatrice turned to go, her smile instantly fading.

"Forget the giants?" said Evie. "She's bonkers."

"Come on, Evie, I could really use a cuppa right now."

"There's something she's not telling us, Maggie. These attacks were much bigger than they said last night. She wants us to trust her, but she's not being honest."

"What are you saying?" said Maggie with a huff. "You're saying I'm not getting my tea, aren't you?"

Evie glanced out at the three enormous, shaggy figures occupying the forest beyond the wall. "I'm saying I want to talk to someone who I *know* is honest."

Smoke wisped out of the crooked chimney atop the sweet little timber-framed cottage that was slowly being swallowed up by the mossy hillside behind it. Evie knocked on the old, knotted door. There was muffled movement inside, and then a voice.

"Who's there?" came the dry croak of Rumpledshirtsleeves, the tailor troll.

"It's Evie and Maggie. We need to talk to you."

"It's about bloody time you turned up!" he barked. His voice was so raw, it was almost painful to hear. "Go round the side! Hurry up!"

"The side?" said Evie to Maggie. Then, loudly, "Can't you just open the door?"

"Go round the side!"

The left corner of the cottage was covered by earth and moss and thick tangles of ivy. The other was a bit clearer, though it, too, was sinking beneath the hillside.

"Look!" said Maggie, grabbing Evie's arm. There, behind an overgrown spotted hemlock bush, poked the oblong head of one of Rumpledshirtsleeves's miniature troll assistants. He had burrowed through the earth, and dirt was smudged across his face and arms. He made a chattering noise, then waved them over with thick gray fingers.

"He can't possibly expect us to go in there," said Maggie.

"I expect that's exactly what he expects." His gray face popped back out with bulging eyes. He made more sharp noises, like a squirrel preparing for a fight.

Evie looked at Maggie, then nodded to the tunnel, urging her in.

"Ladies first," said Maggie, holding out her hand.

"Thanks," said Evie ruefully. She climbed behind the hemlock bush and brushed aside some dangling purple wisteria. She scooped out a few handfuls of the rich, black soil to make the passage bigger. Then, with a grimace, she shimmied in, using her elbows to propel herself through the tunnel. Damp clumps of earth fell onto her face and mouth with every inch she moved. Once her entire body was inside, she began to feel quite claustrophobic—

Suddenly, the troll's face appeared right in front of her, jabbering wildly. "Stop that!" she said, perhaps a bit too forcefully. "I'm coming, all right?"

"You've barely moved a foot," came Maggie's muffled voice behind her, complete with laughter.

"Yeah, enjoy it while you can. You're next, you know." She dragged her elbows ahead through crumbly dirt that smelled of the deep forest. Inch by inch, she shimmied forward until she reached a bend in the tunnel. She took a deep breath to try to calm herself, though the air was thick and pungent and altogether not calming. She willed herself on, bending ever so slowly around the back wall of the cottage.

Before long, the air became warmer, with hints of cinnamon. Finally, she saw a dim light. It was coming from a window in the side of the tunnel that opened into the cottage. She slithered through, landing in a plop on the floor. Her face, her hands, her hair, her clothes . . . all were grubby and grimy from the tunnel. She stood and tried to get her bearings. She was in some sort of storeroom, with crates and debris piled to the ceiling. The only light came from the doorway to the main room. Maggie's face appeared behind her, smeared with mud. A six-inch-long earthworm dangled from her ear.

"Get it off! Get it off!"

Evie hadn't meant to, but she broke out in laughter. She reached through the window and took the worm off Maggie's ear, then draped it over her nose.

"Evie, I'll kill you!"

Evie laughed even harder. She took the worm away, then pulled Maggie's hands until she suddenly slipped free. "We ought to hide out in here. No self-respecting witch would dare go through that."

"Well? Come on, ladies!" shouted Rumpledshirtsleeves from the other room.

"He's in a mood," said Evie. They brushed themselves off, though with hands so filthy it had little effect, then went through to the main room of the cottage. They were shocked by what they found.

Trolls of all sizes lined the far wall. Some were asleep. Others sat listlessly on worn wooden benches. Evie recognized some of them but was surprised to see so many she hadn't even known were on campus.

"Come, ladies, you've much to tell me," said Rumpledshirtsleeves. He lurched toward them from the wan light near the front of the cottage. He was dressed as impeccably as ever, in a sleek black suit with a custom-tailored pink shirt beneath. His face, however, contained an anger unlike anything they'd seen before. "I hear there's now a giant as well?"

"Three, actually," said Maggie. "What's going on in here? What's wrong with your door?"

"There is nothing wrong with my door, except that it has been magically affixed to keep in prisoners. Well-dressed, highly educated prisoners."

"Who would do such a thing?" said Evie.

"Beatrice," he spat. "Your ever-charming Headmistress General. A woman whose hatred of trolls has found new depths."

"*Beatrice* locked you in your cottage?" said Maggie, eyeing the rest of the trolls sitting glumly in the back. "Why?"

"When it became quite clear to me that these attacks were orchestrated by the witches as part of a larger maneuver, I went straight to the Headmistress and told her we needed to act immediately. Her rather predictable response was that the last thing we needed was a panic. I replied that perhaps the very first thing we needed was a panic. She decided our conversation was at an end and locked me and my brothers-under-the-bridge away where we couldn't be a bother."

"See?" said Evie. "I knew she was lying! She's out there telling everyone it was only a small attack on the last three coaches!"

"Come, I've just made tea. I'd offer you a place to sit, but I'm afraid you'd only make my dust dirty." They passed through the dress forms to a small wooden table near the fireplace. The troll poured two more steaming cups. "I'll tell you this, girls, and you know I'm not one for hyperbole, except when it comes to silk tops: that woman will be the death of us all."

Evie and Maggie exchanged a look. Maggie gulped. "Why do you say that, Rumpledshirtsleeves?"

"Because she has no interest in the reality of our situation, the old cow." He slurped some tea, then slammed down his cup. "We've got nothing left, girls. And the coach that was due back today contained supplies of critical importance."

"Why?" said Evie. "What was in it?"

He sighed deeply, then looked her in the eye. "Fairyweed."

Evie was staggered. Her pulse began to race. "Fairyweed? But . . ."

"Do you know how much those fairies eat in a day?" he said. "This year has utterly cleaned them out. They're living on crumbs."

"But if there's no more fairyweed," said Maggie, "then . . . what will they eat? Will they die?"

"If there are no more fairies," said Evie, "then there's no more wall."

"Absolutely correct," said Rumpledshirtsleeves. "And with no wall, there will be no Pennyroyal Academy."

"THEY WEREN'T ATTACKING the coach to get at you, Evie," said Maggie softly. "They attacked the entire caravan to cut the Academy off from the outside world. We're under siege."

"Precisely so," said Rumpledshirtsleeves. "The witches want the wall to fall so they can destroy the Academy before the Warrior Princess can graduate, thus removing any chance of the prophecy being fulfilled. These giants are nothing more than prison guards." He stepped away and began to pace, clucking his black tongue. "Fairyweed is so difficult to cultivate, even under the best of circumstances. Factor in all the extra fairies we needed to handle the new recruits . . ." He shook his head ruefully.

"How much time do we have?" said Evie.

"Days. And all the while Beatrice trilling that everything is fine."

"But why?" said Maggie. "Why is she acting like this?"

"For the most dangerous of reasons. She believes it to be true."

Evie had to sit, despite how filthy her uniform was. She was starting to feel light-headed. "What can we do?"

The troll turned to face them, firelight dancing across his eyes. "I've been wondering that since I began serving this unfortunate sentence. Believe it or not, our new friends, the giants, might hold the answer."

"The giants?" said Maggie. "I don't understand."

Rumpledshirtsleeves hobbled back over to the table. He stared at Maggie for a moment, then at Evie. He took a deep breath and slowly let it out. "My plan is only half formed, and that half is already astonishingly dangerous. There are sure to be many spots along the way where you might very easily fail, and all hope will be well and truly lost. It is also entirely possible that neither of you will live through it."

"Er, perhaps we could come up with a different plan," said Evie.

"To the north of the Dortchen Wild," he continued, ignoring her, "beyond the conjoined rivers known as the Two Brothers, lies an ancient forest so cursed, so haunted, that few dare enter. It is known as Goblin's Glade."

"I really think an alternate plan might be—"

"Centuries ago, the Glade was enchanted by a trio of wicked witches. It quickly earned a reputation for swallowing up all who entered. As a result, fewer and fewer dared try." He lifted the steaming kettle from the flame and carefully refilled all three of their cups. The tea leaves swirled in the boiling water. "The forest sat undisturbed, steeping in that dark magic year upon year, soaking it into the trees and the earth and the water and the air itself, metastasizing into something entirely unique. To my knowledge, Goblin's Glade is the oldest enchanted forest in all the land. That means its magic is also the most potent." Evie studied the gently swirling tea leaves, the water already mirroring their greenish color. "But unlike the Dortchen Wild, it isn't the trees that make Goblin's Glade so dangerous. It is, rather, its citizens. Many questionable beings make their homes there, including no fewer than two of my brothers." He lowered himself into his chair with a run of crackling joints. "There were one hundred fourteen of us in all. And like one hundred and eleven of those brothers and sisters, I am a middle child. Of all of them, only one sister is even worth exchanging a hawk. She does keep me apprised of my brothers, however, and that is how I know where they live."

"You had one hundred and thirteen siblings?" said Maggie. "Blimey, Basil's got nothing on you."

"That is to say nothing of my three thousand cousins. But of that number, only two concern us now." He blew on his tea and leaned back with a grimace. "Deep in the heart of Goblin's Glade lies a dense patch of forest known as the Wood of the Night. And at the edge of the Wood of the Night, there sits an abandoned castle. That castle is where my eldest brother now resides. He, ladies, may well be the key to our salvation. For he possesses an enchanted item that could win the giants to *our* side."

Evie's eyes went wide. She glanced over at Maggie, whose eyes were equally large. "What is it?"

He set down his cup and leaned closer, looking each of them

in the eyes. "The item you must recover is a golden harp." A chill ran through Evie's body, though she couldn't say exactly why. "The harp's music has the unique ability to bewitch giants. With this harp, we could wrest them from the witches' clutches and put them under our own command."

"This is incredible!" said Maggie. "We could break the siege ourselves!"

"Precisely. But, it isn't as simple as walking into the castle and asking to borrow the harp. Both my brothers are heavily involved in the black market of enchanted goods, which is one of the reasons they've chosen to live in a place as lawless as Goblin's Glade. No, parting the harp from my brother's claws will not be easy. And that is where my younger brother comes in. He is by far the more reasonable of the two. You will need his help to steal the harp from the other."

"I don't understand," said Evie. "Why would he want to help us? You said yourself that you don't even speak to him."

Rumpledshirtsleeves stood and sighed. "It is not often that an enchanted item becomes available on the black market. Most who deal in the trade covet their items intensely, hoarding them until something more desirable appears. This mostly happens after a kingdom is plundered or when a witch decides to enchant something new. And when a new piece becomes available, it sets off a chain reaction of fraudulent trades and double-dealings as these rogues try to cheat one another. To entice Rumpelstoatsnout to help us—"

Evie and Maggie both burst out laughing.

"What?" said the troll, affronted.

"Your brother's called *Rumpelstoatsnout*?" said Maggie.

"Rumpelstoatsnout is no one to laugh at, I can assure you!"

Maggie bit her finger to keep from laughing. Evie couldn't even look at her.

"Pay attention now!" croaked Rumpledshirtsleeves. "To entice my brother to help us steal the harp, we must offer him something very valuable in return. And, unfortunately, the thing he covets most is something we must steal from the Academy."

Both of the girls stopped laughing.

"I warned you, my dears, there is danger from the first word of this plan to the last. We must begin by breaking into Cumberland Hall to recover—"

"Cumberland Hall?" said Evie. Her fingers went to her jeweled neckband. "That's where this came from. It gave me back my voice."

"Indeed," said the troll. "Cumberland Hall is one of the largest storehouses for bewitched items in all the land. With the surplus of princesses and knights ordinarily stationed here, and the magic of the fairies' wall, there are few places better suited. Some of the most magical items in all the land are kept there. I happen to have it from my sister that Rumpelstoatsnout has long had his eye on one item in particular. She's been trying to coax me into stealing it for him for years in hopes it might draw him back from the dark path down which he is steadily dancing. Bless her. After all these years, she still thinks he's redeemable."

"What's the item?" said Evie.

"It is called the Bandit's Chair. It is a small, lightweight chair—white pine, I believe—and can easily be carried on one's back with the proper strapping."

"Why would he want a chair so badly? Couldn't we take something . . . smaller?"

Maggie let out a snort. Her face had gone bright red. "Rumpelstoatsnout!" She burst out laughing. Rumpledshirtsleeves rolled his eyes and shook his head.

"He wants the Bandit's Chair because whoever sits down upon it will stand somewhere else. His plan is to lure travelers into his home, providing them excellent hospitality, a straw bed, and a hot bath. Then, once they're at ease, he will invite them to supper, where they'll sit upon the chair. When they stand, they'll have gone, but their belongings will not. He'll be able to rob people blind simply by asking them to sit. He is a thief and a scoundrel, but to save ourselves, we must help him become a better thief and a better scoundrel. If we can deliver him the chair, he'll help us steal the harp from Rumpelstiltskin."

A spray of tea splashed across his face. Maggie coughed and choked on what little remained in her mouth. "Rumpelstiltskin? *He's* your brother?" One of the miniature assistants began to blot Rumpledshirtsleeves with a cloth.

"I'm sorry," said Evie. "I'm afraid I don't know who that is."

Rumpledshirtsleeves sighed deeply and looked down, waving away the assistant. "He has a penchant for . . . eating children." He shook his head, clearly pained by this relationship. "Years ago, I wouldn't have even admitted that he was my blood. But I have finally come to accept that my blood is not me. Rumpelstiltskin's choices, however odious, are his own."

Silence fell over the room. The fire crackled, and several trolls snored from the back of the room. Rumpledshirtsleeves rose once again. He set his gnarled hands on the back of his chair. "As much as I wish it were not the case, ladies, and as unorthodox though it may be, it appears you shall be required to complete your first mission *before* you graduate. And that first mission will be to save Pennyroyal Academy."

The night was black and moonless, the sky blasted with stars. Evie stood in the darkness up the road from the glowing torches of the Dining Hall with the rest of her conspirators: Maggie, Demetra, Basil, and Remington.

"You having a laugh?" came a thunderous bellow from the forest. "Galligantusohn eats first, yeah? What's left over is for you two geezers."

"I only want the crunchy ones," said Blunderbull, his voice echoing up from the darkness beyond the knights' barracks. "I like their metal shells."

The giants had been arguing for ten minutes about the order in which they would eat everyone once the wall fell. For now, they seemed content to hurl threats and insults at one another, though the intensity of the argument had gotten worse.

The third one, the giant that Demetra had nicknamed Scabby Potatoes because of the itchy pink encrustations covering his body, gave a laugh like a donkey's bray.

"And you watch yourself as well!" shouted Galligantusohn. "I'll have you both if you even set your filthy eyes on my meal!"

They went quiet, leaving the crickets to fill the cool night air. "I can't believe we're talking about joining forces with *them*," said Demetra. She was sitting on the stone wall that followed the curve of the road all the way to the edge of Pennyroyal Castle. Basil sat next to her, with Maggie on the other side. Evie and Remington stood on the hard-packed dirt, alternately pacing and staring out in the general direction of the giants.

"The more I think about it," said Maggie, "the more I'm convinced it's a brilliant plan. The witches would never expect—"

"If either of you blokes eats that old bird with the white hair," roared Galligantusohn, "I'll eat you just to get to her, yeah?"

"This is impossible," said Evie. "They won't shut up!"

"You can hardly blame them," said Remington. "Deciding who gets to eat Beatrice is terribly important. They can't leave it too long."

Evie sighed. "It's just so hard to think when they're forever winding one another up."

"I agree that it's a rather excellent plan," said Basil. "Using the witches' own weapon against them is brilliant. But there's still the matter of getting to Goblin's Glade. To turn the giants to our side, first we need to get past them uneaten."

"Rumpledshirtsleeves has an idea for that as well," said Maggie. "He says that many years ago the campus went through a massive expansion where they added on a lot of these third-ring buildings. And they used dwarfs to build them. He says the construction tunnels are still there, criss-crossing beneath campus. Some go well out into the forest, so the dwarfs could bring back lumber and stone from the Dortchen Wild."

"Brilliant," said Basil in awe. "That troll thinks of everything."

"Nearly everything," said Maggie. "There are still two problems with the plan. The first is that there may still be dwarfs down there."

"What?" said Demetra, pulling up her feet from the road. "Under there?"

"He says it's only a rumor, but there's no way to know for certain. And if we do run into them—"

"His exact words were 'You may well wish you'd stayed above with the giants,'" said Evie. The threat hung in the cricket-soaked air.

"What's the other problem?" said Basil.

"The tunnels might be able to get us past the giants," said Maggie. "But we'll still need to get from there to the Two Brothers. There's a sizable stretch of enchanted forest we'll need to navigate with no way of knowing how many witches might be out there."

The silence returned. A wave of muffled laughter came from inside the Dining Hall. Beatrice's attempts to reassure everyone continued apace.

"There are so many places it could go wrong," said Demetra, shaking her head. "How do we even start? They won't very well just let us into Cumberland Hall so we can collect the chair."

"We've got that part covered," said Evie. She took a corroded brass key from the inner pocket of her dress. "One of the trolls locked up with Rumpledshirtsleeves is the custodian for the second ring."

"Once everyone's asleep," said Maggie, "Evie and I will go to Cumberland Hall and get the chair. You three focus on gathering food and supplies for the journey. Only knapsacks, and only the essentials. We've got to move quickly. This wall could come down at any moment."

"Of course," said Demetra. "Basil and I will find some dried meats and things in the kitchens."

"Right. So we're all agreed, then?"

There was a moment where no one spoke. Finally, Remington broke the silence. "Just so I understand . . . you two will break into Cumberland Hall and steal the Bandit's Chair while the three of us are putting together supply kits. Then we'll drop down a well that Rumpledshirtsleeves recommended and follow the tunnels out beneath the forest—"

"And hope we don't get killed by dwarfs," added Basil helpfully.

"And hope we don't get killed by dwarfs," said Remington, nodding to Basil. "Then we stroll past the witches—we still haven't worked that part out yet—and somehow make our way up to Goblin's Glade to locate a smuggler named Rumpelstoatsnout. He will then help us steal a golden harp from Rumpelstiltskin in exchange for the chair. Is that basically it?"

"And then we need to come all the way back," said Maggie.

"Naturally."

"Once we've all agreed," said Maggie, looking at each of them through the darkness, "there is no going back. We're going to be discharged."

"Yes, but at least we'll be alive, won't we?" said Basil.

"It sounds quite exciting," said Remington. "Saving the world and all that."

"I'm in as well," said Demetra. She hopped down from the wall and smoothed her gray Leatherwolf dress.

"Good, then we'll meet in the Pit before dawn," said Maggie, climbing down. "Come on. Rumpledshirtsleeves gave us a map. I'll show you exactly where the Two Brothers are."

Evie's eyes flicked over to Remington, though it was difficult to see his face in the dark. "I'll be along in a minute, Maggie."

"Oh," she said as a smile formed on her face. "All right."

"Come on, then, show us the map," said Demetra, giving Evie a wink as she led Maggie and Basil away.

"Let's take a walk, shall we?" said Remington. They began strolling up the road toward the Pennyroyal Castle courtyard, where the world was even darker without the Dining Hall's torches. Blunderbull's snores echoed through the forest, punctuated with the hoots of owls and the thrum of crickets.

"I can't believe you're here," said Evie. "Why aren't you at home? What were you doing out there in the forest?"

"You didn't really think I'd leave you alone with the Vertreiben, did you?" he said with a grin.

"You stayed?"

"Not exactly. I did go home in the end, and received some rather unexpected news when I arrived. It seems I am now the King of Brentano."

Evie stopped and looked over at him with a furrowed brow. The night was so dark she could only see the faintest reflection in his eyes. "What are you talking about?"

"Well . . ." He took a deep breath. "My father was killed."

"Oh, Remington, I'm so sorry!" She grabbed him and pulled him close.

"A witch got him, quite unexpectedly. The whole kingdom

was in mourning when I got back, so no one really noticed that I'd been discharged."

Evie had no idea what to say, no words of comfort or wisdom. And now the giant's snores were making her angrier and angrier.

"It was quite a shock, to be honest. Not something I could have prepared myself for. So . . . I left. I needed to *do* something, and there was nothing to be done there but weep, so I came back to see if I could help with the Vertreiben. By the time I got here, you were already off on your mad plan to the Drudenhaus. Then when they brought you back to the Infirmary . . ." He shook his head. "I'm only happy they've got such a cracking good medical staff here."

"You were here?"

"Come now, the Infirmary is full of frogs. You never thought to look?"

She smiled and shook her head, astonished. "I suppose I didn't."

"You can be forgiven for that. There were other things on your mind, weren't there?" Something fluttered past overhead. A bat, perhaps. "This is quite another mad plan, isn't it? Hope we can escape these monsters with some underground tunnel and then hope we don't pop up in a field of witches? It's a bit like drowning in the bathtub of a sinking ship."

A chill ran through Evie's body. *Drowning in the bathtub of a sinking ship.* Though Rumpledshirtsleeves's plan had given her a glimmer of hope, it was hard to disagree with Remington's assessment. As unsettled as it all was, and whether she was ready for it or not, her first mission would begin before the sun rose the next morning.

But first, there was a chair that needed stealing.

"Remember, Evie," said Maggie, her voice echoing into the vast expanse of Cumberland Hall, "Rumpledshirtsleeves said not to touch anything but the Bandit's Chair. Everything in here is bewitched, and there's no telling how it might behave."

Evie nodded and held out her torch. Firelight danced across the sweeping limestone walls. Even in the dim light, she could see that the hall was immense and almost preternaturally beautiful. The floor was inlaid with a crisscross of different wood shades that formed a mesmerizing pattern stretching to the distant end of the hall. The walls were dominated by arching pillars of white stone that bloomed into the ceiling, forming a network of carved veins accented with the sculpted faces of beasts. The pillars served as entrances to various anterooms that flanked the wide central hallway.

"Where do we start?" said Evie. "It's enormous."

"I'll take this side. Let's do this quickly, all right? I don't like it in here."

Evie nodded again, her face solemn, and together they moved forward. Each step echoed like a hammer strike across the curves of stone. The air was musty and dusty and thick. As they reached the first set of archways, she stopped and faced

Maggie. "What do we do if we find something that could help us on the mission?"

"Like what?"

"I don't know, weapons? Navigation aids? Things like that?"

Maggie sighed, unsure. "I think we should just focus on the chair and get out of here as fast as we can."

"All right." They separated. Maggie disappeared beneath the first archway on the left as Evie went to the right. Her pulse began to race. It was darker inside the small side rooms. Above her, the pillars bloomed like waterspouts. The room was gray and cold and smelled of wet stone.

The far wall was carved to look like creeping ivy that climbed all the way to the ceiling. There were several stone pedestals placed around the room, some topped with glass domes. Wooden tables along the walls were also covered in glass. Each housed a magical item of some description. Others, like a series of enchanted woodcuttings, adorned the walls themselves. Each had a small placard that described the item. The first pedestal Evie passed held a simple wooden flute. The placard read

## Flute of the Honest Miller

### Oak and brass
### When one who lies should hear this song
### A milling stone he'll be 'fore long

Evie read with skepticism. *An enchanted flute that turns liars into millstones? That can't possibly be true.* Of course, according to

Forbes, a cursed portrait had turned him into a pig, so perhaps some impossible things *were* true.

She moved on to the next pedestal, where a gray moth flitted about beneath the glass. It crawled upside down, the underside of its wings as brown and mottled as bark. An oversized iron lock held the dome shut.

## Dusk Moth

### When evening falls, this moth grows strong
### Lifts newborns to witches who sing its song

A chill coursed through Evie's body, and she quickly moved along. The Bandit's Chair was clearly not in this room, so she headed for the passage to the next chamber. A portrait of a rather severe-looking woman in a green frock met her, glowering down from the wall. Next to her, the table held a spool of twine, a battered and chinked hammer, and a dried leaf in the shape of a skull. Still no chairs. The next chamber was filled wall-to-wall with items used for spinning. Wheels, bobbins and treadles, spindles and needles of all sizes, each of them cataloged and protected beneath the glass. Many of the needles were rusted, and a few were recognizable only by their general shape—

Maggie screamed. Her voice caromed through the hall, sending Evie into a panic. "Maggie!" She bolted out of the spinning room, nearly toppling a pedestal holding a small pile of flax. Maggie was waiting just across the hall, her eyes as wide as soup bowls. "Are you all right? What happened?"

"Evie," she said, and then a smile crept across her face. "You'll never believe what they've got in there." She tilted her torch toward the chamber she'd just been searching. "See for yourself."

"You can't do that, Maggie!" said Evie, her hand going to her heart. "You nearly scared me to death."

"Look!"

Evie walked over and peered inside. The chamber was empty except for a weathered rowboat made from gray and lifeless wood.

"A boat? So what?"

"It's Stupid Hans's boat!" said Maggie. "The *real* Stupid Hans!"

"Stupid Hans?"

"You've never heard of Stupid Hans? Evie, this boat can travel faster on land than on water. Do you know how useful this would be on our mission? We could row our way straight through to Rumpledshirtsleeves's brother!"

Evie turned to her, incredulous. "Through a sea of witches."

Maggie's smile began to fade. "Oh . . . right."

"Come on, Maggie, focus. All we're looking for is the Bandit's Chair."

"Bandit's Chair. Right."

They went back to their respective sides of the hall. After the spinning room, Evie found a chamber that was a dazzle of sparkling rocks and gemstones. Each had a small card that described the stone's power. And yet, still no sign of the chair. She was just about to pass through to the next room when something caught her eye. It was a single gray feather sitting atop a stone pedestal.

"'Bewitched squab feather,'" read Evie. "'When one becomes lost with no way to go / This feather leads true despite how the winds blow.'"

*Leave it, Evie. Remember what Rumpledshirtsleeves said.*

Her heart thumped. She took a furtive glance over her shoulder to be sure Maggie wasn't watching, then carefully lifted the glass dome. It scraped a bit, but she managed to lift it enough to get her hand under and grab the feather. She felt a bit hypocritical, since she'd just chastised Maggie, but the feather sounded incredibly useful. She carefully replaced the dome and slipped the feather into the hidden interior pocket of her dress. As she turned to continue on, something else caught her eye, equally as small and equally as intriguing:

## Needle of the Poorest Maiden

### Silver
### When speak'd the words
### "Needle, needle, sharp and fine"
### This needle makes fabrics in
### almost no time

*"Needle, needle, sharp and fine,"* she thought. *Instant fabrics could be useful if the others get cold at night.*

She held her breath and tried to work the glass free. It popped open, and she nearly dropped her torch. She carefully picked up the needle and inspected it. Nothing special about it at all. She joined it with the feather in her pocket, then began to replace the glass.

*Stop taking things, Evie!* she shouted in her mind. *You're here for the chair and the chair alone—*

"Evie!" hissed Maggie from across the hall, and she nearly dropped the glass again. "They've got the actual ball of crystal here! From the Castle of the Golden Sun!"

"Come on, Maggie, the chair! The chair!" A flush of shame came over her. The feather and the needle felt like lead weights in her pocket, testaments to her hypocrisy.

She made quick work of the next few chambers. One contained only a tree made of bone. She forced herself to hurry past without reading what it could do. The next contained several displays that seemed empty but actually contained minuscule objects. One held only a single grain of sand. According to the sign, it could shine as brightly as the sun. Evie shook her head and moved on, keeping her focus where it belonged. *Bandit's Chair . . . Bandit's Chair . . . Bandit's Chair . . .*

She peered through another piece of glass at a single flower, dull red with a short, thick, grayish-green stem. The placard so confused her that she had to take the flower out of its home and see it with her own eyes. She twirled it in her fingers. It gave off a sweet, earthy smell. According to what was written, the flower could turn all enemies in range to ravens simply by breaking the stem. She held her breath and slipped it into the pocket of her dress, cursing her own weakness.

"*Ahh!*" screamed Maggie. Evie jumped from guilt. "The hands of the Handless Maiden!"

"Maggie, please stop doing that!" She smoothed her dress over her stolen items and continued to the next chamber. There was a pewter stein. A horse's shoe. A wig of white and gold—

Her eyes shot back to the stein. There, just behind the display, sat a small chair made of wood. The bark was still on the branches used to make the legs and back. It looked decidedly uncomfortable, yet as small and light as Rumpledshirtsleeves had said.

## Bandit's Chair
### Pine
### Sit close over here
### Rise far over there

She approached the chair with caution. It was so unassuming, she had almost missed it. Yet all she'd have to do is sit in it for the chair to reveal its incredible power, flinging her off into the world somewhere. She gripped the edges of the seat and lifted. It was as light as driftwood.

She turned to look for Maggie but found herself once again drawn to another magical item. The pewter stein was just in front of her. There were images of people etched all around its dull silver surface. They were jumping over candles and thorny bushes and wolves and all manner of things. She set the chair down and lifted the glass—

The stein pounced off the table. Evie screamed and jumped back, the glass dome shattering on the floor. The stein soared across the room, clanged off the wall, and ricocheted back toward Evie. She dove away as it sailed past, only just missing her head. It smashed into another glass dome, then launched itself into the air. Her torch rolled across the floor, sending freakish shadows up the walls.

"Maggie! Help!" She skittered beneath a table as the stein clattered off the wall and shot straight toward her. It caromed off the floor and smashed through a table on its way to the ceiling.

Maggie appeared in the doorway, her eyes following the darting mug. "Hang on, I've got just the thing!" She vanished, leaving Evie to cower from the rampaging stein. A moment later, she was back. In her hand was a small white doily.

"What are you going to do, polish it?" shouted Evie.

Maggie stepped carefully into the room as the stein whizzed past. When it clanged against the wall and raced back toward her, she lunged at it with the doily, which unfurled like a fishing net to many times its own size. The stein sailed into it and clattered to the floor, captured.

Evie slunk out from under the table, watching the doily with wide eyes. "Thanks."

"Mother Lempert's Doily," said Maggie. "Just reading about it over there."

"Mother Lempert's Doily," said Evie, retrieving her torch. "Brilliant." The delicate lace leapt and hopped like a frog was trapped underneath.

"Hey! You found the chair!" She picked it up. "Rumpled-shirtsleeves was right. It's as light as a feather." She turned to Evie, who was still staring at the trapped stein with shock. "Well? We've got the chair. Let's go."

"Do we just leave that thing there?"

"Yes. If we manage to save the Academy, we'll confess. Until then, let's get out of here."

THE LEAVES IN THE PIT dripped from the showers that had passed through during the night. The air was crisp and piney. Evie and Demetra sat on a log while Maggie paced nearby. Basil stood on the far side of the fire pit. Hunks of charred wood and piles of ash, now sodden from the rain, were all that remained from their second year. This had been the place where Leatherwolf Company had gathered. A place to sing songs and complain about the Fairy Drillsergeant. Tonight, however, it was just the four of them waiting for their fifth.

"This is getting bloody tedious!" bellowed one of the giants rather suddenly, making them jump. Evie knew their voices well enough now to recognize it as Blunderbull. "Someone come out here and play!"

"Blast, they're awake!" hissed Basil.

"Where'd you learn the word *tedious*, matey?" laughed Galligantusohn. "You sound like a wee schoolgirl!"

Blunderbull let out a frustrated growl. Scabby Potatoes

followed with an irritated bellow of his own. The sun had just begun to lighten the dark skies.

"Where's Remington?" said Demetra. "We've got to go before those fools wake everyone else."

Evie looked out at the darkened forest. Her stomach began to flutter as an unpleasant thought entered her head. "Are we absolutely sure about this?"

All three looked at her in shock. "Of course," said Maggie. "It's the only way."

"I just mean that if we all go, the four of us and Remington . . . what happens if the wall falls? It feels like we're abandoning all these people."

"What are we supposed to do about it?" said Maggie. "We can't fight the witches ourselves."

"She is right, though," said Demetra. "We are sort of leaving these people to their own devices. If the wall falls, they'll need a leader with clear eyes, and we all know that's not Beatrice." She took a deep breath and looked around at her friends. "Maybe one of us should stay."

"Don't look at me," said Basil. "I'm not a leader. It should be Maggie if it's anyone."

"Me?" said Maggie, crinkling her face. "Why me?"

"Because you actually are a leader," he said. "Look, if we're really serious about this, you know the Academy better than anyone. You could theoretically help keep them alive. Take them down into the dwarf tunnels. Hide them in a secret passage somewhere. You'd know what to do and where to go."

Maggie looked stunned, wavering somewhere between disbelief and disappointment. "Are you really telling me not to come?"

"It's not that at all," said Evie. "We need you desperately. It's just that these people need someone even more. They'll scatter like sheep if the wall falls and no one's here to guide them."

Maggie took a deep breath and shook her head, considering. "Blimey. Maybe you're right. Maybe I could do more good in here than out there. It's just that I've been building up my courage to do the mission, and now—"

"Now you can share that courage with all of them," said Evie.

"All right." Maggie nodded, but there was pain in her eyes. "All right . . . I'll stay. But I'm still part of this team."

"Of course you are," said Evie. She smiled, though the thought of leaving Maggie behind filled her with panic, both for herself and for her friend, who would have to face those giants on her own.

"Well then . . ." She took a deep, sniffling breath, trying to push back her emotions. "Go on, get over here, all of you. If I'm staying, this may well be the last time we see each other."

"Don't say that!" said Demetra, embracing her friend. "Of course we'll see each other again."

Basil hugged Maggie next, and then Evie joined them. A cold gust rattled the leaves above as the four of them stood and held one another.

"Blast, are we late for the hugs?" said Remington. The four friends startled and looked up. He was coming down the hill with a smile, and he wasn't alone.

"What did you bring him for?" spat Evie.

"I'm an excellent hugger," said Forbes. His humorless mouth and intense eyes gave the impression of a storm cloud threatening to produce a tornado.

"He's deadly with a sword," said Remington. "I've asked him to join us."

"What?" said Evie. "You had no right to do that!"

"Well, he did it anyway," said Forbes. "And believe it or not, I actually agree with what you're doing. Staying here is suicide, and this magic harp idea is as good as any."

"He can't come," Evie said to Remington.

"Ouch," said Forbes with a smirk. "My feelings."

"Evie, listen, we need him. Of course Forbes has an immensely bad attitude and a terribly quick temper and is his own particular brand of torture to be around, but the first two of those things might be quite valuable on this mission."

"Cheers, mate," said Forbes.

"I don't want him—"

"I'm sure you don't. But you do need him."

"Hang on, *he* gets to go and I don't?" said Maggie.

"Why aren't you going?" said Remington.

"What's your father going to say?" said Evie, glaring at Forbes.

"I don't know," replied Forbes. "But I won't be around to hear it."

No one else spoke. Then, Galligantusohn bellowed, "It's been too long since I've had children stuck in my teeth! Get on with it up there!" This led to a flurry of dopey laughter and snorting from Scabby Potatoes.

Evie glanced around the circle and assessed her team, letting her frustration settle. Then she looked up at the sky, which had brightened to the color of days-old ash.

"All right," she said, throwing her knapsack over her shoulder and adjusting her sword. "Let's go."

Evie sat in a loop of rope like a children's swing as her friends lowered her slowly down the well. The coarse fibers were digging into her thighs, even through her uniform. She looked farther down the well, but the flickering orange of her torch couldn't reach the bottom. Above her, a small circle of gray grew progressively smaller.

The outline of Basil's head appeared. "All right, Evie?"

"Yeah," she said. "But hurry."

Lower and lower she went. The pungency of mold choked her. The well was coated with a thin layer of wet, spongy moss. She could hear dripping water somewhere below, and the oppressive quiet of walls that were as close as a tomb's. The rope was swaying a bit, making her legs rub against the slick limestone. Thankfully, the knapsack slung over her shoulder protected her back. She couldn't bear another bit of cold, wet fabric sticking to her body.

She took a deep breath and stared straight ahead as the rope twirled her in space. The stone bricks swirled round and round. She thought again about the plan and how it had gone smoothly so far. *Of course, we did exchange Maggie for Forbes, but aside from that we're right where we're meant to be.*

She glanced down again, and this time, to her relief, her torch reflected off black water. Moments later, her feet slipped into it. Even for someone who had been raised by dragons, the cold was a shock. Thankfully, she only sank to her knees before her feet found the bottom. It was as slippery as if it had been coated with candle wax. She quickly gave the rope three sharp tugs and was pleased to see it lift a few inches in response. She drew her sword and took a deep breath.

*Make sure the area is clear, then signal the others.*

She fished the rope out of the water and secured it around her waist. With the torch held high in one hand and her sword in the other leading the way, she stepped through an arched passageway and into a brick tunnel beneath the earth. Up ahead, water dripped with a haunting echo. She was about to enter a very large chamber.

She swallowed dryly as she sloshed ahead. The rope pulled tight around her waist, then gave as her friends let out some slack. The torch was creating a cloud of black smoke, and the walls were as dark and shiny as tar. Still, she moved ahead. She was listening for . . . she wasn't sure exactly. She was listening for dwarfs.

Her legs swished gently through the water while her eyes bounced around the shadows of the tunnel. Finally, after a few more steps, still holding her breath, she noticed something ahead.

"What?" she said in confusion. Her voice echoed down the tunnel. Now she splashed ahead quickly, no longer concerned about the noise she was making. An iron grate had been sealed across the tunnel, masoned into the brick. Water passed through the grate and continued into a much wider chamber beyond, but Evie couldn't see it. She could only hear it.

"What is this?" She tried to jar the grate loose, but it didn't move in the slightest. She searched the edges for some sort of weakness and found none. *Now what?* She tried to peer past the grate, but all she could see were shadows playing off the brick. *Bin the plan,* she thought. *Find another well. Adapt or die. That's what a trained princess does.*

"Blast!" She sighed, slamming her fist against the grate. She turned and splashed back to the bottom of the well.

"It's sealed!" she shouted up to the tiny circle of light. Her voice sounded hollow, compressed inside the well walls. "There's a grate here! Pull me up!" There was no answer from the top, just her own muffled echoes. She gave the rope three tugs.

Nothing happened. She peered up at the light.

"Hello?" she called. Then she gave it an even harder tug.

There was a soft hiss as the rope began to race down the well, slithering into the water around her. Then it stopped. She was knee-deep at the bottom of a well, and there was no one holding the other end of her rope.

Evie's heart began to pound. She dropped the torch, which hissed into the water, then began feeling along the walls. There were plenty of rough joints in the mortar between stones, but everything was coated with the slippery slime of decades of dripping water. She began to climb, carefully. She knew it was only a trick of the mind, but she couldn't stop picturing a furious dwarf looking up from the shadows beneath her. The face in her mind grew clearer and closer, though she knew it wasn't really there at all. Her foot slipped off a stone and she nearly plunged all the way back to the bottom, but her dragon childhood had strengthened her fingers and legs in ways other humans never knew. Climbing the odd tree or castle tower wasn't nearly so grueling as trying to keep up with Evie's sister. So, despite her growing fear and despite the treacherous walls, she made quick work of the well. After a few minutes of climbing, she glanced up and realized she was only about fifteen feet from the top.

"Hello?" she cried. When her echoes had receded down into the darkness, she heard something from up above. It was the unmistakable baritone of King Hossenbuhr.

"Well? Do something! They're trying to steal my son, I tell you!"

A jolt of panic shot through her. *They've caught us.* She began to climb even faster. Then she heard other voices above, and nearly all of them angry.

"This is an unfathomable disappointment," came the voice of Princess Beatrice, flat and clear and angry. "To undermine the Queen in a time of crisis."

Evie scrambled the last few yards to the top of the well and pulled herself out. Beatrice stood alongside Corporal Liverwort and a handful of her princess administrators staring down at Remington, Basil, Demetra, and Forbes. King Hossenbuhr and his guardsmen sat on horseback opposite where Evie was climbing out of the well.

"And let me guess," said the Headmistress with thin, glaring eyes. "This was all your idea, wasn't it?"

"Headmistress, please," said Evie. "You've got to let us explain—"

"I haven't the patience. I've had more than enough of your sneaking about since you've been at the Academy. Stolen food in your knapsacks. Swords strapped to your belts. Any fool can see that you're planning to go out there. And did you ever consider how it might affect our guests to wake and find you gone? You hadn't, had you? It would set off a panic. Those people are terrified already. If they found that some of our own cadets have lost faith in our security, it would destroy the fragile calm we've worked so hard to establish. There could be talk of mutiny against me and my staff. There could be a mad dash into the forest, forcing us to shift our resources to recovering bodies." She stepped forward again and looked at Evie with a mixture of contempt and sadness. "Who do you think you are to do something like this?"

"But, Headmistress, please allow me—"

"We are here to protect you, Cadet," said Beatrice, her voice rising. "Whether you understand our methods or not, they are in place to *protect you*. We are not required to explain our decisions to you, but you are required to accept them, something you have failed to do time and again. And now, not only have you involved your friends in one of your ridiculous schemes, but you have also implicated the son of an esteemed visitor."

King Hossenbuhr straightened his sloping back with pride. Evie glanced at Remington. His body was tense, yet his face was calm. The rest of her friends looked as though the slightest wind might cause them to scatter like frightened hares.

"Our ridiculous scheme worked last time, didn't it?" said Demetra, a slight quiver in her voice. "It was us who saved Cinderella, not you."

A dark shadow fell over the Headmistress's eyes. Her nostrils flared as she took in a deep breath, then slowly let it out. "Because we are facing such unusual circumstances, I will give you one final chance. Return to your barracks this instant and I will forgive your insubordination."

"You heard her, boy," said King Hossenbuhr. "March."

Forbes's eyes flicked from his father to the Headmistress and back again.

"Move, *now*, or you are all discharged from the Academy. None of you will be princesses or knights."

Evie's heart was racing. "We can't stay, Princess! We're going to die in here—"

"Enough!" bellowed Beatrice. "Seize them!"

No one moved. Confused, Beatrice looked back at the princesses behind her.

"What, you mean us?" said Princess Moonshadow. "We're not guards."

"Well, someone's got to seize them!"

A sword *shinged* out of its scabbard. Evie gasped as Remington stepped forward, his blade at the ready. "You've already discharged me, so perhaps I can speed this along. We have one chance to save ourselves, and this is it. I'm afraid it's time for us to go."

"Come away from there, Forbes!" called King Hossenbuhr. He climbed down from his horse and took a step toward his son.

*Shing!* Now Forbes's sword came free.

*Shing!* Hossenbuhr's face turned to fury as he pulled his own blade.

*Shing! Shing!* The guardsmen unsheathed their swords as well.

"All right!" called Marline. She was hurrying down from the barracks with a giant smile on her face. "I heard you lot shouting down here, and I knew there'd be blades!" *Shing!*

She pulled her own free as she joined the group. "Who's fighting who?"

"Go on, Bas," Demetra whispered to Basil.

"Hmm? Oh, right." *Shing!*

"Enough!" shouted Beatrice. "Put your swords away, you fools. Cadet Marline, get back to your barracks this instant—"

"*Princess* Marline." She gave Beatrice a wink. High above, the dark shape of her hawk circled.

"I'm very sorry, Headmistress," said Evie, picking up her knapsack from the ground. "We didn't tell you our plan because we knew you'd object."

"Has it ever crossed your mind that I might know what I'm doing?" said Beatrice.

"Forbes!" barked Hossenbuhr. "This is not how I raised you! Put that thing away and get over here this instant!"

"You didn't raise me at all, though, did you?" said Forbes. "And a consequence of that is that I don't particularly care what you say."

"I've lost my wife and my kingdom, and I'll not lose my son as well. You two, disarm him and take him to the keep."

The guardsmen dismounted and stepped forward. Marline bounded across the field and jumped between them. Her eyes were wide, her smile hungry.

"Marline, do not . . . Oh, blast it all," said Beatrice.

"You're not the only king here," said Remington. "Perhaps it's time I issued some orders as well. Forbes, you're coming with us."

"Yes, sir," said Forbes.

Hossenbuhr turned to Remington with a furious smirk. "Yes, I heard about your father. A shame. By all accounts, he was a decent man. However, a dead father does not a king make."

"There are witches coming across that wall in a matter of days," said Remington. "I'd prefer to show them my face rather than my backside. And that's why Forbes is with me. He'd rather fight back than cower in someone else's keep."

Hossenbuhr's grin faded into dead-eyed rage.

"We could have avoided all this if you'd only seized them," spat Beatrice to her staff.

"Forbes," continued Remington, "mount that horse and take Evie with you. The giants are distracted. If we go now, we can outrun them." They all looked at the giants on the northwest end of campus, who were busy fighting over a bear.

"Remington, what are you doing?" said Evie, stepping forward.

"Stay there!" he called.

"Listen to him, love," said Marline. "Lots of metal over here."

And that was certainly true. Steel points filled the air, each held by someone whose nerves were thin. As everyone stared at one another, it was Basil who took action. He replaced his own sword and sneaked around behind the small crowd, where he mounted one of the guardsmen's horses.

"Hey!" the man called, but Basil managed to steer the horse

to where Demetra and Forbes were standing. He reached down and helped Demetra up. With the Bandit's Chair strapped to his back, he gave her the reins.

"Come on, Evie! There are two more horses there!" shouted Demetra.

The swords wavered like vipers ready to strike. The guardsman whose horse had been taken was furious. "Get back here with that!"

"Forbes! Choose a horse and go!" shouted Remington. "Now, before we attract the giants' attention!"

"My son is staying here," said Hossenbuhr. "You, however, are free to go. And when you're out there with the witches, you'll know exactly what your father saw before he died."

Remington's jaw tightened. Evie could see in his face what was about to happen.

And that's when the swords did what they had been made to do.

Everyone screamed, even Princess Beatrice. Hossenbuhr arced his blade above his head like an executioner's ax. It came down with a terrific crash of metal on metal. Flashes of silver began to whir through the air, punctuated with deafening clangs. Hossenbuhr chopped down at Remington again and again and again, but each time, his steel was turned aside. Marline found herself battling both guardsmen at once. Blades flew, people screamed, and the already-wobbly mission to save the Academy vanished into the clouds.

"Stop it!" shouted Evie, but her voice was only one of a chorus. She glanced at the giants, who were thankfully still busy punching one another over the bear.

Remington swiped back, catching Hossenbuhr off balance. He knocked the King to the ground, then wheeled to help Marline fight off the other two. "Evie, go!"

Hossenbuhr regained his feet and came straight after Remington, driving him steadily backward with a relentless assault.

"Stop!" screamed Evie again.

Hossenbuhr ignored her, keeping his focus on Remington. "You are better than I expected," he admitted.

"I'm better than I expected," said Remington.

"You're a stellar tactician," said Hossenbuhr. His momentum had stalled, and now Remington was beginning a counterattack.

"Learned it from my father." He switched hands and attacked again, and now it was Hossenbuhr giving ground.

"Stop this instant!" shouted Beatrice.

Marline kicked one of the guardsmen, knocking him to the ground. She leapt onto his back and wheeled to exchange blows with the other.

Remington, meanwhile, had suddenly claimed the advantage. His sword flashed through the air like a hummingbird, coming at Hossenbuhr from a million different angles. Evie noticed something different in his face as well. His eyes were wide, his nostrils flared like a steaming dragon. His lips were set tight and his face was crimson. He seemed to be gaining strength as Hossenbuhr lost his.

With a mighty swing, Remington delivered a blow that knocked Hossenbuhr completely off his feet. The King landed squarely on his back, sword still somehow in hand, but before he could counter, Remington was on top of him. The tip of his blade hovered an inch above Hossenbuhr's neck, his breath coming as quickly as a hunting wolf's. Hossenbuhr looked down his nose at the blade, not saying a word. With the second guardsman distracted, Marline bashed the hilt of her sword into his back, knocking him to the dirt as well.

"That is enough!" shouted Beatrice. She stepped forward, her hands outstretched. "That is enough! Will somebody please seize somebody?"

Remington stood and glared down at King Hossenbuhr. Everything had suddenly gone silent. "Forbes, take that horse. Evie, get on with him."

"Remington—"

"*Get on the horse, Evie,*" he spat.

Forbes walked over and climbed atop his father's horse. He looked down at the King, who was lying on his back in the mud.

"What an incredible disappointment you turned out to be," said Hossenbuhr.

"I feel the same way," said Forbes. He urged the horse

toward the well where Evie was standing. She pulled herself up behind him.

"Go on," said Remington. "I'll be right behind you."

Evie looked at the giants. Blunderbull had Galligantusohn in a headlock.

"Now's our chance!" she said. "Let's go!"

"Hang on, you're not leaving me!" said Marline. She leapt off the guardsman.

"Get back here!" shouted Beatrice. "I gave you an order!"

"Sorry, we're a bit busy trying to save your life," said Forbes.

The horses took off for the western hillside, Marline racing after them on foot. Evie looked back and found Remington's eyes. Half of his mouth curled into a smile.

"Look out!" she screamed.

Remington wheeled and parried the guardsman's attack, but it gave Hossenbuhr all the time he needed to scramble to his feet.

The horses surged down the hill. Evie looked back helplessly as Hossenbuhr lunged forward and planted his sword directly in the center of Remington's chest. There was a dull clang, and his limp body fell to the ground.

"Remington!" she screamed, drawing King Hossenbuhr's attention. He looked at her atop his horse with his son, and she could see the venom in his blood. He shouted something to his men, and they both leapt onto the final horse. The horse Remington was meant to use. Marline bounded down the hill on foot, a huge smile on her face.

Evie's body drained of strength. She felt herself losing her grip on Forbes with every stride of the horse. But then, just as quickly as she'd been flooded with despair, a wave of joy swept over her. Remington leapt up and kicked Hossenbuhr to the ground. He flashed her the rest of his smile and knocked his knuckles against the small patch of stone in the center of his chest, put there by a witch's curse at the end of their first year.

"Look!" shrieked Basil. He was pointing to the north end of campus. There, thundering through the forest, were two of the giants, Blunderbull and Galligantusohn. Scabby Potatoes held the bear in his hand, victorious.

The wall was just ahead. Hossenbuhr's men were bearing down on Marline. Just as it looked like they were about to run her down, she leapt into the air, twisting her body around. She caught one of them by his cloak, pulling him off the horse as she pulled herself on. The guardsman with the reins tried to grab her, but she was now behind him in the saddle. She took hold of his neck and flipped him off, then spurred the horse on after the others. Her hawk soared down from the sky and landed on her shoulder.

"Hang on," called Forbes. "Here we go!"

The giants had rounded the curve and were running straight at them, and now Scabby Potatoes had decided to join. Suddenly, everything lurched upward as the horse leapt across the waist-high pile of stones. Evie held Forbes tightly, her face pressed into his back. They landed with a thud and disappeared into the enchanted forest.

Now the giants' footsteps thundered behind them, trees bending like dandelions. The earth shuddered each time one of their enormous feet slammed down. Evie looked back but didn't see Demetra, Basil, or Marline anywhere. Massive columns of ancient wood snapped at the base, crashing to the ground at the giants' feet. Those beasts, meanwhile, began to turn on one another. There was a deafening exchange of shouting, then suddenly Galligantusohn's body crashed through the trees up ahead, thrown there by one of the others. It felt to Evie as if the world was crumbling down around her.

"No one takes my meat, you brigand!" bellowed Blunderbull. The voice seemed to be coming from directly overhead. Massive legs like the knotted trunks of thousand-year-old oaks pounded into the earth, leaving huge craters of flattened and broken brush.

Forbes kept on. Trees continued to fall in long, arcing swoops. Evie looked up and saw a nightmare. Only it wasn't. It was real. A pocked face leered down from the treetops. Swollen, cracked lips. Enormous, fiery eyes. Fingers as thick as boulders, coming straight for them.

Evie's body clenched, ready to be crushed—

Somewhere high above, there was a deafening crack. "*Aaugh!*" bellowed Scabby Potatoes. He plunged forward and slammed to the ground. There stood Blunderbull, tossing aside the tree with which he'd just struck the other giant. Forbes kept his horse at a gallop as the black-haired giant bounded after them. The horse dove over the lip of a ravine and hurtled down the hill in a spray of tiny, golden leaves. The strides of the giants shook the forest. It was impossible to tell where they were until a foot broke through the trees and crashed down in front of them. It was as big as an ox, covered with layers of filth and cracked calluses. Forbes jerked the reins to the left, and the horse responded.

*There's nowhere left to go,* thought Evie. *The trees are too thick—*

Everything went black as her stomach shot down through her feet. The giant plucked her from the horse and hoisted her in the air, higher and higher, until she crashed through the canopy. She couldn't breathe as his fingers crushed her chest. Above the treetops, the world stretched away in all directions, a sea of gray. Below, Blunderbull grinned. His one eye leered at her above cracked and infected teeth, as misshapen and discolored as the boulders strewn about one hundred feet below.

"Not quite a meal, but you'll do for a starter, I reckon," he said. Then, suddenly, his face transformed, and he let out a shriek. Evie's stomach left her as she plummeted back toward the ground. Marline was there, slashing at the giant's toes with her sword.

Evie spread her arms just as she had at Joringel's Stem during her first year of training. The ground swooped toward her, branches rushing past, but soon her body began to angle forward. She was falling more slowly, soaring ahead through the trees rather than down to the ground. Still, her angle was too severe. She was going to crash.

"Fly!" she screamed at herself. The green sludge of a bog waited in the valley trough, but it was too far away. She tried to will her body forward. The earth raced toward her. The bog loomed ahead like a soft blanket of green. She was almost there . . .

SPLASH! She plunged into the frothy bog with a spray of dark muck. Her nose and lungs filled with fetid water. She thrashed about in a panic, but the thick slime held her like a net. The roars of the giants echoed through the trees.

She hacked and hacked, coughing up water that looked and tasted like stewed frogs. The stench filled her nose, even after she was finally able to take a deep breath. Somehow, she was still alive.

She sloshed toward what she thought must be the edge of the bog. The water burned her eyes. Suddenly, she was jerked back by an arm around her waist, throwing her down into the sludge. It was Forbes. The muck coated him like wet, green fur.

"Stay down!" he hissed. She blinked at him, utterly confused. "They can't smell us in here. Just stay down and keep quiet."

"But . . . Marline!" she said. "And where are Demetra and Basil?"

"Evie!" whispered Demetra. Two sludge-covered faces looked back at her from the edge of the bog. They were camouflaged beneath a rotting stump.

Just then, Scabby Potatoes barreled through the forest in pursuit of something. Trees creaked, then broke apart with furious crackles of splintering wood. The other giants bellowed, the crash of their footsteps rippling the bog water.

"Look!" called Basil.

There, sprinting straight toward the bog, was Marline. She had her sword held high and a demented smile on her face, as though she had just killed all three giants herself. "WOO-HOO!"

Behind her, trees exploded as Blunderbull and Galligantusohn raced after. With eyes as wide as the full moon, Marline leapt through the air. She sailed toward the bog, smashing down on top of Forbes. They both disappeared beneath the sludge as the giants thundered past. One of them stepped in the bog, causing a massive wave of stinking green to splash over all their heads. Then the booming strides began to recede, leaving twin paths of broken, twisted trees behind them. The trees tried to right themselves, but with snapped spines, the best they could do was flop around helplessly.

"I'm eating those children, and I'm going to make you watch!" howled Galligantusohn, shoving Blunderbull to the ground.

"I haven't got them, you muttonheaded lout!"

Scabby Potatoes bellowed in the distance.

Forbes's head shot out of the bog as he threw Marline off. He hacked up more of the disgusting water, wiping the green scum from his eyes. A moment later, Marline popped back up. She whipped her hair back with a smile, energized from multiple brushes with death.

"That was incredible!" she laughed. "Oi, come on back, boys!"

"Marline! Enough!" spat Forbes. "Have you forgotten there are a million witches out here as well?"

"Not here," said Basil. "The witches are farther out. They wouldn't be caught dead this close to the giants."

Forbes gave him a sarcastic smile. "Thank you for your expertise, Princess."

Basil scowled and trudged to the shoreline, inspecting the Bandit's Chair to make sure it had survived.

"I think you dropped your sword when I landed on you," said Marline with a wink. "Check over there."

Forbes scowled, violently swiping the sludge from his face, then waded over to where Marline had been and began feeling around in the swamp for his sword. Evie splashed out of the bog and joined the others on the shoreline. With trails of dying trees thrashing all around them, and the spring wind suddenly feeling quite wintry again, Evie and her friends smiled at one another.

But their moment of relief was short-lived. None of them could say where they'd ended up after the flight from the giants. The mission was a shambles, and the team was a splintered mess of what it was meant to be. Even the horses had gone.

"I'll find them," said Marline. She gave a sharp whistle, and her hawk swooped down from the sky and glided through the trees.

Just as Forbes started to complain about trusting a bird to find their horses, hoof beats began thundering toward them. It was Hossenbuhr's three horses with Marline's hawk in pursuit. Now that the bird had finished wrangling, it arced into the air and landed on a high branch. Forbes, meanwhile, grabbed the horses' tack and tried to calm them after the terrifying run from the giants.

"You're lucky," said Marline, giving Forbes an exultant smile. "I could've had him bring back only two."

Once they'd all mounted up again, Forbes, the most experienced of the group in affairs of the forest—except, of course, for Evie—took the lead. He insisted that the quickest way out of the Dortchen Wild was to head due north. Evie let him give the orders . . . for now. She knew that, according to Rumpledshirtsleeves's map, north was where they needed to go anyway. "Besides," she said to Demetra, "it's only his pig instincts taking over. Believe me, if he steers us wrong, I'll let him know."

They rode for quite some time in relative silence. Marline's hawk kept a constant vigil from the skies. The trees occasionally rustled with hostility, but the cadets still managed to make good progress over the swooping hills and valleys of the enchanted forest. Finally, after several hours, Basil asked for a rest.

The five of them sat in silence, exhausted from what had happened that morning. After a while, Basil spoke.

"The giants aren't all bad, are they?" He took a drink from his waterskin. "They're brilliant at keeping the witches away."

"The witches may be afraid of the giants," came a sprightly voice from the trees, "but I'm not."

The horses whinnied, snorting against their reins, which had been tied to a tree. Evie quickly scanned the forest for confirmation of what her heart already knew. And there, atop a small hill, stood a figure wrapped in a dark cloak.

"Malora."

"LOVELY DAY for a walk in the woods, is it not?" said the witch, her skin as waxen and lumpy as a melted candle.

Marline looked at Malora, then back to Evie and the others, dumbfounded that no one was doing anything. "Well? Have none of you seen a witch before? Because that is one." When no one spoke, she squared her body to Malora's, and a spark of white began to appear. "All right, then, allow me."

"Wait," said Evie. "That's my sister."

The magical light vanished. Marline looked at Evie with astonishment. "That?" She pointed at Malora. "*That's* your sister?"

"Stepsisters, actually. Aren't we, darling?" said Malora, stepping down from the trees. As she joined them near the bog, her features came into view. She had deteriorated even further in the weeks since Evie, Demetra, and Basil had seen her at the Drudenhaus. The skin around her eyes hung loose, and streaks of white ran through the stringy remains of her once-lustrous hair. Still, the thing that sent a chill through Evie was that her sister seemed strangely upbeat. *She's happy,* thought

Evie. *I think I might have preferred her angry.* "Where's your ginger friend?" she said with glee. "Did the witches get her?"

"Maggie's at the Academy, and she's perfectly fine," said Demetra defensively.

Malora's eyes snapped over. Her smile turned to a glare. "You survived as well? What a shame." She gave Demetra one last look of distaste, then turned back to Evie with a smile. "Come, dear sister, haven't you any fun gossip? Nothing to keep me entertained as I wait for the wall to fall—"

"They got Sage," said Evie. In the silence that followed, she realized how cruel it had sounded. "It was right after the attack. She was running toward me, and the witches turned her to stone."

Malora swallowed thickly. Her cheery demeanor faltered. "What are you all doing out here, anyway?"

"What are *you* doing out here?" said Forbes.

"I'm looking for the best possible view to watch the wall come down. Now answer my question."

"We're on a mission," said Evie, and her heart began to race.

"Evie!" Marline jumped forward with her hands out. "What are you doing? I don't care if that is your sister; it's still a witch!"

"It?" said Malora with amusement.

"We're family," said Evie. "She might be able to help us."

Malora let out a shrill cackle. "Again? I just saved Cinderella for you. What is it now? Shall I trim Rapunzel's hair?"

"Take us past the siege lines. We need to go north, out of the Dortchen Wild."

"Evie," said Demetra, taking Evie's elbow. "She only just

got finished betraying us. She tried to hand us over to the Vertreiben, remember?"

"I did do that, didn't I?" said Malora. "Must have been my inner witch coming through."

Evie ignored her. "She helped us in the end. Cinderella wouldn't be alive if not for her."

"Ah, and that would be my inner princess," said Malora. "What a quandary!"

"And your inner jabbermouth takes up the whole thing, doesn't it?" said Marline.

Malora only grinned at her and flashed her eyebrows.

Evie, flustered, waved her group closer. "Pretend you aren't hearing any of this," she said to Malora.

"All right," said the witch.

"This wasn't part of the plan, Evie," said Demetra quietly.

"None of this was. Forbes wasn't part of the plan. Marline wasn't part of the plan. Remington and Maggie *were* part of the plan, and they aren't here. But we've just got to adapt, don't we? Courage, compassion, kindness, and *discipline*. We can't let the unexpected throw us off our mission. We've got to stay disciplined. We're princesses. That's what we do."

"I'm not," said Forbes, raising his hand.

"We've got a witch right here in front of us who can help lead us past the others. Without her, what else are we going to do? This is the part we didn't plan for." Each of them considered her words. "Come on, let's adapt again. Let's stay disciplined and stay on course."

Forbes and Marline exchanged a dubious look. Both were wary of Malora, but both nodded in approval. Demetra did the same. Basil stroked his chin and pondered.

"Well? Bas?"

"So our choices are these. We either have a guide with inside knowledge of our enemy who could help us sneak past but who could just as easily turn around and kill us, or we take the safer route of trying to sneak past a thousand witches on our own? Hardly an inspiring selection. But I suppose we should go with Malora. She is your family, and that's got to count for something, right?"

Evie looked over at her sister, who was watching them closely. "Well? Will you help us?"

"Tell me where you're going and why and I'll help you."

"Hang on," said Marline. "I don't even know that."

Evie stared into her sister's wide yellow eyes. She was trying to read her intentions, but it was impossible. "We're taking that chair to Rumpledshirtsleeves's brother," she said, pointing at the Bandit's Chair strapped to Basil's back. "Then he'll lead us to an enchanted harp that will turn the giants against the witches."

Marline faced Evie, incredulous. "We're out here risking our lives to deliver furniture?"

"So? Will you do it?" said Evie. She had to force herself to look past the decaying face of the witch standing before her to envision the black-haired girl she'd first met on the coach. Her sister.

"What an entertaining choice! I came down here to watch

116

the giants eat all of you, but seeing them turn on Calivigne and the rest might be even better." She strolled along the edge of the bog. "All right. I'll take you as far as Marburg, but then you've got to promise you'll come back with that harp so I can have my show."

"Marburg?" said Demetra. "But isn't it—"

"Controlled by the witches? Yes," said Malora. "But on the other side of that . . . open forest."

Evie locked eyes with Demetra, who was completely on edge, then turned to Basil, Forbes, and Marline. None of them spoke. "Lead on," she finally said.

"Excellent!" said Malora. "Our giant friends are bellowing just over there, so let's set off this way instead." She motioned up the stony hill she'd just come down.

"Placing our lives in a witch's hands because she's 'family,'" said Forbes. "Brilliant."

"Uh . . . Evie?" said Basil in a soft voice. "I realize this is a bit petty, but . . . we've only got three horses. One of us will have to ride with . . ." He flicked his eyes toward the witch, then scratched his head self-consciously.

"My sister and I will ride together," said Evie.

"Oh no," said Malora with a laugh. "Those horses wouldn't let me near them. I always bring my own."

She lifted her hands, and the dead leaves carpeting the forest floor began to rattle. They slowly swirled, rising higher and higher until they were far above Malora's head. Then, in an instant, they all fell. As the leaves fluttered to the ground, the form of a horse appeared in their midst. It looked as though it were made from the dead leaves.

"I suppose I could just fly, but I wouldn't want to make anyone jealous." She gave Evie a wink. Then she lifted off the ground and deposited herself onto the phantasm's back. It snorted and stomped, just like a real horse.

"I'll ride alone, then, shall I?" said Marline. She snatched the reins from Forbes and mounted one of the horses. Her hawk circled down from the tree and landed on the saddle behind her.

Evie glanced at the two horses, then at Demetra and Basil huddled near each other. She closed her eyes, deeply pained. "Fine. I'll ride with Forbes."

"Thank you for welcoming me to the team so graciously," he said, climbing atop one of the horses.

"Who says you get the reins?"

"I'm a far better rider than you. Get on."

Evie's face darkened, but she knew he was right. She'd spent a fair bit of time on her horse, Boy, the previous summer, but Forbes had been riding his entire life. She grudgingly took his hand and got on behind him.

Basil and Demetra gave each other an awkward look. "Well, I'm not really bothered," said Basil. "Do you want to drive?"

"If it's all the same to you," said Demetra. "I still get a bit scared of horses if I'm not in control of the reins."

"By all means," said Basil. He helped Demetra up, then climbed on behind her.

"Shall we get on with it, then, before those monsters return?" said Forbes.

"A word to the wise," said Malora. "It's time for you to start worrying about witches instead." And with that, she rode silently up the stony hill into the forest.

As the day began its final stretch through the late afternoon, someone finally broke the silence. "This is utterly ridiculous," said Forbes. "I've studied navigation under the best mapmakers money can buy, and we're out here traipsing after a witch."

Evie was snatched from her thoughts. The group was still following Malora, but now they'd reached a relatively flat bit of forest. The red leaves carpeting the ground looked like waves in the sea, with strange, curved trees sprouting up all around like fishing hooks.

"Shouldn't we at least *see* Marburg in the distance by now?" he said.

Malora slowed her phantom mount until she was riding next to Forbes and Evie, upsetting their horse. "I liked you better when you could only oink."

He scowled at her but said nothing.

Malora turned to her sister, her eyes as shimmering yellow as topaz gemstones. "Have I told you the worst part of all this, Sister? It's looking back on my childhood and feeling so utterly stupid. The conversations with Mother about the evils of the witch as she prepared me for the Academy—I wish you could have been there for those. It must have revolted her to have to say the things she said. 'Witches are evil, and only princesses can defeat them!'" She chuckled and shook her head. "And she never once talked about what would happen when I actually became a princess. There were no stories of what a great hero I'd be and how I could help save the realm from the horrors of the witch. Because that part was never actually meant to happen. The Seven Sisters say they wanted to turn me into a Princess-Witch, but in truth, none of that mattered. They only cared about getting what they wanted."

Evie felt a cold chill rush through her heart. "What did they want?"

"What they always want. Information. They wanted a way to see inside the mind and heart of a princess so they could learn how to defeat her. I'm nothing but an experiment. An instruction manual for that army they've got up there in the mountains."

"Army?" said Forbes. "What are you talking about?"

Malora's face stretched into a grin. "You were right, Pig-Boy. We should have been in Marburg by now. I've decided to bring you on a little detour, but I think you'll be pleased that I did." Her grin curled down at the corners. "Not far now. Just up ahead."

Against Forbes's complaints, they rode on for the better part of an hour. Behind the clouds, the sky steadily dimmed. Finally, Malora's spectral horse began to move just a bit faster. She rode to the edge of a hilltop and stopped, turning back to face them with a smile. "Come. See."

Evie's fingers clenched Forbes's cloak. The horse walked up the hill and joined Malora's. The others followed. On the far side of the hill, the earth sloped away into a great pine valley. Just below them, in a crease between hills, there sat an enormous pile of sticks. Someone had deliberately put them there, forming a crude structure.

"An old beaver's dam," sighed Forbes. "Well worth the trip."

"Go on," said Malora, nudging her skeletal head toward the structure. "You'll like it, I promise."

Evie swung herself off the horse. After so many hours riding, the ground felt strange beneath her feet. The muscles in her back and legs ached. Malora suddenly appeared next to her, floating to the ground as her horse disappeared in a swirl of leaves.

"You don't have to come," said Evie, looking up at the others.

"Yes, they do," said Malora. "They'll like it, too."

Marline dismounted, as did Demetra and Basil. Forbes, however, sighed and remained on his horse. One by one, they followed Malora down into the furrow. The wooden hut was much bigger than it had looked from above, with sticks spearing out of it like a morning star.

"What is this?"

"Come and see." Malora crept inside through a small doorway.

Evie turned back to her friends, who were all looking at the hut with apprehension. "Wait here. I'll be right back."

She walked slowly to the doorway. As she neared, she could

smell the biting stench of black mold inside. She closed her eyes for a moment, just to gather her courage, then ducked through.

Malora stood to the side, watching Evie. Cracks in the walls of the hut let only traces of dusky sunlight in. The mold spores in the air nearly choked her. A cursory glance revealed several broken tables, shattered vials of many different colors, and parchments scattered everywhere, as though someone had left in a hurry. On the far side of the room, there was an overturned cauldron.

"What is this?"

"Do you remember when I told you how stupid the witches had made me feel? Well, this is where they did it to me all over again." She looked across the ransacked hut. "This is where they planned the whole thing."

"Planned what?"

Malora stalked around the room, glaring at the detritus as she passed. "While you and I were off dancing with the Vertreiben, the witches were here planning their assault on the Academy."

Evie's whole body shuddered. *Calivigne has been here. In this very room.*

"The witches knew what I was doing with the Vertreiben, and they let me go on doing it. They used me to distract you. Me and Javotte and all the other fools."

"What are you talking about?"

"They thought it would be the Vertreiben who would drive you out of the Academy and into their hands. They hadn't expected you and me to have a secret meeting at the Drudenhaus. And yet it somehow still turned out beautifully for the witches, didn't it? Just wait for poor stupid Malora to finish being a distraction, then launch the attack."

Evie's eyes flitted around the hut. There were books and parchments and stacks and stacks of documents. "All this . . . belongs to the witches?"

"Every scrap."

Evie began to leaf through a stack of cracked parchments on the table next to her. There were maps. Lists of names and villages and kingdoms. Portraits and sketches. Handwritten notes and diagrams of carriage coaches. Her mind lurched from one thought to the next. "This isn't supposed to happen. This level of detail . . . of organization. Witches are supposed to work alone."

"Wait until you see the really good stuff."

Her eyes snapped over to her sister. "What do you mean?"

Malora took a casual step over some scattered debris to where a small wooden shelf had collapsed from rot and rain. She picked up a stack of parchments tied with twine and tossed them at Evie's feet. "I believe these are yours."

Evie picked up the stack and pulled the twine open, her heart thumping. She unfolded the first parchment. *Dear Evie,* it read. *I do hope my letters are reaching you. I'm a little surprised you haven't written back yet. I like to think you're too busy writing to Remington.* She quickly scanned to the bottom of the letter. The closing read, *Your friend, Maggie.*

She flipped to another and found the same looped hand-writing. Then another. And another. "These are all letters from Maggie to me, but I've never seen them before. I don't understand."

"The witches intercepted them."

"What? But why? What possible value could these letters have to them?"

"They didn't want the letters," said Malora, smiling.

Slowly, the witches' plan began to reveal itself in Evie's mind. "They wanted me. They thought they could make me worry about Maggie enough to ride south."

"Yes, but then you rode east instead, didn't you? I hear they were none too pleased when they learned you'd gone to see the blond rather than the redhead."

Evie felt a cold pall sweep over her. She had nearly done exactly what the witches had wanted. She even remembered feeling guilty for choosing to go to Demetra's home instead of Maggie's. But there had been one thing, one detail, that had decided it for her, and may have indeed saved her life. Demetra had mentioned in her letters that her father knew Evie's human father, King Callahan. One offhand comment had altered her decision, and may have altered the entire course of her life.

"Evie?" said Demetra, peering in the small doorway. "Are you all right?"

"Yes," she said, though in truth, her mind was still reeling. "Yes. Come inside."

"What is this place?" said Demetra with a cough.

"It's a witch encampment," said Evie. "It's where they planned the siege. All this stuff . . . It could be invaluable to the princesses."

"It certainly could," said Demetra, flipping through some nearby parchments. "But what are we supposed to do with it all? We'd need horses and carts to even make a dent. And it's already getting dark."

"We can't just leave it." She looked around at the wealth of information they'd be forced to abandon. "We've got to search the place. Let's take this stuff outside where we can get a proper look at it. Anything important goes in our saddlebags."

She and Demetra took armfuls of parchments, books, paintings, ledgers, and other ephemera out into the softening daylight. Marline jumped down from the overhang to help, while Forbes and Basil took two horses and patrolled the surrounding forest. Much of what the girls discovered was too damaged to be of any value. The ink had faded away or the parchment was too rotten or brittle.

Malora watched them from a slate boulder nearby, one leg folded across the other. "Don't be too choosy. There must be plenty of valuable information there."

"Shame we can't bring the lot of it back," said Marline. "There's things in here the Queen herself probably doesn't even know." She held up a parchment, shaking her head in amazement. "Look at this." She showed Evie the hand-drawn map. There were black scratches showing routes of attack. "It's the whole bloody ambush right here."

Evie, meanwhile, was nervous. The longer they took sifting through the witches' cache, the darker the sky was growing. And they still had plenty of forest to traverse. She started on a new stack of documents. The first was a list of ingredients for some unnamed potion—lutewart and trolls' tongues and other such unpleasantness. Then, beneath that, she discovered something odd. It was a painting, only slightly smaller than the average parchment. And it was of extraordinary quality, though the edges were water-stained and withered. The painting depicted roughly twenty women in white Pennyroyal Academy uniforms. Each wore a tiara in her hair. The parchment was muddy and faded, nearly broken where it had been creased, yet the likenesses were startlingly lifelike. But none of that was what troubled Evie. What troubled Evie was that all but four of the women's faces that remained had been crossed out with a large red X. "What d'you reckon this is?"

Marline glanced over as she put the map in her saddlebag. "Class portrait. We all get them after we're commissioned. Can't bloody wait for mine."

Demetra looked over Evie's shoulder at the class portrait and gasped. "No!"

"What? What is it?"

She snatched it out of Evie's hands. Her eyes were filled with terror. "No!"

"Demetra, what's wrong?"

"That's my mother! Right there, it's my mother!"

Evie looked at the face in the portrait. It was the same woman with whom she'd ridden from the Blackmarsh to Waldeck the previous autumn. *Cadet Christa*, it said below. Thankfully, her face was not emblazoned with an X.

"What is this?" said Demetra, shaking the parchment at Malora. "Why are they all crossed out?"

"I've no idea," she said with a bit too much elation. "Perhaps they've won some sort of prize?"

"This isn't funny! What are they going to do to my mother?"

"Lower your voice," said Malora. Her smile faded away, and her eyes suddenly became much more intense. "I've no idea why those people are crossed out."

"Look here!" said Marline as she took the portrait from Demetra. "This says Cadet Middlemiss! She was in your mum's class? Aw, blast, the rain's eaten her away." She rubbed the disintegrated edge with her thumb where Middlemiss's face had once been.

"This isn't the time, Marline," said Evie.

"Right." Her excitement fell when she realized how scared Demetra was. "Sorry."

She handed the class portrait back to Demetra and moved off to check some more of the documents. Evie took Demetra's hands. "She hasn't been crossed out. I'm sure she's all right."

"We have no idea how old this is! It could have been sitting here for months! Oh, Evie, what if something's happened to my mum?"

She collapsed into Evie's arms. "We're going to get through this, all right?" said Evie. "We'll figure it out together."

"Mothers are overrated anyway," said Malora.

"Mind your tongue," snapped Marline. "Or I'll mind it for you."

Malora sat back on her stone and cackled.

"Look," said Evie. "Something's written on the back."

Demetra turned the portrait. Scrawled across it in black ink were the words *Beatrice said it was this one—ALL MUST GO.* She and Evie looked at each other in shock.

"Beatrice?"

"Mount up!" came a distant voice. "We've left it too late! We've got to go before it's full night!" It was Forbes. He and Basil were riding up from the forest. Evie only now realized how difficult it was to see them.

"We've done all we can here," she said. "Let's go."

Forbes and Basil reined to a stop, their eyes wide against the falling night. "Well?" said Basil.

Marline began stuffing his saddlebags with documents as quickly as she could while Evie helped Demetra onto his horse. "Demetra's had a bit of a shock, I'm afraid."

"What is it? Are you all right?"

"I'm fine," said Demetra. "Let's talk about it later."

"Of course," said Basil, but now he looked as worried as the rest of them.

"We'll have to go the rest of the way at night," said Forbes.

"It was worth it," said Evie. She shoved the stacks of documents she thought might be the most valuable into the saddlebags until they couldn't hold anymore, then took Forbes's hand and climbed up.

Malora had conjured her phantom horse and was waiting right in front of them, her yellow eyes casting an eerie dim glow. "Shall we?"

"Hang on, not yet," said Marline. She whistled sharply. A moment later, a streak of wind flew through the darkness. The hawk dove straight at Malora. She screamed and fell off her horse as the hawk looped back up into the air. With a shout of rage, a puff of black smoke billowed out from the witch's chest. It lanced into the sky, striking the hawk like a lightning bolt. The bird plummeted, hitting the ground with a stony thump.

Marline stared at the bird-shaped statue planted in the moss. Then she looked at Malora with shock. "What'd you do that for?"

"It attacked me!"

"He did not. I was just having a laugh!" In an instant, she was off her horse and kneeling by her hawk's statue. "What've you done?"

Malora stood with a scowl, brushing the leaves off. She mounted her horse as Marline lifted the stone bird off the ground, then gently secured it to the back of the saddle. Once the final strap had been tightened, she walked calmly over and stood beneath Malora. She pointed a finger that was at once accusatory and threatening.

"The moment we've saved the Academy, I'm going to cut you down. And for the rest of my life whenever anyone mentions your name, I'll cut them down, too."

As she turned and walked back to her horse, a delighted smile bloomed across Malora's face. "Ooh, well, I'll certainly look forward to that."

Marline climbed onto her horse. "It's coming."

"She loved that bird more than I've ever loved anything," said Forbes to Evie in a low voice. A heavy stillness followed as the night finally snuffed out the daylight.

"Let's just go," said Evie.

They rode in silence for hours, over moonlit hills and shadowed valleys. The darkness and the chill in the air and the threat of witches in the trees gave each of them enough solitude to get lost in their thoughts. Evie's went to something Malora had said back at the witch encampment. *I'm nothing but an experiment. An instruction manual for that army they've got up there in the mountains.* Lieutenant Volf had taught them that witches were reclusive creatures who preferred to be alone. But recently there had been more and more instances of witches working together. This, a secret army somewhere in the mountains, would be an entirely new level of cooperation. She wrestled with all the different elements of it as they continued north through the pines. Where had Malora heard about that? And could she be trusted? Could it possibly be true?

Finally, the endless hours of night ended abruptly. Malora's horse evaporated into the darkness, and she floated to the ground. She turned to the others. In the dim moonlight diffusing through the clouds, her face looked like a skull. "Here we are. The jewel of the mountain kingdoms. You can leave your horses here. We've finished with them."

"Are you mad?" said Forbes. "You want us to go on foot?"

"Witches cannot see well, but they can absolutely smell. And horses smell even worse than you people do."

They all exchanged dubious looks, though none of them dismounted.

"Marburg is just beyond this hill," said Malora. "I'll help you through, but there are many witches there. And they will smell your horses, and they will find you and throw you in pots. Is that your choice?"

"You could have told us this before we wasted all that time filling the saddlebags with documents," said Evie.

"Yes, I suppose I could have," she said with a smile.

Evie sighed heavily, then climbed off the horse. "Come on. There's no point in arguing now." Her stomach clenched at the thought of all the documents they'd be forced to leave behind.

Marline dismounted, then began untying the hawk from the saddle. She lashed it over her shoulders and didn't complain once. Basil did the same with the Bandit's Chair. Evie checked the saddlebags for anything else she could carry but decided only on her knapsack. Forbes stayed on his horse the longest. As they all peered up at him, he rolled his eyes. Then he jumped off with a frown.

Malora led them through the trees in a single line. Climbing a rambling hill, Evie began to notice an orange light in the distance. It wasn't long before she realized it was fire.

They reached the summit. There stood the once-grand Kingdom of Marburg, ruined by war. There were flames eating away at some of the interior buildings. The gates had been torn free and burned, leaving only their iron bones. Carriages were strewn in front of the curtain walls, dismantled and destroyed.

Standing atop each lookout, creeping along the top of each wall, loomed the dark forms of dozens of witches.

"They're like cockroaches," said Marline. "Big, magical cockroaches."

She was peering through a slit in the curtains of a carriage window. Malora had found one on its side outside the kingdom walls that hadn't been too badly damaged by the witches. She had righted it and conjured several of her phantoms to pull. The horses looked more like moonlit reflections in the water than actual living beings. Inside, the carriage smelled like a dungeon cell that had never seen the sun, dank and thick.

Evie slipped the curtains aside with her finger and saw a sliver of the kingdom. They were traveling down one of Marburg's twisting back roads. Witches stared with yellow eyes from the windows of the once-grand timber-framed cottages and buildings that ringed the castle. Others lurched down the street, stopping to watch as the carriage passed by.

"What've you got in there?" squawked one of them, a short,

round one whose oversized yellow eyes made her look like an owl.

"Mind your business," said Malora from the driver's box outside. The witch recoiled as though stung. She turned her yellow eyes right to Evie, who leapt back with a gasp. Marline, however, didn't even flinch.

"This whole bloody kingdom stinks of fire," she said quietly. Then she sat back and let the curtain fall closed.

"I'll never understand why they burn things," said Forbes. "Odd choice for monsters who hate fire."

"They're like a lot of things," said Marline. "Attracted to what kills them."

Forbes scoffed. "That's ridiculous."

"It's not, mate. We learned all about the psychology of the witch this year." She turned to face him, the stone hawk on the bench between them. Evie, Demetra, and Basil sat on the bench opposite. "Witches love the rain, yeah? And they also love fire. Two things that could kill them, and they love it. Now why is that?"

"I believe that was my original question."

"Listen, you snotty git, you've got to think about what motivates a witch. She's made up of dead things. Someone's heart. Dried herbs. Crushed bones. Whatever else they throw in that stew. All of it dead. Then, when she comes climbing out of the cauldron, she's born without a heart of her own. Practically speaking, she's already dead, isn't she?"

"You're giving them too much credit with all this," said Forbes. "They're simple animals."

"Just listen, will you? I'm trying to educate you about your enemy."

Evie was most certainly listening.

"Witches are drawn to fire and water because they're drawn to rot and decay. Look at this kingdom here. They've already plundered it, haven't they? Not much left for them, to be honest. But they can't get enough. Because they want to see it in ruins. They *need* to see it in ruins. The destruction fuels them. But on the other side of the coin, fire and water can also kill them, yeah? Why is that? Because they're two essential elements of *life*."

"Fascinating," said Basil. "I'd never thought of that before."

"It's the same reason we've got centuries of stories about princesses and witches. It's never sea captains and witches, is it? Or flower merchants and witches. It's always princesses and witches. We're drawn to each other. It's inevitable. We're blood enemies, but we're forever bumping up against each other, as connected as a moth and a flame. The magic a true princess can create is built with love. Has to be. It's made up of courage and compassion, and what else is love but those? The witch is drawn to it, to us, but we're also what kills her."

Forbes sat with his arms crossed, a sour look on his face. He glanced over at Marline. Evie could tell he was impressed, despite his attempts not to be. "So how many have you killed?"

"Not nearly enough," she said. "I've only been a Princess of the Shield for a few days, haven't I? But I'll tell you one thing: it'll be a few more dead before I'm gone. I bloody hate witches. My stepmother was a witch."

"So was mine," said Evie.

"I've never had a stepmother," said Forbes.

"Human mother here," said Basil.

"Same," added Demetra.

"Two stepmothers, two witches. Not a very good ratio," said Marline.

"Only a fool would put their trust in family, blood or not," said Forbes. "We think we need them as children, but we're better off once we realize we can stand on our own."

A wave of shame crashed over Evie. Though he had phrased it in his own uniquely harsh way, it still hit a bit too close to home. Since enlisting at the Academy, she'd felt herself steadily growing apart from her family. This summer, she'd even decided to abandon them to go to Maggie's instead. The idea that they might see it as her not needing them anymore nauseated her.

"My stepmother was far more than disappointing," said Marline, patting her stone hawk with affection. "She murdered my brother here."

Forbes gave the statue a dubious look. "Your brother?"

"Half brother, if you want to be a slave to the facts. But whatever you'd like to call him, he was the best brother any girl could hope for. We shared a father. A great man, truly. But she bewitched him. Next thing we knew, she was our stepmother. She was cruel to my brother but never to me. It made things even worse. I felt guilty for all the secret torment he went through, but I was just a child. I didn't know what to do, and neither did he. And then one day Dad went off to market, and she finally took it too far. Set fire to my happy family just to watch it burn."

"Who's inside?" came another muffled witch's voice.

"You'll be if you ask that again," snapped Malora. Even through the carriage walls, her contempt for her fellow witches was clear. The axle squeaked as they jostled over a rut in the road.

"All she left of my brother was bones. I found him before my father could, thank the Fates. Wrapped him in linen and buried him beneath the big juniper tree outside our cottage. Then I got down on my knees and said a prayer for him. And that's when something happened that changed my life forever. The tree started thrashing about, you know, in the way enchanted trees do. Only it wasn't enchanted. Next thing I knew, it just . . . split in half. Straight down the middle. And there he was." She looked down at her statue with bittersweet eyes.

"That's remarkable," said Demetra. "He came back as a hawk?"

"Aye. And as soon as he did, he was off. Gone into the clouds. I was absolutely gutted. And there sat my stepmum with this smile on her face. So pleased with herself. Well, about a week or so later, back he came." She sat forward, trying to keep her voice down, though she was clearly excited. "I can't possibly explain this to you properly, but I swear that it happened. When my brother came back, he had a millstone in his talons. I understand that's not possible, yeah? But it happened." She couldn't stop smiling now, the same intense, slightly mad expression Evie had first seen during the ambush. "You know what he did? He flew at her. Knocked her in the river. Then he dropped the millstone right on her head. Pinned her underneath. I'd never been more proud of my brother in all my life."

"I'm so sorry, Marline," said Demetra. "I had no idea that hawk was your brother. No wonder you're so attached to him."

"I promised him the day he killed that witch that I'd never leave him again. And I never have done." She kept her hand on the hawk's back. "We've traveled all across this land, my brother and me. And ever since that day, we've never been afraid of anything. Not one thing." Before she could become too emotional, her melancholy became anger. She thrust her finger toward the front of the coach. "But she should be."

The carriage hit another bump, and Marline settled back, drifting away into her thoughts. With everyone else going silent as well, Evie turned to her window. She eased the curtain aside and put her eye to the glass. The black-cloaked figures were even thicker here on the high road, lurking amongst the burnt walls and soot-clouded puddles. This was the very spot where she had first become enchanted by humanity. And now it was crawling with witches.

They seemed to be growing more interested in the carriage as well, watching it pass with hungry eyes and leering grins. They crept out from the butcher's and the tanner's and the stables and the forge. They crawled through the timber-framed buildings, skulking behind broken windows, hobbling figures with sharp noses and sagging skin, stinking of rot. The only sound was the repetitive squeak of the carriage axle as the wheels bounced along the stone-pocked road.

One witch, her hair the consistency of sun-dried worms, got a bit too close. There was a loud crackle that made Evie wince. The witch flew backward, struck by one of Malora's dark spells. The others backed away, their evil grins replaced by anger and fear.

"Stop, Evie," said Demetra. "It's better if you don't look."

Evie closed the curtain, but it didn't help her nerves at all. Her fists were clenched for what felt like an eternity. What she'd seen out the window was less frightening than what she was seeing in her imagination, so she looked back outside again.

"Nearly there," she whispered with relief. "We're almost through the gatehouse." The witches were fewer near the massive wooden doors. The wheels cracked as they bounced onto the timbers of the drawbridge. "We're outside! We've done it!"

The rumble of the wheels on the drawbridge filled the carriage until at last they reached the other side, where they crunched back down onto gravel and dirt. Evie filled her lungs and let her muscles relax as Malora's creatures spent the next twenty minutes navigating the thin, winding trail down the mountain ridge from Marburg. Finally, the carriage groaned to a stop. Marline opened the door, picked up her statue, and stepped outside. One by one, the rest of them emerged. The fires lit up Marburg on the other side of the valley, but otherwise the night was cool and crisp and clear. Basil piled out of the carriage and ran to the bushes to be sick. When he returned, his skin had gone gray. "Sorry," he said. "I can't tolerate riding backward."

"Well," said Malora, "it seems I've done my part. And I didn't even kill a one of you." She smiled. "Unless you count the bird." Marline just laughed and shook her head as she stepped away.

"Thank you, Malora," said Evie. She stared into her sister's eyes, despite how terrifying she found it. "I mean it. Thank you. You may have been born a witch, but that doesn't mean you have to be one."

"A lovely sentiment," said Malora, "but I wasn't born, remember? I was mixed up in a pot and sent off with a head full of lies." She waved the tips of her fingers dismissively. "Ta-ta."

"Come on," said Marline. "Before those witches up there realize what just happened." Demetra, Forbes, and Basil began to follow her down the hill, but Evie lingered, still staring at her sister.

"I hope we meet again."

A cold smile crept across Malora's face. "You shouldn't."

There was more Evie wanted to say, but she couldn't put it into words. Finally, she turned and walked away. As she and her friends entered a spruce forest, with tall trunks and feathery needles all around them, Evie couldn't help feeling a sense of sadness about leaving Malora. *I know there's good in her... Why doesn't she?* The only road in sight was a thin strip of red earth descending into the fog that hung heavily beneath the trees. They consulted Rumpledshirtsleeves's map and saw that the westernmost of the Two Brothers was just ahead at the bottom of the mountain. The forest was quiet and empty, except for the haunting echo of the wolves singing across the valley. Over and over they howled, joining and rejoining the chorus to create one chilling voice.

"What a beautiful call," said Marline softly after they'd been walking quite a distance. "Beautiful call from a beautiful creature."

Then, in the darkness ahead, they heard Forbes's sword jump from its scabbard.

"Who's there?" Everyone froze as he took a step into the ferns lining the path.

"Forbes!" whispered Evie. "What is it?"

"Come out of there," he said in a loud voice, stopping ten feet short of a copse of ghostly white birches.

Evie watched the shadows. Something seemed to be moving, but she couldn't tell if it was just her mind playing tricks.

"I said come out." Forbes sheathed his sword. "Come on, you. Out."

A little boy emerged from the trees. He was dressed in rags, mud-stained and filthy. He looked to be around ten years old, with short brown hair.

"Who are you?"

"No one," said the boy.

"What are you doing out here in the dark?"

"You're not meant to see me. I'm to stay hidden and report anyone who passes."

Forbes narrowed his eyes. "Report to whom?"


The boy, whose name turned out to be Franz, stopped behind a large spruce tree that leaned perilously over the edge of a cliff. One good storm would send it plunging to the river below. Franz pointed just downstream to where the water bent back to the right and disappeared into the forest.

"That's where we live," said Franz. "Everyone's very nice."

"Is this the Two Brothers?" said Basil.

"One of them," said Franz. "West Brother."

"Look at that, we made it! Go on, Franzie, take us down."

The boy turned and gave the group a sheepish look. "They're going to be cross with me for being spotted."

Demetra stepped forward and bent down in front of him. "They won't be cross when they hear what a hero you've been. Do you see her?" She pointed at Marline. "That's a Princess of the Shield. Who could be angry with you for finding her? I bet they'll all be thrilled."

The worry evaporated from the boy's face. He led them along the river and down the embankment to a small collection of tents and cook fires nestled above the water. Several villagers milled about, each as filthy as Franz. Some roasted fish on spits. Evie's stomach rumbled.

"What's this?" said one of them in alarm.

"That's a Princess of the Shield," said Franz with pride. "Found her myself."

The villager's eyes went wide, as though Marline were a visiting queen.

"My father and sister and I live just at the bottom," said Franz, continuing along. "We've been here longer than most."

"Where were you before this?" said Demetra.

"Up in Marburg. Most of us here are from Marburg, but there are others. Some came from the west, where they say it's even worse than here. The north as well. This place is all right because the witches don't really come down this way. Princess of the Shield here," he said to the people they passed. "Found her on the road." The men and women they passed gave nods and even the occasional smile. Soft snores came from several of the tents. And still the wolves howled across the river.

Evie kept her eyes on the people in the encampment but also on the blackness beyond. It was bold to have fires at night, but the villagers had clearly been there quite some time and knew the risks. When Franz led them to a group of three sitting on stones around one of the fires, Evie stopped dead. Across the river, the wolves' howling ceased.

One of the three, a man, passed a twig with a roasted fish to the person next to him. Evie studied his silhouette, and her stomach did flips. "It can't be . . ."

"What's wrong?" said Basil. He followed her eyes. "Do you know him?"

Now the man felt himself being examined and turned to face Evie. At first, his eyebrows crinkled up unpleasantly, as though he'd eaten something sour.

"Who is this, Evie?"

"Wormwood?" she said, stepping into the firelight.

His head shook, as though it couldn't possibly be true. "You're . . . why, you're the Countess's girl, aren't you? My stars, is that really you?"

"It is. It's me. Evie."

"Evie," he said in astonishment.

"Who's Wormwood?" said Basil. "It's considered polite to answer questions, you know."

"He's Countess Hardcastle's valet." She ran forward and

hugged him. Where he had been plump and doughy when she'd met him before, now his skin sagged from his bones. His crisp uniform was gone, replaced by simple linen clothes and a tattered cloak.

"Evie," he said. "I never dreamt I'd see you again."

"Nor I you." She had spoken hardly a word to Wormwood when they'd first met, yet seeing him now felt like reconnecting with a long-lost friend. "Wormwood drove Malora and me to Callahan Manor after the wolf attack our first year." She looked back at him, unable to contain her smile. "But what are you doing here?"

His jowls sagged below his chin as his entire face fell. A memory had come to him, and not a pleasant one. "It all came apart. I'd known something was wrong for years, but . . . so many strange goings-on at that house. All the other servants left when you and the King died. They couldn't handle it with only Hardcastle and Malora there. I don't know why I stayed. She always treated me decently, the Countess, but it would be a lie to say she didn't frighten the dickens out of me." He seemed to finally notice Evie's friends gathered just outside the fire. "Are you lot from the Academy as well, then?"

"We are," said Marline. "One graduate, three princess cadets, and one angry, bitter knight cadet."

Forbes gave her a cutting glare.

"Well . . . you just keep your eyes on that Headmistress of yours," said Wormwood. "Something's not right with that woman, if you ask me."

"Princess Beatrice?" said Evie. "Why do you say that?"

"She was up to Callahan Manor many, many times. Always had to have the expensive wines decanting when the Headmistress came for a visit. And she seemed entirely too chatty about dark things. I'd hear the two of them laughing on the veranda into the wee hours, the wine vanishing faster than I could pour it. And many's the time I heard whispered words exchanged about . . ." He looked up with distaste. "Witches."

"That settles it!" said Demetra. "She *is* with them!"

"But how could that be?" said Evie. "Wormwood?"

His jaw had fallen open. He stared wide-eyed toward a commotion at the top of the camp. There were screams. Then there were shouts. "Witches! Run! They've found us!" The entire forest seemed to come alive.

"Come on!" shouted Basil. "To the water! Everyone to the water!" But the villagers were in too much of a panic to listen, instead scattering into the forest.

A group of dark figures materialized from the shadows, lurching down the hillside and into the firelight. Evie grabbed Demetra's dress and pulled her away. They scrambled after Basil, down the tree-lined embankment toward a promontory with a view of the whole wide stretch of the river. The water below churned against the rocks.

"What do we do?" he said.

"We've got to jump," said Evie.

"No, wait," said Demetra. "Look!" There, gliding across the

water like a serpent, was a long, slender ferryboat. A boatman stood in the back, guiding his craft with a wooden pole. "Hey! Over here!"

"He won't get here in time," said Evie. "We've got to jump!"

Marline looked back to the encampment. The witches began to toddle over the ridge. "Here they come!" There were too many, and they were too close.

Suddenly, the whole forest burst with a magical white flash. It had come from Marline. Witches yowled in agony. "Get on that boat!" she shouted. "I'll hold them back!" As more witches began to hobble down the hill, she unlashed the hawk statue and shoved it into Basil's chest. "Find a cure."

Before he could respond, she wheeled. Her princess magic bloomed, illuminating the leering faces of the witches coming for them.

"He's here!" shouted Demetra. "Jump!"

Before she had time to think, Evie leapt off the outcropping and landed on the deck of the ferry below. Forbes, Demetra, and Basil all followed. "Let's go!" shouted Forbes. "Move off!"

The boatman calmly steered the ferry back toward the center of the river. White pulses of light burst from the dark forest they'd just left. As they watched the shoreline and tried to catch their breath, the faint sounds of Marline's wild laughter echoed across the river. Then, one by one, the witches began to appear at the edge of the cliff. The white flashes stopped.

Once they were far enough away from the shore, they each

took spots at the sides of the ferry to balance it. The boat was nearly flat-bottomed, the bow curving to a point like a dagger. "Now, how in the world did that happen?" said Forbes, slamming his hand on the boat. "It was Malora. She set us loose, then told the witches where we were. She led them to us like hounds to a hare. How's that for your precious family?"

"No," said Evie. "They must have seen us. Or had suspicions when we passed through Marburg. You saw how they looked at our carriage." She glanced at the shoreline, where several sets of glowing yellow eyes stared back. "She wouldn't do that."

"Poor Marline," said Demetra, and that sent the rest of them to silence. The shore, too, had gone quiet. The ferry slid through the water like shears through silk, the boatman's pole splashing softly as he propelled them along. Evie turned away from the shore. *And now Marline is gone, too.*

The river cut a hard line through the dense pine forests. The water was calm, at least, and the wolves had stopped howling. She glanced over at the boatman. He was tall and lean, wearing a water-stained tunic and leather boots with mold growing on them. But it was his head that startled her. The man's face was covered top to bottom in wavy black hair. She found herself unable to look away.

"How much to ferry us north?" said Forbes. "To Goblin's Glade?"

The boatman turned at the waist, and Evie gasped. His head was on the wrong way round, with his face on the back. He was angular and bony, with patches of silver hair along his chin.

Deep wrinkles furrowed the skin beneath his eyes. A dull red scar ran across his entire neck.

"Goblin's Glade, you say?" he rasped. His voice was even croakier than Rumpledshirtsleeves's, dry and brittle and thin. It sounded as though his throat had gone permanently dry. "Just up the West Brother here. Catch us a rat or two with that blade and we'll be square."

"That's all you want?" said Forbes. "Dead rats?"

"Man's got to eat, and I've had enough fish for a lifetime." His pole splashed through the water as he steered into a gentle curve. "Glade isn't out of my way; I'm following the river anyway, right round to where he joins his Brother. Follow one up, follow the other down, carrying whatever needs carrying. Like you." He shoved his pole against the bottom. "Rats'll square us."

"I've never killed a rat with a sword before, but how hard could it be? You've got a deal."

Before long, the boatman began humming a quiet song. Demetra soon fell asleep on Basil's shoulder. Forbes kept one hand on his sword, even as his head began to bob from exhaustion. Evie watched the ferry's progress as it sliced the smooth black water in two. The rhythmic sloshing of the boatman's pole and the crisp, crystal smell of the river air put her into something of a trance. The shapes of the trees and mountains reflected off the water, as did the thick clouds hanging overhead. The silver orb of the moon had gone, and the sky had turned the color of charred coal. She stared into the water until it had lightened to whitish gray. She couldn't say for certain if she ever fell asleep, but before she knew it, the rest of the night was gone. She looked around the ferry and was surprised to see that everyone was awake.

"Are we nearly there?" said Demetra. Her voice seemed as loud as a dog's bark in the quiet of dawn.

"Not far now," said the boatman.

Demetra turned to Evie, perturbed. "I think we should talk about what happened at the camp."

"I'm sure Marline's fine," said Basil. "Remember the giants? We all thought they got her, and she came through that all right."

"Sure, Bas," said Evie, though the best she could muster was a halfhearted smile.

"I'm talking about what Wormwood said about Beatrice," said Demetra. She took the class portrait out of her pocket and unfolded it. *Beatrice said it was this one—ALL MUST GO* was written there for all to see. "The Headmistress had a hand in the ambush. Isn't that what we're all thinking?"

"It's certainly what I'm thinking," said Forbes.

Basil grimaced. "It's a bit of a leap, isn't it?"

"She's been acting suspiciously ever since we enlisted. Think about it. Do you remember how she reacted when that witch predicted that the Warrior Princess was in our class? I do. She almost passed out cold. Liverwort had to help her out of the castle."

Basil furrowed his brow, trying to remember. "Did she?"

"She did," said Evie. Beatrice's face had gone ashen that night. Where so many other staff members were overjoyed at the news, the Headmistress seemed horrified.

"When Malora attacked me on the wall and Anisette was sent home," continued Demetra. "Remember what happened then? The girl who kicked it all off, the girl who had been causing trouble the whole year long, got to stay. And Anisette was the one discharged. Why? Because Hardcastle turned up."

"So you're suggesting that Beatrice is working in concert with the witches to destroy the Academy," said Basil, assuming his familiar look of seriousness. "Why wouldn't she just lower the wall, then, and let them in?"

"I don't know," said Demetra, folding the portrait up. "But I can't imagine it would be all that easy to take the one step you know will immortalize you as one of the most evil people ever to live."

"Yes," said Basil. "Yes, I suppose that might be difficult."

Evie puzzled through it all and couldn't refute a single thing Demetra said. But how could the leader of Pennyroyal Academy, a woman who had climbed to the highest rank in the princessing service, possibly be working with the enemy?

"Could we perhaps change the subject?" said Basil. "The idea that we might've left Maggie behind with a traitor is making me ill."

"Here's a different subject," said Forbes, eyeing the boatman darkly. "I want to know what's happened to his head."

"Forbes!" snapped Evie.

The boatman shifted his pole and turned backward so he could see them. "I expect it's *my* head you're referring to?"

"Yes, the one that's on the wrong way round."

Evie smacked his leg and gave him a stern look.

"I was a bandit before I gave my life to the river. Spent my days with a murdering band of criminals in a little cottage up there in the mountains. Or rather, they spent their days with me. I was the most murderous and criminal of the bunch."

"Perhaps we should walk from here," said Evie.

"I stole and killed and did whatever else I liked," said the boatman. "The King, he finally had enough of me and my mates causing mayhem in his forest. He sent his best men to hunt us down. I got what I deserved, I reckon, but the Gray Man took pity on me and gave me a second chance."

"Who's the Gray Man?" said Forbes.

"He's a sorcerer." The boatman lifted his hair to reveal that his scar went all the way around his neck. "Gray Man fixed my head back on with his magic. That was enough for me. I gave up my criminal ways and became a pious man, a man of the water."

"If this Gray Man is such a savior," said Forbes, "then why's your head on backward?"

"He wanted to be sure I learned my lesson. This way, I can never look forward, only back at what I once was."

"This Gray Man," said Basil, suddenly quite excited. "Are you suggesting he brought you back to life?"

"Gray Man has all the cures. But they've chased him into the Glade now. Some call him a monster."

"Could he turn stone back to flesh?"

The boatman laughed, his throat as raspy as a rusted chain. "If any can, it's him."

"And he's in the Glade? That's where we'd find him?"

"Basil," said Evie softly. "We've got bigger things to worry about. I'm sorry, but . . . it is only a bird—"

"It's more than just a bird," he snapped. "Besides, what's the harm in popping by for a cure?"

"He isn't hard to find," said the boatman. "It's just that usually no one wants to find him."

"Excellent," muttered Forbes, fixing Evie with an exasperated glare. "Another monster in our forest."

"Plenty of monsters in this forest," said the boatman. "Welcome to Goblin's Glade."

As the river curved around to the right, becoming the eastern arm of the Two Brothers, the boatman began to steer into the current. He was guiding them to the northern shore, where a dark forest rose like an impenetrable wall from the water's edge. As they got closer, they could see a thin trail leading up into the foliage where it disappeared through a mouth of tangled branches and briars. Flanking the trail were three large statues. One was a leopard. One a lion. The other a wolf. The boatman guided the ferry to the end of the path, river rocks scraping its bottom as it came aground.

"Here we are," he said.

Forbes stomped off first. Basil followed, then helped Demetra and Evie across. The forest grew right to the edge of the river, leaving almost no shoreline at all.

"Thank you, sir," said Evie. "We're in your debt." She handed him the loaf of bread from her knapsack. "It isn't rat, but hopefully it'll do."

He took the loaf without a word, then shoved off from shore and floated away down the river. They watched him for a moment, the sun brightening the gray skies to a dull brown color. Then they turned and looked up at the three statues looming above.

"Well, here we are," said Forbes. "Goblin's Glade."

Evie's first impression of Goblin's Glade was that the whole forest was vertical. Her second impression was that it was the rainiest place in the world. They climbed and climbed through sodden, peaty earth that squelched beneath their feet in the relentless drizzle. Giantstoe pines and sprawling beeches proved themselves to be the worst umbrellas ever devised. A white fog as thick as moss sat draped over the mountain peaks. Patches of it hovered between trees. Despite the chill in the air, Evie couldn't tell if it was rain or sweat that had soaked her so thoroughly.

Thankfully, during the first few hours at least, the ancient enchanted forest hadn't lived up to the reputation Rumpledshirtsleeves had described. They had yet to see a single creature, mischievous or otherwise. Even the trees seemed too old and indifferent to bother with the four cadets in their midst.

"I never knew there were mountains without tops," heaved Basil, his hair matted to his face.

"The top's not even the end," said Forbes. "Who knows how much farther once we reach that." He had stopped to catch his breath, eyeing the heavy cloak of fog obscuring the mountaintops. "What's the plan here, anyway?"

"The plan keeps changing," said Evie, "but the mission stays the same: find Rumpelstoatsnout." She climbed past him to take the lead.

They continued on, though the higher they got, the slower they moved. None of them seemed able to catch their breath, except for Evie, whose childhood in the Dragonlands had left her with incredible stamina.

At one break, on a relatively flat slope in the thick of the fog, she started to become concerned with the time, or rather, the light. The other three leaned against trees and drank water and ate dried food from Demetra's knapsack—which, currently, wasn't dry at all.

"The cruel irony of carrying this chair all over the world and not being able to sit down in it," said Basil, rolling his shoulders.

"Just leave the bird," said Forbes, eyeing the statue of Marline's brother.

"No. She gave him to me to look after."

"Him? Look, she's gone, mate. It may be a cruel fact, but it's a fact nonetheless. There's no point in hauling that hunk of stone up the mountain."

"There is if I can find a cure."

"Oh, sod the Gray Man. We're here for only one reason: to give that chair to some troll and hope he doesn't kill us." He took a swig of his water. "Blimey, whose idea was this mission?"

Evie glanced up the mountain to where it sloped into the fog and disappeared. Something was needling her. "Wait here," she said. "I'll be right back."

"What are you doing?" said Forbes. "We can't afford to split up."

She began to run up the hill, which jutted upward and became even steeper. She climbed, much faster than she had with the others. Before long, the mountainside rounded off and began to level out.

"Hey!" she shouted. "The top is just up here!"

"What?" came Basil's voice.

"The top! It's right here! Keep climbing!" She staggered to the base of a ghost pine, a high-altitude tree with a nearly translucent trunk and white needles. The fog began to separate and what Evie saw on the other side made her eyes go wide. An enormous bowl of pines stretched out before her, as black as the fog was white. Huge thunderclouds loomed above the valley, their bottoms disappearing in a relentless spray of gray. Lightning pulsed from within, while thunder grumbled its way from mountain to mountain. She walked forward to where the ghost pines began to thin out. Distant mountain peaks even higher than the one she stood on now looked down like grandparents into a baby's bassinet. She stepped to the edge of a cliff, curved and sharp as a fingernail. The mountaintop should have continued on, sloping down the northern face to the valley below. Instead, half of it had crumbled away in a landslide.

Demetra, Basil, and Forbes hiked over to join her. Their labored breathing stopped when they saw the valley. Clouds billowed miles into the sky, dousing the black forest underneath.

"That is stunningly beautiful and stunningly terrifying," said Basil.

"Unfortunately for us, it looks to be coming this way," said Forbes. He pointed overhead, where thin wisps of cloud sailed past. "I suspect we'll be quite a bit wetter before the night is through—"

"Look there!" said Demetra. She pointed along the curve of the cliffside where the fog had cleared enough to reveal a hulking wall of yellow brick rising up from the rock. Inside the wall stood a castle and tower that looked like they were made from gold. Just then, the first lashing of the storm washed across the mountaintop. It passed in seconds, leaving the unsteady patter of water dripping from the trees.

"Brilliant," said Forbes, swiping the wet hair from his eyes. "To the castle, then."

"Wait," said Evie. She eyed the golden walls warily. "If Goblin's Glade is anything like Rumpledshirtsleeves said it is, perhaps we should just keep going. We don't need beds. We just need to complete our mission and get out of here."

"Keep going?" said Forbes. "Into that?" A jagged flash of lightning cut through the sky, striking something at the far end of the valley. "When night's about to fall and there's a lovely little castle right there?"

Evie stared at the storm in front of them. She knew she

would end up outnumbered if this came to a vote. Perhaps even four against zero. Still, something about the small kingdom made her wary.

"We could have a proper supper there, too," said Basil. "And they might be able to help us find Rumpelstoatsnout."

That was the argument that persuaded Evie, though she still felt apprehensive. As the fog ambled past, she caught glimpses of what lay beyond the exterior wall, where a golden tower rose high above everything. Banners of amber and green snapped atop every turret.

"That tower's got no windows," said Evie. "They're supposed to help you see the enemy, aren't they? What's the purpose of a tower without windows?"

"What's the purpose of a tower up here at all?" said Forbes. "You can see the entire world from the edge of this cliff. It's probably just a decorative tower."

"A decorative tower?" said Basil in amazement. "What in blazes is a decorative tower?"

Another flurry of rain pelted past, drenching them even more. "Right, let's make a decision," said Forbes. "All in favor of the kingdom?" His hand was already up. Basil and Demetra raised theirs next. Evie, still staring at the tower, slowly raised her hand as well. "Good. That was easier than expected. Shall we?" He stalked off toward the kingdom without waiting for the others.

"Forbes, wait!" said Evie. He turned back, annoyed. "I don't think we should mention the siege."

"Are you mad?" he said. "Why would we not ask for help?"

"Something about this place . . . I don't like it."

"We can easily ask about Rumpelstoatsnout without mentioning the siege," said Basil, trying to head off an argument. "We're on official Academy business. What royal would question that?"

Forbes sighed in annoyance. "Fine. Now, can we go before one of us is struck by lightning?" Basil, pleased with his diplomacy, smiled and started off after Forbes.

"I feel it, too," said Demetra, eyeing the kingdom darkly. "I do think we need information, but I'm all for getting out of here as quickly as we can."

The four of them traversed the ridge while thunder echoed across the valley. The kingdom's wall loomed larger and larger as they neared. Its surface was smooth, sandstone bricks inlaid with small colored stones that created a golden shimmering effect. It looked dense, thick enough perhaps to repel a giant. They tracked the base of the wall to the gatehouse, which faced away from the cliff. The portcullis was opened wide. Two bartizans sprouted elegantly from either side of the gatehouse spire. An ornamental carving stretched across the stone above the gates. It read Here May One Live Freely.

"Let me do the talking, will you?" said Forbes as they approached. "It's bad enough to turn up in this state; we don't need to embarrass ourselves with our behavior as well. And whatever you do, not a single foolish word about dragons."

In truth, Evie's family was the last thing on her mind. *There's something odd about how blithe it all seems,* she thought. Even in the best of times, what kingdom would leave its gates open? They passed beneath the teeth of the portcullis. A handful of people milled about the roads as though this day was no different from any other. Men in linen breeches and puffy tunics bowed graciously to women in sleeved dresses. It was a remarkably clean and orderly kingdom, though spotted with puddles, and no one seemed at all concerned about the possibility of witches strolling through the raised defenses. The packed dirt roads had none of the wheel ruts that even Pennyroyal Academy's did. They were perfectly smooth, well tended and even. Shrubs had been meticulously trimmed into small orbs of green, lining the roads at regular intervals. Flowers sprouted everywhere.

"This is stunning," said Basil. "Mum would kill for these groundskeepers."

They followed what appeared to be the main road as it curved around the glimmering golden castle. Everyone they passed gave them a nod and a smile. Evie glanced back at one point and noticed that a man and woman were still watching them. Their smiles had gone.

"Good day, madam," said Basil, grinning at one of the locals. "What a lovely kingdom you have here."

She nodded back.

Evie looked up at the lone tower rising above. It stretched three times as high as the spires atop the castle. *And there are no windows on this side of it, either.*

She felt someone looking at her and turned back to see a

small group watching them. They were whispering amongst one another. "We should go back," she said. "I don't like this at all."

"Of course you don't," said Forbes. "It was my idea."

"To be accurate, it was my idea first," said Basil.

Forbes tromped on with a scowl. The road curved around to the castle's main staircase. It swept up in a beautiful arc that led to the open doors. Standing there was a fat man in a deep purple velvet robe with a sparkling crown atop his head. It matched the glorious castle behind him. Beneath the robe, he wore crisp white breeches and a billowing scarlet tunic. His hair was a bob of white that curled around his ears. He offered them a winsome smile. A small retinue of guardsmen and members of court stood behind him.

"Hello!" he called with a hearty chuckle. "Welcome to the golden kingdom of Stromberg!"

"Thank you very much indeed, Your Majesty," said Forbes.

"All travelers have a home in Stromberg, weary and otherwise!"

Forbes stepped forward and knelt, his head bowed in deference. "I am Sir Forbes, knight cadet of the first class at Pennyroyal Academy. It is an honor to be welcomed into your charming kingdom." Evie had to admit, for as little as he knew about relating to other people, Forbes certainly knew how to speak to royalty.

"I should think the honor is mine!" said the King. "A knight cadet in my home!"

Forbes hissed over his shoulder at the others: "On your knees!"

Evie, Basil, and Demetra dipped to the ground.

"This is Evie, that's Demetra, and that's Basil. They're princess . . ." He stopped himself, coughing with embarrassment. "They're also from the Academy."

"It is an honor and a delight to have four esteemed cadets in our midst." Then, to the people standing behind him, "The future of our great land!" They all mumbled their agreement. "Come, I never interrogate my guests without something steaming in their bellies." He gave them a hearty laugh. "Join me at my table!"

Forbes rose. The others followed his lead. "You are too kind, Your Majesty. It would be our pleasure."

"Well then, it shall be pleasure all around!"

Several of the King's group scurried inside, presumably to begin preparations for lunch. Forbes turned back to the others and muttered, "Do as I do. And try not to offend anyone. This could be a very pleasurable experience if you'd all stop being so paranoid."

"Why didn't you tell him who I am?" said Basil. "I'm proud to be a princess cadet."

Forbes shook his head with disdain and turned up the stairs.

"Forget it, Bas," said Evie. "Let's just ask about Rumpel-stoatsnout and get out of here."

Inside, the grand entrance was dimly lit. Torches flamed

throughout, but there were no windows. Instead, both walls opened into various corridors and chambers via large arches carved into the stone. Suits of armor occupied small alcoves between these archways, each polished and posed. Some were missing parts. Others were covered in chinks and dents from long-ago battles. A crimson carpet of crushed velvet covered the stone floor from end to end. A wide staircase at the back of the hall led to a landing, which flared off in both directions to the higher levels of the castle.

"I must say, Your Majesty, Goblin's Glade doesn't seem nearly so menacing as we'd been led to believe," said Forbes.

The King's laughter bellowed down the hallway. "We do have quite the reputation, though most of it is utter nonsense. The oldest enchanted forest in all the land? Certainly. The most haunted?" He laughed again. "Say, lad, something's just come to me. You say your name is Forbes, is that it?"

"Indeed, Sire."

The King abruptly stopped and grabbed both of Forbes's shoulders, giving him an affectionate shake. "You're King Hossenbuhr's boy!"

"That's right, S—"

The King pulled him into a bear hug with a hearty laugh that echoed off the stone walls. "I know your father well! He's allowed me to hunt his land many times over the years. Such a gracious host. How is he?"

*He's a miserable, sour monster,* thought Evie, remembering his attempt to kill Remington. She kept walking in silence.

"He's well, Your Majesty. Quite well."

"Wonderful! Wonderful!"

Evie kept her eye on the guardsmen standing in the corners. None of them seemed to notice the small group passing by. They kept their eyes forward, their spears straight. The advisers trailing behind offered polite smiles, but none of them spoke.

"Well? What do you think of my armor?" asked the King proudly. "Since you're a Pennyroyal boy, I assume you must have some appreciation for fine workmanship." He took Forbes by the elbow and stopped in front of a massive suit of steel plate armor. It had been cleaned like all the rest, but there was no disguising the black scorch along its left side.

"A Spitzbergen, if I'm not mistaken," said Forbes.

The King erupted in laughter. "A Spitzbergen, indeed!" He turned to his group with more joyous chortling. "The lad knows his armorers!" With an arm around Forbes's shoulders, the King used his free hand to point out the finer features of the suit. "Notice the deep overlay of the plate here. Very difficult to get a sword through that. And there . . . The knight who wore this armor took down three full-sized drakes before he was done in. See the markings?"

"The black stain of bravery," said Forbes, inspecting the char along the armor's left side.

A sharp ache shot through Evie's throat. She would have loved nothing more than to open her mouth and roast these two alive where they stood. Basil must have sensed it, because he grabbed hold of her arm and held it tightly.

"Indeed, indeed. Spitzbergen no longer works in this design. It's quite a rare piece, I daresay." He turned to Forbes and pointed a fatherly finger at him. "And you've a rare eye, my boy. Come, let us dine."

The King led Forbes farther down the hall. Evie, Demetra, and Basil followed with the rest of the group.

"Your Majesty," said Evie suddenly. "Perhaps we could just tell you about our mission and be on our way? We'd hate to be a bother." She could see Forbes wince.

The King turned back with a look of confusion. Evie blushed. She had stepped over some unseen line, broken some unknown rule. "Bother? Have my gates closed without my knowledge?"

"No, Your Majesty—"

"Well, then. Let's eat."

He led Forbes left through one of the archways. Several of the advisers looked at Evie warily as they followed. Basil gave her a shrug, then went through as well.

"That smells *so good*," said Demetra. She and Evie went down an open staircase into a cavernous dining room that was every bit as stately as the entrance hall. A long table of stained pine ran from end to end with chairs carved from the same wood. It was covered in candles spiked atop iron holders. Tall, thin windows lined the far wall, each inlaid with a frame of red stained glass surrounding clear glass. Banners hung from the beams of the ceiling alongside dangling chandeliers made up of arrangements of various antlers and horns. An immense hearth sat unused on the end of one wall, with doorways to the serving rooms and kitchens off the other end. The King ushered Forbes to a seat next to the head throne. Basil sat next to him. Evie and Demetra filed in on the same side of the table, while the members of court took seats opposite them. The bulk of the table went unused. Servants entered with trays and cutlery and drinks and hot cloths, and within moments came the food they'd smelled.

"Eat, please," said the King. "You are my guests, and you are always welcome in Stromberg."

"I must say," said Forbes, "it is nice to be amongst adults again."

Evie had to bite her lip to keep from splashing him with hot soup. Basil, meanwhile, missed the insult and helped himself to a steaming turkey leg, shoving it into his mouth with glee.

"You are a very gracious host, Your Majesty," said Forbes. "Even if my companions are not the most gracious of guests."

Basil stopped chewing, his mouth packed with turkey. His eyes went to the King. "Yuh, 'anks, Sire," he mumbled.

"What's food for if not eating?" said the King. "All of you, tuck in!"

Though her unease refused to leave her, Evie could not deny her hunger. She saw from the corner of her eye that Basil was consuming everything within arm's reach and that Demetra had already finished several poached eggs, so she decided to join in. Beetroot and mutton and turnip soup. Roasted cauliflower and baked lung pie and grilled breast of eagle. It was a feast that never seemed to end. And, apparently, a feast only for five. The King's advisers took just enough as to not be rude and nibbled at it silently.

There was a sudden pattering on the windows as the storm arrived in force. Within seconds, the glass was streaked and everything outside became a gray blur. The steady rain made the dining hall feel cozier somehow, and the low rumble of thunder across the valley only added to it.

"If there's one thing I've learned in my time in this world it's that there's no conversation that cannot be improved with gravy," said the King, dumping the lumpy brown sauce over his entire plate.

"I thought I smelled lunch." A woman entered. She was tall and thin, draped in a frock that stretched to the floor. It was the same purple as the King's robes, spotted with shimmering jewels throughout. An overlong silk wrap trailed off both her shoulders, dragging along the floor behind her.

"Ah!" said the King, mouth full of meat. "The Queen arrives!"

Forbes pushed back his chair to rise, but the Queen extended a slim hand to stop him. She came down the short flight of stairs and walked past the members of court. They looked uncomfortable, as though unsure whether to vacate their chairs to her or not. She took a seat across from Evie and Demetra, giving them a distracted smile.

"My darling, these four travelers come to us from Pennyroyal Academy," said the King. "This is Sir Forbes. He's King Hossenbuhr's boy, you remember Hossenbuhr, don't you? And . . . I'm terribly sorry, but I seem to have forgotten your names."

"It doesn't matter," said Basil, wiping lamb grease off his mouth with his sleeves.

"I'm Cadet Evie, this is Cadet Demetra, and this is Cadet Basil."

The Queen dipped her elegant head. She raised her goblet to Evie and Demetra, who lifted theirs in return. After a drink, thunder cracked just outside, causing the Queen to flinch.

"Right, now that we're all properly gorging ourselves, what's this about a mission?" said the King, slurping gravy off his fingers.

Evie felt the Queen looking at her. She glanced over and saw a look of pity on the woman's face. Sympathy and sorrow. Evie quickly broke the glance and turned her attention back to the King.

"We've set out on a rather dubious mission, I'm afraid," said Forbes.

"How so, lad?"

"Well . . . you see . . . how shall I put this . . . there's been a bit of trouble back at—"

"We're looking for Rumpelstoatsnout," said Evie. The room went silent. Now all the advisers were gaping at her as well.

"I say," said the King. He snorted in disbelief. "Many of the legends of Goblin's Glade are untrue, but any story of that creature is perhaps under-exaggerated. Why on earth would you want to find . . . him?"

"It's a personal matter," said Evie. "His brother is an instructor at the Academy."

"You're joking," said the King, his mouth hanging open. "They let one of them teach the good guys?"

"He's an excellent instructor," said Demetra.

"I've been trying to run those hooligans out of the Glade since I took the throne. Four have gone and never come back, but the two that are still here are the worst of the worst." He dropped his elbow on the table with a clatter and pointed at Forbes with excitement. "My men are closing in on Rumpelstiltskin, though. Won't be long now."

"So you know where he is?" said Forbes. "Could you help us find the brother?"

"My boy, if I knew that, he would no longer be in the Glade. I run a tight ship here. I keep my forests clean. Wild, but clean."

"What about the Gray Man?" said Basil, swallowing his bread.

"Bloody hell, are you looking for him as well? These are dangerous outlaws, children!" Silence fell over the dining hall like a laundered sheet whipped across a bed. The King slowly sat back in his throne. "I'm sorry. I shouldn't have called you children. That was rude of me. You're cadets from the Academy and you're here on official business." He picked up a yellow cauliflower and popped it in his mouth. "Last we heard, Rumpelstoatsnout was somewhere in the Wood of the Night. There's a ravine at the far end of the valley, beneath the Dagger. It's so deep that the sun can't reach it; that's how it got its name. I won't send my men near it anymore, except on very rare occasions."

"W-why?" said Basil. "What's wrong with it?"

"The thing that's wrong with it is exactly what you claim to be seeking. The Wood of the Night is also home to the Gray Man. If you'd like, you can find all your monsters at once."

Basil gulped loudly. Then he took another bite of his turkey leg.

"Listen, chil— er, cadets. Far be it from me to advise you to disobey your orders, but this seems like an awful risk just to reunite two trolls. Especially with this storm. Why not go back to the Academy and tell them you couldn't find him? Might save your own lives in the process."

*We can't go back,* thought Evie. *There will be nothing left to go back to.*

"That's not possible, Your Majesty," said Demetra. "We need to find Rumpelstoatsnout."

"Well," sighed the King, throwing up his hands. "I tried to help you." Another sheet of rain slammed against the windows. "At least stay the night as my guests. We do get some tremendous storms in the valley. And your villains will still be there tomorrow."

"Thank you very much indeed, Sire," said Forbes. Another crack of thunder sounded just outside the castle.

"Then it's settled. I'll have a man take you to the Wood of the Night at daybreak."

*We've already spent one night in Malora's carriage. And now another here. Who knows how many we have left?*

As lightning flashed and thunder rumbled, the conversation turned to other royals whom Forbes and the King had in common. Pudding came, then tea, then more pudding, then cold meat and cheese. Basil piled it all dutifully into his mouth. Evie sat quietly as Forbes told the King stories of his first year of training. The King, for his part, couldn't get enough. The Queen, however, kept shifting her eyes between Evie and Demetra in a way that both found deeply unsettling.

"Are you quite all right, my dear?" the Queen finally asked. The King and Forbes had entered into an endless discussion about hunting and sailing.

"What's that?" asked the King.

"I'm speaking to Evie," said the Queen. "Would you like to lie down? You're looking a bit pale."

"Yes, yes, show them to their rooms! Prince Forbes here will be along in a bit. After he tells me what baitfish he uses for sea trout." He gave Forbes a wink and a rumbling chuckle.

The Queen stood, wrapping her long silken wrap around her shoulders twice. Then a third time. "Come, ladies."

"Thank you very much for your kindness, Sire," said Evie. "It has been a long journey." Suddenly, she couldn't wait to get to a bedchamber where she could talk to Demetra without anyone else around.

"Of course, of course, think nothing of it." He waved his hand to dismiss her, then went right back to his conversation with Forbes. Basil was just helping himself to another turkey leg, so Evie and Demetra followed the Queen by themselves. They went up the stairs and reentered the vast entrance hall.

"It's not often we get princess cadets here in Stromberg," said the Queen. "In fact, I daresay you might be the first." She led the girls to the grand staircase.

"I suppose there isn't much call for us to be around Goblin's Glade, Your Majesty," said Evie.

"I didn't even know this place existed until two days ago," said Demetra.

When they reached the top of the stairs, the Queen led them to the left. She pushed open a wooden door carved with a serpentine dragon from top to bottom to reveal a turnpike stair, a spiral of stone wedges lit with candles that led to the upper floors. The Queen stood aside to let Evie and Demetra pass.

"Did you ever attend the Academy, Your Majesty?" asked Evie. After climbing a mountain earlier, she couldn't quite believe she now had to climb even more.

"I'm afraid I never did," said the Queen. "And I've always regretted it. So many friends trained there, and I always envied their titles. Princess of the Shield. There's something quite special about that."

Evie paused. Her legs were already burning, and her head was thinning from going around and around the stairs.

"Forgive me," said Demetra, doubling over to try to rub the pain from her thighs. "I'm not used to climbing so much."

"Just a bit farther," said the Queen. "Not far now."

Evie looked at Demetra, who nodded back. They started to climb again.

"My daughter has the title," said the Queen. "It was one of the proudest moments of my life when I saw her receive her commission. Though I never managed the training myself, I could not have been more gratified to have raised a Princess of the Shield."

"I suppose she's off somewhere battling witches," said Demetra, trying to pretend her muscles weren't in flames.

"No," said the Queen, and her voice had suddenly flattened. The soft, motherly quality it had had thus far was gone. "She's here. Perhaps you'd like to meet her."

"Maybe later." Evie's footsteps on the stone echoed through the turnpike staircase, but now she thought she could hear the sound of other footsteps as well coming up from below them. "I need to lie down first. Just for a bit . . ."

Her spiraling head continued to swirl as she collapsed. There was a pulse in her vision. Though she could still see things—two advisers hurrying up the staircase, the Queen looking down on her with sympathy—she could no longer speak. She felt herself being lifted into the air, then farther up the stairs. She swirled around and around. Every so often, her head would loll back and she would see the Queen behind her. The same look of pity was on her face, though she said nothing.

Around and around and around. Higher and higher and higher. *Tower,* thought Evie. *Tower.*

It was the only thought that could penetrate the endless,

pulsing pressure in her head. Finally, after minutes or hours or days or years of climbing, the men stopped. Metal latches were thrown and lock tumblers were slid and a heavy wooden door crashed open. Hot air washed into the staircase from the lookout room. The advisers carried Evie inside and laid her down on a soft rug of sheepskin. They gently set Demetra next to her. The Queen stood sideways in her vision, fingers loosely interlocked before her.

"I'm terribly sorry it has to be this way," said the Queen, "but I'm sure you'll grow to love being my daughter's friends."

She straightened and looked past Evie into the shadows. Torches flamed from the walls. Evie could see a table and chairs, some books scattered across the floor. One of the advisers was busy tidying the remains of someone's supper back onto a serving tray.

"I've brought you some new playmates, my darling," said the Queen. "Say hello to Evie and Demetra. They're cadets from Pennyroyal Academy."

Evie heard rustling behind her. The Queen stepped back and a woman emerged. Her skin was as white as the belly of a dead fish, her eyes almost completely black with dilated pupils. Stringy hair wafted from her head. She was barefoot.

"Hello," said the woman. Her voice was as thin as candle smoke. She crept even closer, her crazed smile filling Evie's vision. Evie, paralyzed from some unknown poison, couldn't turn away from that gaunt, skeletal face. "Leatherwolf Company. You're second-class girls."

*First-class*, thought Evie, though she couldn't say it.

"I was an Ironbone girl myself," she continued. "Then it was Bramblestick Company and Crown Company. Of course, that was many years ago. But the Ironbone uniform always was my favorite. Look, it still fits. See?" Beneath layers of dirt and grime, Evie could make out the blue of the woman's dress, hanging loosely from her body and torn off just above the knees.

Then the door slammed shut and the locks clicked and snapped and rattled and there was only the sound of torches burning and rain pounding and the strange woman's breathing as she stared down at her new friends.

THE WOMAN PEERED out from the shadows like a wraith, her teeth brown, her cheeks hollow. "I know you," she said, smiling at Evie with wide, darting eyes. "We've met before, haven't we?"

Evie managed to push herself up. There was no comfortable way to sit, however. The walls had been cobbled together out of jagged fieldstones and hastily applied mortar. With a trembling hand, Demetra passed her a wooden cup. She drank. Her head was still thin and gauzy but becoming clearer by the moment.

"Why have they brought us here?" said Evie.

"Well . . . I suspect you've died. As I have." Her voice was as thin as mist.

"What are you talking about? We're locked in a tower, that's all." Evie glanced around now that her eyes had adjusted to the stifling darkness. The lookout room was small and quite claustrophobic. The only way out was the door they'd come in through. There were no windows, only slim smoke vents at the top of the domed ceiling, and they were narrow enough that she couldn't have even gotten her arm through. The floor was

177

the same fieldstone as the walls, though it had thankfully been polished to relative smoothness. There was a spinning wheel with thread next to the table. Small figures made of straw and fabric sat about the room. There were bears and dogs and dragons and humans. The woman's friends, Evie supposed, before she and Demetra had been brought in to fill that role.

"This is surely a wasted question," said Evie, "but I don't suppose you know a way out of here—"

"Why do you say we've died?" said Demetra, cutting across her. "What do you mean by that?"

"Princesses aren't allowed in the Glade." Her eyes were wide, aglow in the wan candlelight. And no matter how much they darted about, they always seemed to end up back on Evie. "My father keeps things orderly round here."

"So he told us."

"When the witches came, my father struck a bargain with them. He had to. For the greater good."

"What sort of bargain?"

"If he killed me, the witches would leave Stromberg alone. So Mother brought me up here, and I died. And the witches don't come round anymore."

"That's why they drugged us," said Demetra. "Having princesses in the castle would violate the bargain."

The only other time Evie remembered her muscles feeling so paper thin and weak was after she had eaten a handful of strange berries in the forest as a child. She had fallen violently ill, and her dragon mother had wept many tears thinking she was about to lose her youngest daughter. Instead, Evie managed a recovery. But for weeks after, her muscles had trembled like they were doing now.

"Mother always told me, 'Falada, someday I'll find you a friend,' and now—"

"Falada?" said Demetra. "Your name's Falada?" Suddenly, she reached inside her dress pocket and took out the class portrait she'd found at the witch encampment. "Falada . . . Falada . . ." She unfolded it and found one of the many faces that had been crossed out. "That's you, isn't it?"

Falada crept forward, her eyes as wide as a possum's. She studied the portrait. Her jaw began to harden. "And I've been struck out. I am very much dead, it seems." Then she turned to Evie with a jagged smile. "I do know you, don't I? You're in my company as well. I recognize you!"

"No," said Evie with sympathy. "I'm afraid I'm quite a bit younger than you. You've already graduated and I've only just finished my second year."

Falada looked unsure. Her penetrating eyes began to water as she studied Evie's face. "I'm sorry," she said in a voice filled with sorrow. "I've been up here a long time."

"Falada, listen," said Demetra urgently. "This is my mother here. Did you know her?" She pointed to her mother's face, one of the last without a mark. She was only three places over from Falada.

"Cadet Christa," said Falada, and her face changed in an instant. It was as though seeing her old company had given her a thin tether back to reality. "Christa helped me survive the Helpless Maiden. I'll never forget that." She sat up straight as a horrible realization came over her. "Why are so many of us crossed out? What is this?"

"We don't know," said Evie. "We found it mixed in with a load of other papers."

"May I?" said Falada. Demetra handed her the portrait. As she looked at the faces of her childhood company-mates, a bittersweet smile appeared. "Your mother is a remarkable woman." She laughed, a sound as delicate as a bat's wings. "I remember in our final challenge we had to infiltrate a mountain kingdom that had been taken by a witch. When we got there . . . I don't know what happened. The first girls in . . ." She shook her head. "All their training left them. Our plan was ruined. We lost four of our company that day. Four girls who should be in this picture." She handed it back to Demetra. "It was your mother who got us back on track. She took over the whole mission. She reminded us who we were, what we'd trained for . . ." She pointed at the picture of her company. "That group right there defeated the witch. Your mother is a true hero."

Demetra looked down at the portrait in her hands in confusion. "Perhaps this isn't my mother."

"Of course it is, Demetra," said Evie. "Why is it so hard to think your mother could be heroic? Look at you; you volunteered to come on this mission knowing how dangerous it would be."

"You sort of forced me to come—"

"Because I know you. I know how courageous, compassionate, kind, and disciplined you are. And I'm not at all surprised to hear the same about your mother."

"I just . . . I guess I never really asked about her life before my sister was born. Her princess life."

"And you'll ask her once we get out of here," said Evie. "What can you tell us, Falada? There must be something we can use." She tried to stand, but her head instantly began to spin and she fell to the floor.

"Careful!" said Falada, reaching out to rescue the cup before Evie could spill it. "No more water until tomorrow."

Evie pushed herself against the wall, straining for breath.

"Is Princess Hazelbranch still there? She was my favorite of the House Princesses. So many favorites before I died."

"You haven't died!" snapped Evie. "You're here with us. And we're going to find a way out, all right? You and me and Demetra. We'll do it together." She hadn't meant to get angry, but the dizziness scared her.

"Princess de Boncouer was my favorite in second class. And Princess Rottweil. She taught me to speak with animals. I have rats now, but they're not very good company. Not like real friends."

Evie gritted her teeth and tried to pull herself up using the jagged stones of the wall. She made it to her knees, which held despite their violent shuddering. She tried to get to her feet, but the muscles in her thighs felt like overstretched fiddle strings.

Finally, with incredible concentration, she clung to the wall, her fingers scraped and cut.

"Listen to me," she said, staring directly into Falada's eyes. "Pennyroyal Academy is about to fall. There are witches everywhere. If we can't get out of this tower, it'll all be over." She began to press the stones, feeling along the wall for a loose bit of mortar or a hidden trigger. It was as solid as a shield. She glanced around the room, searching the shadows for anything that might help.

*Table. Books. Rug. Smoke vents. Torches. Spinning wheel. Straw figures. Think, Evie, think . . .*

"Every day I remember the witch your mother helped me kill," said Falada. "That's your final trial, you know. Your company has to kill a real witch." Her eyes shot to Evie, then to Demetra. "Don't tell anyone I said that! A Princess of the Shield never reveals Academy secrets! Please don't tell them I told you!"

"We won't," said Evie absently.

"Please! Princess Hazelbranch will be so cross with me."

"We won't say a word, Falada."

"Good. Thank you." She smiled a melancholy smile.

*Table. Books. Rug. Smoke vents. Torches . . .*

"Do you want to hear about your mother's heroism?" She didn't wait for a reply. "It was in the mountains they call the Seven Dwarfs. The range to the east, near Devil's Garden." Falada's voice had calmed as she stared at the floor, remembering. "Lödla, that was the kingdom they wanted us to clear. Not much of a kingdom, really. Just a castle at the end of a mountain path. Do you know snow? They had snow up there."

*Think, Evie, think . . .*

"We found her straightaway. She was sitting on the King's throne. He didn't mind since he'd done a runner long before she came. She smiled when we came in, I remember that. Like she was welcoming old friends." Another chilling giggle escaped her. "Then our advance team . . ." She shook her head, unable to comprehend what had gone so wrong.

*Could this mortar be scraped away?* thought Evie. *We've got the spoon. It would take ages, but perhaps we could carve enough of a hole . . . to what? To jump?*

"They were obliterated. Where our friends had been standing, there were only statues and memories."

Evie glanced around again. *Table. Books. Rug. Smoke vents. Torches. Rats. Spinning wheel . . .*

Her eyes snapped back to the rats. They hadn't been there a moment ago. There were two of them, sleek brown things with pink tails, dining on Falada's scraps.

"Christa was so calm. So brave. She knew how scared we were, but she wouldn't let it take over our hearts. She helped us win the day. No . . . *she* won the day."

Evie couldn't take her eyes off the rats. Their whiskers bobbed as they sniffed each other. "Princess," she said. "Did you say you know how to talk to animals?"

"Of course. Soon, you will, too."

Evie lowered herself gingerly to the floor. She knelt in front of Falada and looked straight into her eyes. "You can communicate with those rats? And they'll listen to you?"

"They're the only ones I've had to talk to for years. And Mother, of course."

"I have an idea about how we can get out of here."

"It won't work," said Falada.

"You haven't even heard it yet."

"You want to send the rats down to bring back help. It won't work. They won't go near anyone who isn't a princess. The cooks have made them terrified of everyone else. And besides, my father will kill any princess who tries to enter the gates."

"Not every princess. There's one down there right now," said Evie.

Demetra's eyes shot open. "Of course! Evie, that's brilliant!"

Falada started to breathe heavily. Her eyes darted between Evie and Demetra. "Please don't give me false hope. Getting out of this tower is impossible."

"Hope is never false," said Evie. "And all sorts of impossible things are true."

Falada stared into her eyes. As hope crept in, a look of physical pain came over her. "What would you like me to tell them?"

Evie moved back and sat next to Demetra to give space to Falada and the rats. "Tell them to look for a boy named Basil." Falada glanced at her in confusion. "It's a long story, but he's every bit the princess Demetra and I are, trust me."

"It's true. Basil has more courage and heart than even he knows," added Demetra.

"All right," said Falada, nodding slowly. "Then what?"

"He should be in bed by now. Tell them to get right up next to his face. I don't want to do anything more than whisper."

Now it was Demetra who looked confused. Evie, meanwhile, pulled a thread loose from the battered rug. Then she unclasped her neckband, tied the thread around it, and handed it to Falada. "Tell them to—"

Falada gasped and recoiled from the neckband, which fell to the floor. "How did you do that?"

"My voice, it's in there," mouthed Evie, her words coming from the jewelry on the floor. "If the rats can get my voice close enough, I can tell Basil where we are."

Falada inched forward and picked up the neckband. She inspected it with wonder. Then she turned to the rats, who looked up at her expectantly. "Good evening, sirs," she said. To Evie and Demetra's astonishment, they squeaked back to her. "Do you suppose you might do something for me? There's a princess in the castle called Basil. I would be ever so grateful if you might bring this neckband to him." She paused, and the rats looked at each other.

Demetra's face broke into a smile as she watched them chatter back and forth. "So cute!" she whispered.

Finally, one of them squeaked something to Falada. "You will? Oh, thank you!"

"Thank you very much indeed!" said Demetra. The rats looked at her blankly.

"They can't understand you," said Falada. "To them, you just sound like a strange animal making strange noises."

"Oh," said Demetra, disappointed.

Falada leaned forward and offered the thread to the rats. One of them grabbed it with tiny pink fingers. It put the thread in its mouth and ran across the room to the door, the neckband dragging behind. One of the rats slipped beneath the gap under the door. The other helped push the neckband through, then followed. Falada turned to Evie and Demetra with a proud smile.

"They're such helpful young gentlemen, aren't they?"

Demetra didn't speak and Evie couldn't, so Falada sat and crossed her legs, her spine straight. Evie grabbed the wall and pulled herself to her feet. Her strength had started to return. She peered up at the smoke vents in the ceiling. The tower walls appeared to be about three feet thick from the inside of the vent to the open air. The small sliver of sky she could see was black and starless.

"The rats will find him. Don't worry about that," said Falada. "They know this castle better than the men who built it."

Evie's head was once again swirling. She couldn't tell if it was from the poison, the heat, or if she was still reeling from being locked in the tower.

"Here," said Falada, handing her the cup. "Drink and rest."

Evie emptied the cup and laid her head on the floor. Her cheeks felt hot, her head thick with pressure. She stared up at the ceiling for several minutes. Rain tapped against the stone outside the smoke vents. Thunder continued to rumble in the distance.

"I'm not going to let them get away with this," said Demetra, staring at the class portrait in her hands. Her voice was suddenly as stern as Evie had ever heard it. "They've got the whole world twisted round, and I've had enough. Your father didn't do this to you out of cruelty, Falada. He did it out of fear."

"What?" Falada's wide eyes reflected the torchlight. "My father isn't afraid. He's never been afraid."

"He is. I've seen people do all sorts of mad things because they're scared of witches. And it isn't your fault that he let his fear win. It really isn't. It was wrong of him to put you up here."

"But he did it for—"

"There is no reason. There's no excuse for letting fear win."

Falada blinked. Tears welled in her eyes and streamed down her cheeks, but her stunned expression never changed.

"I've had enough. I'm not going to be afraid anymore. They want to come after *my mother*?" Evie tilted her head to look at her friend. It was dark and her face was in shadow, but she could still see the fire in Demetra's tear-soaked eyes. "I've been piddling about for two years at the Academy, doing enough to get by and nothing more. Well, those days are over. When Basil gets us out of here, I am going to rain fire on those witches."

She looked up and met Falada's eyes. "And so are you." Neither Evie nor Falada spoke. "Go on, Evie, it's time. We've got work to do."

Evie struggled to push herself up. Her head was still throbbing, but the water had helped calm her stomach.

"Ready?" said Demetra.

Evie nodded. She took a deep breath and slowly let it out. It was impossible to know where the rats had gone, whether they'd made it to Basil or not, but she had no choice but to try. Her lips began to move and nothing came out. It was a surreal feeling. Her vocal cords vibrated in her throat—she could feel it—but there was no sound. *Come up the tower, Basil. We need you. They've locked us up. You've got to get us out of here.* She said it a few more times, then stopped. Then waited. There was a slight whistle as the wind washed over the smoke vents in the ceiling, but other than that, there was only a close, thick silence in the cell. Evie breathed long, deep breaths. *Please hurry,* she said. *We're locked in the tower.* They waited. And waited. Each random chink or drip that echoed up the spiral stairs outside the door gave them hope, but each was followed by more silence. They waited some more.

"It's all right," whispered Falada. "It's not so bad up here. You can still see the snow in the winter." Demetra and Evie sat silently, their ears trained on the door. "Mother brings Christmas pudding as well—"

"Shh!" said Demetra. "There's someone out there!"

Evie listened but couldn't hear anything. Then, distantly,

only as an echo, she heard the soft patter of footsteps. They became more distinct as they continued up the tower. Then they stopped.

Evie held her breath. The tension in the room threatened to choke them all. *Basil? Is that you?* she said.

"Yes, it's me!" he hissed from down the staircase, his voice punctuated with huffing and puffing. "Don't rush me. It's a bloody long way up there!"

*Hurry!*

His footsteps started again as he spiraled closer and closer to the top. Falada stood. Her face was a mask of terror.

"Don't be afraid," said Demetra softly. "He's a friend. We really are going to get you out of here, all right?"

"No, please," said Falada, and her tears began to fall. "Hope is too cruel. Please."

The footsteps stopped just outside. "Right," said Basil. "There appears to be a door here."

"Hurry, Basil!" said Evie. She jumped when she heard herself muffled just outside. Her voice was free while the rest of her was locked up.

"Basil, they'll put you in here with us if they catch you," said Demetra. "You've got to get the door open."

"Right," he said. "Let's see." They heard scraping and metallic chinks as he tried to negotiate the locks. "You won't believe what just happened. These two rats just came into my room and climbed onto my face—"

"Basil!" Evie's voice echoed down the spiral staircase.

There was a bit more scraping, then the sounds of him trying to force the lock open by jerking on it. "There's a rather large lock here."

"You've got to break it!" said Demetra.

"With what?"

"I don't know, but you've got to do it quickly!"

"There's a hearth in my bedchamber," he said. "It's such a lovely room. Beautifully appointed. You just ring for some wood and they—"

"Basil!"

"Right, sorry. There are some implements there I could use. The poker would work quite nicely."

"No!" said Evie.

"Stop talking, Evie!" said Basil. "You're scaring me half to death."

Evie scowled and pointed urgently to Demetra. "You can't go back down!" she said. "There isn't time!"

"I've got no choice. There's nothing here for me to use. I'll be right back!" His footsteps began to recede down the staircase.

"Basil! Stop!" But he was gone. And so they began to wait again. Only this time, the tension was almost unbearable. And Falada wept the entire time, whispering about false hope.

"I can't take it," said Demetra. "Motivate him, Evie."

Evie's lips began to move, and for once she was happy she couldn't hear what she was saying. She wasn't being particularly nice to Basil. A few moments later, they heard his distant footsteps, followed by his panicked gasping for air. "Was that entirely necessary?" he said crossly.

"I'm sorry," said Evie's voice outside the door, "but this is life or death."

"Is he going to be all right?" asked Falada as Basil gasped and wheezed.

"Everyone stand back!" he said.

"Stand back?" said Evie. "Basil, you've got to do this quietly—"

*Crack!* A hard, metallic strike echoed down the staircase.

"Basil, be quiet!" said Demetra. *Crack!* "Basil!" *Crack!*

"Look, do you want to get out of there or not?"

Evie began to pace. He was beating the fireplace poker against the lock like a drum. *Crack! Crack! Crack!* The whole kingdom might have been awakened by now.

Finally, there was a thud on the floor. The lock had come free. "Basil?" said Demetra. She went to the door, but it didn't move.

*Clang!* She jumped back. *Clang!*

"Basil, what are you doing?"

"I got the big one!" he shouted.

"Shh!"

There was one more great *clang* before the iron poker hit the door. Wood splintered and cracked.

"He's not the most graceful of princesses, is he?" said Falada with annoyance.

"Basil, can you be a bit quieter?" called Evie, but even she couldn't hear her own voice over the rending of wood. "Basil!"

Finally, he stopped, gasping for breath.

"Ba—"

*Thud!* He rammed his shoulder into the door. *Thud! Thud! Thud!* Evie threw her hands up in frustration. Outside, another piece of iron clattered down the staircase.

"The whole bloody Glade will be awake by now," said Demetra.

Just then, the door burst open. There stood Basil, red-faced and proud. But his smile fell the moment he saw Falada. From his look of horror, it seemed as though he thought Death himself was standing in the tower with Evie and Demetra.

"Oh, uh . . . hello," he said, trying unsuccessfully to disguise his revulsion.

"This is Princess Falada, the King's daughter."

"Hello, Princess," said Falada with a slight bow of her head.

"Uh, hello yourself, Princess," Basil returned. Then he handed Evie her neckband. "Your voice. Perhaps you can use it to apologize for those things you said to me."

"If you haven't gotten us killed, I will."

Evie's nerves were tight. She expected guardsmen to appear at every turn with axes and swords and chains and ropes and a thousand new locks to bar the tower door forever. But so far that had not happened. Nothing had happened except a dizzying whirl down the stone staircase to where the air was cool and still. It seemed Basil's thunderous rescue might not have echoed all the way down the tower after all.

Around and around they went through the impenetrable dark. Falada had convinced them that they could escape without a torch, and without the possibility of accidental discovery that came with it. So Evie ran her hands along the circular walls to keep her balance. The haze of the poison had mostly cleared, but now she was becoming dizzy from the descent. Basil and Demetra were somewhere behind her.

"Slowly," said Falada in a hushed tone. "We're nearly there."

Evie couldn't see a thing and didn't know how Falada could, either. Perhaps it was some princess trick she'd learned at the Academy, or maybe it was the deeply entrenched memory of a childhood spent climbing the tower. Regardless, Evie began to slow as Falada did, and the next thing she knew a door was being cracked in front of her.

"This'll take us to the kitchens. Unless they've rearranged the entire castle." She chuckle-snorted. Evie could almost feel Basil's incredulous stare. "Once we're through, we'll need to go upstairs. The guest chambers are down the right side of the hall."

"She's right," said Basil, his face red and blotchy from two full sprints up and down the tower. "That's where my room is. You must come and see this fireplace——"

Evie put her finger to her lips to shush him. Falada eased the door open. Torchlight poured through in a wedge of flickering orange. On the other side was a corridor of gray stone bricks. Sconces lined the walls. There were no other adornments. This was a servants' hallway, as Falada had said, where kitchen workers and service staff did the castle's unseen business. Thankfully, it was empty.

They hurried down the corridor. After about fifty feet, it began to slope upward. Crisp night air washed over their flushed cheeks as they emerged into a small room filled with wooden tables and racks of serving utensils. This was some sort of preparatory room, where servants could make last-minute adjustments to the presentation of the food before serving it. And several of the windows were cracked open.

"The air feels like magic," said Falada, closing her eyes and letting it wash over her. "My skin is alive."

"It won't be if they catch us," whispered Evie.

"Right." Falada opened her eyes and focused. "There'll be guards in the hall, but it's the only way. We've got to be quiet as rats." She scrunched her nose and mouth into a rat face, then turned and disappeared into the next room.

"She's bonkers," said Basil.

"She's brilliant," said Demetra.

The three of them hurried after Falada. They were now in the dining hall where Evie's and Demetra's lunches had been poisoned. The table had been cleared and cleaned, all packed away and tidied. *It's like we were never here,* thought Evie. *No one was ever meant to find us.* With a shiver, she crept up the stairs and followed Falada into the hall. They stayed close to the wall, sneaking past the glimmering suits of armor, until they made it to the grand staircase. Rain rattled against the stained glass window at the landing. Falada turned to the others, pointing to the corridor that branched off to the right, and that's when her face fell.

"Who goes there?" came a voice.

Before Evie could see who it was, Basil shoved all three of them behind one of the armor displays. Evie's shoulder slammed into the plinth. She had to bite her lip to keep from shouting.

"Hiya," said Basil loudly.

"Oh, it's you," came the reply. It was a man's voice, grumbly and stern. "You oughtn't be about without a candleholder in the night hours, sir."

"Guards," whispered Falada. "I think that's Patric."

Evie glared at her with wide eyes. Falada smiled back and, thankfully, didn't speak again.

"Forgive me," said Basil, his voice rising to cover Falada's. "I was just looking for the kitchens. As lovely as that mutton was hot, I couldn't sleep without trying it cold."

"Can't say I blame you, sir. Always did like a bit of mutton myself."

"Well? Come on, then!"

Patric's voice softened. "Just this way. Don't tell the King I tried his mutton or he might lock me in the tower."

Basil chortled a bit too loudly. Falada had her hands pinned over her mouth to keep from laughing. Evie implored her with her eyes to keep quiet.

Basil quickly turned to the girls and said in a whisper, "I'll get Forbes. Meet us in the trees." And then he left to join the guard. "Coming!"

Evie, Demetra, and Falada waited a moment longer, then crept out from behind the suit of armor. They hurried down the hallway toward the main entrance. Falada stopped short, motioning for the others to follow her down a side corridor that branched off to the left. Within moments, they emerged from a servants' entrance into the brisk night air. The instant the rain hit Falada's face, she fell to her knees.

Evie was desperate to get out of Stromberg before they were spotted, but when she saw Falada, face raised to the sky, she stood frozen. The princess's body was wracked with sobs, though the rain slapping the stone covered any sound. Evie pushed the hair from her eyes and stood and watched.

"Look at that, Evie," said Demetra. "That's what freedom looks like. *That's* what I want to do." She walked over and knelt next to Falada. She put her arms around the princess, and Falada clutched her so tightly it nearly knocked her over. Evie stood in the driving rain and watched as her friend comforted a Princess of the Shield twenty years older than her. Finally, she said something to Falada and helped her to her feet. When the princess spoke next, she was a completely different person than she'd been in the tower.

"The stables are just round that way. In this weather, we're unlikely to meet any guards, but if we do, let me do the talking."

They crept through the empty roads that rolled gently

across the kingdom until they found the stables. Falada had been right. The guardsmen couldn't be bothered to patrol in the downpour. She led them into the stables and selected five horses, strapped on their tack as expertly as any stable boy, and led them out the hunting gate, an unmanned exit through the curtain wall that was only used when the King and his party wished to make use of the vast forests surrounding Stromberg.

Once they were outside the walls of the kingdom, they slunk back around toward the main gates. If there were any lookouts atop the wall-walk braving the storm, they wouldn't have seen Evie, Demetra, and Falada skulking through the mud directly below. When they finally reached the gatehouse, they splashed across the grass to the edge of the forest. There they found a spot that was well concealed with brush where they could still see the entrance. Evie peered out into the night. Lightning flashes lit up the mountaintop, freezing the rain in place. All was quiet except for the storm. There was no sign of Basil or Forbes.

"Are you all right?" said Demetra, putting her hand on Falada's arm.

"I've never been more all right," she said, smiling at Demetra. "Those things you said up there . . . well, you've inspired me in a way I never thought I'd be inspired again."

"Me?"

"I may never forgive my father for what he did, but you helped me see that it wouldn't have happened if not for the witches. I very much needed to be reminded of that. I'm not afraid anymore. And now I'm ready to rain fire on the witches, too." She and Demetra hugged, and then she went to the horses and rechecked their gear. Watching her, it was difficult for Evie to imagine how the mousy girl she had first met in the tower had become the self-assured princess standing before her now. "They can take everything from you," she said. "They can take your windows. Take your sun. But as long as you have hope, you still have a weapon." She turned to Evie with a smile. "I was just about to lose mine when you turned up." She climbed into the saddle of one of the horses, looking every inch a Princess of the Shield. "Right, let's be off."

"We've got to wait for Basil and Forbes," said Evie. "But it would be wonderful if you'd be willing to join us on our mission."

"No, I'm sorry, that's not possible. The witches are targeting my company. This isn't the ordinary danger we face as princesses, this is an attempt to destroy us all. They already killed me once. I won't let that happen to my sisters."

"What are you going to do?" asked Demetra.

"The same as you. You're coming with me."

Demetra looked over at Evie in confusion. "But . . . I've got a mission. I can't just leave."

"You've got to. I don't mean to sound heartless, but you said yourself you don't know how old those marks are. I hope it isn't too late for Christa, but the fact is we've no idea what's happened since the witches crossed out their last face."

Evie studied her friend's eyes as they flooded with heartache and doubt. Despite the roiling fear in her stomach, she made a decision. "She's right. You've got to go."

"But . . . what about the Academy?"

"Basil, Forbes, and I can handle it. We're nearly there now anyway."

Lightning flashed across Demetra's face. Thunder crackled over the valley.

"Demetra," said Evie, "I never knew my real mother, so you've got to listen to me. Go to yours now. Protect her from the witches."

"Please," said Falada. "I owe your mother my life. I'd do it myself, but I haven't been out in the world in quite some time. I need your help."

Demetra looked from Falada back to Evie, heartbroken at the decision she was being forced to make. "Once she's safe," she said, her voice just above a whisper, "I'll come back. And then the witches will pay."

Evie forced a smile. She nodded.

"Will you say goodbye to Bas for me?"

"Of course." The two friends hugged tightly. Then Demetra mounted a black horse. Evie couldn't deny that she, too, looked strikingly like a Princess of the Shield. Demetra wiped the tears from her eyes as she began to ride off. Then she stopped and looked back at Evie. "We're going to win this war."

"Yes, we are."

"Good luck, Princess," said Falada to Evie, and then she rode silently after Demetra until they both vanished into the darkness.

*May the Fates look after you both.*

"Evie!" came an urgent voice. "Demetra!"

Evie turned and peered through the rain. Two figures stood huddled beneath the words Here May One Live Freely.

"Over here!" she hissed, waving an arm. "Basil! Forbes!"

They ran against the rain until they were beneath the cover of the trees.

"Are you all right?" said Forbes. "Basil said they locked you up."

"Yeah. Fine."

"Brilliant, we've got horses!" said Basil. "Where's Demetra?"

"She's gone."

"What?"

"I'm sorry, Bas—"

"What do you mean she's gone, Evie? Where?"

"The witches are trying to kill everyone in her mother's old company. She's gone to the Blackmarsh to save her."

"What?" He began to shout. "Dem—"

Evie leapt at him, jamming her hand over his mouth. *"Quiet, Basil! You'll get us all killed!"* Above her hand, his wide eyes stared back at her. He looked even more upset than Demetra had been. "Keep quiet, all right?" She slowly took her hand away.

"How could you let her go, Evie?"

"She needs to look after her mother," she said, her stomach suddenly in knots. "All we've got to do is find Rumpelstoatsnout. Her family needs her more than we—"

"You had no right." He turned away and climbed onto one of the horses.

"I didn't tell her to go, Bas. We all decided it would be—"

"Yes, well, you're the only one left to yell at." He looked over at Forbes, who had already mounted his own horse. "Let's go."

Basil began to ride away. Forbes looked down at Evie with a cocked eyebrow. "There you go again, letting family cloud common sense. Your soft heart is going to cost us this mission."

Evie mounted the last horse and wiped the rain from her face, then followed Basil without uttering a word to Forbes.

They rode slowly through the woods, parallel to the mountain ridge. Once they'd gone far enough to avoid being seen, they came out from the trees and stepped to the edge of the cliff. Beneath the nighttime storm, the valley was an endless black void stretched out before them. Pulses of white lit up the billowing clouds.

"There," said Evie, pointing at the horizon. "That must be the Dagger. Do you see it?" In the intermittent flashes of lightning, the faint outline of another mountain range appeared at the distant end of the valley. One peak stood sharp and tall above the rest, like a blade. "The King said the Wood of the Night is beneath the Dagger. That's where we've got to go."

They sat beneath the rain clouds and watched as darts of white light repeatedly stabbed the forest valley. Then, without a word, they began their descent.

"UGH, I CAN'T WAIT to be rid of this bloody chair," said Basil, adjusting the leather straps over his shoulders. He also had the stone hawk to contend with, making him the team's pack mule.

"I can carry it if you need a break," said Evie.

"No, it isn't heavy. It's just so . . . unwieldy."

"It'll be a harp on the way back," said Forbes. "This is the easy bit."

They'd been following the trench down the middle of Goblin's Glade for most of the day, and the rain had not stopped. At best, it was a fine drizzle. At worst, it pounded down so loudly they could barely hear one another speak. But now the sun had broken free for the last hour of daylight, bathing the forest in a glowing green that made it come alive. The pines shook themselves like wet dogs, spraying sodden needles everywhere.

Evie looked up. The clouds were tall and hard-edged, the kind that billowed and plumed like a golden palace in the sky. Behind them was blue sky and warm sun.

"Here's the Dagger," said Forbes. The valley had been closing in for the last half hour, funneling them toward a pass between two towering mountains. Light gray stone fletched with trees bulged up on either side of them, disappearing into the clouds. "Wood of the Night must be through there."

"Bas, are you all right?" said Evie, riding up next to him.

"Yeah. Fine."

The faint trail in the moss that had been serving as a road started to slope downward to a bend ahead. All they could see were walls of green and gray growing closer and closer, steering them into the pass. "I'm sorry about Demetra. You're right. We should have waited and decided as a group. It was all so frantic and we'd just escaped the tower and . . ."

"I understand. I just . . ." He looked over at her with a shrug. "I didn't get to say goodbye."

"You'll see her again. She said she'll come to the Academy once her mum is safe."

Large stones had started to appear on the trail, tumbled down long ago from the mountains. The pass was narrowing dramatically. Still, the sun felt nice on their backs.

Suddenly, Basil burst out laughing. "Do you ever get those strange moments of perspective? When you step back and see how absurd everything really is?"

"Bas, I was raised by dragons."

He laughed again. "I was just sitting here thinking about Demetra, and about you. About how we all met."

She smiled at the memory.

"It occurred to me how utterly ridiculous my life is. Do you realize no one else in the world has had the experience I've had the past few years? Not one. I shouldn't even know you or Demetra or Maggie or Anisette, none of you. And look at us now . . . two princess cadets on the verge of graduation off on a mission to save the Academy." He chuckled in amazement. "You know, I still wake up every morning hoping I'll be sent home, but I must say, if my mother hadn't put me in as a princess cadet, things would certainly be far more ordinary."

"If you weren't a princess cadet, none of us might be around anymore. Demetra certainly wouldn't be here if you hadn't been in the Drudenhaus with her."

They rode on in silence for a moment. "I miss her already."

"Me too."

Their conversation faded away as the horses began to slow. They had reached the bend in the pass, and the trail had gotten steeper.

"Easy coming down," said Forbes from below. "It evens out over here."

"After you," said Evie. Basil's horse began to creep down the trail between the stones. Evie followed. She clung to the reins, far more nervous than her horse.

"Incredible . . ." said Forbes from the bottom of the trail. He was staring through the pass to whatever lay beyond.

"What is it?" called Basil. Forbes didn't answer. Instead, he urged his horse forward and disappeared through the gap in the stone.

Basil glanced back at Evie with apprehension. "Forbes?" he called.

"Come on!" came Forbes's distant voice.

They continued until they reached the thin dirt rut between the mountains.

"Blimey," said Basil as he disappeared through the pass.

Evie's horse walked to the curve and stepped through. She leaned forward and peered around the bend. Her eyes went wide. The path continued into a thick, dense wood that descended like a waterfall as the valley floor fell away. The Wood of the Night reminded Evie of the whirlpools her sister's tail used to cause when she dove into the lake. The forest itself seemed to be swirling into the ground. The warm blue sky ringing the valley met an impenetrable wall of black clouds directly above the sunken black wood. The shadows inside the forest were as dark as if the sun had already set.

"Do you reckon that's the Wood of the Night?" said Basil in astonishment. Forbes looked over at him.

"Right," said Evie. "We don't know what's in there, so let's just find Rumpelstoatsnout, get the harp, and get out of here."

"Where do we begin?" said Forbes.

"The path," said Evie. "If the path is an option, we take it."

"Be ready with that sword," said Forbes. Basil looked over at him, then pulled his sword free.

The three of them rode ahead, following the path as it curved down into the Wood of the Night. But as they reached the edge and the air began to darken, their horses refused to go on. They jerked their heads, whinnying and pulling against their reins.

"Come on!" said Evie. "What's the matter?"

"We'll have to leave them," said Forbes, fighting with his horse. "They're not going in."

Basil jumped off his before it could throw him. "I can hardly blame them."

Evie gave it one last try, jerking hard on the reins to establish control, but it was no use. Forbes was right. The horses were not going to obey. They led them back up the path and tethered them loosely in a fertile bowl filled with delicious green treats.

"I'd rather stay here and eat grass, too," said Basil.

The three of them walked down the path and entered the blackened wood. In seconds, the blue sky and sun were gone, replaced by bracing dusk air. Crickets chirped. Owls hooted. The trail dropped precipitously down into the Wood, with branches spreading off it like the web of a spider.

"Let's try to stay near the top," said Evie. "It'll be much easier to go down if we need to than to come back up."

They left the main trail and followed the rim of the basin as it arced around the sunken valley. The forest was completely dark down there, further shrouded by a thin, hanging mist.

They continued in silence for some time, weaving through the trees, eyes wide against the darkness. After two hours in the difficult terrain, they came across a fast-moving stream that poured down the hillside and drained into the valley. They paused and drank, then sat and rested their legs.

"Does anyone have any idea where we are?" said Forbes. "Or when we are? I can't tell if it's midnight or midday."

Evie's eyes followed the stream back up the hillside, where it sluiced through mud and tumbled over stone. "How in the world did we get this far down? I thought we were at the top of the basin."

"We'd better find this troll soon or I'm going to sit in this chair and there'll only be the two of you left," said Basil.

Evie held her breath and listened. Her eyes darted through the trees. It could have been the wind, or it could have been . . . something else. "Let's go. I don't think we're alone."

"What is it?" said Basil. He swiveled around, scanning the forest.

"Let's go," she repeated. Basil and Forbes followed her down the trail. She stepped carefully to avoid the crackle of the leaves. Though her head remained still, her eyes darted everywhere. She kept thinking she'd seen something in the corner of her vision, but when she turned to look, there was only empty forest.

A gust of wind shook the trees, and now everything was moving. Even when the wind stopped and the leaves began to settle, shadows continued to swirl and bob. Forbes drew his sword.

"You're right," whispered Basil. "There's something out there."

"There are many somethings out there," Evie whispered back. The hairs on the back of her neck stood up. "Do either of you have experience with goblins?"

They both shook their heads.

"You're about to." She herself had encountered them before. It was one of the single most difficult days she'd had in all the years she lived in the forest. She and her sister had been in a race back to the cave. Knowing she had virtually no chance of winning against a creature ten times bigger than her, she decided to take a shortcut. As she dashed through an unfamiliar section of forest, she'd stumbled upon a goblin. It stood around two feet tall, with a bulbous gray body and long, lanky arms. Its head was bald and its teeth were sharp. It was covered in brittle black hair. And when it attacked, the two grappled through the leaves in violent struggle. Evie took a hard thrashing and had even been bitten twice, but when she finally got hold of a stick, she was able to take the upper hand and send the creature scurrying into the bushes. The thing that haunted her about that day, even more than the fight and narrow escape, was the high-pitched giggle the goblin had made as it retreated into the forest.

She heard the same giggle now.

"What do we do?" hissed Basil.

In the next instant, the entire forest filled with laughter.

"We run."

They tore down the hill, bounding through the brush. Evie glanced back. Basil was struggling to keep up, the chair and the stone hawk swinging wildly on his back. Then came Forbes, sword raised. Behind him were about thirty goblins.

"Run!" screamed Evie. It was only the shortness of the goblins' legs that kept them from overtaking the cadets as they barreled down the hillside through the darkness. Then, just ahead, Evie saw something that didn't belong. It was a tin stovepipe. A moment later, she saw the roof it was coming out of, then the rest of the small cottage. It had been built into the side of the valley, tucked away beneath a copse of birch trees.

"There!" shouted Evie. She raced toward the cottage. Basil and Forbes skidded down the steep hill after her, with a wave of goblins pouring through the undergrowth. Their delighted laughter echoed through the wood.

She blasted through a pile of dead leaves at the side of the cottage. The front door was shut but yielded easily when she slammed her shoulder into it. Inside, the air was thick and moldy. It seemed the cottage hadn't been occupied in many, many years. Except, that is, for the piles of treasure strewn everywhere. Furs and boots and shields and scepters, all shimmering with gemstones.

Forbes burst in next, Basil just behind. The chorus of giggles surrounded the cottage as Evie slammed the door shut. She fumbled in the darkness for some sort of lock. She found a board nailed just above that could be rotated to bar the door. She wheeled it down just as a swarm of tiny fists began to bang against the wood.

"The windows!" shouted Basil.

Forbes lunged toward one as two sneering goblin faces appeared behind the filthy glass. They tried to force it open. He leaned his body onto the handle to hold it shut.

Another goblin appeared with a laugh. Then another. And another. Together, they were stronger than Forbes. "Someone help!"

Basil, however, was using the same tactic at another window and getting similar results. Six of the sharp-toothed monsters smiled in at him, their long arms slowly forcing the window up. Evie was occupied as well. Dozens of fists rained down on the door, which was starting to loosen from the jamb. She searched frantically for some way to fortify it but found only treasure, which was proving utterly worthless at the moment.

There was a loud *chink* in the other room, then the flickering orange of firelight. The goblins' laughter poured through the cottage like the wind as the windows kept inching open. The light approached, and a lumpy troll hobbled out from a bedroom. He was rotund and hairy in a coarse sleeping gown, though taller and leaner than his brother. He and Rumpledshirtsleeves shared the same wiry beard, however, and the same ambling stride. Rumpelstoatsnout walked to the center of the room, candle in stumpy hand, and grunted in annoyance. He seemed to not even notice the hordes of goblins that had nearly made it inside the cottage.

"What are you doing in my house at this hour?" he barked. His voice was as dry and rumbly as his brother's but inflamed with hostility.

"Help us!" shouted Evie. "Goblins!"

"Yes, goblins, yes, I see. And what have you brought them here for?"

Evie threw her body against the door as the bit of wood barring it wobbled loose. Across the cottage, Forbes gave one last shout as the window slid open. He dove back to the center of the room, sword raised. Rumpelstoatsnout's candle flickered orange against the sinister smiles of the goblins as they climbed inside.

"Well, don't let them in, you fool!" shouted the troll.

Now Basil lost his battle, and a second window opened. Evie could feel the thumping at her back and knew it was only a matter of moments before the door would fall as well.

"Go on, get them out of here!" bellowed Rumpelstoatsnout. Basil and Forbes backed toward him with their weapons in the air. The goblins fanned out across the room.

Evie's feet slid forward. The wooden brace clanked to the floor. The door eased open and there was nothing she could do to stop it. Laughter filled the cottage. Her mind swirled for a way out and finally landed on an idea. She reached around to her knapsack, fumbling with the clasp. One of the goblins was in now, smiling up at her with teeth like thorns. Another entered.

Evie's hand fluttered around inside the knapsack and found the thick, hairy stem of the flower she'd taken from Cumberland Hall. The first goblin grabbed her arm and opened its mouth for a bite. She ripped the flower from the knapsack and snapped the stem in two.

In an instant, the goblins transformed into a fluttering cloud of ravens. The sinister giggling became panicked squawks. Huge black wings flapped as the creatures banged around the ceiling searching for a way out. Evie threw open the door and dove out onto the mossy ground. Ravens cawed as they poured into the night. Basil and Forbes raced out and crouched near Evie.

The forest was nearly black except for the wavering light of the candle Rumpelstoatsnout held in one hand. In the other, he was swatting at the remaining birds with a straw broom.

"Get out, demons! Begone!"

There were more squawks from the darkness as the ravens found branches on which to perch. Rumpelstoatsnout peered down at the three cadets. They huffed and puffed, amazed to be alive.

One of the troll's rust-colored eyes nearly closed as his mouth curled into a malevolent frown. His ashen skin was even more dotted with warts than his brother's. Strands of thick black hair sprayed out from the top of his otherwise bald head. The ravens continued to squawk.

"Where did you get that flower?"

• • •

When Rumpelstoatsnout's mind was working, his body seemed incapable of standing still. Unlike his brother, who always looked as though he was about to collapse in a pile of bones and loose skin, Rumpelstoatsnout's movements were almost graceful. He had been a doddering, sour-faced old troll until his eyes found the chair strapped to Basil's back, at which point he had transformed into something resembling a hungry fox with an eye inside the henhouse.

"I'll need to inspect it, of course," he said in his customary rasp. "I've lived in Goblin's Glade long enough to have had my trust withered to naught." The troll paced, bobbing up and down with one leg shorter than the other. His eyes never left the Bandit's Chair. "My brother sent this? To give to me?"

"*After* you help us get the harp from Rumpelstiltskin," said Evie. "When we have the harp, the chair is yours."

"Shame I didn't know that before. I could have given you to the goblins, and it would already be mine."

Basil gulped.

"Will you help us or not?" said Evie.

Rumpelstoatsnout stopped pacing. He looked hungrily at the chair, his teeth chewing on nothing. "Rumpelstiltskin will not give up the harp easily."

"Then he'll give it up difficultly," said Evie.

"I think you mean 'with difficulty,'" said Basil.

"No, I don't!" she hissed, keeping her eyes fixed on the troll.

Rumpelstoatsnout considered, and then his lips spread to reveal blocky yellow teeth. "I'll help you, children. But I warn you, if you try to cheat me, you'll never leave the Glade again."

"Agreed," said Evie.

"Uh, pardon me, Cadet Basil here." He gave a nervous wave. "Er—we were told there might be someone called the Gray Man living round here?"

"Will you stop with that nonsense?" said Forbes. "He's just agreed to help us with the ha—"

"The Gray Man, you say?" said Rumpelstoatsnout. Hearing the tension between Basil and Forbes seemed to have ignited his mind once again. He began to pace. "Why, he lives just down the valley. I could take you there now if you'd like."

"Yes, we should like that very—"

"Basil," snapped Evie. "Outside."

"We are outside."

"Over here, then." She pointed away from Rumpelstoatsnout, who watched from the doorway with a grin. Ravens squawked in the trees. "You as well." Forbes came over and joined them. The fog grew ever more dense with each step down the valley, which felt as though it might funnel straight down to the center of the world. "Forbes is right. We cannot afford to veer from our mission. There's no time."

"Especially not for the cursed brother of someone who's not even alive anymore."

Basil stared at the ground. He didn't say anything, but his nostrils flared.

"Bas, what is it?"

"Nothing."

"Look, I know this has been hard, but we're almost there. We've nearly finished the mission—"

"Sod the mission. I've got a mission of my own."

Forbes threw his hands in the air. "Brilliant."

Evie scowled at him, then turned back to Basil. "I know Marline asked you to find a cure for her brother, but that can't be our mission right now."

"It isn't about Marline. It isn't about her brother, either."

"Then what is it about?"

Basil glared at Forbes. "I don't want to say with him here."

"Fine," he said. "I don't care. I'll just go chat with the murderous troll over there."

He stalked off, leaving Evie and Basil alone. She took his hand, but he still wouldn't look at her. "Basil. What is it?"

He took a deep breath as emotions played across his face. Finally, when he had brought them under control, he spoke. "It isn't this bird that I need the Gray Man's magic for." He looked up and met her eyes. "It's my sister."

Evie was astonished. "What did you say?"

"My mother didn't send me to the Academy because she always wanted to have a girl to train as a princess. She already did have one. Her name was Charlotte Amelie, and she was my best friend."

"Bas . . . why didn't you tell me you have a sister?"

"Because I don't anymore." Tears welled in his eyes. "She

215

was turned to stone." A frigid breeze swept across the valley. Ravens sang out as they flew off into the night, bored with the people down below. "It was my decision to train as a princess. I did it as a tribute to her. To at least attempt what she'd always wanted to do but never had the chance." He wiped his eyes. "I never thought I'd last a month, much less two years. Charlotte would have breezed through all three. She was the kindest person I ever knew. She would have made a brilliant princess. And she'd be howling with laughter at the idea that I was only one year away from doing it myself." He chuckled ruefully.

"I'm so sorry, Bas. Why did you keep it to yourself?"

"The only way I could make it through the day was to pretend she never existed. She's right there in our castle, but I haven't gone to see her since they brought her back. It's just too painful." He sniffled and sighed. "That's why I've got to find the Gray Man. I'm sorry, Evie, I know what's at stake, but if I have the chance to bring my sister back to life, then how am I supposed to give that up? I may never get this opportunity again." The loss of his sister was suddenly so plain in his face, in the sadness that had always lurked beneath his bright eyes. "If you and Forbes want to go on without me, I understand. But I can't leave this place until I've spoken to the Gray Man and found out if he really does have a cure."

Panic bubbled in Evie's stomach. She couldn't bear the thought of losing another person on this journey that seemed to be robbing her of one loved one after another. Still, she couldn't imagine trying to convince Basil that he was wrong to try to cure his sister while he had the chance. She nodded, then walked back up the hill. Through the gnarled branches, the sky seemed less black than she'd expected, more ashen, like the color of the end of night. Forbes turned to face her as she approached. Rumpelstoatsnout smiled. It made one of his eyes nearly close, like a wink. "Well? Have we a destination?"

"We'd like to see the Gray Man—"

"Oh, for the love—"

"Quiet, Forbes." She turned back to the troll. "Can you take us to him on the way to your brother's castle?"

"Aye, it's only a short jump out of the way. But why should I agree to that? Our terms were already in place: the chair for the harp. Now you'd like to make use of more of my expertise?"

Evie's mind began to race. What else did she have to offer? Now that the flower stem had been broken, there was only a feather, a needle, and some dried meat in her sack, none of which seemed big enough or powerful enough to entice the troll to help.

"Give him the bird statue."

"Forbes, you are not helping." She took a deep breath. "If you lead us to the Gray Man . . ." She reached up and unfastened her enchanted neckband. She held it out at arm's length, and when she spoke, her disembodied voice caused Rumpelstoatsnout to jump. "You can have this."

The troll ambled forward, and the corners of his smile plunged down. His large, bulging eyes stared intensely at the treasure.

"Evie, you can't give up your voice," said Basil.

"It's all I've got left," came the voice from her hand.

"Say, Stoatsnout," said Forbes, "isn't there a fair round here we could pop by? Or a tournament of some sort? Now that we seem to have this extra time to traipse about?"

"My name is not Stoatsnout!"

"Will you do it?" said Evie.

Rumpelstoatsnout lowered his thick eyelids and looked at the jeweled neckband. "For the chair and the jewels . . . aye. You have a deal."

"Lovely," said Forbes with bile in his voice. "Shall we have some tea before we set off upon our leisurely journey to complete the mission? And I do hope you'll show us the scenic points of interest along the way."

Rumpelstoatsnout disappeared back inside, where they heard the sounds of hammering and windows slamming shut. Forbes glared at Basil. "Any other stops you'd like to make?"

"Forbes," said Evie with a scowl. "Princesses adapt to the circumstance."

"And knights don't. They kill dragons no matter the circumstance."

A surge of anger coursed through her, which, of course, was exactly what he wanted. Rumpelstoatsnout emerged wearing a large hat. The brim was filthy, stiff from rain and sweat. He used a special key to turn the piece of wood inside the door.

He tested it, and it held. With his stolen treasures protected, he began to limp down into the valley. "This way."

They followed him on a thin trail with a gentle grade that wound around the slope of the forest. Evie was behind Basil, with Forbes behind her. As they descended, the air became so crisp, it bit at their skin. The fog stayed one step ahead of them, always obscuring the parts of the valley they were walking into. Ravens cawed from their hidden perches in the trees. *Real ravens or former goblins?* she wondered.

Finally, as she began to feel herself settling in for a long night of walking, Rumpelstoatsnout spoke: "Just up there."

Evie was jolted from her thoughts. "Already?"

"Aye, the Gray Man is my neighbor." He turned back with an evil sneer. "He's going to *love* my new neckband."

"Hang on," she said, stomping her foot. They all stopped and looked at her. She pointed back the way they'd come. "You want me to give up my voice for a short walk in a straight line?" The troll's cottage was still visible on the hillside in the distance.

"Are you trying to cheat me?" snapped the troll, raising his shoulders.

"No one's cheating anyone," said Basil.

"Gray Man won't like hearing I've been cheated. Perhaps I'd better tell him what sort of people you are."

Evie's foot was tapping. She knew she was trapped. "All right, all right. But I need it until we get the harp. I can't talk without it."

"Fine." He pointed a stubby finger at her. "But then I want the chair and the neckband with no trouble attached."

Evie nodded. "Lead on."

Satisfied, Rumpelstoatsnout continued down the trail. The cadets followed him straight to the valley floor. It was a vast meadow of trees and tall grasses beneath a constant drip of rain, and it was dotted with pools of black water. Scattered all across the valley were statues. As the group went on, the scene became even more frightening. The statues were moving. Their stone heads turned to watch as the four of them passed. They were soldiers, each of them, an army of statues frozen on the march.

"Look!" said Basil, a hopeful smile forming. "Look at them!"

"This is the Gray Man's garden," said the troll. "These are the ones he's tending." The frigid water pooled on the valley floor wicked straight into their shoes. Some of the statues turned almost completely around to watch them, while others could only move their eyes. Evie tried to keep her head down, watching Basil's feet splash along the trail, but she couldn't look away from the stone eyes that followed her.

"Gray Man!" called Rumpelstoatsnout. His voice sounded like gravel under a carriage wheel. "Gray Man, are you in?"

The cottage at the back of the stone garden was low and small and covered with moss. Evie could still feel the statues watching her.

"Come out, you old fop!"

They stood in silence for a moment, the sound of grinding stone all around them. Still, neither Evie nor Forbes nor Basil could take their eyes from the cottage door.

"Gray—"

The door opened, just a crack. Evie held her breath. She didn't dare blink. It opened wider. When she saw what stood inside, she nearly screamed.

THE GRAY MAN TOWERED above everyone else, a sculpture come alive. His body resembled an ancient gravestone, its details smoothed by rain and obscured with moss. Evie couldn't take her eyes from his face. His edges were all eroded, leaving him with rounded, ill-defined features—a bump of a nose, two smooth hollows for eyes. But someone, it seemed, had found him rather recently and decided to use him as raw material for a new sculpture. Half of his head, from his right eye to his chin, had been carved into the face of a woman. The cheek, the lips, the jaw . . . all were sharper and more human than the rest of his face. The grooves of those recent chisel marks were still evident as the firelight danced across his face.

"Hello, sir. My name's Basil. Uh, Cadet Basil. That's Evie and that's Forbes. I believe you know Rumpelstoatsnout?"

"Aye, the Gray Man knows me quite well, don't you?" The troll stepped past the tall stone man and began to make himself at home. "Come in, you fools! Tea's on offer!"

They exchanged a look. Basil stepped forward first. Evie

nodded for Forbes to follow, and he did the same to her. Finally, he scowled at her and walked after Basil. They each shrank away from the Gray Man as they entered his cottage. Rumpelstoatsnout was already at the small cooking fire with a kettle of water.

"This old heap of rock always has the best tea, and he won't tell me where he gets it," said the troll with a chuckle. The Gray Man, meanwhile, turned away from the door and took two slow strides into the room. His hands gripped the arms of his chair, and he slowly lowered himself. He sat with his spine as straight as a spruce.

"What's the matter with his face?"

"Forbes!" shouted Evie. "You did that with the boatman as well."

Forbes shrugged. "They have interesting faces."

"After the battle with the witches, back when the Gray Man was only a statue and before anyone knew of the Water of Life, some king found him. He only saw a mound of stone to be carved, and he had a daughter who needed carving. But before he could even finish his precious daughter's face, a sorcerer stole the statue for his own. He was testing the Water of Life against witches' curses. My friend here was the result. When he could walk and think on his own, he stole some of the Water of Life and escaped the sorcerer, then came straight back here to his men. Been working on the cure ever since."

The Gray Man didn't move.

"You'll have to excuse me," said Forbes. "I need some air."

He walked past the man with the stone skin and out into the day-night.

"I won't waste your time, sir," said Basil. "I'm only hoping—begging, actually—that you might spare a bit of this Water of Life for my sister."

The Gray Man slowly turned his head to face Basil. In the soft orange light of the fire, the bit of the king's daughter's mouth that had been carved into the stone looked almost sympathetic.

"He wants you to hear his story," said Rumpelstoatsnout. "I'll tell you. I was there when it happened." He carefully poured steaming water into three mugs, then shook in some dried leaves. "It was many, many years back, when the Wood of the Night was more heavily trafficked than it is now. There were enchanted treasures all over these woods in those days. Most have been found, dug up and hauled away by plunderers and bandits, but there were always more to find. More to sell." The troll hobbled to a small wooden table covered in big black blotches of rot. He set the mugs down, then collapsed into a chair. "This one here"—he tipped his head toward the Gray Man—"came round with his army. That's them outside. When they reached this valley, they happened upon a threesome of witches who were none too pleased to see them. This is their cottage we're sitting in now. My brother and I, we were still on good terms back then, and we watched the battle that followed. The witches made short work of the soldiers, as you can imagine. Turned him to stone right beneath a heavy branch. That's why he's all eaten away like that, rain forever dripping down over the top of him. Well, once the witches finished this lot off, that's when me and my brother fell out. We waited until the hags had gone, then we went down to look for whatever treasures might be left. Quite a lot of it had been turned to stone in the battle, but there were a few things here and there that attracted our attention. And it was I who found the ultimate prize.

"An enchanted sack had fallen from this one's pocket in the scrum. Being something of an expert on enchanted items, I recognized it straightaway, and the sight of it made my mouth water. That sack turned fingers into gold." He waggled his bloated digits. "Drop one in, coins come out. You can see where that's quite the valuable item." Evie glanced at the Gray Man, who hadn't moved throughout Rumpelstoatsnout's story. "Well, as soon as I bent down to pick it up, my brother smashed me over the head with a log. Left me for dead in a puddle while he made off with the sack. Even took one of my fingers to test his new trophy." He held up his other hand, which was missing the little finger. "That was when our rivalry began. But even though my brother turned against me, I did gain a fine new neighbor in this one here. He's even shown me the castle where the Water of Life flows from an enchanted fountain. I never dared venture inside, but I've seen him do it. And each time he goes in, he comes back just a little bit more himself. Water of Life alone won't finish the job, though. Gray Man's tried all different combinations on his men out there to turn 'em back to human.

From herbs and tonics to blood and tears. Some call him a witch for all the experimenting he does. One day, though . . . one day he'll strike the right mix and all that stone will be flesh again."

"Where is this castle?" said Basil to the Gray Man. "I don't even need to take any of your supply. Just tell me where it is, and I can go get some for myself."

"Basil," said Evie. "I'm sorry, but there isn't time for that. And it isn't even a cure, anyway, it's only—"

"Hope," he said. "It's hope. The last thing my sister saw was the face of the witch who turned her to stone. Same as him." He pointed at the Gray Man, who sat as still as a statue, his huge granite hands resting heavily on his knees. "Only difference is, he's found a way to see more."

Evie was at a loss. *Maggie. Remington. Marline. Demetra. And now Basil.* She looked away from him, her emotions threatening to explode out of her like a volcano. "Fine," she spat. "Go ahead and go."

"Evie—"

"Take him," she said to the Gray Man. The statue rose from his chair and clomped to the door, then lumbered outside.

"Well," said Rumpelstoatsnout in a soft voice. "I suppose you'll be needing someone to carry that chair—"

"Take me to your brother. Now." Her eyes were red. All she wanted was to hurt Basil.

"Evie, I'm sorry."

She grabbed the chair and roughly pulled the straps off his

shoulders. He let her take it. She threw it onto her own back and stomped out the door after the Gray Man. Finally, Basil came out, his head hung low, with Rumpelstoatsnout behind him. He closed the door and inhaled deeply. As he let it out, he raked his fingers across his bulging belly.

"Right. You're already carrying my neckband for me; you might as well carry my chair, too."

"Evie," said Basil. His eyes were pinched, his mouth in a frown. He looked so sad and helpless that she wanted to simultaneously hug him and kick him. "I'm sorry. I'll come find you as soon as I can, all right?"

"He's leaving now, too?" said Forbes. "This is quite the team you've assembled."

"He's all yours," said Evie to the Gray Man. Then she turned to Forbes and Rumpelstoatsnout. "Let's go."

"Evie . . . I'm sorry."

She didn't even look at him. She walked back through the moving sculptures of knights, tears streaming from her eyes. But she never turned back to let him see.

The rain was falling again. It soaked the forest in sheets. The good news was that the weather had suppressed the more bewitched elements of the forest. Evie and Forbes had been following Rumpelstoatsnout along a thin mountain trail for a long while and had yet to encounter a goblin, or anything more harmful than a deer for that matter. The most perplexing element of the Wood of the Night was that it always looked like dusk. Since they'd entered it, the sky had been threatening to go dark, yet it never really had.

She looked at Forbes, soaked to the bone. *Of everyone I've lost, why must I be left with him?* As she had the thought, another one entered her mind. An odd thought, and one she never would have predicted: *I'm glad to be with him.* Evie had a strange, complicated relationship with Forbes. They were two wolves drinking from the same puddle. Despite his claim that family was nothing more than a meaningless relic of the past, she could see his cold, cruel father inside him. But she could also see something more admirable. He was strong, even in the face of dreadful circumstances. He'd never spoken of his mother, but perhaps that came from her.

"Nearly there," croaked Rumpelstoatsnout. He paused beneath a pine tree. The earth plunged away next to it, down into the fog hanging in the valley below. "I suppose I ought to prepare you for my brother. I told you how he got the drop on me with that log? Well, he has quite a talent for that, just sort of *turning up* out of nowhere. Even if it looks like he's away, we'll need to be careful. He's very manipulative, so if he does appear, trust me to handle him." Neither Evie nor Forbes spoke. "One last thing, and you've got to believe me when I tell you this." A smile crept across his face. "My brother would rather destroy the harp than let our brother get hold of it. Rumpledshirtsleeves is something of a black sheep in our family, and no one likes him less than Rumpelstiltskin. The quicker we can get out the better." He glanced up the hill ahead. "Right. On we go."

They followed the troll up the trail to where it crested, then down the other side into a basin of marshland. The trees were sparse here, and the sky was a dull, gray mass of clouds. Sharp stone cliffs sprouted up on the far side of the clearing. Beneath them, seated atop a raised mound of mossy earth, was Rumpelstiltskin's castle. Twin towers as round as tree trunks bordered the entrance. A small keep stood behind them. The stone was covered in splotches of black mold where it had killed away the moss. There was no gate in the gatehouse. In all, it looked like nature had won this particular battle against humanity.

"After that unpleasant business with the princess guessing his name—you know, the incident for which my brother is most famous?—well, after that he came to the Glade to escape mankind, which he felt had cheated him. He found this abandoned castle and claimed it as his own. He used to have me round quite often before we fell out. If it's still done up the way it always was, the whole castle will be empty except for the throne room. That's where he keeps all his . . . *winnings.*"

"Lovely," said Forbes. "To the throne room."

"What do we do if he's in?" said Evie.

"I've no idea," said Rumpelstoatsnout with a sneer. "Let's hope he's not." He walked out into the mossy marsh, following a natural path toward the castle. Forbes and Evie followed, both with their hands on their swords. The clouds above the castle were a furious black swirl. The wind whistled through the cracks in the distant mountains, blasting southward across the bog. As they drew nearer, the castle loomed above them, more imposing than it had been from afar. Though neglect and weather had taken their toll, the walls stood tall and strong.

Forbes began to slow, letting Rumpelstoatsnout move ahead a bit. He signaled for Evie to slow as well. "It's time we took control," he whispered above the wind. He reached for the Bandit's Chair, unstrapping it from Evie's back and hoisting it onto his own. "If you see the harp, grab it and let them sort out the chair. No negotiations. Not with Rumpelstiltskin or his brother. Be ready to run." Evie nodded. Her muscles felt twitchy and her heart was racing.

Rumpelstoatsnout crossed a short wooden drawbridge over an ashy moat and walked inside. He lurched across the open-air courtyard to the far wall, where he huddled against the stone. Evie and Forbes hurried over to join him. His smile had gone. His eyes darted about as rainwater plopped all around. Then he turned and edged toward the passageway that led to the throne room. Forbes looked back at Evie. She gave him a nod. Her heart was threatening to leap out of her chest. Rumpelstoatsnout leaned forward and peered into the throne room. After several moments, he stepped out into the open.

"He's gone."

Evie and Forbes took tentative steps to join him. As her fingers shook atop the pommel of her sword, she looked into Rumpelstiltskin's throne room. There were holes cracked through the stone ceiling, with vines sprawling down into the castle. A small straw pallet sat in the darkness on the right side of the vast room. There were piles of spun gold everywhere, along with countless other treasures: statues made of bronze, balls of pure emerald, stacks of gold coins.

"There it is!" said Evie, pointing across the room to the golden harp. It was small, meant to be played on a child's lap, and it shimmered like the sun.

Forbes staggered into the room in awe. He slowed near the dais where thrones had once stood, looking in wonder at the pillowy piles of spun gold. "He's got enough riches and land to be a king. King of a place with no natural enemies."

"Forbes," snapped Evie. "In and out, remember?"

He continued to study Rumpelstiltskin's plunder, only reluctantly hearing Evie's words. "Yes, yes. Of course." He walked through the spun gold and stolen gems until he reached what they'd come for. Then he unstrapped the Bandit's Chair, set it down with a *thunk*, and picked up the golden harp.

"And what've you got there, chap?" came a voice like the growl of a wolf.

The harp clattered to the ground as Forbes's sword jumped free. He scanned the darkness for the one who'd spoken.

"Why, that appears to be my property," said the voice, as sharp as a rusted blade. "By what right do you propose to steal my harp?"

"Were you its rightful owner, I might give you an answer," said Forbes. "But as it currently stands, this harp appears to be more mine than yours."

"You may not realize it yet, my friend, but you have only

two choices." A figure began to move in the darkness. "One is to die. Would you like to hear the other?"

"Oh, go on."

Evie watched, her muscles clenched as tightly as a hangman's noose. Forbes's terrified eyes flicked back to Rumpelstoatsnout.

"Your other choice is to leave here with the harp securely in your possession." Rumpelstiltskin lumbered out of the shadows. One of his legs had been fashioned from a rotten piece of wood, which made his limp even more pronounced than either of his brothers'. He was short and wide, with bulging purple cheeks and needlelike whiskers sprouting from beneath his chin. His mouth was in a scowl, revealing teeth that had been sharpened down to points. "But first you'll have to give me something better."

"Th-the chair," said Forbes, unable to disguise his fear. "That's the Bandit's Chair. It's yours."

"That's my bloody chair!" roared Rumpelstoatsnout, charging into the room.

"You!" growled Rumpelstiltskin. "I might've known you'd be behind this, you moldy cur."

"Give me that chair," said Rumpelstoatsnout. He suddenly seemed much less doddering than he had up to this point. He held out his bulging hand. "It's mine."

Forbes's eyes shot from one troll to the other. He was frozen between them.

"Give me the chair and the harp is yours," said Rumpelstiltskin, eyeing his brother with malice.

"It isn't his to give!" shouted Rumpelstoatsnout. "The chair is mine!"

"To sweeten the pot, I'll give you a bolt of this spun gold as well," said Rumpelstiltskin. "I saw you admiring it. Take two if you'd like."

Suddenly, Rumpelstoatsnout lunged across the throne room. Forbes grabbed the harp, as did Rumpelstiltskin, who also took hold of the chair. The three of them grappled for the magical items. As the troll brothers tried to pry each other's hands from the harp and the chair, they rolled right on top of Forbes. Even as he was crushed beneath them, he kept his grip on the harp.

"Let go of my chair!"

"It's in my castle! It's my chair!"

Evie sheathed her sword and raced into the fight. Rumpelstoatsnout punched his brother, who kicked him in the shins. They lurched forward and back, upending all manner of priceless antiquities. Evie lunged toward the pile and managed to find Forbes's legs sticking out from beneath the trolls. She grabbed hold of his boots and pulled with everything she had.

Rumpelstiltskin, however, was not about to let go of the harp. He flashed his sharp teeth at Evie, then began savagely trying to jerk the harp out of Forbes's grip. She gave one mighty heave on his legs, and he slipped free from the troll pile. He still had the harp in his hands.

"*Give me that!*" shouted Rumpelstoatsnout. He grabbed the

harp and jerked it away, sending Forbes and Evie tumbling across the floor.

"He's got it!" shouted Forbes. Evie scrambled to her feet as Rumpelstoatsnout used the harp to bash his brother over the head.

"He's going to break it!" shouted Evie.

"Get off me!" shouted Rumpelstiltskin.

"You get off me!" bellowed Rumpelstoatsnout. He raised the harp and smashed his brother in the nose. The Bandit's Chair went spinning across the room, coming to rest just in front of the empty dais.

Rumpelstiltskin roared. He leapt at his brother, tackling him onto his back. The decrepit old trolls fought with the ferocity of all tragic brothers. Now both of them were pushing and pulling on the harp, each trying to free it from the other.

"If it breaks, it's worthless to us," said Forbes. "We've got to get it away!"

Rumpelstoatsnout started to kick his brother in the rotten wooden leg. "Rumpledshirtsleeves sent them to *me*! The chair—is—mine!"

"*RUMPLEDSHIRTSLEEVES?*" The mention of his younger brother's name sent Rumpelstiltskin into a frenzy. He used the harp to knock his brother off his feet. "*He* sent you? You dare to partner with the treasonous viper who revealed my name to that princess?"

Evie inched forward. The brothers were so focused on each

other that she thought she might be able to make a grab for the harp.

"I have no partners," said Rumpelstoatsnout. "If our brother chooses to send me a bewitched chair, then who am I to refuse?"

"If the chair comes from that old rat, then I'll burn it and use this harp for kindling!" He tried to wrench the harp out of his brother's hands with such force that Evie thought it would snap in two.

"Now! Grab it!" shouted Forbes.

Evie lunged for the harp, but Rumpelstoatsnout came crashing down on top of her. For a moment, she couldn't breathe. Even when he'd scrambled off and started punching at his brother, she could barely inhale. Forbes lifted her from the floor and pulled her back from the fight.

"Are you all right?"

She couldn't speak, so she nodded. As the air started to flow, she rubbed her throat and remembered the neckband. Her eyes went wide. She unclasped it.

"Whoever brings me the harp gets this as well!" she shouted, her voice emanating from her hand.

"Treachery!" bellowed Rumpelstoatsnout. "It isn't yours to give!"

The brothers raged across the floor in a violent dance, each trying to wrest the harp free from the other's grip.

"It's mine!" shrieked Rumpelstoatsnout, shoving against Rumpelstiltskin.

Locked in combat, the two of them fell as one. The momentum of the battle carried them across the room.

"You can tell our brother what I did with his—"

The words echoed faintly in the sudden silence of the throne room. The brothers were gone. So, too, was the harp. The empty Bandit's Chair tottered onto its back, clanking hollowly on the stone floor.

Evie and Forbes looked at each other in confusion. Rain hissed against the castle's stone walls.

"What happened?" said Forbes. All the air had been sucked from the room.

"The chair! They sat in the chair!" Evie ran to the Bandit's Chair and set it upright. But wherever the trolls had gone when they stood back up, it was far, far away.

Forbes walked over to join her. They both stared in disbelief. "It isn't even a nice chair." He picked it up with one hand, underscoring how light and dead the wood was. "And this bloody thing has just destroyed the world. I don't suppose you've any idea where it's sent them?"

"None," said Evie. "Sit in one place, rise in another. They could be on the moon for all I know. And wherever they are, the harp is with them."

Forbes looked around the silent throne room with annoyance. "So that's it? After the giants and the witches and the goblins and the trolls and the bloody Gray Man? After losing more than half our team along the way? Our one chance at saving the realm, and we come *this bloody close*, only to lose it because of a *chair*?"

"What do we do now?"

"Put your voice back on."

Evie fastened the neckband. "What do we do now? We failed our mission."

They stood there, astonished and gutted. Slowly, Forbes began to laugh. His voice echoed off the stone castle walls. It was a dark, rueful laugh. "They sat in the bloody chair! Of all the idiotic ways to fail the mission! We carried this thing all the way here from the Academy, through all those trials and tribulations, and the troll brothers *sat on it*!" He grabbed the chair. "You cost us the mission!" He slammed it on the floor. "You cost us the mission!"

"Forbes, stop!"

He bashed it down again and again. Within seconds, gray splinters began to fly. He was left with two broken stumps in his hands and an array of broken wood at his feet. He looked over at Evie, his breath coming hard.

"That was a priceless artifact!" she said.

"So what?" He tossed the stumps aside with a clatter. Then he stormed out of the throne room, leaving Evie surrounded by spun gold that suddenly didn't seem to have any luster left at all.

She stared at the broken remains of the Bandit's Chair and let the meaning of it all wash over her. Everything Forbes had said was right. They'd come so far through difficult circumstances, only to have it end in the most ridiculous of ways. Finally, with feet as heavy as granite, she trudged out of the castle.

Forbes was sitting on the drawbridge, throwing pebbles into the murky gray water. She joined him, a wintry wind howling steadily down from the mountain pass on the far side of the castle. Numb, she stared across the marsh, back toward where they'd entered. The mounds of peat and earth and moss looked like great, green beasts asleep beneath the clouds. The urgency, the tension they'd felt ever since the witches had first attacked, had suddenly vanished, leaving them adrift like ships in dead winds. They had lost.

"Brothers," he said, winging a stone into the moat. "It's almost poetic, isn't it? The fate of the world upended because of a petty family squabble. Why can't people understand that family isn't there to help you? They exist to give you one gift— life—and then you've got to move on the first chance you get. Birds leave nests, fish leave eggs, and we should be smart enough to do the same."

"You can't possibly blame this on family."

"Why not? As soon as they were able, those stupid trolls should have shaken hands, turned their backs to each other, and started walking. The world would be a whole lot better off if they hadn't clung to the idea of family."

"You're being ridiculous."

"He just said he'd rather destroy the harp than give it to his brother. We could have calmly negotiated with him if his family hadn't been involved." He fired another stone into the water. "Family's the anchor that drowns us all unless we shed it and learn to swim."

"You sound like your father."

He gave her a sardonic look. "Ha-ha."

"I'm serious. If you think family is some sort of anchor that you've shed, you're wrong. He's inside you now, speaking for you, controlling you. You haven't shed him at all." He threw another stone but didn't say a word. She turned to face him, softening her tone. "Family isn't something we use until we don't need it anymore. It's inside us forever, whether we like it or not. It's up to us to see the good and the bad in them, and then to find it in ourselves. Family isn't an anchor. It's a current that can help to carry you along, or something you can spend your life fighting against only to end up in the same spot."

He sighed and tossed another stone, though this time he didn't throw it nearly as hard. "And how does any of that help us? Even if what you're saying is true, and I'm not agreeing that it is, we're still sitting here harpless and hopeless."

Another wind blew across their backs and howled south over the marsh. Evie's muscles felt quivery, as though she'd just climbed a mountain. But for all that climbing, her view was still the bottom of a marsh. She had been resilient from the very first moment of the mission, adapting to unexpected circumstances every step of the way. Yet she couldn't figure a way forward now. And she was exhausted.

They sat with their feet dangling off the bridge for quite a long time, neither of them speaking. "Should we just stay here?" he said at last. "Save us from having to watch the witches celebrate."

Evie pulled her nearly empty knapsack onto her lap and took out the feather she'd stolen from Cumberland Hall. "If you'd like to stay, I completely understand. I won't hold it against you. But I've got to go back."

"What's that?" he asked.

"An enchanted feather. Supposedly it will lead us where we need to go."

"Why not," he said as he stood up. "What better way to end a ludicrous mission than by following a magic feather?"

Evie twirled the feather between her finger and thumb, watching the wind flutter through its downy barbs. She stared at it and was struck with profound sadness. The depth of their failure was only now starting to sink in. After all the perseverance it had taken to get to Rumpelstiltskin's castle, when she'd finally seen the harp sitting there, she really had believed they'd accomplished the mission. And then, with one foul breath from the Fates, it was over.

She held the feather up into the wind and let it go . . .

It flew straight back, directly into the howling wind. Somehow, instead of catching the gusts and carrying south across the marsh, the feather flew north.

"Ah, that's more like it," said Forbes. "Let's end the mission with a *faulty* magic feather." He walked down the bridge and turned onto the mossy path between marsh ponds toward the way they'd come.

Evie stood alone on the bridge. She watched the feather as it darted and swirled against the wind. It flew past the castle, headed for the gap between the harsh stone cliffs.

"North," she said to herself. She took a step forward, watching the feather get smaller and smaller. "North." Her mind wandered, sailing high above the countryside. Blood pulsed into her head as a realization struck her as solidly as a jousting lance. "Forbes!" she shouted. "Forbes!"

He turned back in annoyance. "What?"

"Everything I've just said to you, I should have been saying to myself!" Suddenly, her body felt like it was full of electricity. She couldn't stand still, couldn't control the words pouring out of her. "I've been so worried for so long . . . ever since I realized I was different, I've been waiting for them to reject me, so *I rejected them first!*"

"What are you on about?"

"But they're my family! They'll always be my family! Oh, I've been such a fool!"

"Yes, and you still are. What are you blathering on about?"

"We haven't failed. Our mission wasn't to find the harp. Our mission was to save the Academy." She turned to face him, her eyes alive. Gooseflesh broke out all across her arms. Another icy wind blasted across the bridge and she began to smile. "Come on," she said. "It's time you met my family."

THIS WOULD BE *so much easier if I still had Boy,* thought Evie. She missed her horse as a friend, of course, but also for his utility. The treacherous mountain pass was littered with rubble from long-ago rockslides that Boy could easily have navigated. Finally, after a tense climb with calloused fingers and cheeks red from wind blasts, Evie and Forbes made it through. The cliffs opened into a vast expanse of rolling green forest cloaked in heavy, unmoving fog. As they paused to catch their breath, a hole opened up in the cottony gray, a small window that revealed a colossal mountain range on the northwest horizon.

The Dragonlands.

It had taken some convincing to get Forbes to agree to this latest adaptation to the mission. "You can't possibly be serious," he said. "You want me, a knight, to go ask a dragon for help."

"Two dragons."

"It's not possible," he said. "Look, at the risk of complimenting you, you have managed to somewhat alter my opinions on dragons. I've always thought of them as mindless beasts, but you've convinced me that they're actually free-thinking enemies with their own agendas."

"How enlightened," she said, rolling her eyes.

"Be glib if you like, but I've just spent two years preparing to kill them. And I have every confidence they know that. They'll devour me the moment they see me."

"Forbes, they're my family. They *will* help us. Trust me, it'll mean a lot that it's a knight asking for help."

"Not a chance—"

"I changed Remington's mind about them. And I've clearly started to change your pig-headed mind. Why couldn't I change dragons' minds as well? Particularly since the dragons in question are my own mother and sister?"

He had stomped his foot and hardened his jaw and refused to go north. So she had left him standing there in the marsh and gone off after the feather by herself. Thirty minutes later, he was climbing next to her, and he was only too happy to let her know how he felt about it.

"I'll kill them both if I have to."

She'd ignored him all the way up the pass. Now, standing above the vast northern woodlands, it seemed he had finally given up fighting. "There's the feather, there." He pointed down the hill to where the trees thickened into a rolling beech forest.

They headed down the mountainside, thankfully a much

more gentle grade than the southern half of the pass had been. They entered the forest and walked in silence for the better part of an hour. The ground was carpeted in the brittle remains of last autumn's leaves. The smell of rain hung in the air.

"Bit of daylight up ahead," said Forbes. "I can hear a river."

Evie listened. There it was, the distant burbling of water. A good place to refill their waterskins. They passed through a rare clearing in the dense forest and came upon a small stream sluicing through the long grass on its way down the mountain. Evie knelt and let the bracing water wash over her hands as she filled her waterskin. She took a deep breath. The air tasted of home. Pine and earth and far off storms. She hadn't planned on coming home, maybe not ever again. Now that she was here, she couldn't believe how foolish she'd been.

When she opened her eyes, something moved in the corner of her vision.

Her head shot over, but the forest was silent and still. Next to her, Forbes dunked his face in the river and gave it a rinse.

She stood, looking off into the forest. She stepped onto a large stone at the river's edge and used it to vault across. Her heart raced as she walked on, eyes opened wide. She could sense that something was there but found only the soft hiss of the wind and gently waving grass. The forest gave way to another clearing just ahead. She moved slowly through trees as still as a painting, and when she entered the next clearing, she gasped.

There, alone in the meadow, stood a whitish-gray unicorn. Its horn was as long as a sword, pure polished white, like ivory. Evie had never seen a unicorn before. She stepped forward, as gently as she could, showing her open palms to prove she wasn't a threat. The creature took a bite of grass and chewed it, watching her.

"Hello there, beauty," she said. The unicorn snorted and waved its head but didn't retreat. Evie extended her hand. She was close enough to smell the familiar horse smell she'd grown to love from her time with Boy. "Easy now, beauty. What are you doing out here?"

The unicorn inched its head forward, blowing warm breath across her hand from its velvety snout. Finally, satisfied, it took a step toward her. Her smile cracked open with a laugh. "Hi there! Well, you're nice, aren't you?" It butted her affectionately with its head. She placed her palm on the unicorn's face. The hair was soft and smooth. Its eyes regarded her, large and expressive and so, so beautiful. She ran her hand down the unicorn's back, and an idea came to her. "Would you like to help me, beauty?" she said in a soft voice. "My friend and I have some urgent business in the north, and it's taking us an awfully long time to get where we're going. Do you suppose I might try riding you?"

The unicorn nudged her again.

She glanced around and found exactly what she needed. There was a small patch of celerywood trees at the edge of the clearing. The bark was dangling off like a snake's skin. She began to tear away pieces and set to work fashioning a crude rope, which she slipped around the creature's neck. It threw its head back proudly as she climbed onto its back. She found the unicorn incredibly responsive to her cues with the rope, and even more intuitive to ride than Boy had been. She ambled back up to the river where Forbes had taken his boots off and was washing his feet. When he looked up and saw her on unicornback, his jaw dropped. She sat just a bit taller. Nothing she had ever done had made her feel quite so much like a princess as riding on the back of a unicorn.

"What do you think you're doing?" he said.

"I've found us some help. She's brilliant to ride." She lifted her handwoven rope. "I used to make dresses out of this stuff. Very easy to weave."

"That's a bloody unicorn."

"I know," she said with a smile.

His eyes rolled back in his head as he let out a long, irritated sigh. "You don't know much about unicorns, do you? They..." He trailed off as his eyes moved past her toward something down the hill. "Ah, here we are. Well done, Evie. We'll never be rid of them now."

She turned to see an entire herd of the majestic creatures walking up the hill with great curiosity. Forbes pulled on his boots and leapt over the stream, waving his arms in the air. "Get on! Get on!" he shouted. They stopped and regarded him warily. Finally, he let his arms drop. "What a disaster."

"Why must you always be so dour? We've got mounts now. We'll be with my family in no time." She jumped off her unicorn and went to a nearby tree, where she quickly began lashing pieces of bark together. "Why are you always so negative?"

He faced her with the same mix of exasperation and anger that she'd come to expect. Behind him, dozens of unicorns stepped forward, each the same smoky color, their horns shimmering in the murkiness of the forest.

"Why am I always so negative? Allow me to enlighten you. Unicorns are the biggest pests in all the . . ." The inquisitive unicorns enveloped him. He sighed again. ". . . in all the land. Now we'll have the lot of them following us all the way back to the Academy."

As Evie slipped the rope over one of the unicorn's heads, dozens of other snouts began inspecting her. "Hello," she said, smiling at all the innocent, soulful eyes looking at her. "You're just determined to be a grump, that's all. I think they're absolutely magical." She remounted her unicorn and smiled down at the small herd in front of her.

Forbes shook his head darkly, then climbed onto the unicorn Evie had prepared for him. "On the positive side, perhaps your family will think they're as magical as you do and eat them instead of me."

Forbes slapped the unicorn on the snout. "Get away, vile beast!"

The curious creature jumped back and disappeared into the herd. They were milling by the dozens around the makeshift campsite set up at the bank of a glassy lake. Evie was eating what was left of an enormous fish they'd caught earlier, after riding well into the night. The unicorns had followed them through the forest, over streams, across thin mountain trails, and around the vast lake stretching out before them now. As they chose a flat piece of ground and set about building a cook fire, the unicorns made themselves at home. They didn't just linger on the fringe of camp; they walked right through as if Evie and Forbes were just two more members of the herd.

The rain had stopped several hours earlier, and now the chirp of crickets and the croak of frogs surrounded them. The sky had cleared into a grand explosion of stars. The smell of the fire and the sounds of the cool evening brought her back to that first night she'd spent with Remington, the night they'd rescued each other from a wicked witch. She had been so suspicious of him then. So sure that, as a knight cadet, he would like nothing more than to kill her and her dragon family. Now here she was willingly bringing a different knight cadet to the family cave. How times had changed.

"You're deadly with a line," said Forbes. "I don't suppose you could pull a bit of chocolate out of that lake."

"Or one of those Friday tarts."

"Mmm, yes, best pudding at the Academy, bar none."

"I never would have rated you a lover of sweets."

"Me?" he said with a laugh. "I would subsist entirely on chocolate if I could. You can keep your salt."

A unicorn strolled between them. Evie held out a hand to stroke it. When it passed, she took another bite of fish and looked at Forbes out of the corner of her eye. "Could I ask you something without you having a tantrum?"

He shot her an irritated look.

"I've been thinking about my family, obviously, and . . . well, yes, they're dragons, but I've always been a human, even when I didn't know it. You . . . you actually *became* a pig. What was it like? I mean, do you remember when it happened?"

He took a deep breath and contemplated. "You can't imagine what it feels like when your bones shrink. Or when bristly hair comes jutting out of your skin. The pain is incredible. But that's not the worst of it. What haunts me is that while all that was happening to my body, I couldn't stop thinking I'd just made a horrible mistake. The panic . . . the helplessness . . . it's . . . it's awful." He stared into the fire, reliving the worst moment of his life. "On the other hand, as excruciatingly painful as it was to turn back into a human after I saw you, the exhilaration of knowing that my mistake was finally over was the greatest thing in the world. Greater than tarts."

One of the unicorns whinnied in the darkness. Evie turned his words over in her head. "What about before that? When you first walked into the room to look at the portrait?"

"Ah, you mean how can we make my traumatic life experience about you?"

"That's not what I—"

"It was you, Evie." He was looking straight into her eyes without a trace of humor. "I know you'd love me to say I was wrong, but it was you in that painting." He picked up a stick, broke off a piece, and tossed it in the fire. "There are a great many things I've forgotten in my life, and a great many more I'll forget in the future, but not a moment of that day will ever be included. I can close my eyes and be right back in that room now. The dread was overwhelming, but I couldn't contain my curiosity. And when I lifted the sheet . . ." He shook his head and blinked away the memory. "It was you."

Evie said nothing. The portrait that had cursed Forbes had been haunting her since her earliest days at the Academy. Despite what he said, she still didn't believe it could be her in the portrait. After all, she'd spent the majority of her life in the forest with dragons, miles and miles from humanity. How could she sit for a portrait and not remember it? Maggie had done some research and discovered that it could have been any number of other factors that caused Forbes's curse, and also his cure. For a little while, Evie felt the weight of that mystery lifted. But then on the last day of her first year, King Hossenbuhr had mentioned the portrait by name: *The Princess of Saudade*. Remington had called her the Princess of Saudade in one of the visions she'd seen in the dragon's blood. The coincidence of that had been too great to ignore, and she had been thrust right back into the mystery.

"I can see you don't believe me. That's fair. I don't know if

I'd believe me, either. But it's you in that portrait. There's not a doubt in my mind." He prodded the embers, sending an orange spray into the air. "See for yourself when we get back. If the witches haven't burned the place to the ground, that is."

His words hit Evie like a splash of icy water. "See for myself?"

He looked up at her. "What, did you think he left it behind when they sacked our kingdom? His most prized possession? It's right there at the Academy in that little fortress he's created for himself." He threw the stick into the fire.

Evie's mind began to whirl. The portrait had been right under her nose. She suddenly felt fidgety, like she wanted to jump on a unicorn and ride south past all the witches and right into Hossenbuhr's keep to see the portrait with her own eyes. To finally put to rest all her questions about it. Or would seeing it only create more?

"I don't want to talk about it anymore," he said, throwing another stick into the flames. "Let me ask you a question. And no tantrums."

She looked over at him, but her mind was a million miles away with King Hossenbuhr and the precious thing he was protecting.

"What do I do if your mother and sister try to eat me? I'll have to fight back."

"They won't, you incredible fool," she said with exasperation. "Not with me there. Just leave your sword sheathed, and you'll be fine. They're very nice."

He snorted. "Nice. They're bloody dragons."

"They're nice bloody dragons. My mother is lovely. So is my sister. We're a very happy family."

"'A person can be great or happy, but not both.' That's what my father says."

"I suppose that makes us great, doesn't it?"

Forbes chuckled. "Perhaps it does. He's also fond of saying that all great leaders end up alone, so we must be two of the greatest of all time."

Another unicorn sauntered between them on its way to drink from the lake, where the water lapped gently against the shore. *I'm not alone,* she thought. *My family is with me. And soon I'll be with them.*

"Why don't you ever talk about your mother?" she said. His eyes shot up. The grim look on his face unnerved her.

"My mother was killed by a dragon." He snapped a piece off a stick and tossed it in the fire.

Evie's mouth fell open.

"That's why I enlisted. All I've ever wanted was to learn to kill dragons. Ever since the day I watched my mother get dragged off into the woods." He paused as the horrible memory bubbled up. "I wanted to do whatever I could to help ensure that no other little boy would ever have to go through what I went through. And now . . ." He chuckled and shook his head. "I'm about to crawl to them for help."

The fire crackled, and the creatures chirped in the darkness.

Evie watched him through the flames, abashed. She had no idea what to say.

"I've never told anyone that. I didn't want to give the dragons any more power than they already had. But it's true. They killed her. They ruined my life. And yet I'll still go along with you tomorrow because I believe what you said is true. She is still inside me, and they're still inside you, and all of us are doomed without their help."

The unicorns milled about, whickering and stomping. Evie and Forbes both stared into the flames and let the song of the crickets fill the silence.

"It's odd, isn't it?" Evie finally said. "How much we'd like to kill each other's relatives?"

Forbes laughed. "Your father's dead and mine is a monster. My mother's dead and yours is a monster."

That was the end of their conversation. The image of King Hossenbuhr's sword striking Remington's chest repeated itself in her memory. If not for the patch of stone Countess Hardcastle had put there, he'd be dead now. She looked up at the stars. What had happened after they'd left? What was happening now?

At some point, as the flames dimmed, Forbes began to snore. King Hossenbuhr's portrait troubled her, as did thoughts of her friends. Had Demetra made it to the Blackmarsh and rescued her mother? Had Basil found the Water of Life for his cursed sister? Was Marline frozen in stone on the bank of the river near Marburg? And what about Maggie? Had the wall fallen or was it still intact? Her mind only touched on Remington and found the memory as sharp as the needle of a spinning wheel. *The dragons must help us break the siege,* she thought. *No more adapting. Now we fight.*

Despite her bone-deep weariness, her mind was whirring. Even if she and Forbes did make it to the cave and persuade the dragons to help save a place whose stated mission was the eradication of all dragons, and even if they did somehow make it back to the Academy before the fairies' magical wall fell, and even if they did somehow turn back not only the army of witches encamped in the Dortchen Wild, but also three enormous, bloodthirsty giants, there were still great challenges awaiting. Even if all those things came to pass and the Academy was saved, she would still have to confront the horrible business with Beatrice. The Headmistress General, second in rank only to the Queen herself, was working with the witches.

Her mind spiraled around those various thoughts for the next few hours until Forbes finally woke and she collapsed into a heavy sleep. She dreamt of goblins, more specifically goblins' teeth, and didn't stir again until the morning sun had risen and a unicorn's soft muzzle tickled her nose. Then she was jolted awake by a snort of hot breath in her face. She sat up, her sleep-addled brain mystified by the herd of unicorns.

"More arrived in the night," said Forbes. He was hidden somewhere in the sea of white-haired bodies milling about the lakeshore. Finally, she saw him peering over them. He had found the two with the flimsy celerywood ropes Evie had made. "Let's be off before they completely pack us in."

He mounted his unicorn. Evie stood and stretched with a yawn. She picked up her knapsack, took a drink of water, then climbed onto hers.

"These things were like weeds in Diebkunst," growled Forbes. "We couldn't get rid of them fast enough. I found three in my bedroom once. *Inside my bedroom.*"

The rest of the herd stared up at her. Forbes spurred his unicorn forward, forcing the creature to push through the others, who filled in the sea of white behind him as he passed. Evie did the same. She followed Forbes up the hillside along the lake that had been too treacherous without daylight. The unicorns followed one by one, a stream of white hair and pointy horns. The going was slow, but the unicorns performed admirably. Within an hour, they had all crested the hill, the entire traveling party. Evie was reminded of what it had been like to journey with Demetra's family and all their attendant servants and guards.

Another mountain stream crossed the slope in front of them. This one was wider, with less defined banks. Still, it didn't look particularly deep.

"We might have trouble here," said Forbes. "I don't know if you noticed yesterday, but unicorns hate the feel of water on their hooves."

"How do we get across?"

He spurred his unicorn forward. It stepped right to the edge of the crystalline water but began to whinny when he tried to lead it through. The unicorn jerked its head and neighed, staring at the river with wide blue eyes.

"Come on!" he said. He kicked the unicorn's sides even harder, but the animal refused to budge.

"They won't respond to that," said Evie. As more and more unicorns joined them at the top of the hill, she gave hers a gentle tap with her feet. It stepped forward and stopped next to Forbes's. "Come on, now," she said in a soft voice. "I know you're scared, but you can do it." The unicorn touched the water with its hoof. Forbes's continued to jerk its head and whinny in protest. "That's it. Just take a step and you'll see it's not so bad."

Forbes yanked on the rope, trying to get his unicorn under control. Several others snorted and paced unhappily. For once, with the gurgling stream in front of them, the rest of the herd was keeping its distance.

Evie's unicorn put a hoof in the water. It shook its head in protest but took another step forward. The stream only came up a few inches on its leg. "Well done, well done. Keep going." The unicorn continued on, even as the water deepened. Once it reached the unicorn's knee, it began to shallow again. Before long, they'd reached the other side. "That's it! Well done!"

Forbes, however, was struggling to calm his unicorn. Finally, it bucked onto its hind legs and threw him into the water with a splash. Evie broke up in laughter. He stood and sloshed angrily across the stream, while his unicorn trotted away and joined the rest of the herd.

"It appears I'm riding with you," he said, wiping the water from his face.

"Not 'til you've dried off," she said with a grin.

"Fine." He gave her a dark look and began to stomp away.

"I'm only having a laugh. Climb on." She offered him a hand. "But I'm driving."

After leaving the herd of unicorns behind, Evie and Forbes continued north through the land of dragons. They crossed a chain of glass-still lakes called Griselda's Tears at midday, then rode west. The mountains seemed closer to the sky here, the land more musical. Though clouds still stretched from one horizon to the next, the pine needles were greener and the air was more refreshing.

Evie was home.

"Watch for dragons," she warned. "It's possible there are some new ones here who don't know me yet."

He grumbled and shook his head.

As the sun moved toward the horizon, they rode straight into the heart of another thick beech forest. The thousand-year-old trees bloomed toward the sky with boughs as bent and craggy as water through a canyon. With darkness falling, wolves sang out all around them. They drew nearer to the cave, and Evie's stomach became a swirling eddy. She hadn't seen her mother or sister since she'd crept away under cover of darkness nearly a year ago. How would they react to her return?

She thought that her sister might possibly understand why she'd left, but her mother would almost certainly not. Then she changed her mind and envisioned her sister in a rage and her mother appealing for calm. Or perhaps they would both be angry. She just didn't know.

Finally, after hours on unicornback, her body sore and tired and wet, Evie saw something familiar from her childhood. Under the softly diffused light of the full moon, a huge sweep of green mountain rose up before them. It was dotted with hundreds of limestone boulders, some as big as cottages. From here, the cave would only be an hour ahead, possibly less.

Her anxiety grew with every hill they crested and stream they crossed. Everything looked familiar now. Finally, they broke through the edge of the forest and emerged at the base of another mountain range. Evie's range. There, a few hundred yards ahead, the side of the mountain was broken away in what looked like a violent explosion of sun-bleached stones and shattered tree trunks. This was where her father had crashed trying to save her life. Seeing it again took her breath away. His blood was still there, splashes of black washed and faded by the elements. Greenish-yellow shoots sprouted up everywhere, new life growing out of the crumbled stone, the decaying trees, the churned earth. She dismounted and ran her hands along the broken wall. Forbes climbed off as well and waited behind her.

"What happened here?"

She didn't answer. Her hands worked across the stone,

hoping that perhaps there might be another dragon scale embedded there, something she could use to replace the one that had crumbled. A wolf howled behind them.

"Uh, Evie? Perhaps we should be going."

She gave the cliffside one last look, then, stomach churning, she led the unicorn across the huge stone plates at the bottom of the mountain. Where she had expected some measure of joy at returning home, she instead felt only dread. Certainty and dread. Something life-changing awaited her up ahead. She knew it in her bones.

They came around the mountain and there it was, barely visible in the moonlight. The family cave. Its mouth was an empty black swoop in the mountainside. Water trickled down through stone teeth and disappeared inside. It looked cold and empty and dark.

"Is this it?" whispered Forbes. He slid his sword out of its scabbard.

"Put that away," she hissed. "It's like you want them to eat you."

She tried to coax the unicorn forward toward the cave, but it had reached the end of its journey. It pulled against the celerywood rope until finally it snapped. Then, with snorts and huffs, it turned and ran back the way they'd come.

"Did I say unicorns were dumb?" said Forbes. "That seems quite sensible to me."

She studied the cave. "Wait here. Let me talk to them first."

He nodded, his eyes wide. He was jumpy and scared. With

him so tightly wound, Evie was worried what might happen if her sister happened to recognize him as one of the dragon-slayers who had tried to kill her in the first year. Things could go . . . badly.

She walked along the stones toward the teeth of the cave. Inside the darkened cavern, echoes turned the gurgling water into a soft rush. The main chamber was empty. Cold and empty. It was an enormous cathedral of water-smoothed stone. Moss grew up the sides of the walls and across the ceiling. There were no signs of dragon life.

As she continued through the home where she had lived most of her life, the surreal feeling sharpened. She'd only been gone since last summer, but it felt like a lifetime ago, the cave a foreign country. She passed through the main chamber and followed the slope into the rear chamber, where she and her sister had once slept side by side on a stone ledge. Despite being smaller than the first, it was still an enormous chamber of stalactites and walls pocked with veins of shimmering, multi-colored mineral deposits. And it, too, was empty.

Evie sighed with some measure of relief. Of course she'd hoped they'd be there so she could go about the business of trying to persuade them to help. But their not being there meant she could put off explaining why she'd run away for just a bit longer. She walked through the chamber, the room where she'd perched every night since the dragons had taken her the day King Callahan had died. She had become who she now was in this cave. She had learned how to live, who to be, amidst these dripping rocks and mossy walls. In spite of her fears, this was and always would be her home.

She noticed something in a pile of stones near the wall. It was difficult to make out in the near darkness of the cave, but she recognized the shape. She pulled it free from the pile. It was a doll lashed together from sticks and bark. She had made it for her sister's birthday many years ago. The shape was crude—two legs, two arms, a head, and a body—but it had been a controversial item ever since the day she'd made it. She remembered an argument it had caused between her parents. She hadn't known then why a simple doll should lead to such strife, but now it was clear. Evie had made a human doll, based on her own shape and not that of the rest of her family. She hugged it close and thought of her sister's face when she had first given it to her. She hadn't cared in the least what the doll had looked like. She had wept, moved by Evie's thoughtfulness. It had been her parents who had struggled with the meaning of the doll's figure.

A tear fell from her eye. Everything had such meaning now. It was as though that old Evie, the one who had eaten crispy goblin with dragons and sung songs with dragons and slept beneath the wings of dragons, had become nothing more than a memory. This was home, of course. But would the new Evie ever truly feel at home? Or would she—

The deafening roar of a dragon echoed through the cave. She fell to her knees, dropping the doll to cover her ears. After the shock had passed, she realized what was happening.

*"Forbes!"* She scrambled to her feet as another primal roar nearly buckled her knees again. She bounded through the main cavern, sending up splashes of water. Brilliant light lit up the cave as flames erupted outside. She could just make out a human voice amidst the crashing booms of the rampaging dragon.

"No!" she screamed. "Wait!"

She burst out into the night. Forbes was on his back, his sword lying nearby. Above him, a dragon towered sixty feet in the air. Her mouth was wide, her eyes filled with ancient rage.

"Sister!" shouted Evie.

The dragon's head swooped down toward Forbes but stopped short. Her fangs, shimmering with saliva, were only a few feet from piercing Forbes end to end. She turned her reptilian head to Evie. And in the hot glow of fire, there was recognition.

"Sister?" said the dragon in a scorched grumble.

Now another dragon floated down from the black sky and landed with a thundering crash behind the other.

"Mother!" shouted Evie. "MOTHER!"

She scrambled across the stone and clung to her mother's talon as tightly as she could. She had spent her childhood hugging her mother in this way. Any time she had been hurt roughhousing with her sister or gotten into a row with her father, she had run to her mother and embraced her talon. And all her life, it had never felt entirely satisfying. Now that she knew what she really was, and how naturally humans were made to embrace one another, she understood why she'd never been able to hug her mother closely enough.

"Daughter," rumbled her mother. "Is it really you?" She studied Evie with wide, black eyes. "We thought we'd never see you again!"

"I'm sorry, Mother. I shouldn't have run away last summer. I didn't mean to frighten you . . ."

Her eyes fluttered open as she heard the *whoosh* of beating wings pushing down a blast of wind. A third black shadow spiraled in the sky above. It pounded its great wings as it whirled round and round, then thundered to the ground and turned to face her.

Evie stood and stared, her mouth hanging open, unable to comprehend what was standing right in front of her.

One of this dragon's horns was broken away. His scales had gone even whiter around the belly and mouth. And his eyes, as deep and black as a mountain lake under a moonless sky, looked down at her with utter shock.

"Daughter?"

## 13

HE WAS REAL. The grooves of his claw pressed against her face. It only made her squeeze harder. "Daddy! Daddy! Oh, Daddy!"

He lowered his enormous head, brushing his snout against her back. "Where have you been?" he growled. "Mother expected you days ago."

"Where have *you* been?" She looked up into his eyes. Her face was red, covered in a sheet of tears. "Oh, I can't believe it!" She lunged at his claw and held it so tightly, the muscles in her arms began to burn. "I thought you were dead!"

"Dead? The Fates themselves couldn't kill me!" He rested his head on the ground. She climbed up his face until she could see herself reflected in his huge black eye. Somehow, she did still look like the little girl he had raised. Yet she also looked like a strong, confident princess. So much had happened since she'd seen him last. "How I missed you, my daughter. Not a day passed that I didn't wonder where you were."

"And I you. Oh, Daddy! I just can't believe it!" She collapsed onto his cheekbone, even more tears pouring out of her. She felt as though she'd been living in a horrible drought and had somehow managed to adjust to the new conditions—not a happy existence, but a manageable one—and now the heavens had opened up again. She was nourished in a way she hadn't been since he'd disappeared nearly two years earlier.

"Before you lot get too blubbery," growled Evie's dragon sister, "why have you stopped me from killing this one?"

Evie had completely forgotten about Forbes. He was cowering near the wall, his wide eyes darting from one dragon to the next, trying to assess which was going to eat him.

"This is the knight who tried to kill me when I took Evie back!" She glowered at him, and he shrank even more.

"I am sorry about that," he said.

"Sorry!"

"Wait!" shouted Evie. She leapt down from her father's face and ran back to where Forbes was standing. "Wait. Don't hurt him."

Evie's sister snaked her green head forward, teeth bared. "He just admitted it was him."

"Yes. It was him. But he's had a change of heart. He's not who he was then."

The dragon glared down, jets of black smoke puffing out of her nostrils.

"Sister, you've got to listen to me." She looked over at her mother and father. "Please, all of you. We need your help."

"What is it?" said her mother. "Why have you brought him here?"

"Pennyroyal Academy is under siege. The witches have it surrounded, and the wall is about to fall. If Calivigne can destroy the Academy, there won't be any new princesses to stop her."

The sister snorted another impatient cloud of black smoke.

"What are you saying, Daughter?" said Evie's father. "You want us to fight in a war that isn't ours?" His voice was as gentle as she had ever heard it. "I've only just made it back. Why don't you forget that place? Forget the witches and the princesses and all of it. Let's go north, just the four of us. Far away from all this. We can be a family again."

"After I eat him," said Evie's sister.

"We can be happy there. Just as we once were here."

Evie could feel herself being pulled apart inside. More than she had in years, she felt like the little girl who wanted to live simply again with her mother and father and sister. But now there was a new force pulling her as well. There *was* a princess inside her, one she hadn't known was there. Her lips quivered. She didn't know what to say. It was her mother who finally spoke.

"This war *is* ours. Witches are as much a threat to dragons as knights are. Or have you forgotten where they'd been keeping you?"

The father sighed, letting out an acrid puff of black.

"The witches had you this whole time?" said Evie. "Daddy, is it true?"

He took a deep breath and raised his head. He looked at his mate, then back to his human daughter. "That day . . . the day you ran off . . . I went after you because the storm was coming, but it moved faster than any storm I'd ever seen. I kept flying, kept hoping I'd catch a glimpse of you down there in the forest. Then a bolt of lightning knocked me clear out of the sky. I crashed somewhere . . . I didn't know where I was, and I was so dazed from the lightning strike. The last thing I remember . . ."

"What, Daddy? What was it?"

"It was a witch. She was smiling at me. I was stunned. I couldn't move. She kept coming and coming. I lost consciousness then. And when I woke . . . there were hundreds."

"What?" Evie turned to Forbes, who looked just as surprised as she was.

"I'd no idea how I got there. Only that there were three other dragons with me. They'd chained us all inside a cave somewhere high up in the mountains. There was snow everywhere, ice as clear as crystal. And the air was so thin." He looked straight into Evie's eyes. "That mountain was crawling with witches. They were training, Daughter. Just as you train to battle them, they were training to battle you."

Evie stared at her father, astounded. *An army of witches. Just as Malora said.*

"We finally broke free, me and some of the others. But it was as if they were collecting dragons, just keeping us there until they needed us for their wicked brews."

"This is our war, too, whether we'd like it to be or not," said Evie's mother. "Once they've finished with the princesses, they'll come for us."

"You can't seriously be suggesting we risk our lives to save a place that trains knights," said Evie's sister. "I'd sooner trust the witches than them."

Forbes looked every bit as terrified as he had when he was about to be eaten. He locked eyes with Evie, and she gave him a nod. He swallowed hard, then took a step forward and looked up at the dragons.

"If you agree to help us," he said, his voice quivering, "I will devote every breath I draw from now until I die to bringing an end to our war."

More smoke vented from the sister's snout. "Might not be many breaths, mate."

"My mother was killed by a dragon," said Forbes, directing himself to Evie's father. "It upended my life, just as your disappearance upended Evie's. I have every reason to hate you and want you dead."

Evie's sister opened her jaw and let out a deep, threatening growl.

"Uh, Forbes . . ." said Evie.

"But I trust your daughter," he continued. "It's difficult for me to trust people, but I do trust her. If she thinks we're wrong about each other, the knights and the dragons, then I'm willing to put aside what I believe about you. Because I believe in her."

A pained look came over him. "Blast. I've just complimented you, haven't I?"

The crickets chirped from the darkness. No one moved.

"This isn't an empty promise, Daddy. He's going to be king someday. And kings have the power to stop wars."

"The power to start wars, too," said her father. "You're asking me to risk my family by trusting a knight!"

"A knight who already tried to kill me, by the way!" said Evie's sister. "Look! See? See?" She raised her wing to show the scar on her side.

"I said I was sorry!" shouted Forbes. "That wasn't me, anyway. I missed."

She roared, buckling his knees.

"You've got to help us," said Evie. "We can put the world back on the right path, but we can't do it without you."

Evie's mother stepped forward. She lowered her head with love in her eyes. "We trusted a human once before, and she became our daughter. Perhaps it's time we trusted another."

Each of them looked to Evie's father. He looked down at his youngest daughter. Then, slowly, he began to nod.

"Oh, thank you, Daddy! Thank you, Mum! When this is over, we're going to make the world a better place for dragons *and* for humans."

"I do hope that's true, little girl," said her father.

She turned to Forbes, then back to her family. "Right, well then, let's go."

"Now?" roared her father. "I haven't had supper!"

"The wall might already have fallen, Daddy. We've got to go straightaway."

"About that," said Forbes, suddenly looking quite ashen. "How are you proposing we get back?"

"My family will take us."

"I'll carry you, little boy," said Evie's sister with a grin. He looked over at her and gulped.

"He can't ride with us," said Evie's mother. "We'll roast him alive."

"She's right," said Evie, crestfallen. "I've been riding dragons for years, but your delicate skin won't be able to handle it."

"My skin isn't delicate!"

Evie was suddenly struck with an idea. "Hang on, I know what to do." She reached into her knapsack and found her final magical item: the Needle of the Poorest Maiden.

"You want to sew me a basket or something?" said Forbes. "That will take—"

"Needle, needle, sharp and fine." The needle jumped out of Evie's hand and began to flit about like a fairy. Yard upon yard of blue fabric streamed out of the clear night air. Finally, when a large pile of material sat at Evie's feet, the needle vanished with a pop. The tail of the fabric fluttered to the ground.

"Are my sewing things still inside?"

"Just where you left them," said Evie's mother.

"Give me ten minutes."

Evie scooped up the material and dragged it into the cave, leaving Forbes to spend those agonizing minutes alone with the dragons. When she returned, she had assembled a crude harness chair out of the fabric and several thin logs.

"Not bad for ten minutes," she said, running a bit of the fabric around her sister's claw. "Go on, climb in."

Forbes reluctantly approached Evie's sister and stepped inside the contraption. There were two handles sewn inside of it, fashioned from woven strips of bark. He lifted them but couldn't figure out what he was meant to do with the drape of fabric hanging below. "What is this? How am I supposed to—"

"We've no idea what to expect when we get there. You may not be able to wait for my sister to land. If there is some sort of emergency, use your sword to cut this piece here and then hold on tight to those handles. You'll come down in a hurry."

"How do I steer?"

"You'll see when you're in the air. It's crude, but it should get you to the ground without dying."

"'Should'?"

"All right, Sister, take him up."

"With pleasure." She stretched out her wings, then blasted into the night. Forbes shrieked as the fabric went taut and he was slung into the air. His terrified screams rained down from the sky as the dragon spiraled higher into the night.

Evie looked over at her parents and nearly broke down in tears again. "I never thought I'd see the two of you together again."

"Aw, this is no time for tears, love," said her mother, giving her a gentle nudge. "Go on, ride with your father. I know how long you've both waited for that."

Evie smiled at her, then bounded across the cave mouth and scrambled up her father's leg. The intense heat of his body was something she thought she'd felt for the last time. She seated herself where his neck met his shoulder and grabbed hold. Even though his scales were almost too hot for her to bear, she put her cheek against him and closed her eyes. A moment later, she lost her breath as the ground rushed away and the dragons plunged into the open sky. Millions of stars shimmered above as the whole world slept below. Her mother sailed next to them, her wings beating rhythmically as she soared through the air.

The great green lands of the west flowed past like a gentle current. She held tight to her father as he glided through the black sky, but her mind wandered to the sprawling world below. Somewhere down there, the innkeeper she had met on her way to Demetra's was sleeping alone in his bed, his beloved wife murdered by the Vertreiben. Somewhere down there, Wormwood had been scattered into the forest after the attack on his camp. Somewhere down there, Remington's subjects mourned their king, slain by witches. With so much evil in the world, she wondered, how would anyone survive without Pennyroyal Academy?

The flight should have been thrilling, a race above the world through the bracing night sky, but Evie's stomach was a twist of dread and fear. What lay ahead? The days and nights had blended together along the way, and she'd lost track of how long they'd been gone. Would they make it back in time to fight the witches and giants off in the enchanted forest? Or would the enemy already be inside laying waste to the campus? A shiver ran through her as she remembered a vision she'd seen in the dragon's blood. It was a vision of the Academy, a charred ruin, smoking piles of rubble. She tried to chase it away and focus on the black horizon, but she couldn't escape that dark image.

*We'll make it,* she thought. *We have to.*

She lowered her cheek to her father's scales. It reminded her of all the times she'd studied the scale she'd found lodged in the mountainside after his crash. It had been her only link to him and then it had crumbled into dust. But she didn't need that scale anymore. She had millions more just like it beneath her now, and all were alive and undulating across her father's body as he flapped his mighty wings. He was alive. And that was where her courage would come from.

Up ahead, her sister dipped and bobbed through the air like a ship in harsh seas. She could only imagine how terrified Forbes must be, dangling below in the harness. And how giddy her sister must be to torment him.

The ground raced past. It wouldn't be long now. She looked for some sort of marker as to where they were. The twisting paths of rivers and great flat black of lakes appeared only as shadows in the forest. Mountains and valleys swept past in rippling waves. She saw castles and kingdoms perched across the mountaintops. Some were dark, nothing more than empty shells of stone, long-abandoned or occupied even now by witches. Others appeared as tiny dots of firelight. So there was life out there still, small lights of hope dotting the darkness. The world seemed so vast from the sky. Her friends were down there somewhere, scattered and alone but not forgotten.

Evie glanced over at her mother, an elegant streak of black against the starry sky. The leading edge of her wings sliced the air, while the membranes propelled her through the sky. *My mother is the most beautiful thing in the world.* They rose higher, soaring over the snow-topped peak of an enormous range, and she knew with sudden clarity just where they were. Up ahead on the distant horizon, tiny red flickers shone through the black. The Queen's Tower, a grain of rice in the distance, radiated its ghostly glow, calling any who could see it. As they soared across the Dortchen Wild, the glowing spear grew bigger and bigger . . .

Then, suddenly, it snapped in half.

Evie's eyes went wide. "*HURRY!*" Somehow, her muscles tightened even more. As they sailed over the treetops, more details came into view. The Academy was spattered with flame. Fire raged across the grassland behind the wall. Her heart pounded in her throat as they neared the clearing. A giant, one-eyed Blunderbull, tore a piece off a castle wall, leaving absolutely no doubt that the fairies' magic had failed. "*Fly on!*" she called. "*The wall has fallen! Fly on!*" Her father swooped down toward the Academy, leaving her stomach somewhere in the clouds. Something bubbled beneath her, and a moment later, her father let out a tremendous roar. Blunderbull wheeled. He shook his fists, a look of fury on his face.

"GET LOST, DRAGON SCUM!" He hurled the hunk of castle into the sky. Evie's stomach lurched again as her father veered to the left. The enormous piece of mortared stone sailed past into the night. "HOW DARE YOU INTERRUPT OUR MEALTIME!" There was a cracking of stone so loud it didn't seem real as the giant broke off another piece, huge boulders slamming to the ground at his feet. He threw this chunk at Evie's sister, who swooped out of its path.

As Evie's father circled for a clean path toward the giant, she saw dozens of other battles happening in the campus below. Arcs of white light flashed inside the windows of classrooms, princesses' courage on full display. Plumes of black magic surged through the roads between training walls. Princesses battled witches in every corner of Pennyroyal Academy.

The dragon bore down on the giant. Pain shot through Evie's body as her father's neck became scorching hot and red flame poured forth into the blackness. When the jet stopped, his body instantly cooled again. He climbed straight into the air, giving Evie a dizzying view of campus. The Queen's Tower lay broken on the ground like a felled tree.

She heard the giant bellowing below but didn't know if her father had gotten him or not. She could barely feel her hands from the heat.

He swooped around, then dove. Evie pressed flat against him, plunging headfirst toward campus as the wind forced tears from her eyes. White flashes exploded in the darkness like lightning bolts inside a storm cloud. Finally, the dragon leveled off and released another stream of fire from his lungs, strafing the enemy inside the Academy that his daughter loved so much. She clenched her eyes against the pain until the heat crested. They flew just above campus now, and she could see individual people atop some of the buildings. The dark figures of the witches were so thick in some places, they looked like a single, heaving mass. Evie's father veered east, sailing above the knights' barracks. Down below, an army of knight cadets did battle with Galligantusohn. He towered above them, trying to smash them with his great fists while they fired volleys of arrows and hurled iron-tipped spears.

And there, at the edge of the fighting, she saw something that nearly knocked her right off the dragon's back. It was Remington. His sword was drawn, and he was trading blows with King Hossenbuhr, just as he had been when she left. She nearly lost her grip again as her father banked through the smoke rising from campus. They flew past Evie's sister, who swung Forbes like a morningstar, bashing him into Blunderbull's shoulder.

"We might work together, you know!" she heard Forbes shouting as her sister flapped her wings and took up position on the opposite side of the giant. He fumbled in his harness and drew his sword. "Get me close! Just not *that* close!"

She rose into the sky, then dove. Forbes sailed past the giant and swung his sword, landing a blow right at the creature's arm.

As Evie's father circled above, diving down for an attack with his talons, she looked over and saw her mother clinging to the side of Windermere's Tower, firing a stream of glowing red into a crowd of witches below. Then she saw something else, and it nearly stopped her heart. The third giant, Scabby Potatoes, was headed toward the tower where Evie's mother was perched. And she was so preoccupied with the witches on the ground that she hadn't yet seen him.

"Father! Over there!"

The dragon thrust out of Blunderbull's reach with three mighty flaps of his wings. When he saw what Evie had seen, he swooped across the sky toward his mate. As he arced toward Windermere's Tower, Evie jumped from his back without a moment's hesitation. Now there was nothing beneath her but the battle-ravaged campus, midnight black, lit up by pockets of orange flame. She spread her arms and sailed above the swarms of witches moving through the grounds and the white flashes of the princesses' magic. Giants and dragons bellowed. Witches and princesses shouted. Fires roared and hunks of stone smashed to the ground. But the only thing on Evie's mind was her mother. She glided above campus without even realizing she was doing it, using her arms to steer through the cold spring winds. In seconds, she landed roughly atop the giant's shoulder.

As he reached up one of the largest towers on campus, she scrambled across his pockmarked back. She finally got to the tangled wisps of hair growing out of his inflamed scalp. She grabbed a fistful and yanked as hard as she could, as though she were pulling stalks of flax straight out of the ground.

"*Yeow!*" he shrieked. She rose into the air as his shoulder muscles flexed and his hand swooped round to swat her. She used a stray hair to swing across his collarbone, landing right on his eyeball. He grunted in pain. As his hand swooshed toward her again, she kicked his eye as hard as she could. Still clutching the hair, she pushed off and swooped across his face just as his palm clapped against his eye. She stuck out her feet and landed right in his other eye. This proved to be enough.

Scabby Potatoes staggered backward, crashing through the roof of a storehouse. Evie was thrown along the ground, boulders slamming down all around her. She finally tumbled to a stop at the base of another tower. Scabby Potatoes writhed on the ground, clutching his injured eyes. She looked up and saw her mother lift off from the tower, swirling through the sky for another attack on the witch forces below.

As Evie tried to get to her feet, she noticed dozens of huddled black shapes moving about in the shadows. They were ducking into every building not in flames, searching for princesses to kill.

She steadied herself against the wall. She looked left, then right. Witches everywhere. *I've got to get to Remington before the knights start attacking the dragons.*

Then, just in front of her, Scabby Potatoes pushed himself up and leered down. One of his eyes was closed, the other leaking tears.

"YOU!" he bellowed. "I'LL EAT YOU TWICE!"

She scrambled into the castle behind her. Everything was muffled, making the raging battle outside seem strangely distant. There was no time to think, so she raced down the first corridor she found. The giant rained blows on the castle walls, trying to get at her. The whole grand structure felt like it was about to crumble.

She emerged into a spectacular hall with fifty-foot windows and a vaulted ceiling. A wall of open archways led outside to the courtyard. And there she found no fewer than thirty witches. They all turned to look at her, each of them beaming with wicked pleasure.

She raced back through the corridor from which she'd entered. Thundering blows continued to rock the castle. She flung herself through a twisting network of hallways and dark chambers, not daring to look back to see what might be behind her. She raced up a spiral staircase, round and round until she reached the top, where she emerged onto the wall walk. The castle's main spire stretched high above her, still flying the Pennyroyal standard. She raced around the parapet and found a wide expanse of brick lined with sawtooth battlements. Witches poured through the door, a blur of grinning hags all coming after her. She was trapped. With nowhere else to go, she ran to the edge of the castle wall and climbed through the crenellation, then scaled down the facade using the climbing skills her father had taught her.

Fire rose in sheets to her right. Her eyes burned from the

smoke. She glanced up and saw dozens of yellow eyes peering down. Then, one by one, fluttering black shapes began spilling over the side, descending toward her. She ran. There was a gateway ahead, and behind it an alley. She knew she was supposed to hide inside to neutralize the witches' ability to fly, but she didn't want to risk being trapped. Perhaps the alley might be narrow enough to keep them on the ground.

She needn't have worried about it after all. A shadow swooped by overhead, unleashing a crackling stream of flame that swallowed up her pursuers.

She raced through an open-air corridor that led past the Tannery, headed for the knights' side of campus, but as she emerged from the archway, a swirl of golden white screeched past in front of her. She collapsed to the dirt, then rolled to her side and saw a witch standing less than five feet away, her skin sizzling into mist as a princess's magic finished her off. She looked behind her to see who had done it.

"Basil! What are you doing here?"

"Saving your life, it seems."

"I thought you were in Witch Head Bay with your sister!"

"I couldn't do it," he said, shaking his head. The torment in his heart was plain on his face. "It'll take years to find the cure, if it ever happens at all. So I went with the Gray Man, got the Water of Life, then rode here without stopping. If we live through this, I'll go back to her." He pulled Evie to her feet. "He's quite a nice chap, that Gray Man."

A harsh cackle sounded from high up on the wall overlooking them.

"What are we going to do?" he said. "They're everywhere!"

"We need to draw them toward us. Centralize them. That way the knights can properly focus on the giants." Basil nodded. "Go to Crown Castle. Gather as many princesses as you can. We'll pull the witches toward the center of campus."

"Right," he said.

"And, Basil, remember that we can't trust Beatrice. She's with the witches now."

Basil gave her a grave nod. "What about you?"

"I've got to keep the knights from killing my family." He turned to go. "Oh, and Bas . . . I'm sorry I was so mean to you out there."

"Mean to me?" he said, incredulous. "Evie, we're in a bloody war here!"

"Right. Sorry." Basil raced off into battle. Evie looked down at the cloak in the road. It was still smoking from his blast of princess magic. What might have happened had he not been there to save her?

With a shiver, she darted down the road, ducking into one of Pennyroyal's gardens that served as a shortcut to the knights' side of campus.

"*Heh-heh-heh-heh-heh* . . ." came a cackle from the shadows.

Evie froze. *Not again*, she thought. She scanned the darkness for the witch but found only the shapes of the dead stalks that remained in the otherwise empty garden. Her impulse was to keep running, but something stopped her. *I'll have to fight sometime. Perhaps now is that time.*

"Come out, witch!" she called. "I'm not afraid of you!"

"*Heh-heh-heh-heh-heh . . .*"

She tried to build her courage and compassion by picturing her friends in her mind and in her heart. Demetra came first, golden hair tucked behind her delicate ears . . . her smile . . . the way she . . . she . . .

But then the panic crept in. She couldn't bring her friend's face into focus. Her mind was a jumbled stew—

A furious crackle rent the air, and the witch's spell struck Evie. She fell to her back, seized by the most extreme terror she had ever experienced. Her mouth hung open, but she couldn't scream. It was complete, blinding fear.

The witch crept out from the shadows and stood at the end of the garden row. Her black spell undulated like a snake below the cracked teeth of her smile. She stepped toward Evie, grinning down at her. *Is this the last face I'll see?*

Evie's eyes fluttered back into her head. She would soon be dead, killed by fear. She could feel her muscles giving up as the witch's spell bored into her heart. She fought to keep her eyes open.

*There's no excuse for letting fear win . . .*

A flash of Demetra's melancholy eyes. It was a memory. A moment, really.

*I am going to rain fire on those witches . . .*

"Heh-heh-heh-heh-heh . . ." The witch hobbled closer.

And then another thing Demetra had said: *We're going to win this war.*

"We're . . . we're going to win this war," said Evie out loud. Her eyes flew open. *"We're* going to win this war!" She could see Demetra's face, as clear as snowmelt. The kindness in her eyes. The courage in her heart.

A surge of energy jolted through Evie's body. She leapt to her feet, knocking the witch backward with an invisible shield that had manifested before her. Her heart was flooded with compassion for Demetra, for all her friends, and for the rest of humanity that she had grown to love so much.

A bright light sparked to life in the darkness. It lit up Evie's face from below. A small golden beam pulsed near her heart, and from its light she could see the witch lying on the ground. She looked like an elderly grandmother might if she had been poached in vinegar and laid in the sun to dry. Her sneering smile disappeared behind a plume of black smoke . . .

Evie remembered Marline. The courage she had displayed when she'd first rescued Evie. The compassion she'd had for her brother when their wicked stepmother had tormented him. Her golden strands of courage began to turn white. With her eyes wide, she looked down at the witch.

*For Marline,* thought Evie, and a tear fell from her eye. *For all my friends!*

She launched a blast of magic at the witch—

Something hit her like a runaway carriage, throwing her

to the ground. She was choking on the horrific fear of the witch's spell, and her courage had been snuffed into darkness. She had lost.

But when she managed to look across the garden, she saw the witch huddled in a ball, slapping at a small flame on her sleeve. Evie lurched to her feet, the fear slowly draining out of her. Her magic had worked. She hadn't lost. It had been more of a draw.

With weakened muscles, she trudged as quickly as she could out of the garden. Before the witch could regroup and finish her off, she turned the corner and joined one of the main roads leading up past the crippled remains of the Queen's Tower. All around her, witches were turning Pennyroyal Academy into a ruin.

She hurried through an alleyway, her strength slowly returning. But a new concern lingered. She had done all in her power to defeat that witch and had nearly died in the process. What would happen next time? Her fear grew even greater.

With the crackling of dark magic all around her, she wended her way through campus, headed east. Finally, she made it to the edge of the moat that served as the last obstacle before the field that stretched out to the knights' barracks. As her mother screamed past overhead, Evie scrambled across a rickety bridge and tumbled through the cool wet grass. Ahead, in a depression beneath a scorched wall, Galligantusohn shielded his eyes from a flurry of arrows. With his free arm, he swatted at the knights.

"All you lot in here is going to die, so you may as well get started!" he shouted.

"AGAIN!" bellowed Sir Schönbecker. The knight forces moved as one, their armor flashing in the firelight of the burning campus. A fresh wave of arrows filled the sky, followed by the furious roar of the giant. "AGAIN! HE CAN'T SEE! POUR IT ON!"

There was a deafening shriek to her right as her sister filled a castle full of witches with flame. *Lieutenant Volf is in there somewhere. And Princess Ziegenbart. And the Fairy Drillsergeant . . .*

Flashes of white and black stained the night sky as princesses and witches did battle. Fires burned and smoke billowed . . .

As she reached the northern edge of the field, she could see Remington and Hossenbuhr still trading blows. Their swords sparked in the darkness, clashes piercing through the sounds of war. Tears welled in her eyes. Suddenly, her loved ones, all those she had lost along the way, were starting to return. First her father, then Basil, and now Remington.

Hossenbuhr's face was a tight mask of rage. He slashed at the former knight cadet from the left, then the right, but each blow was parried away. Finally, Remington began to counterattack. Using his gloves, he grabbed his own blade and used it to trap Hossenbuhr's. Then he kicked the King near his hip and sent him flying.

"*Remington!*"

He turned. The look on his face was one of total shock. "Evic?"

She ran the rest of the way, and they flew into each other's arms.

"Have you two been fighting this whole time?"

"We've had a good break until now, actually. But when he saw those dragons, he flew into a rage. I'm simply trying to convince him that they're here to help. You'd better step back. I don't think I've quite won him over."

Hossenbuhr had regained his feet. His chest was heaving and his face was winched into a scowl. He picked up his sword and aimed it at Remington.

"Stand aside, boy. I'll not let those dragons destroy my portrait."

"That's *King* Boy to you."

Hossenbuhr charged. With every attack, Remington countered. Their blades flashed in the firelight.

When her sister swooshed by overhead, Evie wheeled to make sure none of the knights had turned their arrows to the sky. Thankfully, they were still focused on the giant. Back in the air, she saw Forbes staring down from the harness. But he wasn't looking at her. He was looking at the battle between his father and Remington.

His own blade flashed, and he suddenly began to plummet toward the ground, using the handles Evie had sewn into the harness to steer. The fabric acted as a pair of wings, arresting his fall as he glided toward the field below. Still, Evie could see that he was coming down much too quickly.

"Father!" he shouted as Hossenbuhr chopped at Remington's

blade. "Father!" In seconds, he crashed into them, knocking both Remington and Hossenbuhr to the ground. "Father . . . you've got to stop . . ."

Remington reached for his sword and sprang up. Hossenbuhr had taken a more direct hit and was slower to recover. But before long, he, too, was standing again.

"Where have you come from?" he roared.

"From there," replied his son, pointing his sword at the dragon swirling overhead. He grimaced as he tried to stand. "You're wrong about them, Father. All of us are. We've been wrong about them our whole lives."

"What are you blathering on about?"

"Dragons aren't monsters. I've seen it with my own eyes. They could have killed me a dozen times today, but they didn't. And they didn't because Evie asked them not to. And when she asked them to come and help us win the war, they agreed." He put a hand on his father's shoulder. "Please. Dad. You can help us win the war, too."

"What bloody war? My only concern is preserving that portrait!"

"The war between knights and dragons. Can't you see? We don't need to live in fear of each other. We can end it, Dad. Once and for all."

"He's right, Your Majesty," said Remington. "Whether I'd like to be or not, I now find myself ruler of the most powerful kingdom in the west. I have armies and allies scattered all over this land. I can help you retake your home. But first you've got to accept that dragons aren't our enemies. Together, we can end a war that's been fought since men and dragons first met. With Brentano in the east and Diebkunst in the west united, the others *will* follow."

"These dragons raised Evie as their own daughter," said Forbes. "Her father went missing, and I've just watched their reunion. I saw the love in both their hearts, and I recognized it." His eyes began to well with tears. "I recognized it because it's exactly how I'd feel if I ever saw Mum again."

Hossenbuhr's incensed snarl faded. He stared at his son with something akin to pity. "Your mother was too weak for this world. A trait I see you've inherited."

Forbes winced, but he didn't back down. "Please, Dad. This is our chance to create a new legacy. A chance to live in peace with our enemies. A chance to save lives."

Sir Schönbecker shouted another order in the distance, and Galligantusohn roared with fury. For a moment, Hossenbuhr looked down, licking his lips. *He sees it, too,* thought Evie. *He's got to.*

The king swallowed dryly. His eyes flicked from Evie to Remington to Forbes. "How dare you," he finally said, glowering at his son. "How dare you, you soft-bellied piglet. I would mirthfully have cut him down for standing in my way, but how dare you force me to kill you, too."

Evie looked over at Forbes. All life drained out of him. He looked utterly destroyed, staring at his father with wounded eyes.

"Knights have died protecting this realm from dragons with

valor and honor for centuries. And you two weasely little fools think you know better than they."

"We don't know better," said Forbes. "We know different. Those dragons up there are here to save our lives. To save *your* life. Doesn't that count for anything?"

"No."

King Hossenbuhr lunged at his son. Forbes's blade flashed in the firelight. A man screamed.

Hossenbuhr's sword fell to the grass. He dropped to his knees, clutching his stomach. He snarled at his son one last time, then collapsed to the ground.

With the sounds of war thundering all around, the three of them stared at King Hossenbuhr's lifeless body. Forbes sheathed his blade and stepped forward. He picked up his father's sword. He turned to Remington. His face was red, his eyes filled with wrath. The sword twitched.

"As the . . . as the *King* of Diebkunst . . ." He wiped his eyes with his sleeve. "I accept your partnership." He tossed the sword aside and held out a quivering hand. Remington shook it. Then Forbes turned to Evie and embraced her. She could feel him trembling in her arms.

"You were right," he said. "Family isn't an anchor. I can feel my mother inside me now. It's the lightest I've ever felt in my life."

He looked at each of them once more. The hostility and anger that seemed to be permanently etched on his face had gone. He was torn apart, but he was also free. Without another word, he turned and began to stagger away. He left the giants and the dragons and the witches and the princesses and the knights behind as he walked down the hill toward the forest.

Evie ran to Remington and held him in her arms. The knights shouted and Galligantusohn bellowed, but Evie couldn't take her eyes from Forbes as he receded into the darkness. She saw the faintest movement as he reached the meadow, then watched until he was gone completely, swallowed up by the blackness of the night.

"I'LL CRUSH YOUR BONES TO MAKE MY BREAD!" roared the giant.

"Again, lads!" shouted Sir Schönbecker. "Rebuild the lines!"

"This is complete chaos," said Remington. "We've got to get organized."

"The princesses are falling back to Crown Castle. We'll draw the witches in toward the center of campus. That should leave you clear to handle the giants."

"Cracking plan," he said. "Did you just come up with that?"

"I need you to do something for me." She stared straight into his eyes to emphasize how much she was trusting him. "I need you to keep my family safe. Forbes was right; they're here to help. But the rest of the knights don't know that."

He nodded solemnly. Evie turned to look down at the forest, but Forbes was gone.

"I've got to go help the princesses. There's no point in stopping the witches if the Academy is turned to ash." Her mind raced before finally landing on something. "Calivigne. I've got to find Calivigne. She organized these witches, and witches aren't meant to be organized. If I can stop her, perhaps the rest will fall apart." She realized that Remington's eyes had gone vacant. "Are you listening to me? This is rather important."

He was looking beyond her, and his eyes registered total fear. "It seems you won't have to look far."

Evie turned. There, down the flaming field of grass that led up to Pennyroyal Castle and the main courtyard, where the wall had once protected the Academy and all who dwelt within from the horrors of the world, the night itself seemed to be trickling forward. A wave of witches floated out of the forest and poured across the wall. Dozens of flapping cloaks and bony grins and skeletal hands, all soaring out of the trees.

And there, leading them all, was Calivigne.

**14**

*"WITCHES!"*

The cry circulated down the line of knights, which disintegrated into panic and scattered across the field like ants. They raced past the blinded giant on foot and on horse, looking for any sort of cover from the fresh wave of witches floating up from the forest.

Evie's eyes volleyed back and forth from the witches to the knights. This had been Calivigne's plan all along. Send in the first wave to soften the Academy's defenses, to create utter chaos, and then bring the second wave to finish them off.

But Calivigne hadn't counted on dragons.

Evie filled her lungs with air, cold night air that carried the acrid smoke of battle. Then she shouted with everything she had: *"FATHER!"*

The word rumbled out of her in a primeval roar, even more dragonlike than the one she'd managed during the first year's wolf attack. It shook her from the inside in a surge of immense power.

Her father heard her call. He swerved toward the field, passing above like a leviathan in a sea of sky. He dove across the wall of witches, dousing them with fire.

Evie looked over and realized Remington was staring at her with a slack jaw and wide eyes. "You've got to teach me that."

"Get those knights back up here! You need to drive the giants away!"

Galligantusohn bellowed and clutched his eye, brushing arrows off his skin like pinfeathers. Once the smoke of her father's attack had lifted, the whole hillside was raging with fire. It had slowed the witches, and perhaps even killed some of them, but a huge number were still coming, their black cloaks flapping in silhouette against the ten-foot flames.

"Go! N—" Her words were cut short as Remington leaned down and kissed her. She was silent for a moment, then a wave of embarrassment crashed over her. "Just . . . *ahem* . . . just keep the boys from attacking the dragons, all right?"

"Of course," he said with a smile. "Wouldn't want to get roared at."

Evie dashed up the road to the center of campus. Everything seemed to be alive with flashing magic and crackling flame. Calivigne had gone, scattered by the dragon. She wheeled past the Wolfseye Keep and raced across an empty courtyard.

"Evie!" came a distant voice. "Evie, over here!"

She stopped, searching the shadows for the voice. There, waving from a stable on the far side of the courtyard, was Demetra. *Another one returned*, she thought, and her heart brimmed with gratitude. She raced across the cobbled stones to join her friend.

"You made it back!" she said, clutching Demetra tightly.

"So did you!"

"What's happened? Where's everyone else?"

"We found some more princesses to help us on the way back," said Demetra. "We're desperate to get out there and fight, but there are some really frightened people in here we can't leave behind."

"We?" said Evie. "You found your mother?"

"Demetra!" shouted her mother. "Get inside this instant!" Demetra beamed.

Evie followed her into the stable. Demetra's mother, Queen Christa, and sister, Princess Camilla, were huddled in the shadows with a group of terrified people. The stable was dark and damp and filled with emaciated horses. Even the hay and alfalfa used to feed them had run out during the siege. Evie eyed the group. There were several princesses tending to the others, and a handful of faces she recognized as princess cadets. The rest were parents or siblings.

"Hello, friend!" came a thin voice from the shadows.

"Falada!" She clutched the princess tightly. "I can't believe you're here!"

"Nor can I," said Falada, grinning. "And I've already found my favorite teacher!"

"Hello there, Cadet!" came a sprightly voice from atop a hay bale.

"Princess Ziegenbart!"

A square-bodied goat with eyes splayed out from her head stood heroically above. She hopped to the ground, the bell around her neck clanging. "Will someone please take this bloody bell off me?"

Demetra began to untie the bell.

"So, Cadet Evie, we were just discussing our strategy," said the goat. "What have you seen out there?"

"A second wave has just come up from the forest. Calivigne is with them."

There were gasps from the parents, who hugged their children close.

"The staff will be in the administrative buildings," said Camilla. "If we can find the Headmistress, she'll have a plan."

*Oh, I'm certain she has a plan,* thought Evie. But now was not the time for that conversation. "I've sent Basil ahead to Crown Castle to gather as many as he could."

"Basil's here?" said Demetra with a light in her eye.

"Come on, everyone," said Ziegenbart. "Let's get over there and join the battle."

Demetra hesitated. "Er . . ."

"Yes?"

"What about them?" She nodded toward the people huddled in the shadows.

"I tried telling them being turned to stone was a noble way to go," Ziegenbart told Evie, "but it didn't seem to inspire them. Perhaps not the best message to receive from a cursed goat."

"We can't just leave them here," said Falada.

Evie stepped forward and peered into the darkness. A thick musty smell hung in the stable. Someone was crying. "Listen, girls, I know you're scared. I'm scared, too. But we can't stay here." There were sniffles, but no one spoke. "Fear is just someone putting out the lights. Now we've got to put them back on again."

Outside, a witch's cackle echoed across the courtyard.

"The bad news is we've only got two choices. But the good news is we've got two choices." She took a step forward and knelt in front of them. "When the sun comes up tomorrow, there are two different worlds it can find. In one, we've lost. We've given in to fear and let the witches have it all. We've let them destroy the Academy. *Our* Academy. And without the Academy, the rest of the world is theirs as well. We'll be remembered as the last class ever to enlist. The last class ever to hope."

She could feel their eyes, but it was too dark to see them.

"But there is another world, and it's a world that we can help create *right now*. We're all princesses here, all of us who want to live in a world full of kindness. We owe it to every cadet who's ever come through here, all the princesses who have fought before us. To Christa and Camilla and Falada and the rest. We can do it, girls! Let's watch the sun rise tomorrow and shine down on *us*, not the witches!"

One of the first-year girls stood. Then another. A thundering roar from outside shook the stable.

"Well done, Cadet," said Ziegenbart softly. "I suppose that was a bit more inspiring than the promise of a glorious death."

Evie's heart soared as she saw a few more girls stand. "That's it, stand, girls! They're going to tell our stories no matter what we do. Win or lose, we *will* be remembered. So let's be remembered for our courage, and not for our fear!"

"I'm going," said one of the girls in the shadows. "I'm with you."

"No!" said her mother, clinging to her daughter's arm. "You'll be killed!"

"I have to, Mother. All of us have to."

A few more girls stood. Then, one by one, they stepped forward into the dim light. "What do you want us to do?"

Demetra raced beneath the darkened facade of a castle. She found a vantage point at the end of the wall, then signaled to Evie. She nodded to Ziegenbart, who herded the rest of the team ahead to Demetra's position.

Camilla had volunteered to take those who couldn't fight to the Infirmary. She knew of a highly secured area where they would be safe. The rest had set off into the besieged Academy, moving from one darkened position to the next, working their way slowly and methodically toward Crown Castle.

"It's just round there," whispered Demetra. As soon as she said it, Evie could picture Crown Castle in her mind. And with it came the face of the Headmistress. A surge of red anger filled her belly. Her stomach coiled even more tightly.

But when she leaned forward to peer around the wall, Crown Castle was gone.

Only a ruin remained. One wall stood tall, but the rest had been toppled, almost certainly by one of the giants. Evie stared in disbelief at the pile of stone that had once felt so imposing. Then she ducked back into the shadows.

"It's gone."

"What do you mean it's gone?" came Falada's voice from the shadows.

"Crown Castle. It's gone. We need a new plan." As Christa and several of the others looked for themselves, what Evie had just seen began to sink in. Crown Castle was where she'd first met Countess Hardcastle. It was where she'd learned who the Vertreiben were. And now it was just a heap of broken stone.

"What do we do now?" said Christa.

"I know where they are," said Ziegenbart. "If I know *B-a-a-a-aaagh-agh-agh*—ahem!" She shook her head, chasing away the bleating fit. "If I know the Headmistress, she'll be in the Grandmother's House."

"The Grandmother's House?" said Demetra. "What's that?"

"Follow me!" The goat trotted past Evie and raced across the road. One by one, the princesses followed, avoiding the hungry eyes of the witches. The harsh sizzle of their dark spells rippled through the roads. Stone walls fell in great, thundering crashes. Giants bellowed in fury from the north end of campus. And the princesses slipped through as silently and smoothly as a snake. Finally, once they'd crested the highest point of campus, where the Queen's Tower stood sheared off at half its usual height, they began to descend the south end. Ziegenbart's hooves clopped to a stop.

"It's there," she said. "The Grandmother's House. It's a sort of safe house where the high-value administrators can retreat in an emergency." The rest of them peered through the trees. A small stream wound gently down the hillside. On the opposite bank of a quiet little bend, a well-hidden cottage sat tucked into a grove of willows. Even in full sun, it would have been easy to miss. The windows of the cottage were dark, though a small line of smoke from the chimney indicated someone was inside.

"That's the safe house?" said Evie.

"Look at the stream," said the goat. "There's another beyond that hill. What better protection from witches do you need than a ring of water?" She tore off a bunch of grass and chewed it into a green paste. Then she swallowed dramatically and said, "Courage, ladies!" With that, she bounded out from the trees and splashed across the stream.

One after another, the princesses followed. On the far bank, they scrambled across the small grassy patch to the front door. Falada opened it, and they burst inside.

The cottage was bigger than it looked from the outside. There were several doors off the main room leading to bed-chambers. A steep flight of wooden stairs at the far end led up to a loft. A cozy fire crackled in the hearth. The windows weren't windows at all but were completely opaque.

"Evie?" came a familiar voice. There was a small group

already gathered there, and a flurry of voices followed as everyone began to recognize one another. "Evie!"

"Maggie!" She ran to her friend and gave her an enormous hug. "Basil!"

Demetra joined them with tears in her eyes. "I never thought we'd all be together again!"

Evie looked at her friends and was overcome with emotion. Though she hadn't wanted to admit it, she, too, had thought they'd been together for the last time.

"How did you find us in the Grandmother's House?" said Maggie. "No one's supposed to know about this place."

"Princess Ziegenbart brought us," said Evie. "What are you doing here?"

"We all mustered in Pennyroyal Castle when the wall fell, the lot of us. Everyone who was left. Then the witches came . . ." She shook her head, remembering. "It was so still and so quiet, even the giants. Then we started to see them out there, the witches. They were on the hill. They were inside the wall. We launched an attack. Tried to surprise them."

"You did?" said Evie, impressed.

"We tried. You would've been proud of these girls. Everyone gave it their all. But when the giants came in, we were forced to scatter. The orders were to fall back to Crown Castle, so that's what we did."

"Where's Beatrice?"

"Just there. She's hysterical, Evie. She can't even string a sentence together."

Across the room, a small group of staff members, led by Princess Rampion, was trying to comfort the Headmistress. She was sitting on a chair, and Evie could hear her sobs. "Please! She'll be so cross! Don't let her beat me; please don't let her beat me!" Her skin was as white as bone, the wrinkles like folds in a crumpled parchment. Her haunted eyes were ringed red.

"Ah, good, you're here!" squawked a loud voice. Princess Copperpot peeled away from the rest of the gathered staff members and lurched over to the new arrivals. "Come, Ziegenbart. Leave one of your team with the Headmistress, and let's go. There are witches out there that need sorting."

Evie cut in and explained that the dragons were there to help. She went over her idea to draw the witches in, and Copperpot gave her an impressed nod. Even Lance squawked with approval.

"There is one more thing," said Evie. "It's about Princess Beatrice—"

"Not now, Evie," said Demetra softly. "Let them get out there and fight."

Evie glanced at the Headmistress, her stomach in knots, and nodded in agreement.

"Right," said Ziegenbart. "That's our plan sorted. We'll need four teams. Me, Copperpot, Rampion—"

"I'll take one," said Maggie, stepping forward to raise her hand.

Ziegenbart and Copperpot exchanged a look. Then their eyes went to Queen Christa and Princess Falada.

"I haven't had combat experience in nearly twenty years," said Christa.

"Nor I," said Falada.

"We've been preparing for this, haven't we, girls?" said Maggie.

"We have," said one of the first-class girls, and the rest agreed.

"Good," said Copperpot. "Cadet, you'll take D Team. Follow me up the middle and make sure nothing gets behind us, all right?"

"Yes, Princess," said the whole of Maggie's team at once.

"Ziegenbart, you'll have C Team, and Princess Rampion will take A. Our mission is to cross campus to Pennyroyal Castle to shift the fight north. The dragons will be much better equipped to help us with more open sky." She looked squarely at Evie, her faced pursed and squishy, yet oddly heroic. "You're certain the dragons won't turn on us, Cadet?"

"Yes, Princess. They're my family. We can trust them."

Copperpot nodded, satisfied. "All right. A Team, come round east of the Queen's Tower. Do your best to ignore the giants and keep your eyes open for the Seven Sisters. I'd be gobsmacked if all seven aren't lurking about here somewhere."

Princess Rampion stepped forward, nodding to several of the others gathered. "See you at the castle, Copperpot." They marched out the door and into the chaos.

"See you at the castle. You lot," she said, nodding to the administrators huddled in the corner, princesses who were far more familiar with management than magic. "You're with me on B Team. Straight down the lane to glory. Heavy fire to be expected. Gird your courage, ladies. If ever you'll need it, it's now. Falada, you were always exceptionally courageous. Care to join us on the front?"

"Of course, Princess," said the mousy Falada.

"Good," said the princess with two left hands. Even amidst the mayhem of the day, Evie found herself very much impressed with Princess Copperpot, who was proving to be far better in the field than the classroom. "You, you, you, and you," she went on, using the leftmost of her left hands to pick out several of the recent graduates . . . and Basil.

"Me?"

"Yes, you. You're with Princess Ziegenbart. I want you to sweep round to the west. Lots of rubble over there at the moment, so stay careful and listen sharp. That woman's a goat, and she knows how to climb."

"Team C, with me!" called Ziegenbart. Then she leapt out the door, her team racing after. Basil started off to bring up the rear, but Demetra grabbed his arm.

"Basil," she said. "Wait."

"Wait?" he said, panicked. "I can't!"

"I just want you to know that . . ." She took his hand.

"Demetra? The team's waiting," said Maggie.

"Sorry, I just . . ." She reached up, grabbed Basil's face, and kissed him. He looked at her in shock. He blinked once, and then twice.

"Um . . ."

"Cadet Basil, are you coming or shall we organize a romantic dinner first?" said Ziegenbart with a twinkle in her eye and a twitch in her beard.

"Bye," said Demetra.

"Right," he said, stumbling toward the door. "Right, well, I suppose we can discuss this later—"

"Basil!" shouted the goat, and he raced away.

"What sort of foul tastery is this?" muttered Copperpot. "If we weren't in the middle of a war, I'd discharge you this instant! Now, can we please execute this plan without any more kissing?"

"Everyone else, we're D Team," said Maggie, addressing the patchwork group of first-class cadets, siblings, parents, and leftover princesses. "No one gets behind us."

"Yes, Princess," they said.

Maggie's fierce demeanor faded into a somewhat embarrassed smile. "Well, you don't have to call me that—"

"Let's move out!" shouted Copperpot. She hobbled outside. Maggie and her team hurried after. She paused at the door.

"Evie! Demetra! Let's go!" Those two, Demetra's mother, Liverwort, and Beatrice were the only ones remaining in the cottage.

"I'm sorry, Maggie," said Evie, staring at Beatrice. "I can't leave her here."

"Who? The Headmistress?"

"She's working with the witches."

"Evie, this isn't the time—"

"She belongs in a cell, not a safe house. She's a traitor." Beatrice turned to face her. "Aren't you, Headmistress?"

"What's going on, Evie?" said Maggie. "That's the head of this Academy."

"I . . . I . . . I didn't mean to . . . to help them," stammered Princess Beatrice. Firelight reflected in the tears running down her face. "I was only trying to please her."

"Tell them," said Evie, and Beatrice began to crumble. "No? Then I will. Our Headmistress here has been colluding with Countess Hardcastle for years." She took another step toward Beatrice, her anger rising. "You told the witches about the prophecy in our first year, didn't you? About the Warrior Princess. How else could Calivigne have found out about it so quickly? It's because Hardcastle was not only one of the Academy's biggest benefactors, but also one of the Seven Sisters. And you were in step with her all along, years and years of secret meetings both here and at Callahan Manor."

"What have you done, Beatrice?" said Queen Christa.

"I haven't done a thing!" The Headmistress's voice had gone up in pitch to a frightened squeak. She stood, her jaw quivering as she cast about the room for a sympathetic face. She was wringing a silk handkerchief in her hands. "It wasn't my intention to hurt anyone! Really, it wasn't! She has this way of making me do things!"

Corporal Liverwort staggered back. Betrayal and disgust began to wrinkle her face. "What're you on about, Headmistress?"

Beatrice looked around the room but found herself completely alone. She shook her head feebly, then collapsed into her chair, a small, frail approximation of the powerful ruler she had once been. "I did at one time count Hardcastle a friend. Yes. That is true. But I was as surprised as anyone when she turned out to be a witch."

Outside, there was a great crackling of wood, followed by a thundering crash as a giant tree toppled. In the distance, a dragon roared.

"I can't stay any longer," said Maggie. She marched across the room, leaned down, and pointed into Beatrice's face. "If any of this turns out to be true, I'll feed you to the wolves myself." Then she turned and headed for the door. "See you all later," she said, and before anyone could respond, she was gone.

"Please . . . you've got to believe me," said Beatrice, addressing Evie in a feeble voice. "You're wrong about the prophecy. I never told Calivigne about you. I never told her who the Warrior Princess was."

Now Demetra gasped. "So you admit you spoke to Calivigne?"

"Oh, many times," said Beatrice with an empty smile. "Many times."

"It's all true," said Evie. She was staggered. It was one thing to speculate, but quite another to have it all confirmed.

"She wanted me to lower the wall, but I refused. Oh, she'll be so cross if she catches me!"

"Who wanted you to lower the wall?" snarled Liverwort. "Calivigne?"

"She'll beat me again! A girl must never disappoint her stepmother!"

Silence descended on the room, leaving everyone like they'd been frozen in ice. Evie couldn't breathe. She stared in astonishment at Beatrice, trying to process what she'd just heard.

"That's right," came a soft voice from one of the bedchambers. "A girl must never disappoint her stepmother."

Beatrice shot to her feet, knocking over a small table. Her eyes were wide, her face grave.

Slowly, a figure emerged from one of the dark rooms off the back of the cottage. The wooden floor groaned under her feet. She had to duck beneath the doorway, and when she stood to her full height, she towered over everyone there. Her face was shrouded beneath the heavy hood of her cloak. Two others followed her out of the room. One was Countess Hardcastle, wearing her usual high-necked black frock. The other was Malora.

"Stepmother!" said Beatrice. "How did you—"

"We used one of your trees to make a lovely little bridge. Did you think a bit of water was going to stop me from seeing my stepdaughter again?" Calivigne's voice was soft and melodic, cold and clean as a razor blade.

A wave of dizziness washed over Evie as Calivigne's eyes surveyed the room.

"You're all sodden to the bone." She raised a hand, and the fire flared to life, bathing the room in orange light. Then she reached up with long, bony fingers and gently swept her cloak to the floor. Her hair hung straight down past her shoulders, as brittle black as charred kindling. She wore a simple black dress that covered most of her arms. The skin that did show looked like frosted glass, nearly opaque but not quite. Faint black shadows traveled through her like cockroaches. She looked more like the porcelain figurine of a woman than an actual person. And yet, despite the glassy smoothness of her skin and the vacancy of her yellow eyes, there was a classical beauty to her face, the unfinished sculpture of the world's most beautiful woman.

"Come," she said in her hypnotic voice. "Warm yourselves at my fire."

EVERY INSTINCT told Evie to run. Her mind spun through half-formed thoughts and impulses. Finally, her eyes landed on her stepsister and the words began to flow.

"Malora! Malora, help us! Please!"

"I can't—"

"Don't speak to her, Malora," said Hardcastle.

"Quiet!" roared her daughter. Then she turned back to Evie with a somber expression on her decaying face. "I've done a lot of thinking since I saw you last. You see, I actually felt quite guilty helping you through Marburg. And when I got to the bottom of why, I realized it was because the witches are my family. Not you."

Evie's heart broke in two. She stared into her stepsister's eyes but found no love there. Only emptiness.

"It doesn't matter whether I want it to be that way or not; that's just the way it is. They are who I am. It's in my blood, and there's not a thing I can do about it."

"And blood will never disappoint you the way stepchildren do," said Calivigne, placing a slender hand on Malora's shoulder.

"I only wanted to please you, Stepmother! That's all I ever wanted!" Beatrice's words disappeared beneath her tears. "The day I graduated was supposed to be the happiest day of my life! Three years of training, and you didn't even bother to turn up! I felt like such a fool."

"Oh, Beatrice," said Calivigne in her haunting, motherly tone. "Forever seeking approval."

"And never finding it! My whole life I've tried to win your affection! I worked harder and harder, and it was never enough! Even when I became Headmistress General, it didn't please you!"

"Your accomplishments mean precious little in a sea of disappointment."

"I . . . I asked to meet with you," said Beatrice. "Do you remember that? After the witch gave her prophecy about the Warrior Princess. I wanted to stand before you and look you in the eye and tell you that *I* would be Headmistress when the Academy graduated its most important cadet ever. *I* would be in charge of making her a Princess of the Shield. I wanted you to finally see that I had value! I wanted you to finally recognize who I really was!"

"Oh, Beatrice, it's as clear as day," said Calivigne. "You're the same mewling little kitten you always were."

Beatrice's confidence took another blow. She somehow shrank even lower.

"I asked you one thing," said the witch. "'Who is the Warrior Princess?' But you wouldn't tell me, would you?"

"You belittled me," whimpered Beatrice. "Told me I'd wasted my life. That my father would be ashamed. You broke me apart."

"Yes, and all it got me was that the Warrior Princess's mother graduated twenty years earlier."

"What?" said Christa. "But that's *my* company! Is that why we were targeted?"

"Of course," said Calivigne. "But the Blackmarsh isn't the easiest kingdom to sack. There are a few of your company who have proven quite difficult to kill."

"The old hag told me after she'd made the prophecy," said Beatrice. "She said that the Warrior Princess's mother was in that company from twenty years ago. Of course, that made it significantly easier for me to conclude who it was, but I never told my stepmother! Never!"

So that was what the words on the back of the class portrait had meant: *Beatrice said it was this one—ALL MUST GO.* The Headmistress had betrayed the company, but not the individual who had mothered the Warrior Princess.

"It's true," said Calivigne, addressing Christa. "So, we simply began removing the daughters of your company and then removing the mothers to ensure there would be no new daughters to contend with. Every mother and daughter in one company dead, and there would never be a Warrior Princess."

Demetra ran to her mother and clutched her tightly. They had beaten the odds where so many others hadn't. Until now.

"So much evil from one mistake," said Beatrice, falling back into her chair. "A Princess of the Shield must never reveal Academy secrets. And I have." The repercussions of what she'd done, of all her former cadets targeted and killed by the witches, were only now reaching her.

"And you," said Calivigne, turning her foggy yellow eyes on Evie. "Had you simply died, we might have spared this place. It could have stood as a sort of monument to what the world was like when princesses roamed the land. But somehow you have managed to survive each of our attempts to thwart this prophecy."

Evie wanted desperately to look away but found herself mesmerized by those wide, shimmering yellow eyes. She couldn't move.

"We attempted to create a super-witch with Malora, a creature as dark-souled as any of us but with the capacity to love and to care, and you exposed her. We gave you every opportunity to be killed by the Vertreiben, but you came through unscathed. We ambushed the entire population of Pennyroyal Academy in the open forest, and *you* made it back. And then there is the matter of your mother, whom we have similarly been unable to kill. Where is she, child? We've never been able to find her. Where is your mother?"

Evie's mind was swirling so fast, she nearly collapsed. But before she could, there was an earth-shaking crash. A twisting mass of dark green scales burst through the roof of the cottage. Walls splintered into bits. Where there had been wood, there was now only night sky. The flames from the fireplace scattered everywhere. Evie looked up, dazed and disoriented. Amidst the cloud of dust and smoke, she saw her dragon mother clamber to her feet. Scabby Potatoes towered over them all, a triumphant look on his face. Evie's mother issued a furious roar, then pulled herself out of the rubble and flew straight at the giant, knocking him backward with a thundering boom. *There's my mother,* thought Evie.

"Ahh!" came Beatrice's voice from beneath a pile of broken plaster. Evie ran to her and began lifting the pieces off. She frantically scanned the dust-choked air for the witches, but she could barely see what was right in front of her.

"Come on! We've got to get out of here!" She hauled the Headmistress to her feet, then draped her arm across her shoulder. "Demetra! Christa!"

"Go, Evie!" called Demetra from somewhere in the swirling dust. "We'll look for the witches; just go!"

Evie dragged Beatrice out of the cottage and across the small stream. The night air bit into her cheeks and lungs as she desperately struggled to haul the Headmistress up the road. She glanced back to the Grandmother's House but saw only rising flames flickering out of the broken walls. "Come on," huffed Evie. "Follow the stream."

They continued up the road to where the buildings became more tightly packed. The stream joined others and became a rapidly flowing canal. A large waterwheel turned up ahead, attached to the side of a mill.

*There's someone with us,* thought Evie. She could feel it. She glanced around at her options, then decided to take cover in the mill. Beatrice had gone into a state of shock, which meant she would go wherever Evie led her. It also meant she had little capacity to support herself. Evie struggled and strained and finally managed to get the door open and the Headmistress inside. She slammed the door, then wheeled the wooden brace shut to lock them in. Water splashed over the slow-turning wheel outside the windows, while the wheel shaft inside groaned as it turned a giant wooden gear. "Upstairs!" said Evie. "Hurry!"

Finally, she managed to get the Headmistress to the upper floor. It was smaller, with a domed roof. Water rushed down the sluice outside a bank of windows, splashing over the blades of the giant wheel. An empty grain hopper sat amidst sacks waiting to be filled. Beatrice collapsed on the floor and began to groan in agony.

"Please, Headmistress, you've got to keep quiet! They're just outside!"

"Actually, one of us is inside." Evie spun. Malora was sitting in an open window, backlit by the fire consuming the cottage they'd just fled downstream.

"Malora," said Evie. She moved across the floor, trying to draw attention to herself and away from the Headmistress. "Malora, please, it isn't too late to help us. I know—"

Malora cackled. "You really are incredible. How many times must I betray you before you'll believe me?" She jumped down into the room. "I'm a witch, Evie."

"I know you're still in there. I know there's good in you."

"No, there isn't," she said, shaking her head. "I've been tearing myself apart trying to believe what you keep telling me, but it just isn't true. I'm a witch. I've always been a witch. Fighting it only makes it hurt more."

"'It is certain that hills and valleys always meet,'" said Beatrice, reciting some verse from deep in her memory in a frail voice. "'And it often happens on the earth that her children, both the good and the wicked, cross each other's paths constantly.'"

"What are you babbling about now?" said Malora.

"You are the hill and the valley." Beatrice looked up at them. Her face was barely visible in the darkness of the mill, but she was smiling with something resembling a mother's pride. "It was always you who would solve this, not my step-mother and me. 'It is certain that hills and valleys always meet.' But you don't have any idea what I mean, do you? No . . . I am the only one left who knows that particular story."

"Old woman, have you lost your mind?" said Malora. "What in the world are you talking about?"

"I'm talking about the two of you."

Evie looked over at Malora, whose yellow eyes looked back at her.

"Let me tell it now, children," said Beatrice. "Please. Before she comes for me. There are so many things I'll take to my grave, let this be one less for me to carry."

"Whatever you've got to say, you'd better say it quickly," said Malora, and for the first time, she sounded just a bit frightened.

"It was many years ago when your father appeared in my office. He was frantic, nearly—"

"Hang on," said Evie. "My father? King Callahan?"

"Yes. He had married one of our newest graduates. Princess Vorabend. They were exactly the sort of match you'd imagine from fairies' tales. We were all so happy for them. Truth be told, we were happy for us as well. Two beautiful souls like those uniting would certainly lead to beautiful children for us to train in the future—"

There was a loud crash outside, then some distant shouting. A dragon's roar resounded across campus.

"Get on with it!" shouted Malora.

"King Callahan was in great distress. Vora had indeed become pregnant. The child we'd been so eager to hear word of would be coming after all. He was overjoyed about that, as you might imagine, but otherwise near the edge of madness."

"Why? What happened?" said Evie.

"When he first learned he was to be a father, the King ordered a portrait of his wife as a gift to commemorate the occasion. As certainly as hills and valleys meet, so, too, will good and evil. The artist he'd hired to paint the portrait was a witch in disguise. And she'd used an enchanted canvas . . . enchanted paints. Vora's spirit was captured in that portrait in more ways than one. She was trapped there by the witch's curse, and the woman left behind, though she still looked like Vora, was nothing more than an empty shell. She was alive. She was still herself. But she had no memory of her life to that point. She had no memory of King Callahan.

"The witch made him an offer, as witches often do. When the day came for Vora to give birth, the King could either surrender the baby, in which case she would restore Vora and the two lovers could live happily for the rest of their days. Or he could keep the baby and the witch would take Vora instead. She assured him that he would never again see his beloved should that be his choice.

"The witch vowed to return on the day of the child's birth to hear the King's decision: his wife or his child. In the meantime, she would keep the portrait, which of course meant she was keeping the trapped spirit of our darling Vora. Callahan told me he'd tried everything to restore the shell of the woman the witch had left behind, but nothing had worked. The wife he'd been left with was like a child, unable to fight her way back from the fog in which the witch had placed her. That was when he came to us.

"Vora was on the cusp of giving birth, and Callahan was at a loss. The Queen and I were the only ones who knew what had happened. She sent Callahan and Vorabend away to one of her best midwives. I was to accompany them."

"What is the point of all this?" said Malora. "It isn't going to save your life."

"I know," said Beatrice, "but I'll tell it just the same. We knew the witch would be coming for her ransom; there was no sense in trying to hide. So instead we worked as quickly as we could. The moment the baby was born, the midwife wrapped her and gave her to Callahan. I ordered him to ride back to his home straightaway and to protect that girl with every breath in his body. Which is exactly what he did." She looked over at Evie with a meaningful smile.

"Our plan was to assign Vora a new name and a new identity and send her somewhere the witch could never find her. The King would honor his part of the bargain by choosing his daughter and giving up his beloved, but our hope was that the witch would never be able to claim her prize. Vora would be cursed, but at least she would still be alive. We thought we had planned for every eventuality, but there was one thing that none of us saw coming." With tears in her eyes, she looked straight at Malora. "You."

Evie glanced at her stepsister and felt every bit as astonished as the witch looked.

"There was a second baby that came less than an hour after the first. A twin. The midwife didn't realize it until long after Callahan had gone. The twin was so sickly born, so frail and small, that we were certain she wouldn't last the night. So I stole away with Vora to deliver her to her new life and left the midwife to deal with the baby. The rest of the story was told to me quite later."

"Lies," spat Malora. "I don't believe a word of this."

"The witch came, as we always knew she would. She took one look at the tiny, malnourished creature in the midwife's arms and flew into a rage. She shrieked that she had been double-crossed, that the midwife had switched babies to try to trick her. Nothing the midwife said would placate her. 'Very well,' the witch finally said. 'But I know what has happened here, and one day I shall have my revenge.' In a fit of wrath, she snatched the sickly baby away and fled. From what I've been able to piece together since, the witch who had painted the portrait, the witch who had stolen the baby, was one of the Seven Sisters. And Calivigne used that poor baby's delicate heart, adding it to a cauldron to create . . ." She took a deep breath, then looked at Malora with utmost sympathy. "To create you."

Malora's yellow eyes dimmed. "What?" she said in little more than a whisper.

"The two of you aren't stepsisters," said Beatrice. "You're blood. The heart that went into creating you, Malora, was the heart of Evic's twin. King Callahan is father to you both. Vorabend is mother to you both. You are sisters. You've always been sisters."

Malora looked as though someone had just shot her with an arrow. Her breath came erratically.

"You see?" said Evic. "The witches aren't your family. I am.

And I know there's love inside you. I know you loved me once, and I believe you can love me again. We're family, even if they did try to make you into a witch. We'll always be family, even if we're not. We can find our mother *together*, Malora, you and I."

Evie could barely make out Malora's face in the darkness, but her soft yellow eyes shone through. When she spoke, her voice was as tender as a child's. "I'm a witch, Evie. I may have been made from your sister's heart, but I'm still a witch. To think I could ever be anything else . . . it's not possible."

"Malora," she said, stepping forward. She reached out into the darkness and took her sister's hand. The witch's skin was searingly cold, yet Evie held tight. "I've lived with humans long enough to know that all sorts of impossible things are true."

Beatrice let out a gasp so loud, it made the sisters jump. "She's found us! She's found us!"

There were creaks on the staircase as Calivigne appeared, followed by Hardcastle. "Here you are. We've been looking everywhere."

"Please, Stepmother," said Beatrice. With barely any strength left in her body, she somehow managed to get to her feet. Her arms were stretched out in front of her, imploring the great witch for mercy. "I only wanted to make you proud . . ." She trudged forward, tears streaming down her face. "I only wanted you to love—"

The room filled with noise, a harsh cutting sound, like someone was tearing a board in two. With a spatter of black magic hitting her, Beatrice's skin started to drain of color. She let out a moan as her body began to calcify. Within seconds, her tears had stopped flowing. Her heart had stopped beating.

"Beatrice!" shouted Evie, but the Headmistress had been turned to stone.

"Now," said Calivigne, turning her joyless smile toward the girls. Her eyes were vacant, her features smooth-edged and nondescript. "What are you doing here, Malora? You should have already taken care of all this."

Malora looked absolutely staggered. Once again, she found the sands shifting beneath her feet. "I'm a princess," she finally said. "*You* turned me into a witch, but I came from a princess. I *am* a princess."

Hardcastle pulled her cloak tight around her neck. "Oh, do shut up, you silly—"

A pulse of magic, different from any Evie had ever seen, flared across the room and speared Countess Hardcastle. It looked like a miniature storm cloud, smoky black filled with tiny flashes of light. The witch fell flat on her back, every muscle tensed. Smoke rose from her body. Calivigne barely turned her head to look.

"You took my heart," said Malora. "I was a *person* until you stole my heart . . ."

"I took a dying baby's frail heart and turned it into something so much better," said Calivigne as Hardcastle gasped for breath and scrambled back toward the wall. "You are a witch, my dear, and ever shall be." She turned her glassy eyes to Evie. Looking at Calivigne felt like leaning over the edge of a cliff and stumbling. "And you. You shall not be the fulfillment of any prophecy. You shall simply be the latest princess to die at the feet of a witch."

A slight ripple at Calivigne's chest was the only hint that her black magic was brewing.

"I know who I am now," said Malora from the darkness. "I know who I was before you turned me into this. And that person would have felt so much love for this world. And so much love for her sister." She turned to Evie, and her decomposing witch's face had gone. It had somehow transformed to look as it had the day they'd first met. "I *do* have a heart. I might have been born without one, but I believe I have one now."

"Well then," said Calivigne, "allow me to break it."

There was another deafening strike of magic. Evie flinched, but the blast never reached her. Malora's own black magic was bending Calivigne's spell to her. She was absorbing it into herself, saving Evie. Her skin mottled to granite gray, then back again.

"You wanted to make me a Princess-Witch," she said, her teeth gritted in pain. "Well, you've done it." As she began to lose the battle against Calivigne's magic, as her skin drained of its color and began to harden, she looked at her sister. A tear ran down her cheek. "I love you, Evie. Now let's see how much you love me." With extraordinary effort, she charged straight into Calivigne's blast. Sparks of white arced off her own chest as she countered. She lunged at the great witch, and for a moment the two of them were lit up with magic. White and black swirls exploded out of the air between them.

"Now, Evie! Do it!"

Evie stepped forward and let all the thoughts and feelings she'd been fighting wash over her. All the fear of feeling like she was an intruder in her own life at the dragon cave. All the anxiety for her friends, for Maggie and Demetra and Basil and Anisette, and all the other girls with whom she'd served, those who were still there and those who weren't. All the joy of seeing Remington again, of seeing her dragon father again, of realizing the impossible could be true. All the heartache of a mother she would never meet and a father who had already passed on. And all the pride in the faces of the people she'd seen across the land, people who deserved to live without fear. A blossom of luminescent white appeared in front of her, casting shadows across the mill. Streaks began to flare off into the darkest corners of the room. Inside her own heart, she pushed with everything she had. The white bloom lanced through the darkness and struck Malora in the back, pushing her and Calivigne toward the water sluice just outside the windows. As Malora finally succumbed and her body turned to stone, she embraced Calivigne, locking the witch tightly inside her granite arms. Evie pushed even harder, felt even deeper, until her blast of magic knocked them both through the window. It shattered, and they toppled into the sluice, which dumped them over the side of the water wheel.

Evie raced to the window and looked down. Malora's statue splashed into the water, pulling Calivigne down with it. There was a furious bubbling and thrashing from the water below as Calivigne tried desperately to break free and use her magic. But before long, the water went still.

The wheel continued to turn. Water splashed into the stream, which curled gently down the hill. Though there were still many battles being fought all around campus, a sense of peace fell over this particular bit of stream. At least for a moment.

Hardcastle grunted from the floor next to Evie. She was trying to push herself into position to try her own magic. Evie looked over at her. "It was you who painted the portrait, wasn't it? I saw all the artwork while I was at Callahan Manor; it was you. You took my mother away from me."

"Your father cheated me! She was supposed to be mine! So I found him and cheated him right back. I made him fall in love with me. Then I took his daughter by stealing her name and giving it to my own. Of course Calivigne wanted to exploit the situation to have a witch graduate from Pennyroyal Academy, but all I wanted was what that man promised to me. And I got it after all, didn't I? He tried to cheat me, but I won in the end!"

Evie felt an overwhelming flood of emotion come over her, then in a brilliant flash of white, Countess Hardcastle was no more.

• • •

Evie staggered out of the mill. She walked through campus like she was asleep, numb to the battles happening all around her. A giant stepped over her at one point, only just missing crushing her, but she barely noticed. At the main road, the one that looped around the front of Pennyroyal Castle and ran down the hill to the forest, she paused and did a slow turn, drinking in everything around her. Dragons swooped out of the night sky and into the plumes of smoke streaming up from all around campus. Giants battled with troops of knights. Witches and princesses did battle in every tower. Finally, her eyes came to rest on the forest at the bottom of the hill.

A figure emerged from the trees. It was a woman riding on horseback. She wore a beautiful dress of silver and black with a jeweled tiara in her hair. It was Princess Cinderella, and she had a whole band of others with her. More princesses poured out of the trees, all riding hard toward the hill.

Evie stared at them, mesmerized, as they charged into battle. Halfway up the hill, Cinderella saw her. She smiled. Then she turned in her saddle and shouted to the others, "Come on! Let's take back what's ours!"

The princesses reached the top and thundered around Evie, pouring into campus to join the fight.

For the first time in a long time, she smiled. Then she gave a shout and ran off after them.

THOUGH MUCH OF Pennyroyal Academy had been reduced to a smoldering ruin, even more of it still stood. The sun rose that morning as bright as the dawn of summer, and many of the ancient towers were still there to throw off shadows. The Queen's Tower had been spared after the initial blow. The top half lay splayed across the ground, while the rest still rose high above campus. The barracks and most of the outbuildings had survived, as had the Dining Hall and Rumpledshirtsleeves's cottage. But much of the interior had either been heavily damaged or destroyed entirely. The Piper of Hamelin Ballroom, the place where Maggie had won the Grand Ball during their first year, had been flattened. Schummel Tower, where Evie and her friends had competed in Witches' Night only a few months earlier, was nothing more than a pile of stone.

Not everything was a subtraction, however. There was one huge new addition to campus. As the dawn first started to break, Evie had been coming down the road to deliver the fairies a new fairyweed bush that one of Cinderella's princesses had brought. She turned a corner and found a foot twice as tall as she was made entirely of stone. Blunderbull lay flat on his back, the largest statue the world had ever known. Evie could only imagine what must have happened for the witches to turn him to stone.

Now, in the full, bright light of the morning, with the battle over, Evie looked around and saw help already happening everywhere. Knights heaved stones to free trapped princesses. Princesses rescued knights from damaged towers. Dragons helped move large sections of crumbled wall.

She smiled, feeling as warm inside as her skin did beneath the hard rays of the early-morning sun. There was not a witch left to be found on campus. Not a giant, either, save for the statue. They had won.

She walked toward the knights' side of campus. Though everyone was exhausted, they were all still outside helping to search or take inventory or gather weapons and gear. She saw Remington and another knight pulling hunks of limestone off a collapsed stable. As she approached, they managed to roll a boulder aside. It curled to a stop. Moments later, a donkey came trotting out. Then a horse carefully stepped through. Then another.

"Well done, mate," said Remington to the other boy. He was huffing and puffing, sweating from the exertion. "Ah, Evie. How's everything up there?" He nodded to the main bit of campus up the hill from the field.

They'd found each other again in the night, hours after

they'd parted. Remington and the knights had finally managed to drive Galligantusohn back out into the forest. As he ran off, crashing through the trees, Remington said he had shouted, "I'll never take money off witches again!"

Now, with the fighting over, she'd come to find him again. And she had something very specific on her mind.

"What is it?" he said, still catching his breath. "Are you all right?"

"I need you to come with me."

"Of course. Where are we going?"

"Show me where King Hossenbuhr was staying."

He gave a slow nod as her motives became clear. "You want to see the portrait."

"I do," she said, "but I'm absolutely petrified."

"Right." He brushed his hands on his breeches. "This way." He led her through the war-torn training field toward Copperhagen Keep, the fortress the King had been using during the siege. The doors were torn off and the walls marred by black smoke stains. Mostly, though, it seemed intact. Evie studied the structure. Her heart began to race. Now that she knew exactly what the portrait was, it scared her even more than when she thought it might curse her to look at it.

She felt something and looked down. Remington had taken her hand. He gave her a compassionate smile. "Take your time. Whenever you're ready."

She breathed in deeply. "I'm ready."

They walked to the entrance of the castle. Some knights were sitting in small groups inside, drinking tea and recovering from the fight. Evie and Remington walked right past them, hand in hand. They entered the main keep. It was dark inside. Sunlight filtered in at an angle. The air was thick with dust.

"I think he took a chamber in the back," said Remington.

They crossed through the hall and found the door to another room. It was flanked by piles of armor and weaponry. Remington looked at her and she looked back. Then they stepped through the door and entered Hossenbuhr's room. There were footlockers and more weaponry, a small table and a bunk of his own, all plundered from the barracks. And there, shoved into the corner, stood a wooden crate, wide and thin, with a chain locked around it.

"That's it," said Evie. She stepped over and lifted the lock. "Great."

"Found the key," said Remington, walking over with a battle-ax. Evie moved back, and he swung down. There was a metallic clang. Then another. With the third blow, the lock clattered to the floor. Evie raced over and pulled off the chain.

"Give it to me," she said. Remington handed her the ax, and she used the blade to wedge open the crate. She dropped the weapon and pulled the wood apart with her bare hands. When the lid fell, she took a step back and gasped.

There, nestled into a bed of straw, was the portrait Evie had been longing to see since her first day on campus. It was just as it had been described, but also so much more. The detail, the color, the vibrancy in the face . . . The portrait was so stunningly beautiful, it appeared to live and breathe.

"My word . . ." said Remington. "Evie . . . it is you."

The girl in the portrait had the same wide green eyes as Evie. The same flowing brown hair. The same face. The same cheeks. The same lips. The same spirit.

"No," she said. Then she leaned forward to get an even closer look at the detail. There was immeasurable kindness in the girl's eyes, vibrant and alive to the point that it seemed to radiate from the canvas. Evie reached out a finger and touched the girl's face. She ran it gently down her cheek. It felt like touching a mirror, so exactly did the two of them match. Then she let her finger slowly fall until it was pointing at the girl's stomach. "That's me. Me and my sister."

After several more minutes, she closed up the crate and lifted the portrait out of Hossenbuhr's things. Remington ran off to find the donkey he'd just freed, then led it back to the keep. The donkey carried the portrait of Evie's mother across campus, back to the Leatherwolf barracks. There, she propped it at the head of her bed, sat down on the mattress and crossed her legs, and stared at it for hours.

Girls came and went as they moved through their first day after the siege. Parents, too. Some stopped to talk to her, commenting on the beautiful portrait someone had done of her. Others just gave her a smile and left her to it.

At some point, she knew there was more work to be done,

though she would have liked to have stared at the portrait straight through the rest of the day. Her mother—her real mother, Princess Vorabend—had been trapped inside that image. Her body had continued on through life as a witch fighter with no recollection of ever having given birth to Evie or Malora. She studied the painting of her mother's eyes, which seemed to twinkle beneath the oils. Even if Evie somehow managed to find her, would her story be dismissed? Would her mother turn her away as a crazy person saying crazy things? Would she ever know the feeling of being held by her mother, or would that most human of experiences be forever out of reach? With her head spinning and her heart in knots, she closed the crate and slipped it under her bunk, then went out to help with the efforts.

Later that day, after a meager lunch in the Dining Hall that tasted better than any she'd ever had, Evie and her friends returned to the barracks, and she showed them the portrait. Each of them was sufficiently awed by the work.

"I can't see one single difference," said Basil, his head swiveling from the portrait to Evie.

Demetra was so close her nose was almost touching the canvas. "It's extraordinary. It almost looks like she's alive."

"I'm so happy for you, Evie," said Maggie, giving her a hug.

"Thanks." Evie couldn't help but smile as she stared into her mother's eyes. Of all the people she'd lost, and all the people who had, impossibly, come back to her that day, here was someone she'd only known for a matter of minutes. Someone who had been snatched from her in the very moments after she was born. And now it was as if she were back, too. Evie's heart threatened to burst.

"Right. You. Over there." It was the familiar, snarling voice of Corporal Liverwort. They all turned to look at her, and she was pointing straight at Maggie.

"Me?"

"Come with me. Queen wants to see you."

Maggie stared at her, mouth hanging open. She didn't say a word. Liverwort snarled and stormed toward them.

"Well? Come on, then! This is the Queen we're talking about!"

"The Queen? Wants to see . . . me?"

"That's what she said." Then she called out to everyone inside the barracks. "All of you, get washed up and be behind the main castle in thirty minutes!"

The rest of the people in the barracks began cleaning up from the long day's work. Maggie, meanwhile, was having a hard time following the order.

"What will I need? Surely a new uniform. I couldn't possibly—"

"You'll wear what you're wearing," said Liverwort with a sigh. "Queen wants you straightaway."

"Of course," said Maggie. "Let me just put a few things in my knapsack. There must be time for that, right?" She buzzed around her bunk, exploding with nervous energy and talking to herself.

"Corporal Liverwort," said Evie.

"What," she said. She turned to face Evie, her face a mask of lumps and scowls and angry lines.

"I just wanted to tell you how sorry I am about Princess Beatrice. I know what she meant to you."

Liverwort's face began to go slack as the lines that had been etched into it from years of frowning relaxed. Evie hugged her. She felt as stiff and uncomfortable as a log in Evie's arms, but within moments, her body began to shake. She was crying, Evie knew, and that made her hold on even tighter.

After a moment, Liverwort pushed Evie away and wiped her eyes, trying to put her sour face back on.

"Come on, Cadet, Queen's waiting."

"Ready!" said Maggie.

"Hang on," said Evie. "I'm coming, too."

Now Liverwort truly did get angry. "She didn't ask for you. Just this one."

"She can discharge me if she likes, but she might be the only person alive who can tell me about my mother. I'm coming along."

Liverwort sneered at Basil and Demetra. "Fine. Let's go."

She led them through campus. Now that several hours had passed since the final witch was defeated, a celebratory atmosphere was beginning to take hold. It had come at great cost, but they had won. And that was the part that was now beginning to sink in.

They reached the Queen's Tower, or what was left of it.

Liverwort showed them into a thin, curving staircase. It curled around the outside of the Queen's Tower in a gentle contour, passing a beautifully carved doorway at each floor. Finally, she reached the one she wanted and stepped through. Evie and Maggie followed. They walked down a short corridor made of stone and reached another wooden door. Liverwort knocked, then opened it. She stepped inside. "Here she is, Majesty." She turned and nodded to Maggie, then froze Evie with her eyes. The door shut, leaving Evie alone in the hallway.

She waited and waited, pacing along the smooth stones of the floor, wondering what the Queen could possibly be talking to Maggie about. She was there long enough to start questioning whether she really should have come at all. What if the Queen was even colder and meaner than Beatrice?

Before long, the door opened. Slowly, in a daze, Maggie stepped out. Liverwort appeared behind her and pointed a crooked finger at Evie.

"Wait there while I tell her what you want." Then she slammed the door.

"Maggie? Are you all right?"

Maggie stepped toward her, lost in her thoughts. "It's her, Evie." She met Evie's eyes. "What they said was true. The Queen is Rapunzel."

"*What?*"

Maggie nodded, a smile blooming wide across her face. "It's really her!"

"What did she want?"

Maggie shook her head, still unable to comprehend what had just happened to her. "She wants me to apprentice with her. To learn how everything works. She said she's been watching me, Evie, and that she thinks I've got a place on the staff!"

"Maggie, that's incredible!"

"There's a lot of work to be done before that, of course, but she said that if I train as hard as I have been, she'll keep an eye on me for Headmistress!"

Evie gasped and clapped her hands over her mouth. She grabbed Maggie's arms, and Maggie grabbed hers right back. Both of them jumped up and down and screamed.

"Mum used to read me stories about this place when I was a girl! And now I'll be working here! I get to train the next generation of princesses, Evie! Can you believe it?"

They jumped up and down and screamed again. The door flew open, and Liverwort glowered at them. "Get in here!" she spat.

"I'm so happy for you, Maggie," said Evie.

"Thanks."

She hugged her friend once more, then walked toward the door. She stepped past Corporal Liverwort into a dark stone room with a low ceiling. There were windows all along the curved walls looking out over campus. A spinning wheel and a stool sat near the wall. A wooden desk, a bench, and a neatly organized bookcase were the only other objects in the room. An ancient woman in a golden dress sat in a wooden chair with large wheels near one of the windows. Waves of sleek silver hair cascaded from a waterfall braid around the back of her head. A thick, jeweled crown sat above that. She had kind eyes and a sweet smile, and she was ushering Evie closer.

"I hear you'd like to speak with me about your mother," she said in a small voice. "It's all right, Corporal, you may leave us. Thank you very much indeed for your help today."

Liverwort bowed her head, then left the room. Evie stepped forward, her fingers fiddling in front of her. "Before she died, Princess Beatrice said that you and she were the only ones who knew the whole truth about my mother. I was hoping I might become the third."

Queen Rapunzel closed her eyes and sighed. "Poor Beatrice. She not only broke a vow by revealing Academy secrets, but also broke my heart. She allowed herself to be overwhelmed by her stepmother. But, as difficult as it all is, I forgive her. Who amongst us hasn't made mistakes when it comes to our families? Come. Sit." She motioned toward the bench. Her fingers were curled and twisted into a permanent fist.

Evie sat. The old woman's eyes were so tender, so full of love, that it put Evie immediately at ease. "The Headmistress told me about my father coming here and about the bargain with the witch and my birth. But all she said about my mother was that she was taken away before the witch came for her and given a new life somewhere else."

"Indeed," said Rapunzel. "And it was no small feat, mind you. Here was a girl trained as a Princess of the Shield but who had lost herself to a curse. Imagine the bottom falling out of a glass. That was what the witch left us. To protect her from the Seven Sisters, we needed to erase her from the world. But we also needed to explain a fully trained Princess of the Shield. So," she said with a soft chuckle, "I altered history. You've had Lieutenant Volf, correct?"

"Yes, Your Majesty. In my first year."

"Then you know what a stickler he is with Princess History. Somehow I managed to persuade him to change the truth. That might have been the most difficult part of the entire affair." She laughed softly again. "With the Lieutenant's help, the Headmistress and I set about erasing every trace of Princess Vorabend from our records." A wave of dizziness shot through Evie's head as she remembered looking at the Registry of Peerage in the Archives and finding her mother blacked out from its pages, leaving King Callahan alone. "Of course, there was still the matter of her old company-mates. I summoned each of those girls back to the Academy and told them we were changing Vora's identity to save her life. Without hesitation, without any further questioning, each of them accepted it. They took solemn vows to protect her secret to their dying days, which, unfortunately for most, came far too quickly. But a Princess of the Shield always protects Academy secrets. We knew those girls could be trusted.

"Princess Vorabend had therefore been expunged. I worked very closely with your father on assigning her a new identity. He was such a wonderful man. He wanted to ensure that the life we gave her was a good one, even if he would never be a part of it. In fact, it was he who chose her new name. He asked us to call her Princess Middlemiss."

Evie gasped. Her hands went to her mouth. Princess Middlemiss was the one she'd been reading about since she first cracked a book, the one whose stories had inspired her since she'd discovered them back in her first year. *That* Princess Middlemiss . . . was her mother.

"He chose the name because he saw her as someone stuck between two lives, between the Vora he had known before the portrait and the Vora she might one day be again. He was a hopeful man, your father, and I think part of him hoped he might someday make her his Vora again. Middlemiss was, to him, a temporary condition. So, with that business sorted, the only thing left to do was assign her a kingdom. We needed a real kingdom, one that wouldn't arouse suspicion, but one that also couldn't be easily found. Beatrice herself came up with the idea to assign her as the Princess of Saudade."

Another dizzying wave passed through Evie's brain. The Princess of Saudade. The woman in the portrait. Neither of them were Evie; they were her mother.

"Saudade is a long-dead water kingdom. Little of it remains except the ruins of a castle and some local villagers. It is quite remote, and they were only too happy to have their own princess. We thought she could live out her days happily near the sea, never to be bothered by a witch again. But then . . ." She looked at Evie with a knowing smile. "Things changed.

"Our hope was for her to live quietly, but she just couldn't bring herself to do it. The witches began to spread across the land and her training was still in her bones, even if the rest of her had been stripped away. She refused to let the witches near the coastal kingdoms. In fact, she became one of our most reliable princesses. At first it made me terribly nervous how she attracted so much attention. She even became quite famous after she led a counterattack on one of the kingdoms up there. But the more she proved herself, and the more she built her own name and identity, the safer she became. The witches would never have expected us to disguise someone they were looking for as a highly visible princess of the north. So . . . life went on, and Vora truly did become Middlemiss.

"Countess Hardcastle, meanwhile, had taken not only your sister but also the portrait. From what my sources have told me, she wanted to sell it to the cruelest, most hard-hearted person in all the land. What better way to get revenge on someone who had cheated her, I suppose."

"King Hossenbuhr," said Evie.

"Precisely. She sold the portrait to King Hossenbuhr with the explicit order that he must never look at it, for it had been cursed. He proved to be the perfect accomplice to her crime, however unwitting. Hossenbuhr was driven solely by the desire to amass wealth and treasure. He didn't need to see the portrait; he only needed to *possess* it. By placing it with someone of such extraordinary greed, the witch had ensured that no one would ever find Vorabend again. What she hadn't counted on, of course, was a young boy's curiosity. Until

Forbes snuck into that room and looked at the portrait, not a single human eye had ever seen it."

"Then she came up with her plan to make my father fall in love with her."

"Indeed. She created the Countess Hardcastle disguise and did what witches have become only too adept at doing. She tricked her way into your family and became your stepmother. When we were introduced, she came across as a perfectly acceptable candidate to be King Callahan's second wife. Over time, they became our greatest benefactors, though for entirely different reasons. The King was forever grateful for our help in protecting his wife. The Countess, however, was hoping to create a smooth surface here for her daughter to glide across. She wanted Malora to become a princess as seamlessly as possible. That witch, Countess Hardcastle, has been troubling your family since before you were born."

"Not anymore."

"Indeed."

"Is it really over?" asked Evie, after everything had sunk in.

"It is," said Rapunzel. "You have performed in an exemplary manner, Cadet. I can say with great certainty that both your father and your mother would be immeasurably proud."

Evie's mind was swirling. She could scarcely understand everything she had just been told. "Your Majesty," she said. "Could I ask one more thing?"

"Of course."

"We were due to have Princess Middlemiss's royal wedding

here in a few months. Does that mean she'll become a queen?"

"Quite so," said Rapunzel with a smile. "Which means, of course, that as of this autumn, you shall be the Princess of Saudade."

Everyone had gathered beneath the old oak tree behind Pennyroyal Castle. Despite the devastation, it remained standing tall. Green shoots had already started to appear on its boughs. Soon, they would form branches and then leaves and then acorns would drop and it would all start again.

Evie was there with Maggie and Basil, of course, but none of them could find Demetra. When they saw that Christa and Camilla weren't there, either, they realized that the whole family must have gone off somewhere together. The rest of the crowd was composed of the heroes of the siege of Pennyroyal Academy. There were princess and knight cadets, staff and administrators, parents and siblings, as well as the Princesses of the Shield who had ridden from all across the land with Cinderella. Even the fairies were there, slowly regaining their strength. All had gathered in front of Corporal Liverwort, who was standing above them on a broken piece of wall.

"Everyone here?" she snarled. The crowd mumbled. "The Queen wants to say a few things, so pipe down."

Everyone fell silent in respectful anticipation. Evie and Maggie exchanged a knowing look. Unlike the rest of the people gathered, they'd both seen for themselves that the Queen really was Rapunzel. And then she appeared, pushed in her chair by Rumpledshirtsleeves. There were awed whispers amongst the crowd, and even some gasps. Sir Schönbecker, Commander Muldenhammer, Princess Rampion, Princess Cinderella, Sir Ramsbottom, Princess Copperpot, Lieutenant Volf, Princess Ziegenbart, and all the higher-level instructors had little reaction. But the newest members of staff and recently graduated Princesses of the Shield stared with wide eyes. Queen Rapunzel's silver hair billowed down from her braid, but even that couldn't distract from her sparkling crown. Rumpledshirtsleeves helped her stand, then slowly climb up onto the broken wall. Finally, she faced the crowd with a tender smile.

"Good afternoon," she said. Her voice sounded a bit stronger than it had earlier. "Pennyroyal Academy has taken a punch, ladies and gentlemen. A mighty punch indeed. Yet Pennyroyal Academy still stands—"

*Crack!* A hunk of stone broke off the battlement across the road and crashed to the ground in a billow of dust. The crowd screamed and dove for the ground, then began to laugh when they realized what had just happened. Rapunzel looked over her shoulder, then turned back to the crowd. She, too, was laughing.

"*Most* of the Academy still stands!"

They all laughed again.

"Now, in recognition of the feats of bravery and heroism shown throughout our long, dark night, I should like to do something rather unorthodox. But if ever there was a time for unorthodoxy, this is it. You see, cadets, I know everything there is to know about each and every one of you. I pay close attention to your files and the words of my staff. The battle we survived last night was more difficult training than one hundred years at the Academy could provide. As such, and knowing what I know about you all, I should like to advance everyone who was here to defend our beloved Academy. If you were preparing to enter your first-class training this fall, you may now consider yourself a fully commissioned Princess of the Shield. When your fairies are feeling up to it, they will administer your vows and distribute your assignments."

Evie and Maggie stared at each other in shock. Maggie's hands were shaking. She looked as though she might pass out.

"Uh, Headmistress?" said Basil, raising his hand.

"That's the bloody Queen, you idiot!" snarled Liverwort.

"Sorry, Madame Queen?"

"Yes, Cadet, what is it?"

"I'm sorry, Your Majesty . . . but I'm afraid I can't accept my commission."

"Basil! What are you doing?" said Evie.

Rapunzel, Rumpledshirtsleeves, and Liverwort all looked at him in astonishment. Then Rapunzel's face softened.

"Cadet Basil, isn't it?"

"That's right, Your Majesty. I've loved my time here at the Academy. I've loved training to be a princess more than I ever could have imagined. And there's a part of me that really does want to become a Princess of the Shield. But something happened the other day, and I can't possibly ignore it. You see, I found the Water of Life. It's the first step toward a cure for those who've been turned to stone. I need to be home finding that cure, not off on assignment. I'm very sorry." He turned to face the crowd. "I'm sorry, everyone. I don't want to disappoint you. I just need to find a cure for my . . . my sister." There was a buzz in the crowd. Basil turned to Evie and Maggie with heartbroken eyes. "I'm so sorry."

"Did you say *sister*?" said Maggie in confusion.

"It's all right, Bas," said Evie. Then she turned to Maggie. "I'll explain later."

"Forgive me, Your Majesty. The last thing I want is to seem ungrateful. But the first thing I want is my sister back."

Rapunzel gave a slight nod, her smile revealing nothing. "Cadet Basil, am I to understand that you are refusing your commission?"

"I'm afraid I am, Your Majesty."

"Then you leave me no choice. Step forward, young man."

Basil made his way onto the wall and stood before her, his spine as straight as a pine, his chest held high.

"Cadet Basil, it is with . . ." She paused, studying his face. "It is with . . . complete humility. With awe. With pride. And with the full acknowledgment that you possess a surplus of all the things that go into a true princess, that I hereby dismiss you from Pennyroyal Academy." Her hand rose to her forehead in a salute.

"Thank you, Your Majesty."

"Thank you, Basil." She stepped forward and hugged him.

One of the girls from a second-class company whispered, "Should we applaud? That seems like a bad thing, right?"

Basil descended the wall and came through the crowd to join Evie and Maggie. As Rapunzel continued her speech, he stood next to them with red eyes. He looked absolutely destroyed.

"Are you all right, Bas?" said Evie, holding his hand.

"I'm not sure," he said. "I've been waiting for this day for two and a half years, but now that it's here . . . it's a lot sadder than I expected."

Maggie gave him a hug. Tears fell down his cheeks. Then Evie hugged him. "I love you, Basil."

"I love you, too, Evie."

"Now," continued Rapunzel, "before we retire to the Dining Hall to feast as we have never feasted before, there is one final order of business I should like to address. Corporal, if you please."

Liverwort jumped off the back of the wall and disappeared. The crowd murmured with anticipation.

"What more could there possibly be?" said Basil, wiping his tears on his sleeve.

"Everyone, please remain calm," said Rapunzel.

Liverwort returned, and she was holding the sleeve of a hobbling figure in a tattered black cloak. They made their way up onto the wall together, and that was when the whole crowd began to gasp.

It was the hag from Evie's first year at the Academy, the blind witch who had issued that fateful prophecy.

"Bring the Warrior Princess to me," she said in a thin, brittle voice.

Evie gulped, and her insides began to quiver. Everyone turned to look at her. Several people stepped aside to clear a path.

"Bring the Warrior Princess to me. Her battle is still ahead."

"It's all right," said Rapunzel. "Come. Come." She waved Evie forward.

Slowly, with her heart in her throat, Evie stepped toward the old witch. She could feel the cold air coming off her, could feel her reading the crowd with her black magic. She stepped up onto the wall and went to stand before the witch, whose eyes were fused shut. The witch smacked her lips and moved her head back and forth as though unaware Evie was standing right in front of her.

"I said bring me the Warrior Princess!" she croaked. "Bring her before me!"

Evie furrowed her brow. She glanced out at Maggie, who shrugged. "Uh . . . I'm right here," she whispered to the witch. "I'm right in front of you."

The witch jumped, a scowl on her face. "What are you doing there, trying to scare me? Get away, urchin! I want the Warrior Princess!"

Evie looked back at Rapunzel, who was herself utterly perplexed.

"Forgive me, ma'am, but . . . I *am* the Warrior Princess." Now her own conviction began to falter. "Aren't I?"

"No!" yelled the witch. Then, suddenly, her expression changed to one of reverence. She extended a gnarled, bony finger toward the back of the crowd. "She is here! The Warrior Princess approaches!"

With a great murmuring, the crowd began to part to see whom it was she meant.

"Hurry up, Mother, it's already started! We're missing it!" Demetra took a huge bite of the doughnut in her hand, then, with stuffed cheeks and sugar residue smeared across her face, realized everyone was looking at her. Her mouth was so full, she could barely speak. "Wha?"

"Bring her before me!" said the witch.

Evie crept down from the wall, her mind a blur.

"What's happening?" said Maggie.

"It's Demetra," said Evie. "Of course! My mother was in the company from twenty years ago, but so was hers! *She's* the Warrior Princess!"

The crowd pulled Demetra forward with happy congratulations. She, however, was utterly baffled. "I'm sorry! We were just so hungry, we couldn't wait for supper!"

Before she knew what was happening, she was standing on the wall in front of the witch, struggling to swallow her doughnut. Liverwort stepped forward and slapped the rest of it out of her hand. "Straighten up!"

"What's going on?" said Demetra.

"You, my dear . . ." croaked the witch. "You are the Warrior Princess. And now that the Queen has declared you a Princess of the Shield—"

"She has?" said Demetra, astonished. Then she turned to look at the Queen. "Blimey, you're Rapunzel!"

"Your final battle awaits you, Warrior Princess, and there shall be no excuse for letting fear win. A great victory was secured here today. Calivigne is finished, but there is more to be done."

Demetra looked dubiously at the witch, then the crowd. "You don't really think *I'm* the Warrior Princess, do you?"

Everyone began to cheer. Demetra's mother, as flabbergasted as her daughter, listened to the applause with shock. Camilla began to clap and whistle along with everyone else.

"I can't believe it," said Maggie. "Demetra's the Warrior Princess."

"I knew it," said Basil, clapping loudly. "I could have told you."

Evie stood near the back of the crowd and shouted and applauded and exalted in the victory they'd won, and the victory Demetra had yet to win. It was an afternoon of triumph, and of friendship, and of hope.


"Uh . . . Father? Mother?" Evie shifted from one foot to the other. She looked up at her parents, who were glaring down at her from the height of a respectable waterfall with cold dragon faces. Her sister stood behind them, looking skeptically at something to Evie's right. "This . . ." She took a deep breath. "This is Remington."

"Hiya," he said, raising a hand and giving an easy smile. Then his face fell. "Sorry, I mean, hello there, very good to meet you . . . er . . . what do I call you?" He turned to Evie. "What do I call them?"

"Remington is king of one of the most influential kingdoms in all the land. And he's going to help stop the war with the dragons."

"He's also your boyfriend, isn't he?"

"Sister!" said Evie, her cheeks already reddening.

"And how do you propose to stop the war?" said Evie's father with a grumble.

"He's already convinced one king from the Eastern Kingdoms, Father."

Remington stepped forward. "Uh, look, uh . . ." He gazed up at them and found their eyes. "I've just lost a very important part of my family. As it happens, it's the same part that Evie has just had restored to her family." His eyes met her father's. "I much prefer her experience to mine, to be honest, and I . . . I just don't want to see any more families dismantled. I'm going to help you because I believe in this with all my heart. The only thing keeping knights and dragons from living in peace is that no one has ever said, 'Enough.'"

Evie's mother and father looked into each other's eyes and both knew what their answer would be. "We'll get started trying to change minds on our side," said Evie's mother with a nod. "I imagine we'll find an awful lot of dragons who will be only too happy to see this war end."

"Brilliant," said Remington. "It won't be easy, but this is already a better start than anyone's ever had before, isn't it?"

"It is indeed," said the father. "Thank you for looking after our daughter so well."

"It has been nothing short of a pleasure."

"Then stop with this boyfriend business," he barked.

"Oh, uh . . ." Now it was Remington's turn to blush.

"Well then," said Evie's father, puffing up his chest. "If you'll excuse us . . ."

"Yes, of course," said Remington. "Safe travels and, uh, lovely to meet you." He gave them an awkward wave and walked away toward the Dining Hall. Evie stood at the edge of the hillside with the three dragons as the evening sun bathed everything in gold.

"So? Will you be coming home?" said her father.

"Of course I will," she said, "but only to visit. I'll get my assignment soon, and then I'll have to go out and do my duty."

He lowered his head and softened his eyes. His voice became gentler, too. "Will you come visit soon?"

"I will. I promise." She ran forward and threw her arms around her father's chin. "Oh, I love you, Daddy. I love you, too, Mum. And you, of course, Sister. I love my family as much as I've ever loved anything in this life. You'll always be with me, no matter how far apart we are."

The other dragons nuzzled in, squeezing Evie between

them. They stayed there on that golden hillside for another forty minutes. Evie told them about the Academy and about what her days were like, and they were genuinely interested in hearing it. Her sister even admitted to feeling a bit jealous by the end.

"Why not a dragon princess?" said Evie. "I say you enlist!"

They all shared a laugh. Then the three dragons gave Evie one last nuzzle before lifting off into the deep, dark blue sky, elegant black silhouettes against the falling night.

The next morning at breakfast, Evie and her friends moved to the Crown Company table, the only first-class princess table, an experience the siege had stolen from them. Maggie had a small stack of parchments with her.

"I was tossing and turning all night trying to work something out," said Maggie. "What did the witch mean when she said Demetra's battle still lay ahead? If Calivigne is gone, Hardcastle's gone, and the rest of them are scattered to the wind, then what victory hasn't yet been won?"

Evie took a bite of toast but realized something before she could chew it. "The training facility!" Crumbs flew out of her mouth and into Basil's eyes.

"Do you mind?"

"The training facility!" she said, choking down the toast. "The witches have their own training facility!"

"They do?" said Demetra.

"My father said he'd been taken somewhere like that and

held. He said there were hundreds of witches there, all together. And they were training for battle, just like us."

"Then that must be it!" said Demetra. "Where is it?"

"He didn't know for certain," said Evie. "Only that it was cold. And there was a lot of snow."

"Hang on," said Basil. "Are you saying Demetra has to go and destroy a witch version of Pennyroyal Academy?"

"Exactly right," said Maggie.

"Wait, what?" said Demetra, suddenly looking quite terrified.

"And I think I've figured out where it is," said Maggie. She turned to Evie. "Do you remember all those letters I sent you last year? The ones you said the witches intercepted?" She reached into her parchment stack and took out a map of the realm. "Look. Here's the Dragonlands here, where the letters were meant to go." She put a finger in the northwest corner of the map. Then she put her other finger straight to the south, several inches below the map itself. "Sevigny, where they were sent from, is here."

"My word, you really do live in the middle of nowhere," said Basil.

"My parchment hawks would have taken this route," said Maggie, running one finger north toward the other. She stopped when it reached an enormous range called the Glass Mountains. "That's where they are. That's where they were holding Evie's father. And that's why it was so easy for them to intercept my hawks. I was sending them straight into the witches' lair."

They all stared at the map in silence. The Glass Mountains were huge, stretching out beneath Pennyroyal Academy and continuing west until they ran straight off the map.

"That's where my final mission is," said Demetra.

Once they'd all agreed that Maggie was right, they decided to act quickly. Evie packed up her things and found a strong horse on which to tie it all. Demetra and Basil did the same. Maggie, however, would stay and try to get the Academy operational for the new class in the fall. She stood in the courtyard near the fountain and said goodbye to her friends. But this goodbye had an entirely different tone than the last one.

"Good luck, Demetra, I know you can do it. And when you do, we'll never have to worry about witches as an organized force ever again."

"Thanks, Maggie. And good luck to you. There's so much to be done here." They hugged each other, and then Demetra mounted her horse. Her mother was there, Queen Christa, as was her sister and a team of other elite princesses she'd chosen for the mission, including Princess Falada. "Goodbye, my friend," said Demetra, giving Maggie a smile. "I'll see you soon."

"Goodbye, Demetra." The princesses began to ride off, leaving only Evie and Basil.

"Look after my portrait," said Evie. "I'll need it when we've finished with this."

"I'll protect it with my life," said Maggie solemnly.

"Thanks, Maggie." She gave her friend a hug, then went to mount her horse as Basil did the same.

"Good luck, you two," said Maggie. "Bravely ventured is half won."

"Goodbye, Maggie," said Evie. With a smile, she and Basil turned and rode off after the princesses. A moment later, Remington raced past on his horse.

"Sorry! They just brought out a blackberry tart, what was I to do?" He galloped down the hill and joined the rest of them as they disappeared into the Dortchen Wild.

The group rode for many hours through a placid, magical forest. There was not a witch to be found, and the air was as clear as glass. When they finally reached Marburg, they found the ruins of the once-great kingdom at long last occupied again by people. The witches had abandoned it when the Academy's wall had fallen, and now its citizens were back, setting things to rights and working to get back to normal, everyday life.

The party stopped to buy some food at the inn, then rode through the kingdom and out into the great, wide world beyond. Finally, the sun began to set, and the air turned golden. They rode to the top of a flat hill overlooking rolling, grassy fields that stretched on for miles. Evie stopped her horse and gazed out across the land. Demetra rode up next to her. Everyone else continued down the hill to get their horses some water except for Basil and Remington. The four of them sat silently on horseback and admired the light-soaked hillsides before them, where the grass seemed to glow green and the air was crisp with possibility and hope. Despite the sun and the warm, wildflower breeze, Evie felt a chill run through her.

"This is where we part ways," said Demetra.

Evie's eyes swung over to her. "What?"

"We're going on without you."

"What are you talking about? I'm with you to the end."

"No, Evie. From here, we ride south. And you ride north."

Evie looked to the north, to where the meadows seemed to stretch on forever until the valleys met the hills, and then the pine mountains beyond.

"Go to your mother, Evie. Go and find her."

"But I can't leave the mission—"

"Evie. It's all right. You wouldn't let me abandon my mother when we were in Goblin's Glade, and I won't let you abandon yours now. Go and find her. Go and be with her. Tell her about the portrait and see if she remembers. If she doesn't, then start over anyway. Just go to her."

Tears began to form in Evie's eyes. "Thank you, Demetra."

"I'll ride with Evie," said Remington. "You know . . . muscle."

Evie laughed, then turned back to Demetra. "Would you mind? He won't be any use to you against witches anyway. Trust me, I've already had to save him several times."

"Of course he'll go with you. I'll feel better knowing you're not alone out there."

"I'm not alone. None of us are ever alone."

A gentle breeze whispered over them.

"Well then," said Evie.

"Well then," said Demetra.

She and Basil spurred their horses on, riding down the gentle glade to join the rest of the team. Evie and Remington didn't move, or even speak. They sat on their horses, watching in silence as the sun rolled slowly down the western sky, warmed by the wind as it sifted through the long grass.

# Acknowledgments

THIS WILL BE ROUND THREE of appreciation for most of these people, but the Pennyroyal Academy books wouldn't exist without them. Immense thanks to Alexandra Machinist, my agent. I will never forget the day you called and told me you wanted to represent my first book. It was life changing, and I will always be grateful. A huge thank-you as well to Sally Willcox for so many calm, brilliant ideas. And a cascade of gratitude to Michelle Weiner, Jon Cassir, Kimberly Jaime, Deborah Klein, and everyone at the various agencies and firms that helped me find the perfect publishing partner in G. P. Putnam's Sons.

To my publisher, Jennifer Besser, and my editor, Arianne Lewin, thank you for all of your care and thoughtfulness and ideas and fun phone calls. I couldn't imagine better collaborators. And my unending thanks to everyone else at Penguin and Puffin who has helped to get these books into the world.

Thank you to my family and friends (especially my lovely wife and patron-of-the-arts, Hannah) who have supported me as I learned what it meant to be an author, and to all the teachers and librarians who have welcomed me into their schools, either in person or in book form. It means the world to get an email from a student who tells me that you put the books in their hands, and that they have found some small piece of the courage, compassion, kindness, and discipline for which the cadets at the Academy strive. It's a reward that I never imagined when I began work on the first manuscript.

I would also like to recognize some of the sources that helped me to better understand the importance of the fairy tale. Bruno Bettelheim's *The Uses of Enchantment* opened my eyes to hidden depth in stories that I had taken for granted since childhood. Dr. Allan Thexton's insights into giants and their place in literature helped to shape this third book. And, of course, Jacob and Wilhelm Grimm's dedication to folklore and cultural preservation have influenced so many, myself included. I was fortunate to spend some time on the Brothers Grimm Trail in central Germany, experiencing the places and sights that forged and inspired them, and it helped me to understand how dedicated and passionate these two great men were. They taught me that although fairy tales may seem frivolous and childish to many in their teenage years and beyond, they are anything but. Fairy tales will always have an important place in our world, and I will be forever grateful for that.

TURN THE PAGE FOR A LOOK AT WHERE
EVIE'S ADVENTURE BEGAN!

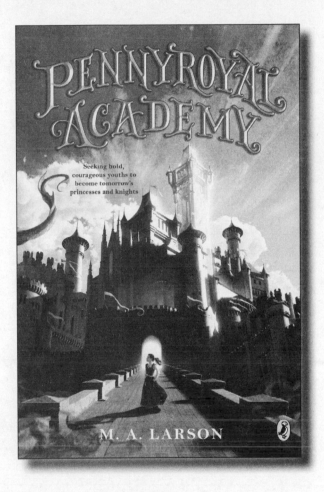

"A breathtakingly exciting novel!"
—*The New York Times*

*If I'm still in this forest by nightfall, I'll never leave it again.*

The girl's eyes darted through the misty pines. The air was wet, though it wasn't exactly raining. Everywhere she turned she found dull gray shadows, and her mind put monsters in all of them. The only sound was her own frantic breath. No birdsong. No tumbling water. Nothing.

A leafy tendril snaked up from the undergrowth and began to slither around her ankle. She tore her leg free and raced into the mist, her bare feet crackling through a carpet of dead leaves and fallen needles. Towering trees swayed overhead like mossy giants, and the small patches of sky she could see were black with clouds. Night was coming. And so were the things that lurked in the fog.

As she hurdled over a rotting stump, a heart-sized dragon scale necklace bounced against her chest. A matted drape of spiders' webs covered her body, her only protection against the elements. The rest of her was streaked with mud. She had been lost in this forest for three days. Had seen and heard things that still didn't seem real—a weathered thighbone so thick and long it could only have belonged to a giant; the deafening thunder of thrumming wings and the shadow of an enormous dragonfly passing above the canopy. Three days lost and she knew, one way or another, there would not be a fourth—

*CRACK!* The girl jumped at the sound, then heard the popping crackle of splitting wood somewhere above. She wheeled just in time to see the hairy branch of a beech tree swooping down. It slammed into her, knocking her over the edge of a hill. She tumbled through moldy black sludge to the bottom, where she collided with a pine trunk. She eased herself up, rolling her shoulder to be sure her arm wasn't broken.

The first day, the day she had left home, she had taken a savage beating from the trees. Her father had always warned her to stay out of enchanted forests, but she was still taken aback by the trees' ferocity. She had slowly begun to learn their moods and patterns, and before long was able to anticipate their attacks. She tried to avoid beeches especially, as they seemed the most malicious.

Today it wasn't the trees that frightened her. The sun and moon and stars had all gone, along with chirping birds and skittering goblins. In their place, the clouds and mist, and the distinct feeling that something else was out there.

*But what?*

She listened, silent and still, though all she heard was wind shivering through leaves. As she stood, her emerald-green eyes narrowed. There, faintly visible through the dusk, was a distant pinpoint of light. The window of a cottage.

She had always been cautious, much more so than her sister, but once she saw that light, she ran for it. The cottage was small, its timbers frayed and soggy. This was the first shelter she had seen since leaving home, and yet something inside her screamed to turn back and run and then run some more.

*Would I rather be out here when the sun is gone, or inside?*

She ignored her instincts and edged to the window, grabbing hold of the sill. Clumps of rot crumbled off in her hands. She wiped them away, then leaned in again.

Firelight washed across her face, and her stomach roared. At the far side of the room, a thick, brown liquid bubbled over the rim of a cauldron, sizzling on the embers. She couldn't see anything else, but that was enough. Her hunger drove her to the door, but as she clutched the handle, panic swarmed up through the soles of her feet like a million wasps.

*Something's not right here—*

A wolf's lonesome howl echoed down from the mountains, and she knew she had no choice. She gave the door a hard shove, but it didn't budge. She threw her shoulder into it and finally it barked open.

"Hello?" she said with a small, shaking voice. There was no answer, only the soft pop of the fire. The floorboards screamed as she stepped inside and shouldered the door shut with a resonant thud.

The cottage was warm and tidy. Beneath the lone window sat a wooden table, where waterflies buzzed around a pile of blackish-red slop. Next to that were a rusted hand-crank machine and several neat stacks of multicolored candies. A chill ran down her arms.

In the corner, beyond the hearth, next to the open door of a small bedchamber, stood a large cage, oranged with rust and age. It was just the right size to hold a person. Next to it, a small pile of children's shoes spilled across the floor.

She turned to run, but the door that had just been so solidly stuck now hung open. And outside, footsteps crackled through the leaves.

She looked for another way out, but it was too late, so she dove under the table and hugged her legs to her chest. A thick drip of red slid through the slats of the table and plopped on the floor at her feet.

*Oh please oh please oh please . . .*

A pair of muddy riding boots clomped across the floorboards, shoved along by an old woman draped in layer upon layer of decaying black robes. The door slammed shut behind them, though no one was there to slam it.

The girl's blood ran cold. She was trapped.

The old woman, hunched and bent like a river, shoved her prisoner into the cage and rattled the latch home. He was around the girl's same age, and wore a dark gray leather doublet embroidered in burgundy. His dark hair was in knots from countless hours on horseback, and his arms were bound behind his back.

The cage was too small for him to stand, so he threw his shoulder into the door. The frail metal clanged, but held fast.

His captor went to the cauldron to stir her bubbling broth, which hissed against the flames like a chorus of angry snakes. "Now then, what have I done with my jars?" Her voice was full of contradictions, soft and sweet, but with a knife edge of menace. "It's been so long since I had a heart to put in them. *Eh-heh-heh-heh-heh* . . ." She leaned her ladle against the stone gently, like a kindly grandmother might, then shuffled into the bedchamber.

*Now! Now! NOW!*

But the girl sat frozen in place, watching as the boy strained and writhed against his bonds. He leaned back to give the door a solid kick, and that's when he saw her.

"*Hey!*" he hissed, jerking his head toward the latch. Tears welled in her eyes, and she suddenly felt as though she might faint. "*I know you're scared, but open this cage and you'll leave here alive. I swear it.*"

She pulled her legs tighter, clinging to them like the last jagged stone before a waterfall. But as her tears fell and her heart thumped in her chest, she noticed something in his eyes that calmed her. He wasn't afraid. When he said he could keep her alive, he believed it.

Somehow, before her own fear could stop her, she began to scoot forward. Each creak of the floorboards made her want to scream and run for the door, but she kept her eyes fixed on his and crept closer and closer to the cage.

"*Hurry!*" he whispered.

Her trembling fingers reached for the latch. She tried to work it free as gently as she could, but the metal had become violently angry over the ages. It screamed open.

"What's this?"

The girl wheeled and fell back against the cage. She had never seen a witch before, but there could be little doubt that that was what stood before her now. The witch didn't move, just stared at her with milky yellow eyes and a wide, toothless grin. Her skin was the color of a worm after three days' rain, and it drooped from her bones like a melted candle.

"Open the latch!" shouted the boy, slamming his shoulder against the door.

But the witch's gaze paralyzed the girl. The hag's eyes bored straight into her own, slicing through her brain and down her throat. The girl gasped for air as the witch stared deeper, deeper, straight for her heart. She was choking on hate, anguish, fear . . . the feeling that she had already seen the sun for the last time without even realizing it. The witch was *inside* her—

"RUN!" shouted the boy as the cage door finally crashed open.

The girl snapped free of the witch's gaze. All that choking awfulness slid out of her throat and she could breathe once more. The dragon scale whipped round to her back as she sprinted for the door. She threw it open and burst out into the night. The blackness of the woods and the swirling fog made it seem like the witch was everywhere at once. Even in the open forest, the girl was trapped.

"Over here!" The boy stood next to a massive white horse that glowed in the moonlight like a ghost.

"What? On that?"

"These are her woods! We'll never make it on foot!"

She grimaced, but knew she would have to trust him. As she raced to the horse, the flickering firelight inside the cottage was suddenly extinguished. Smoky blackness, darker than the night, wafted from the door.

"*Eh-heh-heh-heh-heh-heh-heh-heh-heh* . . ." The cackle was no longer that of a feeble old lady. It had morphed into something elemental and terrifying.

The girl swung onto the horse's back. Beneath the smooth white needles of hair she could feel sweat and muscle and knew the boy was right: this was their only chance of escape. She reached down and grabbed the rope binding his arms, hauling him facedown across the horse's backside. Black smoke billowed from the door, and the cackling reverberated through the forest like it was coming from the fog itself.

"Let's go!" grunted the boy, but the girl was transfixed by the figure floating out of the cottage. The witch's body had distorted into something monstrous, long-limbed and inhuman. Her tattered robes billowed smoke. The skin around her mouth began to crack and split as her smile grew ever wider.

"Take the reins and go!"

The girl wrenched her eyes away. Straps of leather tack dangled from the horse's head and neck. She didn't know what any of it was, so she gripped the mane instead. With her other arm twisted behind her, she clutched the rope around the boy's hands.

"Ride," she whispered, and they lunged away into the night. Every muscle in her body clamped down as she felt the horse's power beneath her. Her fingers clutched the mane so tightly, the knuckles had already gone white. As the horse sailed across uneven ground, each stride threatened to break her grip.

"I can't do it!" she screamed over the thunder of hooves. "I can't!"

"Please . . ." was all the boy could muster. His midsection slammed repeatedly against the horse, forcing the air from his lungs. He couldn't draw breath.

The girl closed her eyes and ground her teeth. *I will not let go. The horse or the rope may slip free, but on my father I will not let go.* She glanced back, and what she saw made her gasp.

The witch, a billowing, spectral fiend, swooped through the trees like an enormous owl. Waves of frigid air swept up from behind as her bony fingers reached forward.

The horse leapt a fallen tree. The landing nearly ripped the mane from the girl's fingers. Her legs, pinned tightly around the horse's shoulders, felt frail and insignificant. Her entire body hurt, but the truly ferocious pain was in the fingers holding the boy's binding. It sawed deeper into her raw skin with each stride. *I can't hold on . . . It's all coming loose . . .*

"Water . . ." he croaked.

She scanned the darkness until something in the distance caught her eye. The pale reflection of moonlight on water. A river.

She jerked the mane, steering the horse toward it. The boy's weight pulled the rope to the final joints of her fingers. She was going to lose him.

Suddenly, she released the mane and grabbed the boy's vest just as the rope slipped from her fingers. Now her legs, locked around the horse's neck, were the only thing keeping them both alive. She lay twisted along the horse's back, and the headlong gallop was driving the leather saddle into her side. The boy was barely on the horse, and she had no way of knowing if he was alive or dead.

The bristles of the horse's coat scraped farther down her legs. Lower . . . lower . . . nearly to the ankles. Behind them, a wall of pure terror rose up. The witch was enormous, wraithlike, her arms extending from a cloak of swirling smoke.

Then, in an instant, the girl lost all sense of gravity. Her body soared through the air. The boy was gone. The horse was gone. And in the next moment, her lungs filled with icy water. With shocking clarity, she realized she had made it to the river. As she began to panic for breath, she found the rippling moonlight beneath her. She righted herself and kicked toward it until her head popped into the crisp night air, and she coughed until her lungs were dry.

The witch had gone, hiding no doubt in the fog at the

shoreline. On the opposite bank, where the air was clear and stars painted the sky, the white horse staggered out of the water.

She swam toward the bank until finally her feet touched the rough, slimy stones of the river bottom, then pulled herself ashore like some ancient creature, sobbing and gasping for breath.

*I made it. A miracle's happened and I'm still alive.*

Her legs buckled and she dropped to the pebbly shore. She forced herself onto her back, filling her lungs with the night until her panic began to recede. As she lay there, astonished to be alive, a strange thought crossed her mind. This night sky, a pale swipe of purple-white across a black field of untold numbers of stars, was the single most beautiful thing she had ever seen. Crickets chirped rhythmically from the trees. The choking mold stench was gone. Somehow, she really was alive.

"Here . . ." came a weak voice from farther down the gurgling river. She sat up. The horse stood at the waterline nuzzling a dark figure. It was the boy, arms still bound behind him, lying facedown in the sand, his legs dangling in the current. She went to him, but her fingers were too stiff and sore to grip the crude knot. She tried pulling on the rope, and it suddenly crumbled away like it was a thousand years old.

The boy, battered and weak, pushed himself over, too dazed to drag his legs free of the water. His teeth chattered, his whole body shuddering in the steady night breeze. "You must be . . . f-frozen solid . . ."

The girl, barefoot, sodden to the bone, and wearing only a thin covering of spiderwebs, said nothing.

"What . . . what's your n-name?"

Her eyes fell to the rocks. "I don't have one."

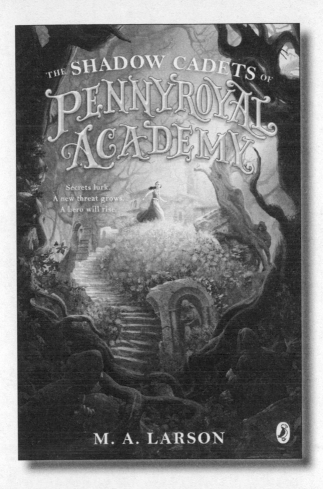

Evie's back at Pennyroyal Academy for her second term, but every-thing isn't as it should be. She witnesses the vicious attack of an innocent woman—by a trio of princesses. Pennyroyal's Headmis-tress General, Princess Beatrice, is dubious about what Evie saw—princesses are enforcers of truth and justice, not thugs. But Evie isn't so sure. Then, amidst piles of mail, she finds a letter with an ominous threat. A secret society has come out of the shadows with a wicked plan, putting the Academy in peril. It's up to Evie and her friends to unravel the devious plot and save Pennyroyal Academy.